Leaving Missouri

"Ellen Recknor is without a doubt one of the funniest, most versatile writers in the business today. Her books are smart, sassy, tough and tender, filled with heart and humor."

—Anne Stuart, author of *Moonrise*

"Tone up the laughing muscles and break out the caffeine; Clutie Mae Chestnut has arrived! *Leaving Missouri* sticks in your heart and keeps the pages turning. Ellen Recknor is a devilishly good storyteller."

—Cindy Bonner, author of *Lily*

"Recknor has created a real original in Clutie Mae Chestnut—gutsy from beginning to end . . . dusty, dramatic, and damned fun. I loved her!"

—Jerrie Hurd, author of
Miss Ellie's Purple Sage Saloon

leaving
Missouri

Ellen Recknor

BERKLEY BOOKS, NEW YORK

LEAVING MISSOURI

A Berkley Book / published by arrangement with
the author

PRINTING HISTORY
Berkley edition / April 1997

The Putnam Berkley World Wide Web site address is
http://www.berkley.com/berkley

ISBN: 0-425-15575-7

BERKLEY®
Berkley Books are published by The Berkley Publishing Group,
200 Madison Avenue, New York, New York 10016.
BERKLEY and the ''B'' design
are trademarks belonging to Berkley Publishing Corporation.

PRINTED IN THE UNITED STATES OF AMERICA

10 9 8 7 6 5 4 3 2 1

prologue

Cat's Claw, Colorado
August 1899

Dear Son,

Robbie, your mother is a liar. I don't mean I ever sat you down and told you a whopper. Not exactly. I mean, I sort of left things out. Things I promised your daddy I'd say out plain when the time was ripe, about my people and raising up, and how I came to better myself. And make you.

Almost thirteen years have passed since I left you, all of twelve years old, with your Aunt Penelope. Nigh on thirteen years, and most of a continent and an ocean between us. It near to broke my heart to leave you, but like you told me at the time, twelve is old enough to know. I believed you. I had done a passel of living by the time I was twelve, and I wasn't near so smart or educated as you.

I believe your Aunt Penelope and you pointed that last part out. Several times.

But you're near twenty-five now, and your Aunt Penelope's dead as a post and past being shocked, and there comes a time for saying the truth. Robbie, this is it.

For the telling to make sense, I've got to go all the way back to Jukes Holler, back to when I was a tyke and the war was on and Chigger first came and the Bug Boys were off fighting.

My aunts were in the whoring game with thievery on the side, and my granny was a full-blown witchwoman with a buckeye in both pockets, hexes on her tongue, and an apron full of potions. My uncles, rot their ornery hides, were the most no-account, scalp-happy lot of peckerwoods that ever stained Missouri's name, both during the war and after. Probably before, too.

There. You're shocked, aren't you? Well, sit tight, because that's just the bare-scratch beginning.

Growing up a Jukes was no waltz through the strawberries. There was Beetle pounding on me all the time, and the Bug Boys bartering me off for livestock and trade. But then, there was Chigger John sneaking in to save me. Also Mr. Frank James himself, who was my angel.

I was ruined at twelve, and wed against my will at fourteen. I went west at sixteen, and shot my husband on my way out the door. I will swear till Judgment it was pure accident, but between you and me, nobody was more deserving than Spider Clyde Jukes.

There'll be about Prometheus, of course, and the Spanish Kid. The slavering puke dogs from Paris, France, and how Chigger struck gold in the cellar, and how I came to be a genuine duchess and live in England in practically a castle.

I swan, it sounds like a lot when you say it all out that way, doesn't it? Well, I aim to make sense of it for you. I promised your daddy.

And there's one other thing, Robbie. Don't you ever believe anybody is dead, not unless you see them lowered and the dirt go on top of them. I made that mistake three times in my life.

Don't you go repeating it.

Love,
Mother

I was born under the constellation Leo, when the sign was in the heart. And in the family Bible, under the date of August 5, 1857, my name is writ as Chrysanthemum Mae Chestnut—or would have been, if any of my kin could have spelled for spit—though I was always called Clutie or Clutie Mae.

My last name was Chestnut, but I was a Jukes on my mama's side, and the Jukeses were the lowest kind of trash. All the menfolks were named after bugs, and were known as the Bug Boys by peace officers and the local wags. Before the war there had been a lot more of them, but the conflict took their numbers down considerable, leaving just my uncles Beetle, Glow, and Wig, and my cousin Spider. Well, the twins, Nit and Gnat, too, but I don't know that you could count them.

I do not remember the Bug Boys much before they went to war, although I recall Uncle Beetle busting my arm when I was two-and-a-half, and I recollect the stench of donk brewing in the barn. But that's about it.

Now, you may think it strange that such a bunch of worthless no-accounts as the Bug Boys would be eager to take up arms—which they did at the first call—but like Granny Wren used to say, the Jukeses were fighting men.

Crazy, more like. Jukes folks came to this country from old England way back in the seventeen hundred and somethings, and I suppose they were all right then. But not long after that, they took up the habit of marrying each other exclusive, likely because they were so lunatic-mean nobody else would have them. A hundred and seventy-odd years and several wars had taken the Jukeses down from nigh on two hundred to just us few.

This was a good thing, if you ask me, because a more cross-eyed bunch of runty, orange-headed, dingle-brained, ornery sons of bitches you would not want to meet.

Now, I would like to say right here that I was not pure Jukes, not by a long shot. I had brown hair, not that brittle, orange, stick-out kind, and big dark blue eyes instead of light blue and watery. And my eyes weren't the least bit wandery or crossed or squinted, still aren't. They're like my daddy's, Mama said. She only said it the once, and since Mama didn't ever say hardly a thing, I remembered the comment. Also, I got a full bucket of brains, if I do say so myself.

The rest of my family looked so much alike that folks got them confused all the time. Not me. I expect I stood out like a plow horse in a chicken coop, being so big-boned and brown-headed and all. Sometimes Granny Wren would stare at me and shake her head, like if she thought she could get away with it, she'd just throw me to the hogs.

This was because my blood was tainted on my papa's side, on account of Mama having broken with custom when she took, for her second husband, a man of foreign blood, "foreign" meaning non-Jukes.

Now, don't get the wrong idea about Mama. Her first husband had been the right sort, being her quadruple cousin, Inchworm Jukes; and by him she had the twins, Nit and Gnat. She was bereaved shortly after their birth, Inchworm having got himself shot through the neck whilst performing a holdup.

When Nit and Gnat were about three, Mama met he who was to be my daddy, and eloped straight off to the bright allure of St. Louis. His name was Ugar Chestnut, and he was half-English and half-Hungarian and a traveling sales representative for the J. R. Whippet Button Company of Lancaster, Pennsylvania.

I never met Mr. Chestnut, as he drowned in a beer barrel not long after my conception. Mama, having used up all the brave inside her, packed up herself and the twins and came back home to Jukes Holler to throw herself upon the family's mercy. Granny Wren took Mama in, but out of sheer mean-ness did not speak a solitary direct word to her until I was near three years old, and that is a fact.

They had to keep me, though. Live-born Jukes babies, even the half-Jukes kind, had got to be a real rarity.

One time I heard Granny Wren remark that it was a God-given miracle if a full-blooded Jukes lived a week past chris-tening. She sounded fair perplexed by it, too, although it seemed to me that anybody with a lick of sense ought to know you can't breed hogs that close for that many gener-ations without getting a bunch of stumpy runts that are mostly born dead, or too stupid to find the teat. I don't know why people should be any different.

Anyway, by the time Mama ran off and begot me, we lived in Missouri and had for a real long time—since around about 18-and-10, when Granny Wren was a girl of fourteen and only had two babes, and walked all the way up from Arkan-sas with all the granddaddies and grannies, six in all, to what became Jukes Holler Farm. They were all dead now, ex-cepting Granny Wren. She used to tell us stories about the olden times, about all the Jukeses.

I guess the farm we ended with was good enough, though it never had much chance to prove itself. Grandpappy Adder was the only motivated Jukes in the lot and the yellow jack-ets took him before he got five acres cleared, let alone a crop in the ground.

In winter Jukes Holler was all gray and misty and the sun never shined, and the naked tree trunks in the woods looked like a million black teeth all coming to chomp you. Anyway, they looked that way to me when I was little. But it was hilly and practically all in timber, and in summer fruity with critters for the table, and healing plants, and the witching herbs for Granny Wren, and so green overhead you could hardly see the sun. I liked it fine.

At the edge of the clearing, facing south, was a one-room cabin with a rickety, peeling porch. Down the slope to the west was the barn and the corn patch and such, and out back, edged on one side by a big berry bramble, was the little wash yard where Mama and Granny Wren boiled up laundry every

Monday, in season. The whole rest of Jukes Holler was woods, all dark and cool and deep and whispery, and calling my name.

Like I said, the Bug Boys took off for the fighting straight off, which left us at home to fend for ourselves. Granny Wren outdid herself on hexes and spells. She hung charm bags full of witching herbs and protecting hexes, and nailed Bible pages to the trees. Also, she had our every pistol and rifle loaded and ready at all times. Granny was a powerful witchwoman, but you cannot be too careful when it comes to war.

Missouri had it gruesome bad in those years, especially along the border farther west, and we were past fortunate in that the war did not much touch us on our farm. It came to our county, though, that was for certain. There were no big battles close by us, but I was told that off and on troops came through town—both Union and our side, depending on who was in charge that week. Sometimes, at night, I could see the sky-glow of flames far beyond our woods, the fires of houses burned out or crops put to the torch.

Sometimes there would be the thin cracks of distant rifle fire, and Granny Wren would say, ''There go them Yankees again, huntin' down poor little Missouri young'uns to throw on the cook fire.''

I would cry and hide under the porch.

About the only good thing that happened during the war was that Chigger John came to live with us. He was delivered to Jukes Holler by the Reverend Preston Spottle (a name I have always remembered on account of its beauty, and also because he was the first person I met, besides me, who wasn't named Jukes) in the spring of 1863, and he was the offspring of my aunt Carnation. She was one of the aunts we were not allowed to talk about on account of she and her sister, Myrtle, had gone off to the sporting life before I got born.

The Reverend Spottle was all dressed in black and skinny as a bean pole and had a nose like an axe blade, but cut an imposing figure. He read a letter out to Granny Wren. It said,

"Mama, a preacher writes this for me. Are you good? I am good. I'm settled for now in Liberty with Myrtle Marie and the man she has took up with. I want you should take this baby. He is mine, his name is Chigger John Jukes. The remedy didn't work this time, ha ha," and it was signed "Your daughter, Carnation Jane."

For me and baby Chigger, it was love at first sight. He was magic to me, like one of my rag-and-sawdust poppets come to life, and even though he was only five years younger than me, I guess I felt about him like a mama feels for her own babe.

You might think that I was just taken with him because he was the only one who would let me talk to him all I wanted without hushing me all the time, or because he was a baby and I had never seen one before. But I did not feel the same about Cousin Violet when she was born, nor about any other baby for a real long time.

I have been told that I started in speaking out plain words at eight months and long sentences by ten months, and that by the time I turned a year it was orations with opinions and they could not shut me up. Now, a fondness for social discourse was not a real strong trait in my family, for most of them would rather knife a body than say hello, and so most of what I got back for my efforts was "Hush up, Clutie Mae" and the back of a hand.

I don't know why I was so noisy, for as I have said, it was not the Jukes way to have much truck with conversation. I later discovered this was because they were too ignorant to string together more than two dozen words in a row, but back then I had yet to figure this out, and was filled with admiration for their closemouthed ways.

Still, I was a fool for chatter. I am told my yammering half drove the womenfolks mad when I was closed in the cabin with them during bad weather, and finally they sent me to school, which was the other good thing, besides Chigger, that happened to me during the war.

They did not do it out of kindness. They were just sick of shouting "Hush up!" and wanted some peace and quiet. This was an unusual thing for the Jukeses—school, I mean, not "hush up"—since girl children never got any formal learning at all. The boys seldom stayed longer than it took them to learn to sign their names and cipher, which meant a couple of them were in school till they were close to ten.

Now, I had never been off our land in my life, and never met any strangers other than the Reverend Spottle. I do not want you to think we never saw folks, though. Sometimes, back before the war, folks had come to our farm to apprehend one or another of the Bug Boys or to buy donk or potions—they still came for the potions, which was how we got most of our war news. It was just that I had never talked to any of them.

On the first day, Mama rode me to the schoolhouse on the one poor horse we had then, an old gray who was twenty if he was a day, and so swaybacked no saddle would fit him. We went by way of the road, and Mama said it was six miles, near all the way to town.

All along the way, I got more and more nervous. Being so nervous, I guess I talked up a storm the whole way in.

By the time we got there, Mama had about worn herself out with all the times she had to say, "Hush up, Clutie!" She dumped me off at the school, then she rode off, just like that, leaving me on the edge of a yard full of strange kids.

I eyed them and they eyed me, and I had just about decided that they were too awed and humbled by the presence of a Jukes to speak up, when one kid pointed and said, "Bug Baby!" and then a bunch of them laughed right out loud. Somebody threw a rock that landed at my bare feet in a little puff of dust, and then several kids started saying "Bug Baby, Bug Baby, Bug Baby" over and over.

I was shocked. Here Granny Wren had always taught us that the Jukeses were the best and the smartest folks, not to mention the most clever and deadly and admired. And even though my family had always been fair vile to me in word and deed, had called me stupid and ugly and worse, I had believed Granny. I had spent the whole of my first six years on this earth aspiring as best I could toward the lofty ideal of Jukesness. But right then, standing in that schoolyard, I all of a sudden knew in my heart that I'd been lied to.

A boy in a brown shirt picked up a bigger rock and was just cocking back his arm to throw it, when a dark-headed lady came out on the stoop and rang a bell. The boy dropped his rock, the kids stopped chanting, and everybody went inside. I followed along. I didn't know what else to do.

Everybody sat down at one of the desks set up in rows. It got real quiet, and everybody fixed their attention on the bell-clanging lady.

"Good morning," she said. "For you new children, my name is Miss Alvinetta Hanker, and I am your teacher." She wrote it on the chalkboard. It just looked like squiggly lines to me, but I took her word for it.

Next, she asked all the pupils to stand, one by one, and say out the whole of their Christian and family name, real formal, and where they lived and what their families did.

Everybody took to their feet serious-like when it was their turn. They said things like "My name is Jonathan Henry Turnbull, and I live at Turnbull Farm west of the crossroads by Dick Toby's bridge, and we raise up corn, mostly, 'ceptin' this year our fields was burned out," or "My name is Agnes Ann Roebuck, and I'm from out to the Roebuck hog farm on Hickory Creek."

By the time it got to be my turn, I was so nerved up that I'd gone all quivery inside. But I stood up, took a real big breath, and said, real fast, "My name is Hush Up Clutie Mae Chestnut from Jukes Holler Farm, four mile down the pike, and my uncles cook mash when they ain't in jail or off givin' misery to Yankees."

Everybody laughed, especially that Agnes Ann Roebuck, and I ran outside.

Miss Hanker came out and found me hunkered behind the woodbox, weeping over the Bug Boys and how everybody knew I was a Jukes. She wiped my tears and then she explained, real kindly-like, that I would just have to live with the Jukes part, but that "Hush Up" didn't have squat to do with my name.

I didn't believe her at first. I'd been hearing "Hush-Up-Clutie-Mae" all run together for so long I had got persuaded that it was the full and fancified version of my Christian name. But eventually she got me convinced.

Miss Hanker and me got to be good friends. She was little and skinny and real sweet—smart as a whip, too. She liked it that I talked all the time, because most of my talking was questions. She said I had the thirstiest mind she had ever known, and that she would be my guide to the well of knowledge.

I determined then and there to raise myself up to be like Miss Hanker, and get an education and talk good, and I guess I did all right considering where I started. She said I excelled at spelling and penmanship, and was the best at drawing in the whole school. Sometimes she would take drawings I had done of birds or critters and put them up on the wall. She left them there for a long time, too.

Agnes Ann Roebuck was my enemy. Her folks had a big place and money. Even with the war raging, she was always dressed better than anybody, with honest-to-Jim ruffles and pleats and layers of petticoats, and her corn-yellow hair curled just so.

She was two grades ahead of me and she never addressed me direct, but when she knew I could hear—and Miss Hanker couldn't—she'd say my name real snotty, like "Cloo-oo-tie," making it into extra syllables with the middle one real high-pitched. And then she'd laugh and so would everybody else.

I suppose I could have just hauled off and slugged her—I was an ace fistfighter already, and strong—but by then I had too much respect for Miss Alvinetta Hanker to make a scene. Also, despite my feeling that a person shouldn't dress so fancy when brave men were dying elsewhere, I had a secret envy for all those ruffles and frills.

Punching her out would have got them all mussed.

Agnes Ann's papa had two nigra slaves, and right up till the end of the war she got walked to school each morning by one of them. Cicero was his name, and he would come back in the afternoon to walk her home, too. Rain or shine, snow or 'skeeters, when that bell rang he was always standing out there beside the swing under the big sycamore, hat off, rolling its stained and floppy brim between long, dark fingers. He hardly ever spoke a word to anybody. But a couple times, when she was teasing me bad, I caught his eye. And he gave me this look that said yes, he surely did understand.

By the time the war was over and the Bug Boys came home, Cicero had stopped walking her to school. I overheard Agnes Ann tell another girl that him and their other slave, a woman called Old Bev, had just walked off and didn't even say good-bye or thank you. I was real tempted to ask her just what she thought Cicero should have thanked them for, but I bit my tongue.

Being not long out of the hills, our family kept a number of the old ways in one fashion or another, and this was mostly because of Granny Wren. She was the head of the Jukes clan, on account of there were no menfolks of her generation left living.

Wren was not my exact granny, being more like my great-double-aunt if you looked at it one way and some kind of quadruple cousin, a time or two removed, if you looked at it another. I called her Granny anyway. She was real old for a Jukes, having been birthed in the year 1796, but she still had a terrible quick temper and most all of her hair, and it was still orange, pretty much, until the day she died. She said she owed this to never having run a comb through it except by the light of the moon, and also that she relied solely on cornstarch for cleaning her hair, which she had never got wet on purpose.

Granny Wren was a great one for potions and charms. Even though folks called us Jukeses the lowest kind of trash, many's the time I spied some town lady or a neighbor's wife sneaking up to our place at dusk. They bartered Granny for remedies to bear a child or lose one, or to leash a wandering husband. They called her Old Witch Jukes behind her back, and Granny or Miz Jukes to her face, and they always left faster than they came.

On account of the Jukeses were so fair-skinned, Granny Wren fought freckles like a preacher fights Satan. It was her only vanity. Summers, when the sun brought mine out in a spray across my nose, she would rub my face with the blood of a fresh-killed black pullet. If a black pullet could not be had, she'd make up a paste of cow dung and smear it thick all over my face, as well as hers and Mama's.

I can't say that either of these treatments did much in the way of fading our freckles, but the cow dung did draw the skin up real tight.

She was also a strong believer in the powers of talismans. All the grown-ups carried a pocket buckeye—that being a big old seed, kind of like a horse chestnut—to ward off piles and the rheumatiz, and just for luck. Buckeyes are good for keeping away all manner of other ailments, too, and it's said that no man was ever found dead who had a buckeye in his pocket.

Red onions, when she could get them, were hung beside the sleeping pallets to keep us from catching cold. She sewed the stones from deer bladders into our clothes to keep us from cuts and scrapes and mayhem. Though, what with the Bug Boys around, it didn't do much good.

Winters, she made little pouches stuffed with asafetida to hold off sickness in general, plus a green penny for lung trouble and a scrap of black silk to prevent the croup. We wore the pouch at our necks, strung on a necklace of iron wire, which was for whooping cough. I am not sure of the reasoning for the latter, since each of us kids had been forced, as babies, to swallow a live minnow, which is supposed to prevent the whooping cough for a person's whole life.

There was a papery-skinned, brittle look to her and she would've had to stand on a nail keg to make five-foot-even, but Granny Wren had magic, that was for sure. She was about as mean as her hide could hold, and she could slug you as hard as any man. And would, at the slightest provocation.

It was a powerful combination. She was the only person I ever saw Beetle take his hat off to. Well, almost the only one. Thinking back on it, I fully believe it was only because of Granny Wren's restraining influence that the Bug Boys held themselves down to petty robbery after the war, and didn't go out on a full-fledged spree of murder and mutilation.

She was tough. Not just in fighting strength, but in her heart. When we received the news that Roach Jukes had been kicked in the face by a mule and died instant at the Battle of Wilson's Creek, his wife—that was my Aunt Iris, and Granny Wren's own daughter—threw herself down the well.

Did Granny carry on? No siree. All she said was, "Damn that Iris, al'ays torturin' over her own problems," hauled up the body, and boiled all the water for two weeks.

She lost a son and two nephews to the war. Her boy Chinch perished at Pilot's Knob. I already said about Roach. Tick just sort of disappeared, and we never heard from him again.

Uncle Weevil was gone, too, but since he ran off to the west before I was born, we weren't allowed to talk about him. Not that we were allowed to talk about any of them, which I thought was kind of funny, since Granny Wren was real big on stories from the olden days. "Dead is dead and the same as gone" is what Granny Wren used to say. "Don't do no good to go conjurin' up spirits."

I guess you could only talk about dead relatives who had been dead a real long time.

There was a story in our family that in late 1860, Granny Wren dreamt of a gigantic snake, coiled tight around the cabin, and she knew by this dream that war would soon be upon us. In the spring of 1865 she dreamt the snake again, stone dead and rotting, and sure enough, pretty soon our boys came home. She only ever dreamt that snake four times in her life, twice for the War of 1812, and twice for the War of Succession. Honest-to-Jim.

Towards the end of the hostilities, things got real bad for both sides, and not just the soldiers. We were starving, too. With my own eyes I saw Granny Wren poison one deserter, and slit another from crotch to lung for stealing our next-to-the-last chicken. He died right there on the dirt coop floor, holding all his purple, ropy innards in his hands and crying for his mama.

We buried him in the corn patch.

In the wet and mucky summer of '65, when I was coming eight and we had pledged our grudging allegiance to the Union, Uncle Beetle came limping home. He was minus his right leg, it having been severed just below the knee. In its place he sported a thick oaken peg, in which he'd embedded a section of saber blade, sharp edge toward the outside, for use in close fights.

"I already sliced me up three Yankees, a grass widder, and a drunk Cajun with this leg," he'd growl at me, drunk on his own homemade donk and scraggly-chinned and slouched on the big oak stump down by the barn. "Come too close, you friggin' little shit-for-hair half-breed, and you'll lose some fingers."

At five-foot-seven, Beetle was a giant amongst Jukes men. He was mean, having been born in the sign of the crawpappy when it was afflicted. And, as you probably know, when one of those crawpappy folks lets out their mad, it is Katie-bar-the-door.

Beetle was the oldest uncle, and because of that he would be in charge of the whole family when and if Granny Wren ever died. Tough as she was, I always prayed Granny Wren would live forever, for Beetle did not think girls were worth much. Maybe that was because Aunt Petunia, who had been his wife until she was took by exhaustion to her Greater Reward, had only birthed girls—eleven of them—and they had all been born dead. This was just as well, according to Granny Wren, for some of them had had terrible things wrong with them.

Anyway, Beetle had started out with Quantrill, but he'd spent most of the war under "Bloody Bill" Anderson's command, and he came back with souvenirs. Anderson's men had got infamous for removing the scalps—and sometimes other body parts, too—from the Union boys they killed, and Beetle claimed to have taken over forty before his leg got shot off and he had to recuperate in Texas.

About the first thing Beetle wanted to know when he came home was about Chigger John. "Whose is it?" he said, honing his knife.

And after Granny Wren told him, he said, "Lord a-mighty, now we got all our kin dumpin' off their rubbish! Has we got us a sign saying 'Jukes Foundling Home' out front? Come home to find the place overrun with woodscolts and sonsabitches." He looked at me real menacing. "And that brown-headed little bastard's still here."

I said, "Uncle Beetle, I'm not a bastard. My daddy was Hungarian!"

"Hush up, Clutie!" snapped Granny, and punched me in the arm.

Beetle growled, "C'mere and let me wring your ugly neck. Boy woodscolt's pure trash, but he's a site better than a gal."

He belted me a good one on his way out the door, by way of punctuation.

Just a few days after Beetle's return, Uncle Wig—that being short for Earwig—rode in on a handsome blood-bay gelding he said he had swiped off a Union officer. Wig was my favorite of all the uncles, no contest, and I was pleased he had made it through the struggle with no parts whatsoever shot or blown or chopped off.

And Wig brought me a present.

"Close your eyes up, Shortcake!" he said, and then he put something warm and furry into my arms.

It was a kitten, all soft and stripedy and yellow as fresh-churned butter.

I let out a squeal. "Uncle Wig! For me?"

"You take good care of her, now." He tousled my hair. "What you gonna call her?"

I studied on it for a minute. The kitten purred and rubbed up against my face, all tickledy. "Daisy," I said, giggling, " 'cause she's so cheery. Daisies are a cheery weed."

"Daisy it be, then," he said.

Before the conflict, Wig had been a pickpocket and a confidence man, and the other uncles and Granny Wren teased him for having entered into a sissy profession. But Wig had been born in the sign of the arms, which makes for nimble fingers as well as a quick wit and tongue, so it seemed to me that he had just applied his native talents.

"Make me some magic, Uncle Wig!" I'd say when there was nobody else around to tell me to hush up. "Make the presta—presto—"

"Presty-digitatin'," he'd say, and then *poof!*, smoke would come out of his ears, or maybe he'd pluck a hen's egg or a flower from behind one of my brown braids. He could dance a coin back and forth across his knuckles and never drop it once. He was orange-headed and short like all the Jukeses, about five-foot-three, and his left eye wandered a little. But he always dressed dapper and took baths regular and waxed his mustache, and next to the other uncles he seemed out of place, like a wild poppy sprung up in the scallions.

Uncle Wig had stayed with Quantrill for the whole of the hostilities, and so I suppose he must have done his share of scalping and burning and murder, too, but I did not like to think about it. I just wanted him to pull another pansy from behind my ear.

About the first thing Beetle and Wig did when they got home was to start up the mash cooker again. It had got pretty dusty and rusty and falling-down during the war, but they fixed it in no time—the Bug Boys were bone lazy over everything besides a good fight and that still—and pretty soon they were up to full production.

When they flung open the barn doors, the stench nigh on knocked you over.

two

About a month or so after Beetle and Wig got home, Uncle Glow came dragging in. Glow was short for Glowworm, and he was Beetle's younger brother. Glow had fought in the regular army, having joined up under General Sterling Price. He returned to the farm with all his limbs intact, but with only twelve teeth left in his head, all of them grinders, after having been shot square in the bugle.

He blamed his misfortune on the haircut he'd got the day before the battle, and vowed to never have it cut again. He wore it in a skinny, frizzledy orange braid, no bigger around than my thumb, that snaked down past his belt when he forgot to tuck it under the grimy Johnny Reb cap he favored.

The jolt he took when bullet hit bugle affected more than his teeth, because Glow would get confused in his brain sometimes and think he was back in the war. This happened especially when he was soused.

The boys would sneak up on him when he was sleeping it off and yell, "Yankees, Uncle Glow! Yankees in the corn patch!" He'd leap up and grab a rifle and sometimes he'd get as much as a mile down the pike before he'd come to his senses and wander on home.

He had been wed to my Aunt Nuthatch. Nuthatch went crazy and hanged herself from a barn rafter not long after her middle boy, Fly, jumped out of the hayloft and landed on an upturned pitchfork. That I remember—her hanging herself, I mean—for I found her, swaying slow in the dusty light one frosty morning, and ran up to the cabin, pitching a fit. It took about six "hush ups" before anybody'd listen to me.

Anyway, besides Fly, Glow and Nuthatch had produced six stillborns and two surviving issue: my cousins Violet and Spider.

Violet was the youngest, and she was cross-eyed and simple and never, in all the time I knew her, got past the baby-talk stage. She was real sweet, though, and when she got older she could cook up a batch of cornbread that was sweet as honey and tender to the tooth. I had to admire her, for this was a Jukes talent lost on me. Everything I cooked turned out burnt or raw or doughy or worse. But at least I never drooled in the batter, which Violet did sometimes.

Violet's brother Spider, who was six years my senior, rivaled Uncle Beetle for meanspiritedness. Maybe this was because they were both born when the sign was in the craw-pappy, or maybe it was just because they were extra Jukesish.

Being just a kid, Spider had not marched off with the uncles, although he ran off to join up during the last year of the conflict. He was only twelve, but I guess they were desperate. And by the time Wig and Glow and Beetle had been back on the farm for three months, we had about resigned ourselves to counting Spider among the perished.

I hope I can be excused for saying that I did not weep over this one bit, for Spider had been my special bane. He walked with a swaggery roll to his narrow hips, partly from bravado, and partly because he was pigeon-toed. One of his eyes—the right one—stared in toward his nose no matter what, and it was understood that when I came of age, we were to be wed.

I had not much zeal for the prospect.

So I felt no particular joy when, on a frosty fall morning more than five months after Appomattox, Spider—not yet fourteen, but sporting a tied-down hip gun, and decidedly alive and breathing—rambled up our lane astride a jug-headed roan.

I had been up in the wash yard, playing with Daisy. Though she wasn't full-grown yet, she was catching her share of mice, and how she loved it when I'd twiddle a string for her! But when I spied Cousin Spider coming, I loped down so as to hide and watch without having to say hello or act friendly right off.

I had no more secreted myself in the hollyhock patch next to the barn when Uncle Beetle banged open the doors and walked out into the sun, stretching his arms and rubbing his chin whiskers. About two seconds later his head cocked toward the lane, and he shouted, "I believes your boy's back, Glow!"

Uncle Wig joined him straight away, and Uncle Glow staggered out about the time Spider whoaed his horse in the yard.

"Lookee here," Spider said, about five seconds after he'd slid down to the ground and they had all pounded one another's back. He yanked his shirt down off one shoulder. "Beauty, ain't she?"

What it was, was a big old tattoo of a black widow spider hanging in a web. It was so coarsely drawn that I could have done better, and I was only eight.

He was real proud, though. "Got that in Loo-siana from a tame niggerwoman," he said with a worldly sniff. "Spoke Frenchie-talk, she did."

"I's staggered," said Wig. From where I was, he did not appear all that impressed.

"Was that where you fit, son? Down to the swamps?" asked Glow, goggle-eyed at the tattoo. Well, he was pretty much goggle-eyed, anyway.

Spider squinted up the slope. He spied Daisy. "Is that a goddamn cat? I hates me a cat."

"It's Clutie's," said Wig.

"Proud'a you, boy," said Beetle, who was still on the subject of war. "Who'd you get to take on a cockeyed little runt like you?"

" 'Bloody Bill,' " Spider said. He forgot about Daisy, for which I was grateful. "I took me some Yankee hair. You wanna see?" He pulled down his saddlebags and went to work on the buckle. I stood on my tip-toes to get a better view. I had heard a lot of bragging on scalps from Beetle, but I had never seen one.

But Beetle grabbed the bags away from Spider and tossed

them over his shoulder, like he was saying that any booty brought home belonged to him. He raised up one brow. "I rode with Bill up till a year ago when I lost my leg. Never heard tell'a him fightin' down to no froggy swamps."

Spider patted the butt of his holstered pistol, real cocky-like. "Ain't all swamps," he said, avoiding Beetle's eye. "I been around some, I guess. What happened to your choppers, Pa?"

"Bugle," said Glow, his smile wide and gaping. "Come on in the barn and we'll take us a look-see at them scalps."

Two days later, I found Daisy out back of the barn, tossed on the dung heap and mutilated terrible. All the Bug Boys expressed surprise at the news except for Beetle, who said, "Goddamn thing was underfoot all the time, anyhow. Save me the trouble of kickin' it."

I was in hysterics. I sobbed, "But she was all cut up!"

"It's them rats," said Spider, his back to me.

Uncle Wig said he would bring me another, but I told him no. It seemed to me, young as I was, that any critter I owned and loved was doomed to perish horrible.

I cried and cried.

Over the next few years was when the James-Younger gang started to get well known, and the Bug Boys got to be great admirers of the Jameses, Frank and Jesse. I was told that Uncle Wig rode alongside Frank during the war, under Quantrill. Whenever one of the Bug Boys happened upon a wanted poster for the James boys or any of their crew, he would take it down real careful and bring it home, and tack it up inside the barn door.

Us women and girls were not supposed to know about this, even though there were plenty of chinks in the barn walls to peek through. The men were convinced, though, that they kept the inner workings of the barn private, like a secret club.

Now, from the minute they came home from war and discovered Granny and Mama had been sending me off to school, the Bug Boys were dead set against it. Not that they'd say so to Granny Wren, of course. But they taunted me terrible fierce until one day, in the spring of '68, Uncle Glow stuck up a man on the road and for a change got clean away with a booty of seven dollars cash, a gold-dipped watch, and a beat-up nickel book about the James-Younger gang.

It was called *Jesse James, The Fist of God,* and I had to read it out to them so many times that it finally fell to pieces. I guess the Bug Boys felt my schooling had been worthwhile after all, and thereafter they didn't ride me so much.

I was ten, almost eleven, then. Miss Hanker was still our teacher, and we had more kids in school all the time, what with Yankees moving down from Illinois and such to steal the farms good Missourians had been run off of during the conflict.

As poor as most everybody was in those days—so poor that being dressed in my patched Jukes clothes didn't make me stand out hardly at all—Agnes Ann still had her ruffles and curls. Now she had a white hired hand to bring her to school each day in a dogcart drawn by a handsome sorrel pony. Once, when she came up behind me on the road, she took the reins from her man and tried to run me over. I jumped for the ditch, and she laughed and called back "Trash!" over her shoulder.

It was the first time she had ever spoke to me direct.

That was the spring we studied on the California Gold Rush, which was mostly boring to me—though not as boring as reading the Jesse James book out loud for the twelfth time—except when we got to learning about California itself; how green and verdant and fruity it was, and how there was a whole blue and beautiful ocean right there at the edge. We learned about how the Spanish had settled it and how there were still some of the old giant ranchos left.

Sometimes I would get to daydreaming about that. I'd picture herds of speckled Spanish cattle grazing on knee-high grass in pastures that went forever; peach orchards rowed in sun-dappled trees that were heavy with fruit and serenaded by buzzing bees; and best, I'd see myself—all rigged out in a dress of Spanish lace, with one of those fancy combs set high in my dark brown, un-Jukes hair—standing on the balcony of a tile-roofed hacienda like the one in the picture Miss Hanker showed us.

I guess that's when I took it in my head that one day I would see California for myself. I knew all along, of course, that it would never happen. I was destined to marry Spider Jukes and live out the rest of my life on Jukes Holler Farm, fetching Spider's boots and being told that I was dumb and big and ugly. But that knowledge did not stop me dreaming of the Golden State and Spanish lace.

When the weather was bad, whatever of the Bug Boys were home would open a jar or a jug and gather in the barn to practice quick draws and snappy sayings in front of that wallful of wanted posters they had collected. They'd get pretty skunked and pretty loud. Sometimes you could hear them from all the way up to the front porch.

"Stand and deliver!"

"Hand down your purse, and there'll be no killin'!"

"I'll take that money poke, Mr. Bank Johnny!"

Sometimes me and Chigger would sneak down the slope and into the hollyhocks, from which we'd peer through the knotholes in the barn wall to watch the quick-draw practice. It was spiderwebby and thick with caterpillars in there, but the show was worth getting crawled on.

Usually the Bug Boys kept this to a pantomime, seeing as how they were in the barn and there was nothing to aim at but each other and the livestock. They would pull their pistols fast and then pretend to fan them, shouting, "Bang! Bang bang bang!"

But sometimes they'd get carried away with the quick-draw practice, and a gun would go off. Before the Bug Boys had been home not much more than a year, Uncle Glow failed one day to clear leather and shot off his own baby toe. After that they used unloaded pistols, mostly so as not to waste ammunition.

Sometimes they'd talk about the legendary Weevil, my uncle who had run off long before I was born. Uncle Weevil was either brother or double cousin—at the least—to all the other uncles, and they'd whisper about him when Granny

Wren was out of earshot. They had conjured him up into a real hero, as they had once heard a rumor that Weevil had a big horse ranch out to Arizona, and was a rich man and a powerful force in government.

I found this hard to swallow, but they'd get real puffed up about Weevil, as if one Jukes in such an exalted position— imaginary or not—elevated the rest of them up out of the hog wallow, too.

Every once in a while a couple of them would actually ride across the county line to try their hands at being high-waymen. But seeing as how in our part of the world most folks didn't have neither a pot nor a window, they rarely made off with a purse worth the effort, and they got caught more often than not. Any time a victim reported having been waylaid by a short, orange-headed man, somebody would come out to Jukes Holler and cart off one of my relatives.

Now, you might think that this sort of thing would lead to a lot of pitched gun battles at our farm. But it never did. Provided they had not been apprehended at the scene, whatever Bug Boys had just done a crime would come on home, pleased to overflowing with themselves and too strutting and full of braggadocio to even hide out in the woods. A few days later, men with badges would ride in straight to the barn, and shortly thereafter ride out with one or more Bug Boys in tow. Usually they'd help themselves to the corn liquor on their way out.

Once I asked Granny Wren why they did not put up any fight, or at least try to hide. She just shrugged and said, "Some'a them jails is nice and has good vittles."

Because they had weak eyes, the Bug Boys were bad with firearms, and couldn't hardly hit a bull in the rump with a fiddle. But it was them who got me started with guns.

That same spring that they got hold of the Jesse James book, me and Chigger John happened to be down back of the barn one soggy afternoon, watching the Bug Boys target practice on rusty cans. They were about halfway through a jug and were not hitting much of anything because of weaving and falling down a lot, and also because they were some distracted by this big argument they were having over who was the fastest gun, Frank or Jesse James.

They had this discussion a lot. Beetle claimed it was Jesse, Glow was pushing for Frank, and Wig, who was the only one of the three to ever have more than passing contact with either of the Jameses, claimed he did not care much one way or the other.

On this particular day I was in a foul mood. First, it had rained all morning, which meant I was stuck in the cabin for the duration. Second, just minutes before it cleared up, little Violet had snuck into the corner with some sulfur-tips and my geography book, and set it afire. And when I got after her for it, Granny Wren whacked me over the head with a broom about ten times.

I was still picking the straw out of my braids.

So there they were, practically all the Bug Boys, calf-deep in wet spring weeds and mud and an argument going nowhere. It was Beetle's turn to fire. He emptied his rifle and hit exactly nothing, then stood there, looking puzzled. He said, "By Christ, Glow, I believe you nailed them peach tins to the fence. I knows I hit 'em."

"Mayhap your sights is off," said Glow. He had stood up, and was staggering over to take his turn. He was sozzled. "If my boy Spider was not locked up in the St. Joe jail, he'd knock them cans off like that!" He went to snap his fingers, which threw him off balance. He fell down with a splat.

I was thinking that if Spider was such a good shot, he probably wouldn't be in jail for the second time in six months, but I knew better than to say so. Instead, I picked another piece of Granny Wren's broom out of my hair and said, "Me and Chigger came down here to see some shooting, and nobody has knocked a can down yet. I guess I know now why we lost the war."

Sometimes my mouth just ran away with me, and I realized, even as the words tumbled out, that this time it was galloping in the exact wrong direction, even if the direction was wholly Jukes in nature.

"Shut your damn hole, Clutie Mae," Uncle Beetle shouted. He made a fist and shook it.

Chigger John had been skipping round my legs for a game, and I pushed him to the back of me. It had been a stupid thing, mouthing off to Beetle like that. But the worst thing I could do would be to run from him. I stood my ground and closed up my mouth.

He took a step closer. There was a serious mad on his face. "Seems like all I done since I come home a hero is listen to your mouth flap mornin', noon, and suppertime," he snarled, watery eyes squinted up and red with drink. "Well I ain't a-listenin', Clutie. I'd like to know how you come to think you's so fancy with that goddamn school talk. And I'd like to see you shoot better, you big ol' mud-headed girl-turd."

The twins, Nit and Gnat, were flopped in the weeds a few feet away, laughing like loons. They were identical but had different birthdays, the delivery having slopped over midnight, and Granny Wren was fond of saying that they looked "more Jukes than Jukes." They admired Beetle and thought he was real witty, which will show you just how smart they were.

Uncle Glow was crawling out of the puddle he had stumbled into. "Give 'er some iron, Beetle!" he remarked, wringing muddy water out of his braid, then that rebel cap of his. "Don't believe she can do no worser'n you."

Uncle Wig, who had been home, off and on, several times since the close of the hostilities and who, on this occasion, was freshly released from the Sedalia jail, laughed right out loud—even louder when Glow stumbled over a root and plopped back into the puddle. The twins' loon laughs went to donkey brays—they might have only been fourteen, but they were sozzled, too—and this got Beetle all the more irate.

He took another pull on his jug before he clumped over to me, his bladed peg leg slicing weeds like a scythe, and shoved his big old long gun at me, stock first. "Go ahead, Miss Loud Mouth," he said. "Miss Ugly Face. Miss High-Talkin' Horse Hockey for Hair."

Behind me, Chigger John started to giggle. "Horse hockey, Clutie!" he chirped. "Horse hockey!"

I shushed him.

"Now, that ain't entirely equitable, Beetle," Wig piped up. He had picked up some real ten-cent words on his travels, and I was proud to have such a refined relative, although on this occasion I think he just did it to get Beetle's goat. Beetle was always ragging me because he thought Miss Alvinetta Hanker's influence had made me too highfalutin in my speech.

Anyway, Wig put away the coin he'd been walking across his knuckles, then strutted over and gave me his twenty-two. "This'un here's more her match."

I was some scared by then, Beetle being so close and in such a foul temper and everything. If you got in bad trouble with Glow, you could usually holler "Yankees!" and point the other way and have enough time to clear out before he realized you'd fooled him. But Beetle? He'd knock you silly.

I took the twenty-two from Uncle Wig, said "stay put" to Chigger, and nestled the stock back into my shoulder. I stared down the sights and set my legs wide like I had seen the uncles do when they were sober.

Then I took a deep breath and pulled the trigger.

Not only did I miss, but the kick knocked me clean off my feet.

Beetle growled, "See?" and made to grab away the rifle, but Wig stayed his hand.

"She nicked the board, Beetle. I seen it splinter." He helped me up and whispered, "Try 'er again, Clutie. Squeeze the trigger, don't go a-yankin' it. And you might try keepin' your eyes open this time." He patted me on the head and took a step back, but not before he added, real soft, "Don't you listen to old Beetle, Shortcake. I think your brown hair is real purty."

Then he snatched Chigger off the ground, and with a cry of "Whirligig! Whirligig!" gave him a spin high in the air and plopped him up on his shoulder. Chigger was laughing to beat the band.

Beetle cussed, but he stepped aside.

I raised the rifle again and did like Uncle Wig had said, and I'll be dad-blasted if that rusty old peach tin didn't fly off the rail like I'd whacked it with a hammer!

"I hit it, Uncle Wig! I honest-to-Jim hit it!" I don't mind saying that it gave me a truly powerful feeling. I hadn't fallen down that time, either.

"By gum, Clutie," Wig said with a grin, "I do believe the James boys could use you a marksman like you!"

Beetle said a long string of bad words I will not repeat, and then he stomped off, his peg leg mowing the weeds. Glow and the twins trailed after him like buzzards after a gut wagon. Uncle Wig stayed, though. He let me shoot four more times, and I hit all four cans left on the fence. Maybe not dead center, but I knocked them over.

"You got the gift, Shortcake," Wig said as he relieved me of his twenty-two and reloaded it.

"The gift? What do you mean?" I was enjoying the conversation.

"Your Grandpappy Viper, he had it, too. I never seen him use more'n one ball to bring down game in all the time I knowed him. Clean kill every time."

He pulled an oily rag from his back pocket and gave the barrel a wipe. "You keep practicin', and one day, you maybe could start bringing in game when I ain't around to shoot it." Then he winked at me, said, "One more time?" and went down to set the cans up again.

My shoulder was sore from the kick, but I didn't mind.

Before Uncle Wig took off again, he showed me all about how to take a firearm apart and clean it and put it back together again, all about building ammunition, and how to lead a moving target. After that, nobody said boo when I shot cans, and it was understood that when Wig was away, I was free to use whatever firearms he had left behind at the farm.

It was not long, either, before I did start to bring in meat. You might think that after having seen Granny gut that deserter, and after all the chickens and hogs I'd seen butchered in my life, that I would not be squeamish about such things. Still, it was a hard thing the first time I shot something living, and I remember I cried and cried over my first squirrel. But

I learned to harden my heart, and prided myself that I always made a clean kill and the animal did not suffer.

The Bug Boys sold me off for the first time later that summer, after their still blew all to pieces and took with it the back half of the barn, not to mention the kennels and Mama's truck patch.

It was a real gollywhopper of a blast, and tossed busted boards and dog chains and squash and cowcumbers over the whole of four acres' worth of corn patch and clear back into the woods, and spooked the bejesus out of two saddle horses and our cow, which happened to be in the corral at the time. It would have blown up Beetle's hounds, too, if he hadn't had them out after possum that night.

Wig did not get caught in it, having left for Jefferson City the week before. And the only reason Glow did not perish was because he was out front of the barn, soused. The explosion roused him, though, and he went racing round the yard, leaping back and forth over the old oak stump, waving his shotgun and hollering, "Yankees! To arms! Yankees!"

When Uncle Beetle came running down through the trees—well, as good as a man with a peg leg can run—with his hounds on his heel, Glow was still carrying on by the light of the conflagration, which all the rest of us had just about got put out.

"By damn, Glow, you's a idiot!" Uncle Beetle hollered, although he did not have much room to talk.

Then he clipped Uncle Glow a good one alongside the jaw with the butt of his rifle. Glow went down and stayed there, and Beetle plopped himself on the old stump in the barnyard and there he sat, cussing and polishing off Glow's jug while he watched us smother the last of the flames.

Now, out of as many acres of timber as Jukes Holler covered, you might have thought that the Bug Boys would just go axe down a few trees and plane some boards and hammer them up and that would be that. But a Jukes mind did not work thataways.

After lengthy deliberation, they rebuilt the still in the same exact place: that is to say, where the back of the barn used to be. They made Nit and Gnat clear up the rubble. Then they commenced to plot a larceny big enough to get them lumber money.

I guess they could not come up with a good plan, because about two weeks later they swapped me to a family named Stubbins for a spavined cart mare named Naomi and two pounds of sugar.

I was pretty offended, I have to tell you. You'd think they would have held out for at least a five-pound sack. I was, in fact, so insulted that even though Uncle Glow cautioned me to stick with them for ten miles and then hightail it home, I waited until me and the Stubbinses got most of the way to the county line before I dropped off the tail of the wagon and started walking home to Jukes Holler.

And then, after I walked all that way—barefoot and with nothing to eat except three boiled eggs and some cornbread I swiped—the Bug Boys had the gall to be mad because I hadn't stole Mr. Stubbins's bluetick bawlin' hound, a dog greatly admired by Uncle Beetle especially.

There was just no pleasing him. He dragged me down to in front of the barn and commenced to wallop me, like usual, and I commenced to holler. Also like usual. "But they loved that hound, Uncle Beetle! Their kids raised him from a pup on a sugar tit!"

He gave me a thump to the shoulder with his fist, then a poke to the thigh with his peg leg, and I went rolling in the weeds, more to try and gain distance than from being hurt. Growing up around the Bug Boys made a body tough and I was that, but you had to watch out for Beetle's peg, for he was not loath to use it. I guess all us kids had scars.

"But he was too big for me to swipe!" I yelped when Beetle yanked me up off the ground by my braids.

Uncle Glow, who was watching me dangle off the end of Beetle's fist, took another pull on his jug, peeked up with his goggle eyes from under the bill of his old Reb cap, and drawled, "Aw, Beetle, we gots ourselves that limpy mare in the trade. Swapped her for a keg of nails and six dollars cash."

"Kill your own snakes, Glow," Uncle Beetle snarled, then thumped me atop my head.

"Uncle Glow's right!" I said, swinging wild and punching nothing but air. "You got that sack of sugar, too!"

"I ain't a-listenin', Clutie," Beetle said, and popped me across the ear.

He wearied of beating me a couple minutes later. I was sprawled in the weeds and holding onto my arm, the one he'd broke when I was two-and-a-half and which still hurt unnatural if it got knocked hard. He grabbed away Glow's jug and plopped himself on the stump.

"You is a idiot, Clutie," he remarked, and tossed back a swallow of donk. "Sometimes I has me a hard time believin' you got any Jukes in you at all."

I took it for a compliment.

They did not stop selling me after the barn got fixed. At first, I thought it was all their idea, making extra pin money this way, but I later discovered Granny Wren had hatched the scheme. The Bug Boys had a pirate's swagger, but it was Granny Wren who captained their boat.

Some folks will think it strange that I did not attempt to scuttle Granny Wren, seeing as how she was so set against me. I mean, I got sold and sold and sold, and still they kept selling me. And still, I kept on coming back. I expect I was afraid to do anything but that, and Granny was the reason. I figured that if I took off she would just witch me home.

I tried spells. I would go up in the woods and face the east with my hands behind my back, and hold my right thumb with my left hand, and my left thumb with my right. I would turn in a circle three times, shut my eyes real tight and say:

> "Breath and flint make air and fire,
> Earth and water make black mire,
> The Holy Ghost is with us all
> But I shall rise and you shall fall."

Now, that is a one-hundred-percent-guaranteed charm to drive out witches or protect you in a fight—especially that Holy Ghost part—but as many times as I said it, Granny Wren did not so much as get the sniffles. After a while, I gave up on having success with her. But I always carried a pocket buckeye to protect me.

The Bug Boys only swapped me off to strangers—pilgrims bound for the promise of the West. Before I snuck off, I always traveled with them far enough that they wouldn't want to waste the time coming after me. Also, nobody was apt to make a ruckus over what had been a real illegal transaction in the first place. And by the time I hightailed it, those folks were usually glad to be shed of me.

This was my fault, I expect. At home, I never could get a real conversational steam built up before somebody hushed me with word or fist. Strangers were different, though. I could talk at them about whatever I'd been studying in school, or discourse on the best way to cure hollowtail in cows, or rhapsodize about California for hours on end, intoxicated on the beauty of my own speechifying and encyclopedic knowledge.

Sometimes they would not tell me to be quiet for a real long time. Although it did not always mean they were enjoying my topic. One man threw me off the back of his ox cart smack in the middle of a mud road ten miles outside of St. Joe, hollering, "I can't take no more'a your jabberin'!" Then he whipped his oxen into a dead run—and oxen can run faster than a body'd expect—and called over his shoulder that my uncles could keep the sheep, but that if I tried to follow him he'd shoot me.

I will admit that it did give me a chance to see some country. Also, sometimes the folks I went off with were real interesting, and would tell me about where they had come from and what it was like there. Once my mouth ran down and they had a chance to talk, that is. I got to feeling kind of worldly after a while.

The Bug Boys did not sell me off often—not more than two or three times a summer, usually, and only that because there was not what you'd call a real high demand for bond servants—but after the first few times I kind of got to resenting it, especially the way they'd march me out and make me show my teeth were good, or tote an armload of firewood to demonstrate my strength.

And I felt bad about Chigger John. He did not understand about larceny or deceit, and would always pitch a fit when the bartering started. One time, right in front of the buyers, he cried out, "Don't go sellin' my Clutie again, Uncle Beetle! Not *again*!"

The transaction turned ugly, and after that Beetle took to locking Chigger in the smokehouse before the dickering got under way. They would leave him there until me and my new owners were long gone, so that he would not know where to follow. Mama told me that he would weep and sniffle and sit under the porch and refuse food until I got back.

To tell the truth, though, I sort of got to enjoying the adventure of it. The travel part and the sneaking off part, I mean.

And then, when I was just turned twelve, something happened that made me not like it so much anymore.

three

It was late August and real sultry weather when Uncle
Beetle indentured me to a pilgrim couple by the name of
Foot. Mr. Foot was a big-bellied fat man of about fifty
or so. He had shaggy salt-and-pepper hair, thick mutton-
chops, and was well set for livestock. I had a bad feeling
about him right off.

His wife was so terrible sickly that she did not leave her
bed in the wagon or say nary a word while her husband was
dickering for me.

"Mrs. Foot has got the stomach troubles," Mr. Foot said,
looking all concerned and just a tad too pious, considering
what he was haggling for. "I keep a Bible beneath her pillow
to draw the Lord's attention to her plight," he went on, "but
she seems to fare no better. If this girl of yours is as good a
worker as you claim, she will be a real blessing."

But once we got a ways down the road, he seemed un-
troubled by his wife's condition. Pasty and gray, she just lay
in the wagon, one leg drawn up real odd beneath a thin,
soiled counterpane. It did not appear to me that she had
changed her clothes or combed her hair for maybe a week.
She was a lot younger than him, and a skinny thing, and she
was either asleep or unconscious most of the time, rousing
only to nurse at a bottle of medicine or bat at my hand when
I poked her.

From up front on the driver's bench, Mr. Foot saw me
watching her. "Tend your own business," he said. "Mrs.
Foot can take care of herself." Then he patted the seat next
to him and added, "Why don't you crawl up here and ride
beside me, Clutie. That's your name, ain't it?"

Instead, I hopped down off the wagon's tailgate and started walking along beside it. I said, "Thank you, Mr. Foot, but I would not want to crowd you."

Now, I was feeling uneasy. Often, when I felt that way, a good conversation would put me right. But I did not want to have a conversation with Mr. Foot. So, as I walked along beside the wheel, I said, "Have you ever heard the story called 'Raw Head and Bloody Bones'? It's a good scary one my granny tells and is better in the dark when the wind's moaning, but maybe you would like to hear it now. Here is how it starts: Far, far back in the piney, piney woods, in the olden days of yore, there was a family who had spent the whole day butchering hogs. Come nightfall, they were—"

"What was their name?" said Mr. Foot. He did not look like he was being entertained.

"Whose name?" I said.

"The folks butchering hogs."

"Smith," I said, although Granny Wren had never named them when she told the tale.

Mr. Foot grunted, and I went on.

"Come nightfall, they were plumb wore out—the whole Smith family, I mean—and were happy to rest in their beds. But then there came a voice in the inky-black night, saying, 'Where'd you put the feet off'n my hogs?'" I made my voice all wobbly and spooky-like for that part. "Well, the father, he got up, all stumbling in the dark, and—"

"Enough," said Mr. Foot. "I have heard this before. And their name wasn't Smith, it was something else. If you think you are too good to climb up and sit here beside me on the seat, then you walk up a ways, by the lead team, so I can keep an eye on you without the plague of your babbling."

Now, I was newly come into my womanhood. Not three weeks before, Granny Wren had pulled me aside one morning as I climbed down the loft ladder in my shift.

"Tulip," she had said to Mama, lips pursed up in the center of her dried-apple face, "I believe we'll be makin' up a pallet for Clutie Mae in the lean-to. She's comin' too ripe to be a-sleepin' up to the loft with them boys. And you'd best be learnin' her how to bind them dinners up."

By "dinners," she meant my bosoms, which had been sprouting to beat the band over the last months, and which I was embarrassed of. I didn't like the way Spider stared at my chest. And it occurred to me, as Mr. Foot ordered me up ahead, that he had been looking at me just like Spider, which was less than wholesome.

I had figured to stay with the Foots until we got about twenty miles from home, just to be on the safe side; but right about then I decided I'd slither out and head for home that very evening, as soon as they had gone to sleep. I just hoped he would not tie me up. The ones that bought me sometimes did.

We made camp alongside a creek. Mrs. Foot did not come out of the wagon. Mr. Foot kept me busy making supper while he leaned against a wagon wheel and sipped from a flask. It was good and dark by then.

He spat out the stew I served him. "Bah! This is half-burnt and half-raw!" He stuck out his tongue and rubbed it on his sleeve. He shoved his plate at me. "I thought they said you could cook!"

"I can cook," I said. "I just can't cook good." That was sure the truth. Granny Wren said I had the least talent with vittles of any Jukes woman in living memory. I had been banned from kitchen work at the age of eight, which was fine with me.

I scraped his stew back into the pot, then nodded toward the wagon. "Doesn't she want any food?"

"My wife has retired," he said after a long drink of coffee. Coffee was about the only thing I could make decent. "You get this supper mess cleaned up."

I did what he said, all the time wondering how soon he'd join his wife and fall asleep so that I could hightail it. He had me so skittery that I was not even capable of making any sort of distracting conversation.

He followed me down to the creek when I went to rinse out the plates and such, and I was bent down by the water, scrubbing stew out of the pot, when I felt his fingers touch the back of my neck.

I sucked in my breath hard, but I did not jump. That came

from habit. If you jumped when Beetle grabbed you, you were likely to suffer a worse whipping than if you just stood still and took it.

So I stayed crouched there on the muddy bank, holding my breath, the stew pot in my hands, cold creek water coursing over my fingers. As loud as the frogs and crickets were chirping, it seemed to me they were almost entirely drowned out by the sound of Mr. Foot, breathing heavy behind my ear.

After a real long minute, he said, "I bet you'd look purty in a dress. You bring one with you?"

My mouth had gone dry. I said, "No, sir." In fact, I had no extra clothes with me at all. I'd brought my traveling poke, but like usual, there was nothing in it but a borrowed book and one of Uncle Wig's old pistols. That, and a little jerked meat and cornbread for the walk home.

"Bet you'd look purty," he said again. His fingers were still on the back of my neck.

Then, so fast it startled me, he let go of me and grabbed away the stew pot with a slosh. He grabbed the plates and cups and shoved them at me, put his hand on my shoulder, and pushed me through the weeds, toward the wagon.

"Get up inside," he said, once we got there.

I stuttered something about not wanting to wake his wife, but he said, "She won't know you're there," and made me go on up. Then he told me to open the small trunk and take out a dress. I took out the one on top. It was too dark to tell what color it was.

"Put it on," he said.

"But I—"

"Put it on," he said again, "and don't go wearin' it over them lumpy farm clothes. I want it to fit you good so's I can see your true figure. I will turn my back, and you throw out them rags you're wearing. If you ain't got that dress on in three minutes, I'll beat you like you ain't never been beat, and then I will put it on you myself. I didn't trade a good nanny goat for you just so's you'd question my authority." He stepped away, but I could hear him cracking his knuckles on the other side of the canvas.

I bent down to his wife. "Mrs. Foot!" I whispered. I gave her a shake. "Mrs. Foot!"

It was dark in the wagon and I couldn't see her good in the shadows, but the smell of death was upon her. She roused, but only waved a hand at me. "Go 'way," she slurred.

I was wishing I had my poke—and within it, Uncle Wig's pistol—but Mr. Foot had thrown it down on the ground near the wagon when he laid out my sleeping blankets.

"That's one minute gone by," he said from outside the wagon. Beside me, Mrs. Foot made a little groan and turned over, her leg still drawn up.

I got busy with my shirt buttons and called, "I'm hurryin' as fast as I can."

To Mrs. Foot, I whispered, "Wake up, please! Your man's got me wearin' your dress, and I think he plans to do me bad!"

"Shut up," she said. I could not tell if her eyes were open or not. "Let a dyin' woman have her peace."

"Mrs. Foot, please! I've got to find me a pistol or a knife! Something!"

"That's two minutes," came Mr. Foot's voice.

She wasn't answering me. I started chanting, fast and under my breath. "Breath and flint make air and fire, Earth and water make black mire . . ."

I tossed my shirt out the back of the wagon, then yanked the dress on over my head, fastening it up as I tried to kick my britches off over my boots. They would not go, and when Mr. Foot stepped round back of the wagon again, I was only half-buttoned into the dress, and my trousers, rope belt and all, were pooled around my feet. Along with them, my lucky buckeye.

He just stood there for a minute, watching me fumble with those dad-blamed little buttons, and then he said, kind of choked-up, "Sit down on the tailgate. I'll get them boots for you."

My insides had gone all cold and shaky. I did what he said, my feet dangling off the edge, and he took off my boots, real slow, then pulled my britches off over my feet and threw them up inside the wagon. I had about all the dress buttons done by then, though I don't know how, since I had sort of lost track of my fingers. Then he lifted me down off the wagon and led me to the fire. He had dragged my blankets over there. I could not see my traveling poke in the shadows.

He must have seen my eyes flicking, searching the campsite, because he said, "If you're lookin' for your leather sack, trouble yourself no more. I found that Navy. It is an old pistol, but too nice for you. Mine, now." And then he laughed. He held me at arm's length, by my shoulders. "How old are you?"

"Twelve," I said. "Twelve, two weeks past. What're you going to do, Mr. Foot? Shouldn't we all be asleep? It must be real late. Mrs. Foot must be a short woman when she stands up. This dress doesn't go but halfway past my knees, and I fear I will bust these buttons. I can't hardly breathe, it's so tight. Don't you think I ought to get back into my own things before—"

"Turn around," he said, and when I didn't—on account of I was about froze up with nerves by then, and fretting terrible over my buckeye—he pushed on my one shoulder and pulled on the other to make me turn.

My backbone might have gone to ice, but my mouth would not quit flapping. Like somebody else was making the words come out, I heard myself say, "I know another ghost story—one not about the Smiths, I mean—if you would like to hear it. It's one I learned in school, about a headless horsebacker."

"Shut up." His voice broke a little. He had turned me all around in a circle by then, and we were face-to-face again. He licked at his lips. "That dress is snug on you. Mrs. Foot is a small woman."

"Yes, she is. And I am big." Of course he already knew that, but the words were just falling out of me right and left, whether they made sense or not. I said, "I'd better change back into my own rig before I split her seams. Is there something wrong with your wife's leg? It's pulled up real odd, been that way all day."

He was not listening. He was not looking at my face, either. He said, "Them kin a'yours—they been at you much yet?"

I was insulted that he'd ask. "Not ever," I said, and that was the Lord's truth. It was a Jukes law that a Jukes woman went to her marriage bed untarnished, and no man in my family, no matter how low in other matters, would have done me that way. Besides, I was five-foot-six and still growing, bigger than everybody except Beetle, and I could've whipped most of them.

"Not never?" said Mr. Foot. "A trashy outfit like that? I bet they been at you plenty. I reckon they're already after that nanny goat I traded for you."

He laughed, and the hairs on the back of my neck went to prickle. I tried to step back, but he held me firm.

"Can't cook for spit," he muttered, not to me at all. "Mouth always running off. Guess it don't matter so much, though."

Then, before I knew it, he had pushed me down onto those blankets and shoved up my skirts.

I started in hollering for help and pounding at his shoulders with my fists, but he was a big man, maybe three hundred pounds, and I could not budge him.

He had his pants undone. He jammed one of his fat knees between mine, and was shoving my legs apart.

I was rolling that chant in my mind as fast as I could.

Then the gun went off. The slug popped up dirt and weeds not two feet from my head, and I said thank you, Jesus.

Mr. Foot rolled right off me, all startled. Behind him, her torso half off the wagon's tailgate, was Mrs. Foot. Uncle Wig's pistol dangled from her fingers.

"Ezra Foot," she breathed, so faint I could barely hear her. "You sonofabitchin' bastard." Then she went limp.

I was too shook and too wobbly to stand up, and tried to crawl away, but Mr. Foot gripped my elbow and dragged me over to the wagon, over to his wife. He had his pants done back up by then. He took the gun. He felt her neck.

"Now look what you've done," he said to me. "You've

killed Mrs. Foot.'' And before I could think of an answer, he slugged me square in the jaw.

I woke up later in the middle of that moonless night, still dizzy from the blow and lashed tight to a wagon wheel spoke, my jaw aching terrible where he had walloped me. I don't believe I had ever in my life wanted my mama so much as I did right then, though Lord knows she was never much comfort. I believe I would even have thrown myself upon Granny Wren's dusty bosom for what meager consolation it might have afforded, that's how dirt low I felt.

Finally, I got back to sleep, and what woke me again was the sound of digging. Squinting against the rising sun, I looked under the wagon and spied Mr. Foot, about twenty yards away and at work with a shovel. He saw I was awake, put down his shovel, picked up his shotgun, and came over. He began to tug at my wrist ropes.

I pulled away from him and he slapped my face so hard it brought water to my eyes. ''Quit squirmin','' he said.

He worked at them some more, jerking me around and cussing a streak. Finally, he spat in exasperation, then reached round to the back of his belt and brought out a great big old knife, the kind the Bug Boys called an Arkansas toothpick. If he had been toting it the day before, I had not noticed.

He cut the bonds from my wrists, then hauled me up to my feet. He said, ''Waste of good rope. You have to make water?''

I nodded. He slid the blade back into its scabbard, then hoisted his shotgun. ''Go behind them bushes,'' he said. ''Don't try runnin'. I can shoot you before you make the woods.''

My hands were full of pins and needles from the ropes cutting off my circulation, but by the time I came out from behind the bushes I was getting back some use of them. He gave me back my boots and put me to work digging deeper the grave he'd already started. It was hot, rough toil, but I guess I did not mind so much, considering what other labor he might have put me to.

I dug and I dug, and while my blisters rose I thought about what I would do to Mr. Foot if given half a chance. I thought about Mrs. Foot, and wondered why she had shot. I thought about Granny Wren, too. All my life she had been ninety-nine percent trouble to me, and now that her naturally vicious ways could do me some good for a change, she was nowhere around.

Plus, I had about given up on that chant. The Holy Ghost one. It seemed to me it had got me out of the fat and into the fire. If only I could get my buckeye back, I told myself, things would be different. Well, they'd be more different if I could get Uncle Wig's gun, but the buckeye would be a start.

Chewing off and on at an unlit cigar, Mr. Foot sat Indian style in the grass a few feet away. The shotgun was across his lap, bumped up against his fat belly. He had long since drained his flask, and was putting to waste a pint of store-bought.

Now, that dress of Mrs. Foot's was way too snug on me. Since Mr. Foot had put me to labor in the grave, I had popped three little buttons off the midsection so that my bare skin showed, and one of the side seams, just under the arm, was giving way. I had sweated the bodice through, and it was stuck to me tight. I said, "I would appreciate some water."

"In a minute," he replied, then hoisted himself up off the ground and came to peer down into the hole I was standing in. I was down about three-and-a-half feet by then. He said, "Deep enough. Get up out of there."

He did not offer his hand, which was just as well, for I would not have taken it.

He set a coin on each of Mrs. Foot's eyes, then I sewed shut the counterpane he'd draped her with. "Are you sure we should lay her to rest here?" I asked as we settled her in that shallow grave. "She would rest better in a town, in a real cemetery. This is bound to be somebody's farm, and—"

"Shut up," said Mr. Foot.

I covered her with dirt while he read the Bible over her,

just like he was decent. I said a quick, silent prayer to ask Jesus to be good to her, and to congratulate her on finally escaping Mr. Foot.

The minute I finished patting the mound, he snatched away the shovel, tossed his Good Book in the wagon, and ordered me to water and feed the livestock. I thought of making a dash, but there was not much cover, and every time I glanced back toward the wagon, he was watching me from the tail, his rifle across his knees as he sat upon the gate, polishing off that store-bought.

He was pretty well lit up by then, and he got to talking. He rambled on about Mexico, for that was where he was headed, to go into the ranching business with his brother, Lester. I did not attend his words with any great care, being too busy trying to think of an escape, but then he started talking about Mrs. Foot.

"I'll tell you two secrets," he said, his words slurry. "First, Mrs. Foot had a bad tumor inside her. Supposed to croak six weeks ago, but she just kept hangin' on. Reckon she was too mean to die. Probably waitin' her chance to take me to the grave with her. Bet you thought she was shootin' at you last night, didn't you? Well, maybe she was. More like me, though. Sneakin' wench has been tryin' to kill me off, one way or t'other, since the day I bought her off her kinfolk back in Kentucky."

He stopped just long enough to drain the last of the store-bought. He tossed the bottle out into the weeds. A little cloud of milkweed rose up from the spot where it disappeared. He wiped his mouth with the back of his hand, then ran a sleeve over his brow. It was getting fiercesome hot, and he was sweating more than most on account of being so fat.

"And that's the second secret, little lady. Mrs. Foot weren't Mrs. Foot at all. She was just like you, a bond-woman, and never much use at it, neither. Ain't nothin' worse than a cold female except one that's cold and whining, too. Kept tryin' to run off or sneak up behind me with an axe or whatnot, and I had to hamstring her."

He bent over that big belly to make a quick, slicing motion at the back of his leg with one finger. "Then she weren't even no good for work, except the kind what comes at night.''

He climbed down off the tailgate about then. ''Ain't that cow had enough to drink yet?'' he asked, kind of testy and mopping at his brow again. ''Get on up here. There is business to attend before we move on.''

Even in the terrible heat of that August morning, it felt like ice had overtaken my spine. I could not move or breathe.

''What's the matter with you?'' he shouted.

Somehow I got my feet to move, and I had no sooner come even with the wagon than he grabbed hold of my wrist and wrenched away the cow's lead rope. One-handed, he looped it through the wagon wheel, and then he turned to me.

He said, ''I believe I will need a little womanly comfort from you.''

I guess I must have tried to jerk away, because he hauled me closer. Through clenched teeth, he said, ''Don't you go backin' up, girl. You come to me nice, or I'll take care of you for good. I already hamstrung one gal, I can do it to another.''

''Please, Mr. Foot,'' I said, surprised when my voice came out so tiny. ''Please don't do me that way.''

In reply, he jabbed his fingers, real quick, inside the gap in my dressfront where I'd popped the buttons, and gave the fabric a jerk.

A slew of those teensy buttons flew off in a spray and my dress popped open. I tried to close it, but he grabbed my other wrist and forced me down to the ground.

Just like that he was on me again, shoving at my skirts and prying my legs apart with his knees. I remember the sun being in my eyes and then his head and shoulders blocking it out and then him poking at me, down below.

I screamed when he did it to me, it hurt so bad. And then right away he grunted and stopped, and I was trapped under him, crying.

There was something in my hand. Mr. Foot's weight was crushing me, but I choked back a sob when I realized that the thing in my hand was his knife. My Jukes half had not been frozen with terror, that was for sure.

I brought it right up and jabbed the tip of it against his neck, right where his jaw met his ear. The Jukes part had kicked in and taken over, all right, because all of a sudden I felt just as cold and calculating and deadly serious as a timber rattler. I said, "Get off me, Mr. Foot."

He froze. His eyes, wide in their sockets, rolled toward the knife at his throat. "Put that down."

I wiped quick at my eyes with the back of my free hand. "I will not. You are foul and disgusting and you have ruined me." I was whispering. It was hard to talk on account of his weight. "Count yourself lucky that I don't drive this knife home right now."

"You couldn't." Sweat from his forehead dripped on my face. "You don't have the sand."

"You real sure of that, Mr. Foot?" I pressed the knife point more firmly into his neck. A little spot of blood welled, a little dot of bright red. "Let me up."

Real slow, he sat up straight, and I finally got a deep breath. My arm was not long enough to keep the blade at his ear. I brought it down between us, the blade pointed right for his belly.

"You are making a mistake," he said, and his face was red with fury as well as drink and the heat. He fair shook with anger. "You'll not get away from me. I'll hamstring you and take you on to Mexico, and me and my brother Lester will have at you at our leisure. Then when we tire of you, we will toss you out to perish in the elements."

I gave the knife a little jab—not enough to draw blood, but enough to let him know I meant business. "Stand up and stand clear, or I will gut you like a deer. Don't think I can't do it."

He blinked at me, his eyes narrowing, his hands closing into fists at his sides.

"Get off me," I repeated. "Now." I have to admit it was a heady feeling, being the one giving the orders for a change. I was wondering where he had stashed my gun. I was wondering, too, if once I found it I could really shoot a person.

Maybe I would just tie him up to the wagon instead, and leave him there.

"You'll be sorry you did this, girl," he said at last, soft and mean, although he was sweating something terrible and his lips were a-tremble.

I said, "I don't think so," and poked him again.

Well, he went to take his feet, but I guess he got his foot tangled in my skirts or the weeds, or maybe he was just too drunk to stand proper, because he fell right on top of me, all catty-wampus.

There was a terrible punching pain in my stomach and I hollered, thinking he had got the best of me after all. But he pushed himself up right away and, still between my legs, sat back on his heels. His face had gone white and his mouth was open. He was looking down.

I looked there, too. The blade jutted from his belly. A red stain spread fast over his shirt. There was blood on my dress, too.

I scrambled out from under him, and I couldn't hold back my screams. He moved his mouth once, but no words came out. And then he fell forward, right on the knife.

He didn't move any more.

If I had been thinking halfway straight, I probably would have found my poke and my gun and my clothes and just took off. But at that moment I was not exactly overwhelmed with logic. I just sat down on the ground and started in to weep.

four

I did not hear the horsebacker until he was practically upon me. He did not look to be local, for his mount carried a traveler's fat bedroll and bulging saddlebags. "Goodness gracious. What's happened here?" he said from the saddle.

I clutched the top of that poor torn dress together and bit at my lips. My stomach hurt terrible from where the knife's grip had punched me when Mr. Foot stabbed himself, my jaw still smarted from getting punched last night, and I was fiery sore betwixt my legs. I stared at him, too flummoxed and too achy and weepy to put words together.

"Can you talk?" he asked. "I heard somebody scream. I am guessing it was you, as there looks to have been a ruckus here." He got down off his gelding, a rifle swinging from his hand, and went over to Mr. Foot. He nudged the body with his boot, and it tumbled to the side. Tugging on his strawberry mustache, he turned to me again. His sharp blue eyes looked down to where I was holding the dress together, then back up to my face.

"Was he after you, little sis?"

I nodded. I couldn't stop crying.

"He wasn't your pa, was he?"

"No, his name was Mr. Foot," I sniffled. "I was traded to him for a goat." The stranger raised a brow, and I added, "My uncles trade me off for goods sometimes. I sneak out and go back home."

He said, "I didn't know anybody was still on that old game. You put the knife in his belly?"

"I didn't mean to," I said between sobs. "I meant to plug him with my uncle's gun."

His mouth made a little twist at one corner, and then he said, "Well, I reckon you still can, if you're of a mind."

I shook my head. "I would just rather go on back home." And then I started crying harder. I remembered the stories of how mean Granny Wren had been to Mama after she ran off with my daddy and got herself soiled by a non-Jukes. I figured that her and the others would have no more kindness for me.

The man was still standing over Mr. Foot's body, except now he was staring out toward Mrs. Foot's grave. Slight of build and fair haired, with a broad forehead and narrow chin, he was not any taller than me, maybe a tad shorter, but he looked to be a man you would take serious in a scrape.

I said, "If you are the law, I suppose you should just take me in. Now that I think on it, I have nowhere to go."

He laughed, right out loud. "You have a name, sis?"

"Clutie," I said. "Clutie Mae Chestnut."

"Well, Miss Clutie, I am not the law and you will not go to jail. You will go home to your family, and they never need know what has befallen you here, if that's what concerns you. If they ask about that big bruise you've got coming up on your jaw, you tell 'em you fell."

He walked back over to his horse and slid his rifle into the boot. "You had best change into different clothes, and then you can explain to me who this man is, and who is buried over there, and how you came to be with them."

It was real slick, how he did it.

After I told him about Mr. Foot, and how poor Mrs. Foot came to die and be buried—all quick and stuttery—he had me bury the bloody dress on the other side of the creek and hide the place real good. When I got back from that, he had already made a cross from sticks and put it at the head of Mrs. Foot's grave, and was inside the wagon, rummaging through a trunk. Me, I felt a heap better just getting my clothes and my buckeye back.

He stuck his head out the back and asked, "Can you write?"

I nodded.

"Good," he said as he climbed down. "I have found some papers. Are you any good at forging? I will do my best if need be, but I am a bad hand at it."

Although I wasn't sure what he had in mind—and it didn't strike me until later to wonder how he would know whether or not he was any good at forgery—I said I would try. He handed over a pencil stub and a couple of lists and a letter penned by Mr. Foot, and after I practiced copying the wide scrawl, my new friend had me write a note. It said, "My dear wife is dead. I cannot go on." And then I signed it "Ezra Proctor Foot" just like his signature in the letter.

"I believe you are an artist," said the blue-eyed man after he studied my handiwork for a few seconds. "I believe you might find a future in forgery."

Then he folded up the paper and stuck it in Mr. Foot's shirt pocket. He fastened up Mr. Foot's britches, bent his hands round the knife grip, then tipped the body back so it looked like he had fallen on the knife on purpose. While I burned up my practice sheets, he put the other papers back where he'd found them, neat as a pin. He unharnessed Mr. Foot's team and shooed them off.

"I'd give you one of those old croakers to ride home," he said, "but I believe it might cause some suspicion. Are you all right to walk?"

I said I was.

"Are you sure?" he asked again. "You have hardly said a word since I rode in."

I was so shocked to realize he was right that I couldn't think of a dad-blamed to say.

He shrugged. "Maybe you're just naturally quiet." He gave me a packet of fried chicken and another of fresh biscuits out of his saddlebags before he gathered up the lead ropes of the milk cow and the goat.

"I know a widow close by who will be glad of the livestock," he said. "And I will ask her to send her son out later to discover this tragic suicide." He climbed up on his horse and made to leave.

"You never told me your name," I said at last. "I would like to put you in my prayers."

"Get on home, now, Miss Clutie, and just tell your folks it was business as usual. I am sorry for what happened to you. But, whether you know it or not, you were lucky. I have seen some bad things in my time. If your kin tries trading you off again, you'd best carry a concealed weapon. Better yet, get new kin."

And then he jogged off into the trees, the goat and cow following along.

If I acted odd when I got home, nobody noticed. Nobody except Chigger, that is. He was seven that summer and my shadow, and never has anyone seen a more comely child, if that word can be used for a boy. He had the light blue eyes and red hair of the Jukeses, but he made those attributes angelic. It seemed like his long sorrel lashes covered half his cheeks when he closed his eyes. Sometimes I would sit for hours and just watch him sleep, he was so beautiful.

The day I got home, it was Chigger who came up to me as I sat on the porch steps. Usually he was the first to greet me, throwing himself into my arms and jabbering about all the things he'd done while I was away. He'd tell me the same things five and six times because he'd forget he'd said them two minutes before. Chigger John's brain just got the hiccups sometimes.

But that day he didn't say a word, not even hello. He just stared at me, real serious, for maybe a minute, then put his little hand soft upon my knee.

I threw my arms around him, trying to stave off the tears but having little luck.

Into my ear, he whispered, "If'n they makes you go again, Clutie, I'll follow you along. I'll bring my gun."

I hugged him all the tighter. Against his curls, I said, "Chigger John, you don't have a gun."

"Then I'll bring me a stick."

I started the seventh grade the next day. I tried to act normal, but those next weeks were a scary time, for I lived in terror that Mr. Foot's seed had taken root in me. Nightmares plagued me, and I would jolt out of sleep, all sweaty and trembling and certain Mr. Foot was there in the dark, sitting atop his wife's grave, sipping at that flask and ready to pester me again.

Every day on the way to school, beside the same thistle bush, I did the chant to stop a baby:

> "Owl in the tall pine,
> Raven in the brush,
> Spit three times on a thistle-berry bush.
> Fish in the deep pool,
> Squirrel up a tree,
> Twice right, once left, flee, babe, flee!"

After watching Granny Wren for so many years, I knew how to flush a baby from the womb, and I started to collect roots and berries and such. Just in case.

I had no need of remedies, though, for the chanting worked and my flowers came of their own accord. When they did, I was so joyous that I let out a whoop and had to lie to Granny Wren, telling her I shouted because I'd stubbed my toe in the outhouse.

I started spending more and more time by myself. Maybe it was just because I was growing up, or maybe it was because I'd finally had enough of Uncle Beetle hollering "Hush up, goddamn it!" and backhanding me.

Or maybe it was leftover shame from Mr. Foot.

Now, I might not have been much of a cook, but I was a good quilter—the best in the family, when I could get decent cloth scraps. I had even won a prize at the county fair. And that fall was when I started the only genuine brain-tanned deerskin quilt ever made by anybody, ever. Leastwise, I never heard of another.

It was a modified star pattern, real pretty. I made it on the sly, out in my secret place in the woods, and it took me almost the whole year that I was twelve. I shot the bucks over a six week period in the fall—which left us better fixed for smoked and dried venison than we had been for any winter in living memory—stretching and scraping the hides as I went, and waiting until the first freeze to tan them. Freezing makes the fibers open better, to suck up more brains.

Now, brain-tanning is a real disgusting process, which I will not plague you with. But I simmered and soaked and scraped, and simmered and soaked and scraped some more, until the brains were worked in real good. And after, when the hides had dried again and I'd got them softened up again by pulling them back and forth across ropes and poles, I made a smoker out of a couple of buckets and a chunk of old stovepipe from the trash heap, and smoked the hides to make them waterproof and give them color.

This makes for a real soft skin with a wonderful smokey smell that's not like anything else in the world, and you can get different shades by the kind of rotted wood you pick to put on the coals in the smoker. Of course, they are all different shades of brown, but I like brown just fine, and variety is good when what you have in mind is a quilt.

Nobody ever questioned me about being off to the woods. They were just glad I did it; without me, we would not have had much meat. So when I went out after game, I would always take an extra day to go to my secret place to read in peace or fiddle with my quilt, or just be alone.

The place I went to was called Tickled Bear Hill. It was the highest point on our land, and from the upper limbs of the grandpappy oak that grew upon its crown, you could see for miles and miles. On clear days I could see all the way over to Agnes Ann Roebuck's farm, and after I swiped Uncle Glow's spyglass, I could even see the wash yard where the Roebucks' serving woman hung out all those frilly dresses of Agnes Ann's. They were like little bits of rainbow, all strung in a line.

Though Granny Wren said Tickled Bear Hill was barely a bump in the ground compared to where she'd been raised, it seemed impressive to me. Low on its south side, under a broad umbrella of hickory and maple and poplar and beech, there jutted a long, shelf-shaped outcrop of pale yellow limestone. Rain and wind had eroded the dirt beneath it to make a sort of shallow, dirt-floored cave with the limestone shelf for a roof. It was not fancy, but it was shelter, and it was all mine.

Farther below ran Little Shy Creek, whose shallow waters sent little glints and sparkles—all shimmering and silver— through the forest's dark trunks and sun-buttered leaves. Once I had my quilt finished, I would stretch out on it beneath the overhang, breathe in its rich, smokey smell, and read or draw or watch the squirrels skitter, or just listen to the trickle of the creek below.

Sometimes I would daydream that I was in California, where it was always warm and everything was golden. A real handsome Spanish man in a fine suit with ruffles on his shirt would take my quilt from me and say, "Señorita Clutie, this is the finest leather quilt I have ever had the pleasure to see, and you are by far the most beautiful woman in the world. How nice it is that your hair is not orange! We will hang your beautiful handiwork here on the wall for all our important guests to see, and you must marry me and be queen of my rancho!"

Over the years, I had got myself into a state of confusion about being half Jukes and half Chestnut. To tell you the truth, I was a little stupefied about what to aim for. When I was at school and had got a good grade or when Miss Hanker put one of my pictures on the wall or commended me, I felt real smart. Almost special, in fact, even though the other kids still would not speak to me. During those times I wanted to be like Miss Hanker—book-smart and mannered and smiling—and I felt like a traitor for it, none of these being Jukes traits.

But then I would come home, and it seemed most everything I did fell short of the Jukes standard, and I would try to steel my mind to being crafty. I attempted to make myself think of Miss Hanker the way my family did—that people like her were soft and fools, and existed only to be bamboozled by Jukes cunning. And then I'd feel bad for having such unkind thoughts about a nice person like Miss Hanker, who always let me borrow books to read in the summer, and who had never been anything but good to me.

It had occurred to me that I was struggling under two different sets of rules for what was smart and right——the Jukes kind and the Miss Hanker kind, which might have been the Chestnut kind, too, although it was hard to say without ever having met my daddy. It seemed to me that I didn't measure up to either standard, as if each half of my blood had ruined the other and left me good for nothing.

In the end, I decided that it didn't much matter what I wanted. I could go to school and learn about the Great Wall of China and multiplying fractions and the hexameter narrative of Mr. Henry Wadsworth Longfellow all I wanted. But the real world, for me, was going to be Granny Wren and the Bug Boys, forever and ever. And I was never going to be very good at it.

I steeled myself to being a half-baked Jukes, but I did not stop daydreaming about California, or the man who had aided me after I killed Mr. Foot. Fanciful as it was, I got to thinking that maybe he had been a heavenly spirit sent to help me.

The more I thought, the more I convinced myself I'd witnessed a supernatural manifestation, horse and all, and that I'd met none other than my very own honest-to-Jim guardian angel. Of course, he'd been a little scruffy and in need of a shave, but wouldn't that be a smart disguise for an emissary of the Lord? And if he had come once to help me, mightn't he do it again?

It was a weighty subject, but I had made myself a lot of silence in which to think it over.

Our winter that year was fairly peaceful, if bitter cold. Even the Bug Boys came up from the barn and stayed in the cabin for a while. This put a strain on everybody, though the extra body heat warmed the place considerable and almost made up for the stink.

Uncle Wig was with us for the whole month of December, which cheered me up a good bit. And for once, all the Bug Boys were out of jail for Christmas, a fact which put them in such a warm glow of family feeling that they hardly robbed, hit, or knifed anybody for something like three weeks straight.

I worked on my quilt in secret, read stories by Sir Walter Scott in Miss Hanker's classroom, and pondered on the mystery of my guardian angel.

In the spring, I got a surprise. May had just arrived, bringing with it a lot of rain and mud and therefore extra washing for me to help with after school.

I was out in the yard behind the cabin, where Granny Wren and Mama had the big laundry cauldrons cooking over slow fires, when I saw the horsebackers come in. There were a half dozen men, all clad in long white dusters like cattle buyers wear, and not one of them rode a horse worth less than three hundred dollars.

Beetle, Glow, Spider, and Nit were down in front of the barn, talking to them. To get a better look, I snuck to the edge of the wash yard and crouched behind the berry bramble.

Chigger was on my heels as usual. "Who's a-visitin' us, Clutie? Is they come to buy donk?" He peered over my shoulder. "Is it John Law come to call again?"

From what little I could hear, the riders were looking for Uncle Wig, who we had not seen since New Year's Day. Uncle Beetle was acting real funny. He had his hat off, and kept ducking his head, all apologetic.

The men got off their horses. By then, I was pretty well convinced that they were lawmen. Many's the time I'd seen deputies ride off with one of my uncles in handcuffs, and those deputies usually acted as cocksure as these boys did, though they did not ride anywhere near such fine horses. I was sort of hoping that since they hadn't found Wig, they'd cart off Beetle instead. Maybe Spider, too.

I had no such luck, though. Beetle spied me lurking up behind the bramble and hollered, "Clutie, get your carcass down here and see to these gentlemen's horses!" Then, to Mama, he shouted, "Tulip! Hotten up the coffee!"

I sent Chigger back to the cabin with Mama, and then I skirted the bramble and trotted down the muddy slope to the barn. Nit kicked me in the leg as I walked by. I ignored him and commenced to collect the riders' reins. I kept my eyes down and did not look any of the riders in the face until I got to the fourth one, and I only looked up then because he put his finger under my chin and lifted it.

It was all I could do not to shout "Glory!" when I saw his face, for it was none other than my guardian angel: he who had come to my aid after the demise of Mr. Foot.

Just like that, all my limbs were washed in gooseflesh. And just as sudden, I was sure in the knowledge that these other men must be angels in disguise, too, and that they had come to lift me out of the Jukes mire and spirit me off to Heaven, or maybe even California. I was in such awe that I just stood there with my mouth hanging open.

A smile tickled at the corner of my guardian angel's mouth. Soft, he said, "Clutie, is it?"

I had forgot my fingers entirely, and a couple of the reins slipped from my hands. Uncle Beetle smacked me, hard, between the shoulder blades. That was one of Beetle's favorite things, as he thought it was real funny if it knocked the air out of you.

This time it didn't knock out my wind, but I guess you could say it shook me out of my trance. I stumbled, and landed on my hip in the mud between two horses, one of which made a halfhearted attempt to step on my arm.

Above me, Beetle said, "You be polite, Clutie, or you's in for a whippin'. I's real sorry, sir. I 'pologize for the gal's clumsiness."

The angel picked me up real gentlemanly, then glared at Beetle. His eyes were so fierce I thought heavenly fire might shoot out of them at any moment. But there were no flames. Instead, he said, real quiet, "Don't you ever raise a hand to a female in my presence again, Jukes. I trust you understand my meaning."

You should have seen Beetle's face! If he'd had a second hat, I bet he would have taken that one off, too. He said, "Yessir, yessir," and flicked specks of mire off my shirt, almost gentle. "It sure won't happen again. It's just that this gal is nothin' but—"

"Don't you believe you had better introduce us?"

I couldn't imagine how Beetle could ever know an angel well enough to introduce him, but it looked like he was going to take a stab at it.

He stood up real straight. "Why sure, sure." About as formal as I'd ever heard him say anything, he said, "Clutie, this here is Mr. Frank James. Mr. James, this gal's my niece, Clutie Mae."

I guess my mouth dropped open all over again. Frank James, his very own self, lifted my hand and shook it, real serious. Tipping his hat, he said, "Honored."

I heard myself whisper, "You're not an angel?"

He gave me a wink, one Uncle Beetle and the others couldn't see, and then he turned me toward another of the riders. This one was lean and blue-eyed, too, but taller than Frank, and with dark auburn hair.

Frank said, "Miss Clutie, allow me to introduce my brother, Jesse. And he's no angel, either."

five

I never met Jesse James again after that day—and he didn't say more to me than "Pleased t'meet you, Miss"—but I will never forget the solemnity of his eyes, or the way he carried himself, all quiet and deep and serious. Kind of crazy, too. Frank James, my angel, gave me another reason to be grateful to him, too, because for a whole month after his and Jesse's visit, Uncle Beetle did not hit me once.

In early July, Beetle sold me to a Baptist family named Rudge. We made a good distance that day—a far enough piece that I felt it would be safe to light out that very night. Also, Mr. Rudge had chosen to camp near the edge of a wood—good luck for me, for woods are good for hiding in if you are being pursued.

I would have slipped out easy, except that at the last minute Mrs. Rudge insisted that her husband rope me to the wagon. She said it was just to be on the safe side, but personally I think she did it just out of spite on account of I burned their dinner so bad.

Now, since the trouble with Mr. Foot, I always brought along a knife of my own. I kept it tucked down inside my boot in a special sheath I sewed for it, on the theory I'd be able to slice myself out of almost any difficulty. It wasn't that I wished to repeat the grisly death of Mr. Foot. It's just easier to conceal a knife than a pistol.

But Mr. Rudge had tied me in such a way that I could not get to my blade. I was therefore pretty annoyed with both him and myself that night—especially when it started in to rain, which left me in the wet grass roped to the wheel, with all of the Rudge family asleep and snoring, dry and cozy in the wagon above me.

I was trying to take my mind off the torrent and the rest of my troubles—including a bad itch on my ankle—when I heard a squishy, scuffling noise in the brush. I swallowed hard and hoped it was only a stray cow. But I made ready to yell anyway, although if it was a bear or a cat I would probably be dinner before I could scream. I had no sooner opened my mouth than it was covered by a small, wet hand.

"Don't holler, Clutie!" Chigger said, a lot louder than need be, right next to my ear. "I come to rescue you." He took his hand away. I couldn't see him as he was in back of me, but I could feel him fumbling with the knots at my wrists.

"Chigger!" I said softly. "You about scared the puddin' out of me. Reach down there into my boot—no, the other one. There's a knife. How'd you get here, anyhow?"

He found it and gave me a big wet grin before he ducked round behind me again and began to saw at the ropes.

"I give you the frights, Clutie?" He stopped cutting. "You mad?"

"No."

The knife went back to work again. I blinked pelting rain out of my eyes. It was turning into a real goose-drownder. Lightning flared in the sky, turning everything stark and bright for a half a second, and right after that the thunder boomed real loud. Above us in the wagon, Mr. Rudge's snores stopped. I froze, and felt Chigger's hand squeeze hard on my arm. I think we both held our breaths for the minute it took for the snores to start up again, even and slow.

"I thought maybe you were a bear," I said, once we were both breathing again and Chigger was back at work on my ropes. "I just wish you'd given me a warning."

"Like a signal?"

"Yes. How'd you find—Chigger?"

Just like that he was gone. I could feel the emptiness behind me.

Louder, I whispered, "Chigger!"

And then I heard it. Through the battering rain, the sound came from the sodden brush and tall grass on the other side of the wagon: a soft whistle, like the call made by some strange bird that had never breathed on this world. That, or maybe a ghost. Beneath the sopping shirt plastered to my skin, gooseflesh puckered my arms.

"Chigger? Chigger John?"

"You're supposed to do it back!" came the reply from the long grass.

I took a deep breath. "I can't. You'll have to teach me later. Come now and finish cutting my—"

He was already behind me. I felt the knife's cool blade lay against my forearm for a moment, then the pressure as he went back to work on the ropes.

"If I didn't know better, Chigger, I'd say you were part Indian, you move so quiet. What was that whistle you made?"

"Bet I am, Clutie." He got real quiet and the knife stopped. I couldn't see him, but I had observed Chigger in the throes of a revelation often enough to know exactly what he looked like just then: face lifted, lips parted, eyes big with wonder, like an angel in a painting, an angel who has just glimpsed the face of God.

Sometimes it did not take much to put Chigger John in this frame of mind.

Lightning flashed again, and Chigger and I counted together, "One-Mississippi, two-Mississippi, three-Mississippi, four—" before the thunder boomed again. The storm was moving away, and then all of a sudden it was barely a drizzle.

The knife began to move again. "Bet I am part Indian. What's the kinds of 'em, Clutie?"

"There's Cherokee, Creek, and Kickapoo. Sac and Fox, Sioux, Osage—"

The wet rope popped and I shook my right hand free, then my left. In a couple of seconds I had my ankles undone and was on my feet, my traveling poke slung over my shoulder.

"Your knife." Chigger slid it down into the sheath inside my boot and then, still bent over, he braced his hands on his narrow knees and shook himself like a dog. Water flew every which way, mostly onto me. "You reckon we could make off with their team?" he asked after he stood up straight.

I pulled out my soggy kerchief and wiped my face, then his. I ran my fingers through his hair, pushing it off his forehead. Between the moonlight and the wet, you could barely tell it was red at all, just darkish. He looked like a half-drowned angel.

The rain had stopped altogether, and without the blanket of its noise, I whispered softly, "We're not stealing any horses, Chigger John. That's a hard and heinous crime. I don't believe we're up to it yet."

He stood his ground, trying to look serious. "A man can't never have too many horses."

"No."

We had put about two miles between us and the Rudges— and their horses—when we came across an old rutted lane, and began to follow it along. We'd been done with the rain long enough to dry the parts of our hides that were exposed, although not our clothes.

Beside me, Chigger began to sing soft. It was an old song called "I Loved You Better Than My Dog, and Now You've Broke My Heart," and it was real sad.

Now, about all of the Jukeses except me were musical and played an instrument, whether it be zither or fiddle, ocarina, mouthharp, or our old harmonium. Evil as Beetle was, if you'd ever heard the sound of his fiddle floating up from the barn, you would have been paralyzed with emotion. Most were fine singers, too.

Chigger had one of the best Jukes voices, a clear and rich soprano, and it was eerie to hear him singing there, in the middle of that wet and lonely wood, especially such an old-time, mournful song. It made the hair on the back of my neck go prickly, it was that beautiful and that unearthly.

"Chigger," I said, after he had finished the last verse, "how in the blue-eyed world did you find me? How'd you get out of the smokehouse, anyway?"

He shrugged. "I'm hungry. I wish I had me a candy. I wish Uncle Glow had got more."

The year before, Glow had stuck up a traveler and made off with the gentleman's case and purse. The purse was empty save for forty-three cents, but the case turned out to be filled with lemon drops and peppermints and jelly beans. According to the card inside, the man had been a drummer for the Sweet Indulgence Confection Company of Little Rock, Arkansas. Uncle Beetle gave Glow a hard time about it, but this was probably everybody else's favorite robbery that Glow had ever pulled. Chigger's, especially.

I started digging through my traveling poke.

"You gonna marry up with Spider?" Chigger asked, just like it was a normal, everyday question.

I stopped dead in my tracks, one arm stuck into my poke. I knew I'd have to someday, but I said, "I'd sooner eat a wasp's nest. Why?"

He stopped, too. "I heared Granny Wren and Aunt Tulip. You gonna have you a baby? Can I play with it?"

All my insides went kind of queasy. "What do Granny and Mama say, Chigger?"

"When?"

"When you heard them talking about me and Spider."

"What you lookin' for?" He stood on his tiptoes and peered inside, like a pup nosing a caterpillar.

I felt around a little more until my fingers touched crumpled paper. I drew out the little sack and handed it to him. He opened it.

His eyes went wide. "Oh, Clutie!"

They were the soft kind of peppermints, the big pillowy white ones, almost powdery, that stick in your teeth and are wonderful sweet. He popped one in his mouth and let out a satisfied sigh.

"I swiped them off the Rudges this afternoon," I said. "Don't reckon they'll miss them."

"Mmm," said Chigger, and helped himself again.

"What else did Mama and Granny Wren say?"

He chewed thoughtfully for a moment. Pale flecks of peppermint dotted his lips. " 'Bout what?"

"About Spider and me."

He shrugged. "You think I's maybe part Indian, Clutie?" He puffed out his chest, and nearly tripped over a root on the path. "That was my secret Indian whistle I give you back there," he said. "Every time you hears it, you'll know it's me."

"That's good, Chigger," I said. I was feeling real low, what with the looming prospect of becoming Mrs. Spider Jukes and all.

Chigger shoved the candy sack at me. He must have been stuffing those things in his face by the handful, for the bag was already half-empty.

"Oo ahnt un?" he said, his mouth full.

I took the sack from him. "No, thanks. But I'm going to put this away. You'll make yourself sick."

"I don't mind." His tongue, white with peppermint, darted out to lick his lips again. He grabbed the candy back. "I likes me a good puke."

"No, you don't." He opened his mouth to argue, but before he could, I said, "Besides, Chigger, if you get sick on the trail, Mr. and Mrs. Rudge could get themselves a puke dog and trail us."

His little brow puckered into soft furrows. "A puke dog?"

I propped my hands akimbo and shook my head. "Chigger John Jukes, you mean to tell me that nobody has ever told you about puke dogs?"

Slowly, he shook his head.

"Oh," I breathed, "they are the hound dogs from hell. They can find where a human has puked, and once gaining that scent, they never fail to trace their quarry."

Chigger stopped chewing. Now, I suppose I am expected to say that I hated fibbing to Chigger, and that I only did it because sometimes it was just a lot easier to tell him a story than to spend a half hour trying to make him understand the real reason for something. And I suppose that was the original reason I fibbed to him so much. But the truth of it was that over the years I sort of got to enjoying it.

I'd made up about the fire-belching dragon in Potter's Pond when he waded out too far—and half-drowned me when I pulled him out. There was the tale of the terrible plague of suppurating boils that beset boys who didn't shut the outhouse door. And when he took to wandering too far into the eastern woods, I came up with the Jukes-eating wampus-cat of Rossiter's Ridge.

It was sort of entertaining for both of us, and I don't think it did any harm. Chigger usually forgot most things pretty quick, anyway.

Right then, his eyes were wide as saucers. "What does they look like, Clutie, them puke dogs?"

"Oh, they're big, Chigger John. Bigger than any of Uncle Beetle's hounds. They don't bay or yodel, so you can't hear 'em coming. They're solid black so you can't see 'em at night. Unless, of course, you know to look for their eyes."

Chigger peeped, "Their eyes?"

"They're red," I confided as I stepped over a root. "They glow in the dark. You don't ever want to meet up with a puke dog, Chigger. They are big-boned, thick-skinned, razor-toothed, slavering hounds."

He swallowed hard, and this time it was not candy. He whispered, "Slaverin'?" I don't guess he knew what it meant, but it must have sounded ominous to him.

"Yes," I said. I was having a pretty good time by then. "They trail their prey by the gastric method. That's French, Chigger, from Paris, France, and it is a way of training that makes a dog—especially a purebred puke dog—always dead on target. Why, I've heard it said that if Jesse James would just once toss his supper, he would be apprehended within the week!"

He handed me back the candy sack. He said, "I sure hope Jesse don't get sick."

Right about then the little lane left the woods and we followed it into a meadow. A score of sleeping cattle, their white patches silvered by the moon, dotted the grassy slope to our left. We kept to the ruts across the pasture, and came right up against a rail gate, which Chigger crawled under and I climbed over, and then we started east again, down the road.

"About two miles yonder," I said as we followed the road up a gentle rise, "we can leave the road. There's a creek. I've got some jerked venison in my—"

Chigger stopped short and grabbed my arm. He was turned around the wrong way and still as stone.

"Chigger?"

He pointed into the distance. I was scared, thinking maybe he'd heard Mr. and Mrs. Rudge coming after us. But he said, "Puke dogs, Clutie! Puke dogs!"

He bolted, but I grabbed his collar. "No, Chigger, it's all right. It's just a farmhouse, way off. Their windows. They've got a lantern lit inside, that's all."

Chigger was shaking hard, and all of a sudden I felt bad about having made up that puke dog story. I was kind of surprised he still remembered it, too, as it had been better than a quarter hour since I'd told it. I knelt down and put my arms around him.

"Chigger, I was just making you up a story. There aren't any puke dogs, not really. And besides, those lights are yellow, aren't they? Not red."

He relaxed some, but he said, "I think there *is* them kind'a hounds, Clutie. Feels to me like there is, someplace."

"Not here," I said, and stood up.

"In France," he said with some surety. "With them French people."

"Maybe," I said. We started walking again.

"Clutie?"

"Yes?"

"Where's France?"

"Pretty far." I reached into my poke and felt around until I found the dried venison. I stuck a chunk in my mouth and handed another to Chigger.

He took it and jammed a corner into his mouth, then paused, mid-chomp, to roll his eyes at me.

"No," I said. "It won't make you upchuck."

He began to gnaw.

"A few more minutes, and then we'll be at the creek. You didn't say how you got out of the smokehouse to trail me."

"The smokehouse?"

"Never mind."

Twenty minutes later we left the road for another stand of trees, through which ran a shallow creek. I made Chigger give me his muddy britches, which I rinsed out and hung over some bushes to dry. Then, the tails of his patched, hand-me-down shirt hanging most of the way to his pink, dimpledy knees, he helped me cut some leafy branches for a mattress to keep us up off the muddy ground.

As he curled up in my arms, his sweet head upon my shoulder, he whispered, "If'n you and Spider get you a baby, will you love it better'n me?" He yawned wide, his jaw working to the side and back.

I brushed a kiss over his forehead. "Chigger, I'm never going to love anybody better than I love you."

"OK," he breathed, as his eyes closed and his mouth curled into a soft smile.

I had been awful sleepy, but the reminder that I was teetering on the brink of becoming Mrs. Spider Jukes sort of woke me up again. I lay there until the sun was almost free of the horizon, holding Chigger and pondering the nature of destiny, and what a mean-spirited thing it could be.

When I finally fell asleep, I dreamed of California and golden sun on speckled cattle, and of a faceless Spanish man who loved brown-haired girls who could quilt.

six

T hat fall, one week before school was to start up again, Granny Wren smeared a cow dung poultice thick on my face in a last-ditch effort to fade my freckles, and then she and Mama commenced to give me a lecture on how the time had come for me to fulfill my bounden Jukes duty to marry with Spider as soon as him and Nit and Gnat got back to the farm. They had set out upon a spree of highway robbery a fortnight earlier, and were due home any day.

I sat there at the old oak table, that stinking poultice tugging at my face skin, and ran my fingertips over the table's knife scars while I listened and nodded my head and listened some more. And when they finally ran down—well, it was Granny Wren, mostly—I said, "I'll do it, Granny, because you are the head Jukes."

She gave her head a curt little nod, like that was understood. She had a poultice smeared on her face, too, and when she nodded, a little clump fell into her lap.

"But I have got to tell you," I went on, "that I've got no love for Spider. He's mean and stupid. But you don't care how I feel. You just want more Jukes babies, and all I am to you is the vessel."

Right about then, Granny Wren forgot about the cow dung and slapped my face. Let me tell you—for an old lady she packed a pretty mean wallop.

I got up off the floor and climbed back into my chair. She was wiping her hands on a dish towel and looking at me like it was my fault. Tears burned at the backs of my eyes just as surely as the mad in me was kindling bright. My limbs trembled with it. But I stayed sat and kept my voice as even as I could.

"All my life," I said, picking each word careful, "you and the Bug Boys have been slapping me around, and I have never once seen any of you except Beetle beat hard on the boys. Maybe y'all like hitting me so much because I'm a girl, or maybe because I'm only half a Jukes and you don't guess I matter so much. Well, I have got no intention of bringing into this world any kids who'll get knocked silly twice a day for nothing more than being just three-fourths Jukes, or for having the misfortune to be born female."

Mama had taken a couple of steps back. She was mudded up, too, and she was wringing her apron between her hands. Granny Wren's face was fury. Well, what I could see of it. She came nose to nose with me and growled low, "I can see we ain't beat you enough to knock good sense into your head."

"Knock the sense out of it, you mean." I was kind of shocked at myself, talking back to Granny Wren that way, something even Beetle was afraid to do. But I could not seem to shut myself up. "I told you I'd wed him. I expect I don't have any choice. But I won't have his babies."

She stood up straight and gave a snort.

"I won't let him in my bed."

She put her hands on her hips and stared at me down her stubby Jukes nose, down that lumpy, smelly mask of cow dung. It was not a sharp angle, for she was not much taller standing up than I was sitting down.

"And if he gets in and gets me heavy," I went on, "I know the chants to say and what to do. I've seen those town women sneaking out here to buy your remedies. For years I've watched you grind the powders."

Just then Uncle Glow, staggering a little and reeking of raw liquor and old sweat, stepped in the door. Granny Wren whirled toward him. Well, as fast as a seventy-three-year-old lady can whirl.

"Glow!" she barked.

He snagged off his hat and ducked his head like a whipped dog. "Ma'am?"

"Take Clutie outside and cut you a fat switch and use it hard on her till I tells you to stop."

"Yes'm," he said, brightening.

I jumped up out of my chair, knocking it over with a clatter. Glow latched onto the front of my shirt and started pulling me toward the porch at arm's length, I expect to stay back from the smell of the poultice.

I followed my Jukes-half instincts, which is to say that I hauled back and slugged him square in the jaw, just as hard as I could. And I'll be danged if he didn't just fold up and fall down and stay there, his skinny orange good-luck braid flopped over his face like an extra mustache, the tattered brim of his old Johnny Reb cap tilted forward to cover one eye.

"Yankees!" he breathed just before he passed out.

I heard Mama, who had by this time retreated clear back to the corner, mutter, "Merciful Jesus."

I could understand her shock. I was a little rattled myself; out of respect, I had never before hit any of the uncles back when they were beating on me. Also, I felt a twinge of remorse on account of Glow was a whole head shorter than me, not to mention drunk.

"Devil child!" cried Granny Wren, like she had room to talk, and made a sign against evil. Mama, her back tight against the corner hutch, started in to weep, her tears running little rivers through the drying dung.

I grabbed my poke off its nail by the door, took a running leap over Uncle Glow and another off the porch, and didn't stop until I was far away, at Tickled Bear Hill, with my face washed clean in the cool clear water of the Little Shy.

By the third day in my cave, I was awful hungry and terrible low, berries and roots not going too far to quiet a hungry stomach. I supposed that the Bug Boys were all rubbing their bony little hands together, waiting for me to get back so they could gang up and take a whack at me, but by that time I guessed it didn't much matter.

I decided to go home.

A couple hours later, I walked down in the farmyard, pre-

pared for the worst. It was real quiet, especially considering
that it was wash day, and I had expected Granny Wren and
Mama to be out back boiling up clothes. For a minute there
I thought maybe a miracle had transpired. Maybe some deputies had come and arrested all the Bug Boys on the place,
and taken Granny Wren and Mama along as witnesses or
something.

Then I noticed smoke wisping out of the chimney, and
reality came home to roost. I put my hand in my pocket and
found my buckeye, and with it firm in my fist, I squared my
shoulders and marched down toward the cabin.

They were all inside. Violet and Chigger sat up on the
edge of the loft, swinging their legs. Chigger looked real sad.
Violet was just as vacant and cross-eyed as always, poor
thing, rocking her poppet and babbling.

Beetle, Granny Wren, and Mama sat round the table. Mama's head was pillowed on her arms, and her shoulders
shook with weeping. Beetle and Granny both appeared real
solemn. Nobody noticed me at first, not until I heard a scraping sound from the floor across the room. It was Uncle Glow,
back in the shadows, just sitting up on a pallet.

He pointed his finger at me. I could not make out what
he was trying to say, since bandages were wrapped tight
under his jaw and tied off atop his head in a big silly bow,
and he could not seem to open his mouth good.

Beetle shoved his chair back and stood up fast. "He says
you busted his jaw, you half-breed sow."

I suppose it's a bad thing to say, especially since it sounds
so Jukes, but the truth is that pride flooded right through me.

The feeling didn't last long, though, because Beetle hauled
off and slammed me alongside the head with the butt of his
fist. It sent me flying. I landed with my shoulder against the
hearth and dropped hard to the floor. By the time I sat up
and grabbed the places that hurt, he was on me, hauling me
up to my feet and cocking his arm back to punch me a good
one.

Well, I had already coldcocked one of the Bug Boys. I
figured I could get into no worse trouble by trying for two.
I kicked his peg leg out from under him and he went over

backward. He was still hanging on to me, though, and I toppled, too, landing crosswise atop him.

He hollered ''Sonofabitch!'' and ''Goddamn woodscolt!'' and grabbed my hair and slammed my forehead against the floor, whereupon I flailed out with my fist and hit him in the face.

Something went *crunch.*

He yelped loud and cursed things I can't write here, and jerked my head up in order to slam it down again, when all of a sudden something bristly crashed down upon both of us once, twice, three times before I realized it was a straw broom. Somebody cried out, ''Stop! Stop it!''

It took me a second to realize it was Mama. I had never heard her raise her voice before.

Slow, both me and Beetle got up from the floor. He looked shocked, too, and there was a lot of blood running from his nose. Mama, her eyes red and her thin body trembling, stood before us, the broom cocked over her shoulder, business end up.

''Just stop it,'' she said. This time it was a whisper.

Granny Wren's mouth was open. Uncle Glow was still on his pallet, but he had scooted to the far side, against the wall, and both his hands were clamped over his ears like one of those ''hear no evil'' monkeys.

We all just stood there for maybe ten seconds, though it seemed longer, and then Mama slowly lowered her broom. Soft, she said, ''I already lost me one'a my young'uns to the Reaper today, Beetle. I'll not see you harm a second.''

He stared at her for a moment without expression, and then he lifted a hand to his face.

''Mama?'' I whispered. ''Who's dead?''

''My nose!'' Beetle yelped, staring at the blood on his hand before he raised it to his face again. ''Ma?'' he said, kind of whiny, to Granny Wren. ''That stinkin' little she-bastard's done busted my nose!''

Muffled giggles drifted down from the loft. I didn't look up. I stared at Mama. ''Who's dead?'' I asked again.

''Titus Holbein come out here this morning,'' she said at last. She looked terrible weary. ''He said they got a wire from down to Arkansas. Said the twins and Spider tried to stop a coach, and—''

''Didn't *try,* Tulip,'' Granny Wren snapped. ''They stopped 'er and shucked the passengers of wallets and watches.'' There was pride in her voice. She lifted her head high, full up with glory, and did not even seem to notice that Beetle's nose was dripping scarlet all over her apron. ''You oughter be proud of them boys, Tulip, instead'a snivelin' over it. Our Nit died a Jukes, and them other two boys'll do their time like Jukeses, with pride.''

''Mama?'' I said. ''Is that true? Is Nit gone?''

''I knowed it was a-comin','' Granny Wren said, all sanctimonious, and not looking at either me or Mama. ''They was an owl at the winder six day back. Bangin' its wings, it were, and screechin' wondrous fierce . . .''

I whispered, ''Mama?''

Her face twisted up. ''Nit's shot dead, shot dead on the road like his daddy . . .'' It came out in a weak wail, almost a sound like a hurt animal makes. With a clatter, the broom dropped from her hands just as her knees buckled. I caught her before she fell all the way to the floor, and helped her to a chair.

I hadn't known that Mama cared so deep for the twins. She had always let Granny Wren do them just like she had done me, and never said a parental word. I saw then that she had secret feelings. Me, I never thought about the twins one way or another. They might have been my half-brothers, but when it came down to it, they were just more Jukeses to torment me.

''Guess that means you ain't got to wed Spider for a while, Clutie,'' said Uncle Glow, real snotty-like, from his shadowed pallet. ''Him and Gnat's got to serve a year. Eight months with good behavior.''

Granny Wren stuck her nose up and drew in a thin breath. ''They'll do their year,'' she said. ''They's good Jukeses. Unlike somebody else in the room who I ain't gonna mention on account of her mother might get up on her high horse again and try beatin' us all to pulp with a broom.''

Mama whispered, "Clutie, you 'pologize t'your uncles. And say you won't never do it no more."

Normally, if Mama had asked me to apologize for something, I would have done it, just like that. I loved my mama and did what she asked, since she asked so little.

I guess I had felt sorry for her. She was under everybody's thumb, Granny Wren's especially. We all were that. But on this day she had shown me, for the first time, that she noticed bad things happening in our family, that she cared. Now that she was backing off, it made me kind of mad at her. I couldn't make my mouth work. I just stood there, grinding my teeth.

"Clutie!" Granny Wren barked. "Mind your ma!"

I said, "Seems kind of strange, you telling me to mind my mama when you've never let her have any say-so over me in practically my whole life."

Mama clutched my sleeve. Uncle Glow was cackling soft, back in the corner. Mama whispered, "Clutie, please. They's already grief enough for one day."

I shook her hand off, more rude than I meant to. I said. "All right. Uncle Glow, I'm sorry your jaw is broke. Uncle Beetle, I'm sorry you got a bloody nose."

Granny Wren wiggled it, and Beetle let out a yelp. "Broke for sure," said Granny.

"Broke," I said. "But I'm not going to promise I won't fight back again."

Mama hissed, "Clutie!"

"No. I won't promise. I'm thirteen, and I'm weary of beatings. I'm bigger than you, Glow. I've come better than even with Uncle Beetle, and I'm strong. And things are going to be different. I may only be half-Jukes, like everybody is always reminding me, but remember that the Jukes part is a fighter, and has already busted both of you up. It could happen again."

In the shadows, Uncle Glow lay giggling upon his pallet with his cap on sideways. I hadn't noticed till just then that he had a jar of donk back there. He sat up far enough to take a sip, and started in tittering again until Beetle shoved a chair over on top of him.

I was about to lose my nerve and run from the cabin when Granny Wren turned away from me. In a real everyday voice, she said, "Clutie, take yourself down to the smokehouse and bring me up a mite of ham."

Mama's shoulders sagged down, and she touched my hand. I said, "Yes, Granny." And I knew right then that I had won. Nobody—at least, not the uncles—would ever try to whip me again.

All the rest of that night I pondered on the death of my half-brother Nit. I hadn't known him real well, for him and Gnat never had time for anybody else, other than to plague them. Being identical, Gnat and Nit had been thick as thieves, finishing each other's sentences and farting at the same time and such. I bet that Gnat was feeling low as he sat in that Arkansas jailhouse.

Nit's body arrived by freight wagon three days later. We buried him right away, as the salt packing wasn't doing much to keep the stench down. He went into the ground at the south end of the family plot at the bottom of the hill, with an empty space saved on the one side for when Gnat would join him in the Great Beyond.

Mama cried.

I finished my eighth-grade schooling, and Miss Alvinetta Hanker presented me with a bona fide diploma on genuine parchment paper with my name writ real swirly and grand in the blank space. I folded it careful and stuck it in the family Bible. This was the safest place, since at our house stray sheets of paper tended to end up doing business in the privy.

Miss Hanker also gave me a present to commemorate the event. It was a small heart, gold-dipped and no bigger than the nail on my little finger, and strung on a fine chain. Honest-to-Jim, it was the most beautiful thing I had ever seen in my life, let alone touched or owned, and my eyes got all wet when she gave it to me. Although it seemed a sin to wear such a delicate thing with my rough clothes, I wore it constant, under my shirt.

Sometimes, when nobody was looking, I'd sneak it out to

look at it or just rub it between my fingers, all small and solid and cool.

I was still having some bad dreams about Mr. Foot. Not so many as before, but even one was bad enough. I would wake up all cold and sweaty and striking out with my fists. I guess I must have made sounds, too, because Granny Wren, whose cot my pallet was next to, would wake up long enough to slug me.

Nobody ever spoke of the day I'd broke Beetle's nose, or of what had been said. And though they'd still put a foot out to trip me, or maybe slap me as I walked past, neither Beetle nor Glow had tried to beat serious on me. Between that and Gnat and Spider still being off in prison, it was almost nice in Jukes Holler.

Beetle did barter me to a couple of families headed west. I didn't mind. I even put on that I was a little simpleminded when the buyers expressed concern about such a big girl as me being hard to handle. Chigger came after me, sounding his eerie Indian whistle from the tall grass, and we walked home together, feasting on the sweet biscuits or fatback I swiped on our way out.

Back on the farm, I came and went as I pleased, brought in wild meat for the table, and weeded the garden. I spent time in my cave, too, reading and sketching and staring at that little gold heart and dreaming about California.

Sometimes, when I was up to Tickled Bear Hill, stretched out on my quilt and fingering my necklace and listening to the Little Shy trickle along, I'd congratulate myself on having the Jukeses "handled." I'd pretend that they were all dead or gone away, all of them except me and Chigger John, and that I was the head Jukes.

I would have fancy clothes—real dresses—like Agnes Ann Roebuck, and Chigger would have store-bought britches without holes, and we would both have new shoes, and when we went to town, people would nod their heads friendly and say, "Good morning, Miss Chestnut! How are you and Chigger today? My, isn't that a pretty dress you have on!" instead of snickering behind their hands or crossing to the other side of the street. I would fix up our cabin and put real curtains—

blue-and-white checked ones—in both windows, and cut flowers on the table in a blue glass vase.

By the time August and my fourteenth birthday rolled around, I guess I had started living in that pretend world even when I wasn't in private. "Quit your woolgatherin' and get to shuckin' them peas," Granny Wren would snap as she jabbed me with her elbow. I'd say "Yes'm" and then go right back to thinking about how I'd put a swing on our porch and paint it white.

Looking back, I think I really did get to believing that they would be true any minute, those things I daydreamed about. I don't know if I can be excused for it or not—getting so caught up in imaginaries, that is—but it made me awful happy.

And then Spider came home from jail.

He came with a human ear, all wrinkledy like a dried apricot, in his pocket. He said he'd cut it off another prisoner that had sassed him back.

He also came home alone. "Gnat's servin' extra time," he told us, "on account'a he ground hisself a stone knife and stuck a guard."

Granny Wren lifted her apron to daub her eyes. "Now, there's a Jukes for you," she said proudly, and then went back to peeling spuds.

Mama went out behind the chicken coop and cried. Chigger said he saw her.

Considering Granny Wren's matrimonial plans for me, I was understandably jittery about Spider being home. But when two weeks went by with not a mention of the subject from either Granny or Mama—or Spider—I relaxed.

"I guess they took me serious," I said to Chigger one day when we were out after rabbits. I had started letting him tag along when I hunted, and he was real careful about keeping quiet and staying out of mischief.

" 'Bout what?" he asked. We were stopped for a bite of lunch at the time, and he was up in a big old tree, swinging his legs and wiggling his bare toes and gnawing on a fat chunk of rat cheese.

"Serious about that they couldn't mess with me any-more."

"Mess with you?"

I could see that he had forgot all about me busting up Glow and Beetle and my fight with Granny. I said, "Never mind. You'd better not eat all that cheese, Chigger. Have some cornbread, too."

"I likes cheese."

"You'll get all stopped up again. Remember what Granny Wren did to you the last time?"

His face screwed up and he kind of squirmed on the limb, and then he dropped the cheese. It landed in last year's powdery brown leaves, at my feet.

seven

Ｂy late September there was a nip in the air by day and
a chill by night. Our woods were showing off their
bright autumn dress, and for most of the day I had
been up at my secret place sketching squirrels, and wishing
I could afford real paints so as to capture all the scarlets and
golds and oranges before they were gone.

It was a Saturday, I remember, and by the time I got back
home and walked down out of the trees and past the berry
bramble, the sun was most of the way down and the air was
cold enough that vapor came from my nostrils. I didn't see
any of the family, not even the kids, but as I strolled toward
the cabin I heard soft laughter coming from down by the
barn.

I squinted for a second before I made out Uncle Glow.
Squatted in the dirt out in front of the barn, his back against
a stump, he had a jug crooked in one arm. He was pointing
at me with the other, waving the tip of his braid and giggling
soft and kind of silly. It made my skin crawl.

I called out, "You better lay off that donk."

His only answer was a soft "Hehehe." It came out with
three little puffs of vapor. He took another pull on the jug.

I don't know why, but for a second I was half-tempted to
just turn around and go spend the night out in the woods.
But I didn't, mainly because my stomach was growling, and
I knew Granny Wren and Mama would be putting supper on
the table anytime. I could already smell the possum sim-
mering. I turned my back on Glow and went on down
through the dusk, to the cabin.

I had no sooner stepped up onto the porch when hands—

a lot of hands—grabbed me. I started in to flail, but they had my arms pinned good. My first thought was that the law had come to finally clean out the Jukeses for good and all, and I was about to holler that I never took anything more costly than tinned peaches, when I realized it was Spider and Beetle who were dragging me into the cabin.

"Leave me go!" I shouted. I was pretty mad, and scared, too. "Somebody else want his face busted?"

"You ain't gonna bust nobody today, Clutie," Uncle Beetle said with a sneer. "Wouldn't be fittin'. Not on your weddin' day."

Spider was behind me, yanking at my arms behind me, binding them above the elbows. Spider stepped around where I could see him. "Hi, honey girl," he said, real smarmy, and then he kissed me right square on the lips with his old mossy-toothed mouth.

Granny Wren came out of nowhere, it seemed to me, and shoved him away. He landed on his hip against the hearth, but he did not stop smirking, even when Granny scolded, "Not till after the nuptials, boy!"

My hands not being free to wipe my mouth, I spat his kiss upon the floor. "You do that again, Spider Jukes," I said, tears heating the backs of my eyeballs, "and I swear I'll puke all over you."

From up in the loft came a thin wail. "Clutie, no! They'll get them dogs!"

Uncle Beetle dragged me over to stand in front of the table. I said, "What have you done with Chigger?" I could still hear him up there, but now he was just crying, real soft.

Granny Wren wiggled her finger at Spider to come stand next to me. She said, "I got him tethered to the beam. He were makin' an ungodly fuss." She turned up the lantern a touch. "Beetle, you bring me a chair. Tulip, start up the music."

Only then did I notice Mama, seated at our scarred harmonium. She looked all hunkered and small and beat down, and I knew this had not been her idea. But just the same she began to move her feet on the treadles and to play and sing a chorus of "Dreams of Youth Have Flown the Coop But

I've Still Got My Darlin' Dear.'' Her voice was all broken, like she was crying.

"That's enough," Granny Wren said, halfway through. Beetle had dragged over a chair by then, and lifted her up to stand on it, so that she was a little taller than me. "Spider, boy, get hold'a her hand."

That's why they'd tied me above the elbows. My hands were free, although I couldn't do much more than flop them at my sides. Spider grabbed my hand, and I didn't have the leverage to get it away.

Granny Wren held the family Bible in front of her, closed, between her hands. The edge of my diploma stuck out on along one side. To Beetle, she said, "Bring me the cord out'n the chifforobe."

I heard him rustling around behind me, and then he came round and handed her a finely braided leather cord, about two feet long, with three scratched green glass beads at each end.

She laid it over the Bible, real solemn, and said, "This marryin' cord has brung together Jukeses in holiest matrimony for more generations than can be counted. The braided hide is the tie that binds, tough as leather, and the green doo-bobs is for fruitfulness in the marriage bed. Beetle?"

Beetle draped it over our wrists, then stepped back.

Granny took a deep breath. "Spider Clyde Jukes, does you take Clutie for to be your wife, for to cover her and make us some more little Jukeses, to keep her in line and be a good man to her without an overment of beatin' so long as you is both breathin'?"

"I does," Spider agreed, real formal. He had my hand so tight that I didn't believe there could be any blood left in it.

"Chrysanthemum Mae Chestnut, you take Spider, here, to be your man forever and all, to bear his young'uns, to cleave to him, nurse him when he's sick or shot up, and to not sass him back or punch him in the face?"

I said, "The only thing real about this wedding is the Jukes cord, Granny, and I don't hardly believe in that. You're just making this up as you go along. I am not going to stand for—"

"Hush up," she barked, and made a motion at Beetle. Just like that, a gag was in my mouth.

"Nod an 'I does,' Clutie," she said, her brows scrunched. "It's gonna get did, one way or t'other."

I shook my head hard and bolted toward the door, but Beetle and Spider dragged me back. Beetle picked up the marriage cord from the floor, where it had fallen, and looped it back over my and Spider's wrists again.

"You take him?" Granny Wren repeated.

Beetle grabbed hold of my head and made me nod a yes.

"Then it's did," announced Granny. "You is wed."

Beetle took the cord away and gave it to her. Then he removed my gag. Before I could say a word, Spider was kissing me again, real wet and sloppy. Up in the loft, Chigger cried, "Don't puke, Clutie!"

Right about then I noticed Uncle Glow. He must have followed me up to the cabin, for he was leaning in the doorway, laughing soft. Spider said, "Hey, Pa, I's hitched!"

Glow raised his jug, took a long gulp, then handed it to my new husband. The two of them and Beetle repaired to the porch for some serious celebrations and left me standing, still bound, beside the table.

Mama was behind me then, removing my bonds. A tear drizzled hot down my cheek. Kind of snotty, I guess, I said, "Aren't you going to say congratulations?"

Across from me, Granny slammed the Bible down on the table with a bang. "Don't you sass your ma!"

My arms were free then, and I rubbed at them. "I thought the only one I wasn't supposed to sass was my husband."

Mama didn't say anything. She climbed up the ladder to the loft—to untie Chigger, I supposed.

Granny Wren glared up at me. "You is the devil's own child, Clutie Mae. I's always knowed it. But Spider, he'll whup you into line. Once he gets you swole with child, you ain't gonna be so smart no more."

They threw me and Spider in the barn and closed it up behind us. Spider was pretty drunk and fell off his feet right away. He sat in the straw, watching me bang my fists on the doors and demand my freedom. But all the while I was hollering, I could hear Beetle and the others pushing our creaky old wagon up against the doors from the outside.

Finally I gave up. Spider was sitting in the middle of the floor. His right eye, like always, was fixed toward the bridge of his nose, and he was breathing hard, with his mouth open. Big snorts of steam rolled out of his nose and mouth. He blinked slow, then looked up at me and said, "We is wed, woman. Get yourself to seein' to my needs."

And then he passed out.

Although I had peeked in the cracks from time to time, I had not been inside the barn since the end of the war. In the lamplight, the walls were gray and splintery looking where they didn't sink back into black shadows, even the part they had fixed after the still blew up. Back by the still, a few dusty sparkles came off the jars and jugs they stockpiled for donk. It smelled like the inside of a garbage pail, only worse, and that was with nothing in it. The still was six times as sour when it was stoked up and cooking.

Hay bales had been dragged here and there, with old saddle blankets thrown over them for more comfortable sitting. On this night, there was a lantern on one, and, to my surprise, a jar with some pretty fall leaves stuck in it.

Somebody—it had to have been Mama, for she was the only one who would have cared, I think—had made a mattress of straw in the corner and spread clean linens over it. A quilt, one I had pieced when I was maybe ten, was folded up at the foot of this makeshift bed, along with my nightshift. To one side was a bucket of water and an old chamberpot and a couple of clean rags.

Spider curled into a ball on the ground and commenced to snore. I had just picked up the lantern to have myself a look-see around the barn when somebody banged a fist against the doors.

It was Beetle. He hollered, "Your granny says to tell you that come mornin' she wants to see evidence. You understand me, boy?"

Spider twitched a little in his sleep. I hollered back, "Go away and leave people with some privacy."

He laughed, and then I heard him walking away.

I guessed I knew what Granny meant by evidence. When Mr. Foot had got me, there had been blood, and I supposed that's what she wanted to see, as proof I had been ravished for my first time.

Spider looked pretty far gone to me, and I didn't believe I was in any danger of ravishment at his hands that night. But as I paced around him, I got to thinking that maybe he wouldn't know if he had husbanded me or not.

The first thing was to get him over to the bed. I put the lantern back on the makeshift table and commenced to grip Spider under his armpits and drag him over to where the sheets were spread out. It was not hard, for he was a few inches shorter than me and skinny.

The next part wasn't so simple. I went over and sat on a hay bale, hugging myself against the chill, and stared at all those yellowed-up James gang posters the Bug Boys had pasted to the inside of the doors, and tried to think where I could get some blood to stain the sheets. If there'd been a chicken, it would have been a simple matter, but they had shooed out all the livestock except for Johnnycake, Beetle's fancy new saddle horse. I could hear him in the far stall, passing wind and nosing hay.

No good ideas came to me right off, and I guess I got a little lost in my thoughts.

The Bug Boys had expanded their poster collection to include every two-bit outlaw who was even rumored to have ridden with Frank and Jesse James. Since that was a real popular thing for scofflaws to brag on, true or not, they had assembled a goodly assortment. Most of the men in the drawings (besides the Jameses themselves, of course) looked mean or scruffy or stupid or all three. But my eye kept going back to one in particular.

He was dark-haired and real handsome—well, as handsome as a poor line drawing can make a man—and the only name given him was the Spanish Kid. He was worth just one hundred dollars, so I guess he couldn't have been much shakes as an outlaw; but I kept staring at him anyway, wishing I could have got to the West and married somebody like that instead of Spider Jukes.

After about a half hour of daydreaming about Spanish men and Spanish haciendas, I was no closer to a solution to my problem. Finally I got up and walked back to Johnnycake's stall, intending to prick his neck for some blood.

Johnnycake was a real pretty buckskin, about two shades off a gold bay, but he was in terrible shape that night, all welted and cut up. It was Beetle's idea of schooling, I guess, to beat the bejesus out of a horse. I put the knife away and salved Johnnycake's wounds.

Once he was seen to, I went back to my bale to stare at the Spanish Kid and think. "What would *you* do?" I asked the poster. He didn't answer—not that I expected him to, being a drawing and all—and so finally, I decided there was only one thing for it. I slid out my boot knife, rolled up my sleeve, closed my eyes, and cut my arm.

It was not as bad as I thought it would be, but it stung like the devil. And because of trying so hard not to make any sound, I bit my lip till it bled, too. If I had known I was going to do that, I would have just bit it and not cut my arm.

But what was done was done. I smeared my arm on the bedclothes, then washed, and bound it up with a rag. I had not cut it deep, and it had almost stopped bleeding by then.

I didn't much relish the idea of sleeping next to my new husband. But even the way Granny Wren starched them, linens were a lot less scratchy than straw. Also, I reckoned that when Beetle or Glow came down in the morning to let us out, they would think it odd if they didn't find me there.

Careful not to disturb Spider, I blew out the lantern, stretched out along the far edge of the sheets with my back to him, and fell asleep.

What woke me up was Spider, on top of me. I must have been sleeping awful hard, for he already had my britches undone and my shirt pushed up. I was freezing. I shoved him off of me and punched him hard, in the middle of his chest.

It knocked the air out of him, and as he lay there gasping out little clouds of vapor, I fixed my clothes. And then I hit him again, just a little one in the shoulder.

"You try that again and I'll murder you," I said.

He mostly had his air back by then. "You got to," he wheezed. "We's wed! You got to let me."

I sat up. "No I don't. I don't have to let you do any such thing."

He sat up, too. I smelled vomit mixed in with the stench from the still and the odor of Johnnycake's manure, so I figured Spider had been up for a while. He had taken off his clothes, and was buck naked. Moonlight filtering through the gaps in the walls painted pasty stripes over his thin, goose-bumpy Jukes chest. I could just make out a blurry shape where the black widow tattoo rode his shoulder.

"Reckon you don't got to at that," he said, which surprised me. I had expected more of a fight. "Reckon you don't got to do nothin' you don't want."

And then, just like that, he yanked the knife out of my boot and held it to my throat. Spider could be awful fast sometimes.

He whispered, "Bet you didn't think I knew about your sticker, did you?" and then he chuckled low. He sounded way too much like Uncle Beetle for my taste, and I held real still.

He started drawing the blade's tip back and forth across my throat, slow. "Nope, you don't gotta do nothin' you don't want. But I think you want to."

"You think wrong."

He smiled. "You's awful fond of Chigger John, Clutie. Seems to me you can't always have him in pocket. Be terrible if somethin' was to happen to him."

I was shocked. I said, "He's your kin, too!"

He stopped moving the blade and pressed the tip of it under my ear, just like I had done to Mr. Foot two summers before. I had a quick thought of Mr. Foot, laughing at me from down in hell.

Spider smiled, real evil. "I wouldn't kill him or nothin'. But he could have accidents. Bad accidents. You know what I mean, Clutie? You recollect that little cat you had?"

My stomach jolted. I think I stopped breathing.

"What'd you call her? Dopey? Dummy? Damn Cat? You

don't want Chigger should end up like that. It'd happen slow, but it'd happen."

I swallowed my tears. I would not let him see me cry. "If it's the last thing I do on this earth, Spider Jukes, I'll—"

He poked me again with the knife. "Think about Chigger, Clutie."

I would have died before I let anything happen to him. And Spider was one who would do him bad and enjoy it. All I could see was my poor little Daisy, who never hurt anybody excepting mice, killed dead with her guts strung out and her little soft paws cut off, left on the manure pile. And then Chigger.

I said, "You don't need the knife." And I let him do it.

Being under Spider was not so bad as with Mr. Foot. That's probably because Mr. Foot was the first one, plus he had been a big man, and there was nothing much to Spider in any department. Besides, it never took him more than maybe two minutes, and I guess a person can stand almost anything if it's only for a minute or two. Also, I had Chigger John to think of.

For the first few weeks after the wedding, he nastied me all the time, night and day, and Granny Wren was all smiles. I heard her tell Mama that every time she looked out the window she saw Spider pulling me back into the trees or into the smokehouse or out behind the barn. She said it wouldn't be long before we had a whole new generation on the ground.

That wasn't the case, though, for I did not get with child. I attributed this to the fact that every time, after Spider was done with me, I ran up in the woods to a big thistle bush, chanting and spitting to beat the band. Spider started to get bored with me after a few months, and began to leave me alone for longer and longer periods. Pretty soon he was only pestering me maybe once every other week. This was a good thing, since the path to my thistle bush was beginning to get beat down.

"Law, Clutie," he said to me one day, while he was buttoning up his britches, "you is a dead end if ever there was one. I wisht you'd catch and do it quick. Ain't like I enjoy doin' it to you. I got me purtier fish to fry, and more willin'. Not no mud fence like you.''

I got kind of offended. I said, "You got something better, Spider Jukes, you go to it and good riddance. If you'd promise to stop pestering me forever, I'd dance for a week solid.''

"Only two reasons I keep on, Clutie," he said, real evil. "One,'cause Granny Wren is set on you droppin' the next crop. Second,'cause you hates it.''

When six months came and went and I had failed to conceive, Granny Wren went to work. First, she took nine little switches and tied a knot in each, then burned them up and made me eat the ashes, baked into a tart. When that didn't work, she commenced to dose me with mistletoe. This only made me sick, and thereafter she stuck to magical sayings and doodads.

She gave me and Spider each a charm to wear in a little pouch at our waists. I did not ask what was in mine after Spider took his apart and found it was the dried-up privates from a raccoon.

Eventually, she threw up her hands and said we'd just have to trust in the Lord. My life, except for putting up with Spider every other week or so, went back to normal.

Nobody but me noticed my one-year anniversary as Mrs. Spider Jukes. I celebrated it by sketching a real good likeness of him, which I then pounded through with nails and burned up. This is a spell that sometimes drives out witches. I had hoped, Spider being so terrible vile and all, that it would work on him, but I had no such luck. If anything, he was more hale than before and just as black-hearted.

My married state had not stopped the Bug Boys from bartering me to travelers. I looked forward to these adventures. They got me off the farm and away from the Jukeses, and gave me a sniff of the West. I guess California was calling to me stronger and stronger.

Of course, I was pretty well Jukes through and through by then, being married to Spider and having given up on my dreams of blue-checkered curtains and haciendas and Spanish men and all. But sometimes—sometimes when we'd get a ways out, far from Jukes Holler—the horizon would call to me and I'd think maybe, maybe I could do it, just go all the way out there with one of those pilgrim families. But then there'd come Chigger, giving me the secret Indian whistle from the bushes and urging me east again, to home.

I never did have another problem like what I suffered with Mr. Foot, except in one case. His name was Mr. Cochran, and just as he shoved me up against the wagon to do me mischief, Chigger tiptoed up behind and whacked him over the skull with a shovel.

I always felt real safe after that.

I did not feel very married, though. Me and Spider did not even live together under the same roof. He slept down to the barn with the rest of the Bug Boys, and I remained up at the cabin, on my pallet betwixt Mama and Granny Wren. This was just fine with me, as I don't reckon I could have stomached sleeping next to him, what with his nits and fleas and all. At least he didn't try to kiss me anymore.

I kept up with my drawing and sketching. I stopped keeping my good pictures out at the secret cave after wood rats found them and chewed them all up. I think it was wood rats, anyway. After that, I kept them at the farm, hid in a big envelope of flat leather I stitched together, and tucked up high on a little ledge I made in the chicken coop.

The reason I had to hide them was that Granny and Beetle—and probably some of the others, though they didn't say—believed there was a powerful evil in the way I caught an image. Once I had made the mistake of sketching a portrait of Granny Wren and giving it to her, real proud. She let out a shriek, made some hexing signs with her hands, spat to the right and then the left, and then chanted over it for a good hour before she thought it was safe to destroy without doing herself harm. Then she made me sleep in the smokehouse for three nights as penance.

All I can say is that it's a good thing no traveling photographer ever came to our farm and took their pictures, as Granny Wren probably would have nailed him upside down to a tree for the Antichrist.

eight

One clear spring day I climbed up in the big oak at the top of Tickled Bear Hill to have a look around the countryside with Uncle Glow's spyglass. I did that sometimes just to remind myself that there was more world out there beyond Jukes Holler. For a while I watched our neighbor to the south plow a field. That got dull pretty quick, and I cast my gaze over toward Agnes Ann Roebuck's house to see if any of her pretty dresses were strung on the line. I never got that far, though, because as I swung the glass over the field that abutted their wash yard, my eye caught a little movement. Something orange.

When I realized what it was, I was so staggered I nigh on fell out of that tree. There was my very own husband, Spider Clyde Jukes, naked as a jaybird with that blobby tattoo on his arm, thrashing around in the tall grass with none other than Agnes Ann Roebuck and doing the nasty to beat the band!

Strange as it may seem, it made me mad. I called Agnes Ann some bad names, I guess, and Spider, too. But then, as I watched them doing it, I started to get kind of tickled, and pretty soon I was laughing right out loud. Agnes Ann might have been too highfalutin to speak to me, but she was not too fancy to strip stark and roll around in the weeds with Spider when she thought nobody was looking.

Every once in while they'd tumble over and her big white backside would reflect back so much sun it near to blinded me. Then Spider'd roll on top, all bony and already rosy with sunburn. Thinking of the misery he'd suffer once he pulled his britches back on over that burnt butt gave me no end of pleasure.

After a while, I got kind of bored and went down to my cave to think. I guessed I knew what Spider had meant that time when he said he had prettier fish to fry. I wondered just how long he had been meeting secret with Agnes Ann, but I guessed it did not much matter. What mattered was that now I knew about it. I had once heard Miss Hanker say as how knowledge was power, and it suddenly occurred to me that she had not known how right she was.

That night, after everybody was asleep, I snuck down to Beetle's kennels and gathered up about a pint of hound hockey, which I mixed up with some dried grass and a few pinches of sulfur in a paper bag. I took off through the woods, and after a time reached the Roebuck hog farm.

I tiptoed quiet past slumbering sows in the hog pens, past the outhouse, up across the wash yard, and to the house. Agnes Ann had a real house, not a cabin like ours, and it was painted white. I knew which window was hers, having spied her head sticking out of it a couple times from up in my tree, and I put that sack of dog leavings directly under it.

I guess I had not been as quiet as I thought, because as I was digging in my pocket for a match, Agnes Ann herself—yellow hair all bound up in curling rags—popped her head out the window. Her mouth opened up: maybe to call me trash again, maybe to holler for help. In either case, she decided not to say anything.

I don't know why, but something about it—her expression, I mean—got me to feeling cocky. I put my hands on my hips and said, "Good evening, husband-stealer."

Just like that, her eyes got all big and she covered her mouth with both hands.

I said, "Speak up."

She took her hands down from her mouth. She whispered, "What do you want?"

I hadn't thought about that. All I'd planned to do was toss a little homemade stink bomb through her window.

"Anything!" she whispered, louder this time. "You can't tell! Please!"

She looked right on the brink of a tizzy, and I almost felt sorry for her. I said, "All right."

She didn't believe me, though. "You can't tell," she said, more like an order this time. "If you tell, I'll . . . I'll . . ." She pursed her lips like she was trying to think of something horrible enough, and right then I realized she had not even pretended to be sorry. She just didn't want anybody to find her out.

I said, "What are you gonna do, Agnes? You gonna threaten to hurt me? I'm a Jukes, remember, and there's nothing you can do to me that I can't think of and do to you first, and worse. You gonna say you'll stop carryin' on with Spider? I don't think so. That big white fanny of yours was shaking too enthusiastic for you to give him up voluntary."

Her face went dark with a blush. "Then what?" She asked it through clenched teeth.

"Well, I don't want that you should stop seeing Spider. Fiddle with him all you want."

She cocked her head and scrunched up her brows.

"A dress," I said, without knowing I was going to say it. It just came out of my mouth.

Agnes Ann's mouth set into a line. "Fine."

She disappeared for a second, then came back with something bunched in her arms. She threw it out the window and I caught it.

I said, "This one's pink. I don't believe I care for it." I threw it back at her.

She went and got another one and tossed it out. "Yellow?" I said, working the fabric between my fingers. "I don't think so." I tossed it back.

We went through that two more times, and by then she was looking real annoyed, which pleased me no end. Every single one of those dresses she had offered had been a thing of beauteous workmanship; you could tell it just by the feel of them. But when she threw that first dress at me, like both me and it were trash—well, mayhap I was, but the dress wasn't—she had just plain acted too Jukesish.

It had occurred to me right then that she and Spider were likely well matched. She probably would have got on fine with Granny Wren, too.

Agnes Ann brought out yet another dress, and she was just about to heave it at me when I said, "I don't want that one, either. I know which one." I had admired it on the line, all sky-colored with a gingham bodice and honest-to-Jim ruffles at the yoke and hem.

I said, "The light blue one. The robin's egg blue."

She had the nerve to get huffy. "That's my best frock!" she said, maybe a little too loud, considering her folks were likely sleeping in the next room.

I shrugged my shoulders. I said, "Fine. Keep it. Tell your ma I'll be coming by for tea tomorrow."

I turned on my heel and had not taken even one step when she whispered, "All right, all right!"

Ten seconds later that dress was in my arms, and Agnes growled, "Now go away! And if you say a word, I'll say you're lying to cover up that you stole my dress."

I shook that blue beauty out and folded it over my arm. "Agnes Ann," I said, "you are sure uppity out of all proportion for somebody who lives on a pig farm."

Law, but she looked irate! She stood up real stiff, made a little huffing sound, said, "Good night, trash!" and stepped away.

I did, too, but only to the side. I squatted down beside a bush and pressed myself against the side of her house. A few seconds later Agnes Ann poked her head out of the window and looked around. I was in the shadows, so she did not see me.

I waited until I heard her bed creak, and then I waited ten whole minutes more, and then I went back under her window and found that sack of dog mess and set fire to it and tossed it inside. Then I ran down the yard, past the outhouse and the hog pens, across the pasture, and into the trees as fast as I could, that dress tight under my arm.

I expect I was cackling like a fool.

• • •

Three days later, before I had a chance to make a second good use of my newfound knowledge and power—this time with Spider—he went and got himself arrested. I can't remember exactly what it was for, although I think there was a stolen ram mixed up in it someplace. But the main thing was that he went to jail, and stayed there for several months.

Maybe five weeks after Spider went away, another woman came lurking through moon and shadows to buy one of Granny's remedies. I knew what kind for I watched her make it, and out of curiosity I snuck down to the lane to see which of our neighbors was trying to lose a baby.

She had on a long cloak and her head was covered, and I could not see her face at first, for she had it ducked while she listened to Granny Wren's instructions. She lifted her face at about the same time the moon came out to show her plain.

"Thank you, Miz Jukes," said Agnes Ann Roebuck before she turned and scurried back down the lane.

A couple months after the second anniversary of my wedding—upon which I had drawn another picture of Spider, this time dousing it with horse piss before I burned it up and dumped the ashes down the outhouse hole—Uncle Beetle rode out to do a crime.

This was a real unusual thing, for although Beetle talked and acted tough around the farm, he usually kept himself to the position of mastermind, so far as Jukes crimes were concerned.

But over that past year he had got a bee in his britches about Frank and Jesse James and how the Jukeses were such small potatoes compared to them and the Younger brothers and such.

"Now, Beetle," Granny Wren would say, "they ain't so fine. They's just a lot more of 'em. You does fine with what you gots to work with, son. Ain't you brought them young boys up good for sneakin' and skulkin', and didn't you barter Clutie Mae three times this past summer? Why, ever' single one'a them boys has been to jail at least three times exceptin' Chigger John, but he's young yet. You done us proud."

But her soothing didn't help. Maybe deep down Beetle knew she didn't really mean it, and that she was disappointed, too.

Anyway, Beetle had spent most of that fall just sitting on the stump down in front of the barn, drinking donk and smoking wild hemp and grouching, and looking like somebody had let the air out of him. He hardly had the strength or the inclination to beat his hounds.

Then, one day in November, Spider came home from jail. He didn't come alone, though. Titus Holbein—he was one of Beetle's best customers for donk, despite his being the local deputy and having arrested most all of the Bug Boys at one time or another—came out to the farm to pick up a few jars of whiskey. Spider scurried straight over to Agnes Ann's on the pretext of hunting, even though I had just brought in two rabbits. I was out at the side of the barn skinning them, so I heard Titus and Beetle talking.

"Been a big robbery up to Ashville," Titus remarked.

"That so?" said Beetle, without too much enthusiasm. They had stepped inside the barn, and I scooted a little closer to listen.

"Yup," said Titus. "Three'a them pint jars'll do me, Beetle." There was the clank of jars. "Gang of men stopped the Flyer and got clean away with near twenty thousand in new currency."

There was a pause, and then Beetle said, "Twenty thousand, you say?" All of a sudden he was sounding more like his old self. "They know who done it?"

By then I had my ear plastered right up to a crack in the barn wall. I heard a jar lid twisting off, and then Titus gave out with a long wheeze.

"Say, Beetle," he remarked after a minute, kind of hoarse, "that's the smoothest yet. Better make 'er four jars."

Another clink.

"You didn't say who they's after for it."

"Who the hell knows? They say it was the James boys, but then they al'ays say it's the James boys. Reckon if that outfit did half the crimes they's labeled with, they'd have to be about forty of 'em in the gang, and all of them'd have to be triplets. Here's your dollar.''

After the deputy rode out, Beetle went back in the barn. I could hear him pacing in there, slicing up straw with his peg leg and muttering.

The next morning he announced he was going out to do some villainy. Granny Wren threw her arms about him, made him an extra big breakfast, and put a special extra-luck spell on his pocket buckeye.

''You two stand back,'' he called to me and Chigger when Spider led out Johnnycake. We were perched on the good rail of the corral fence, watching. ''How many times I got to tell you to stay clear'a my Johnnycake horse? He's liable to strike and murder you, not that you ain't deservin' of it.''

Now, Beetle was hell on a horse, and there'd been nothing I could do to keep him from beating on poor Johnnycake. But for the past two years, ever since my wedding night, I had been sneaking into the barn whenever I could to doctor his wounds. Also to take another peek at that poster of the Spanish Kid.

I had got to daydreaming about him a lot more than was probably healthy, and had given him all kinds of grand attributes that were most likely pure fiction. I talked to him, too, and though he never answered me back except in my head, imaginary-like, I thought he was real understanding. I had even got to comparing the way Spider and the rest treated me to the way I imagined the Spanish Kid would have done. The Jukeses came out losers every time.

Anyway, I would clean and salve Johnnycake's poor bruised flesh, but I could not salve the hatred that had grown in his heart. He nipped and cow-kicked something terrible, and he was worse with Beetle. I can't say as I blamed him.

Between the two of them, Beetle and Spider got him saddled and bridled, and then Beetle tried to get on. He was not good at it, what with his peg leg throwing him off balance, and he fell down about four times in the effort.

Beetle got the whip and lashed Johnnycake a few times, Spider put a twitch on his lip so he wouldn't bite, and at last Beetle got himself into the saddle. He took off down the lane at a trot, Johnnycake swinging his head from side to side trying to bite. Beetle, hat in hand, swatted at his head—first one side, then the other—cussing up a storm.

I had never seen anything quite so stupid in my whole life. Beside me, Chigger set into giggling, but clamped a hand over his mouth when Spider gave him a dirty look.

I said, "When Beetle first got that horse, he was decent. Too bad he's ruined."

"A lot you know," said Spider. We all watched Beetle and Johnnycake move away from us, Beetle's hat swatting Johnnycake's head: left, right, left, right. After a couple seconds, Spider added, "Stupid bangtail. Beetle'll whup him into line."

I said, "Someday some horse is going to murder Beetle. It's only fitting."

"A lot you know," Spider repeated. He was not one for snappy quips. To Chigger, he said, "Get you on up to the cabin. Granny wants you."

Chigger said, "No, she don't." He had grown some in height if not in smarts. I was sixteen then, and had leveled out at five feet and eight inches; at eleven, Chigger was about to my shoulder and still so pretty he made your heart hurt.

"Yes, she does," said Spider, dead vile. "I heared her."

Chigger never took vileness personal, being used to it, I guess. Real cheery, he chirped, "OK," and dogtrotted up toward the cabin.

"Get to the smokehouse, wife," Spider said. "I's got me an urge."

I can't say I was surprised, but I was ready for him. I planted my feet and crossed my arms. "Seems to me you took care of that urge yesterday, Spider Jukes."

He gave me a real odd look. Well, odder than usual. But then surly overrode puzzlement, and he said, "What do you mean?"

I just stared at him and tried my best to look Jukes mean.

He stared back at me for a second, and then he hollered, "Chigger John, get back down here."

I was thinking that if the Spanish Kid had been there, he would have just shot Spider. And then he would have danced with me, maybe. One of those flamenco dances, and I would've had a rose in my teeth, and a high Spanish comb in my hair. But the Spanish Kid wasn't there. Nobody like him—or at least nobody like the person I'd made him up to be—was ever going to be there.

"Never mind," I called to Chigger, who was almost back down to us. "Spider was only fooling. Go on up to Granny."

Spider smiled at me real vulgar. "Get you to the smoke-house," he said.

I kept my feet planted. "If you've got the urge, Spider, you can just go see your lady friend. Because I'm never going to the smokehouse with you ever again, nor to the bushes nor up in the woods. And you're not going to touch Chigger John."

His bad eye, the one that always looked at his nose, gave a little twitch and he hollered, "What?"

"You heard me. If I have to say it again, I'll say it to Granny Wren. And then she'll know that the babe she remedied right out of Agnes Ann was half a Jukes and her very own great-grandbaby. Probably a full-blown, orange-headed, cross-eyed one. Prime Jukes. How you think she'd take to that, Spider? It's my opinion that she'd lash you bloody. Maybe even cast you out of the Holler for good. If you lived through the beating."

His narrow, cockeyed face went bright red. He tried to say something, but nothing happened except his cheeks puffing out a few times. Finally, he waved his fists in the air, turned on his heel and stalked off to the barn. He slammed the door behind him, and did not come out until the next day.

He never pestered me again.

Three weeks later, after a cold and heavy December rain, a stranger rode up through the mud to our place, leading John-nycake behind him. He tied his bay out front of the barn and handed over Johnnycake's lead to my brother Gnat, who had come home from jail four days earlier with a wrist tattoo that said "Mother." He was also missing his left thumb, which he claimed had been bit off in a prison fight.

"This the Jukes farm?" the stranger asked, looking around

and frowning. He was a well-dressed man, with a heavy gray coat and a shiny, gray, narrow-brimmed hat, and he did not seem happy to have climbed down from his nice dry saddle to our miry barnyard.

"What if it is?" said Gnat.

I was watching from the corner of the corral, having just come from the chicken coop and stowing some drawings. Gnat had got real hardened by losing his twin, Nit, and then spending so much time in prison, and I was afraid he'd pull a knife on the man before he had a chance to answer. I stepped forward, half-frozen mud going squish under my boots.

"Mister? How come you've got my uncle's horse?"

The man took off his hat, and when he moved I saw the glint of a shiny badge beneath his coat. He said, "Miss, is there somebody in charge around here?"

Up at the cabin, over coffee, he told us the story.

It seemed Uncle Beetle had stopped a coach over by Independence. He'd made a big haul for a Jukes crime, taking over sixty-two dollars in booty off the passengers, and he would have got away with it, too, except that just as he put his foot in the stirrup to make his getaway, Johnnycake reached right around and sank his big yellow horse fangs hard into Beetle's knee bone.

Beetle let out a yelp and hopped down, but his boot got caught in the stirrup. Before the coach caught them up, Johnnycake had dragged him a good mile through the mud at a slow jog, Uncle Beetle's peg leg whipping the air but never making contact with horseflesh. One of the passengers, who turned out to be a U.S. marshal on his way to a new post, took him into custody.

The gray-suited deputy, whose name was Cyril Pennyworth, said that he had to make a trip east to visit his ailing mother, and had volunteered to bring Johnnycake to us on his way there. "My mama lives only about twenty miles past here," he said, pointing northeast. "She has the lung trouble."

Granny gave him more coffee and a wedge of pie, and a little poke of the ground-up root of butterfly weed, from which she told him to brew a tea for his mother.

"Course, blood's the thing," she then confided in a low voice. "This here tea'll ease 'er, but the bestest cure for lung troubles is fresh blood, still warm, drunk twice a day. I don't suppose your ma lives nigh a slaughterhouse, do she?"

For a minute he looked like the pie he'd just swallowed was going the wrong way, but then he seemed to get hold of himself. He nodded real polite and said, "I'll sure look into it, ma'am."

After he cleaned his plate and pushed away from the table, he said, "I thank you very much for your hospitality." He gathered up his herb poke, stuck his funny gray hat on his head, then paused on the porch.

"Miz Jukes," he said to Granny, "that buckskin I brought back is a fair horse. But if I was you, I'd sell him off before your son finishes his time at the jail, for I have never in my life heard a man plot such evils against a dumb animal."

Granny Wren did no such thing, however. Later that day she had Gnat cross-tie and hobble Johnnycake in front of the barn, and then she took after him herself with a thick willow switch. I did not see this myself, but it was reported to me by Chigger, who I found weeping over it when I came down out of the woods with a few squirrels I had just shot for supper.

"Poor horse," Chigger sniffed into my shoulder. "Poor Johnnycake." He looked up at me with that sweet, open face, rubbed his eyes with a fist, and said, "Clutie?"

I ruffled his hair. "What?"

"Clutie, you reckon I'd go to hell if I wished the puke dogs would get Uncle Beetle?"

It was the dangedest thing, him remembering that puke dog story for so long. It had been years. He hadn't remembered the Jukes-eating wampus-cat of Rossiter Ridge for more than a half hour, and it was one of my best yarns.

I said, "I reckon the Lord wouldn't blame you, Chigger John. And I reckon that one day or another, whether we wish it or not, the puke dogs are going to get Beetle anyhow."

That night all the Bug Boys on the place—that being Glow, Spider, and Gnat—took themselves down the pike to the roadhouse three miles west of town. They did this on occasion, mostly to drink whiskey that somebody besides them had made, and also to pay attention to loose women. Spider was not allowed to partake of the last, though, since he was a married man and it was a Jukes rule. Course, he was creeping off at least once a week to lift Agnes Ann's skirts, so I doubt he felt real deprived.

After they went on their way, me and Chigger sneaked into the barn. Granny had done a job on old Johnnycake, all right. His face was laid open in a few places, and there were welts and cuts all over his body and legs. Chigger had said she'd used a willow switch, but I would have taken odds that she'd changed over to a buggy whip about halfway through.

I cleaned him up, then showed Chigger how to salve the cuts. He did one side of Johnnycake and I did the other, and then I let Chigger give him a measure of oats, since it didn't look like anybody had bothered to feed him. Maybe Granny Wren had told them to starve him to death.

"Say again about Uncle Beetle," Chigger said from the far side of Johnnycake's flank.

For the fourth time, I did.

"How long will he be gone?"

"Like I said before, Chigger. About a year, maybe."

He wandered out to the middle of the barn and plopped down on a blanketed hay bale. He stared up at the posters stuck on the doors. "I wisht *they* was my uncles, Clutie."

I shifted quick to avoid Johnnycake's choppers. He was not keen on gratitude. I said, "Who?" For a second I thought he meant the Spanish Kid. I happened to be thinking about him at the time. Then I saw where he was looking. I said, "The James boys?"

Chigger nodded. "They was nice."

This surprised me. I said, "You remember when they were here? That was years ago!"

"Who?" He stared at me, all blank and open.

"Never mind, Chigger."

nine

January came. Out of frustration that my union with Spider
had borne no Jukes fruit, Granny Wren married off little
Violet, only eleven-and-a-half, to my brother Gnat. Violet
and Gnat moved into the loft—Violet and Chigger having
been the only two kids left sleeping up there anyhow—and
Chigger John was sent down to the barn to sleep with the
Bug Boys.

This meant that all night long, every night, I had to listen
to Gnat and Violet thumping around up there and giggling
and doing the nasty, even though Violet was swole with child
by March. I guess she had taken to married life better than
I had. Maybe it's easier to be married to a Jukes if your brain
doesn't have two marbles to rub together.

Soon it was spring and Chigger John turned twelve, upon
which occasion I gifted him with a double-bladed pocket
knife of his very own, brand new and shiny, and with genuine mother-of-pearl grips. He was plain crazy over it.

That May, Uncle Wig came to stay for a couple weeks. I
guess I have already said that liked Uncle Wig the best of
any of the Bug Boys, mostly on account of he had never hit,
maimed, or shot anybody that I personally knew, and also
because he was extra good to Chigger John.

He told us stories of his exploits in big cities, tested me
on my marksmanship, and gave me a whole silver dollar of
my very own when I hit every single can and target bang-
center. He exclaimed over Violet's growing belly, and at the
end of every meal he'd push back from the table and pat his
little stomach and say my, my, wasn't it good to have some
of Granny Wren's home cooking for a change.

As nice as it was to have him around the place for a spell, he brought bad news with him. On his way to the farm he had stopped to see Uncle Beetle in the Independence jailhouse, and learned that, due to overcrowding, Beetle would be set free sooner than we had expected.

Beetle's release was scheduled for the middle of June, which gave us only another month without him. Considering the way Beetle held a grudge, it also likely meant that old Johnnycake had not much longer on this earthly plane.

It was a sin, the way the Bug Boys had done him. Ever since the deputy had brought him home, poor Johnnycake had been left to stand in his stall, cross-tied, with no exercise. The Bug Boys watered him and threw hay into his manger when they thought about it, and by some miracle one of them had the mercy to trim his hooves every now and then and muck his stall; but if it hadn't been for me and Chigger sneaking him a smidge of grain now and then—and me spell-charming him—he probably would've been dead already. As it was, we did not get many opportunities and he was bones and skin, and just stood in his stall with his head down all the time.

A few days after Uncle Wig went on his way, and about a week before Beetle was scheduled to get released from the hoosegow, Spider, Gnat, and Glow took it upon themselves to try and barter me on their own. I let them do it, and helped a good bit by acting slow and dragging one leg, and showing how much firewood I could tote in my strong arms.

The fact was that I had a plan. I had been secretly plotting it for weeks, ever since I had snuck into the barn to take care of Johnnycake and discovered they'd papered over the Spanish Kid's poster with one of some two-bit no-good by the name of Green Liver Bob, who was only worth twenty-five dollars and was bald to boot.

Did you ever have this one moment when everything gets real clear? Like you've been looking at it your whole life through mired-up isinglass, and all of a sudden the mire is washed away and everything gets crystal? That's how it was for me.

I was real tempted to just go rip down Green Liver Bob's

paper, kind of symbolic-like. I knew that if I stayed, it was never going to get any better in the Holler. It was just going to go on, day after day, year after year, getting worse and more mucked up until I couldn't see anything clear. Until I was pure and full-blown Jukes, and couldn't even dream of being anything different, anything better.

Funny how some little thing like that can push a person into changing her life.

I was thinking to put my plan into motion later in the summer, but by selling me, the Bug Boys gave me a chance sooner than I'd expected.

Just as I was about to set off with the new family, this batch named Suggs, Chigger came running down out of the woods, calling "Clutie! Clutie!"

I wrapped him up in my arms before he could spout something that would queer the deal, and whispered to him, "Chigger, I have got a place in the woods I go to sometimes. I've got some things there, and I want you should get 'em for me and bring 'em along, all right?"

He nodded.

"Can you listen close and remember?"

"OK." He was sniffling a little.

"It's up to Tickled Bear Hill. You go straight up through the woods until you get to—"

"I knows. The cave, up from the Little Shy. They sellin' you off again, Clutie?"

"Yes. How'd you know where my place was?"

He frowned, like I had asked a real stupid question. He said, "You goes there a lot."

"You follow me?"

He nodded.

"How come you never—"

"Hurry up!" Spider shouted from behind me, down by the corral. He made an angry come-along motion with his hand. The Suggses were ready to go.

I pulled Chigger close. "You get yourself up there and grab my quilt," I whispered. "It's in an oilcloth sack up in that first elm tree. Don't spill it, or you'll let out all the magic." I had been collecting buckeyes. "You get that sack, and you swipe some extra vittles from the cabin, and you bring them along when you come after me, OK?''

"OK."

"Repeat it."

He did, almost word for word.

Over to the wagon, Uncle Glow shouted, "Dad-gum it, Clutie!''

"Promise you won't forget, Chigger?''

He nodded.

I stood up. "Comin','' I said, and started toward them, doing my best to drag one leg and look stupid.

So off I went with the Suggses. There was a mother and a father and two boys, and they had a nice team of oxen and a milk cow and a decent saddle horse, and a big black watch sow named Bertha. They looked almost prosperous and had traded my uncles an old pistol plus thirteen dollars for me, which was not a bad haul.

Except for Mr. Suggs, who went astride his horse, we all rode in the wagon. The oxen were well fed and fast steppers, so we made good time. So good, in fact, that I worried about Chigger John, who would be following on foot and with a heavy burden.

On the first night out, Mrs. Suggs got up in the night to make water and discovered me sawing at my bonds with my boot knife. She and her husband relieved me not only of my blade, but of my boots as well. I thought it was pretty rude, leaving a person in her bare feet like that, but I didn't have much say in the matter. To make matters worse, they were then overcome with suspicion and went through my traveling poke. They did not take it from me, for which I was grateful since I was using it for a pillow, but they removed Uncle Wig's pistol and put it in the wagon.

I suppose it didn't trouble me too much, though. I was in a heady state that even their thievery could not erase. When Chigger caught me up, we would have a good head start. Granny Wren and the others would not even realize we were gone for good until we were halfway across Kansas.

By the second night, me and the Suggses had made it all the way to the banks of the Missouri. As I sat there, listening to the frogs and the crickets and the solid rumble of the Big Muddy slapping her banks as she rolled on south, I was getting fair concerned. Not just about how I was going to get myself free, but about Chigger John.

When I was younger, I had sometimes let my buyers haul me a good distance. I had done this out of adventurous spirit, and had once ridden all the way to Lincoln, Nebraska, just to see what it was like. But since Chigger had started tagging after me, I had always parted company with the people before we hit the big river. I did not know how good Chigger would be at finding a way to cross all by himself. He would just as like forget how wide it was and try to wade across.

Anyhow, that second night I was lying there under the wagon with my hands tied together in front, the ropes looped through the wheel spokes and knotted tight. Bertha the sow snored next to me. Maybe she had taken a liking to me, or maybe she had me pegged for the treacherous sort. In either case, she had cuddled right up next to me both nights, and it was not real pleasant.

It was some past midnight, I think, and I had dozed off to the sow's snoring, when I felt something tickle at my shoulder. I went to bat at it, and came up with Chigger John's hand.

I swan, no living person has ever been quieter sneaking up than Chigger John Jukes.

He held a finger to his lips, then held up his new pocket knife to show me. With a smile, he went to work at the rope that tethered my hands to the wheel.

As he worked at the ropes, I was all bubbly in my head and my stomach. I could scarce believe it, but we were finally going to be free, Chigger and me.

Chigger sawed through the first rope in no time flat, which came as no surprise since he could never remember if he had sharpened it or not, and so spent most all his spare time whetting the blades. They were like razors.

I sat up real slow, so as not to disturb Bertha, and held out my hands for him to finish cutting me free. But when I moved, I guess I bumped him off kilter, and just like that he fell smack on top of that pig.

Well, I am here to tell you it was Katie-bar-the-door. I never ran so fast as I did to get away from those folks and that squealy sow-hog, and me with my hands still bound in front of me. Barefoot, too, because my confiscated boots were back in the wagon with my knife and pistol. At least I'd had the presence of mind to snatch up my poke on the way out.

That sow could run at a pretty fair clip, and I'll bet she chased me and Chigger for more than a mile-and-a-half through waist-high weeds, then fields of sprouting corn, and into a stand of timber, before she wore out and turned back. I guess Mr. Suggs, who had come leaping out of the wagon in his butternuts, had gone on back with her, for about the time we stopped hearing the angry squeals behind us, the shouting and cussing stopped, too.

We went on some farther, though, just in case, before we slowed down to catch our breaths.

"Whee!" said Chigger, and laughed.

I suppose it is easy to laugh at things like that when you are uncomplicated in the brain and have your boots on, but I was not feeling so chipper. My feet were all cut up and scratched, and I had stepped on something that was still stuck in my heel. I did not think it was safe to come to a full stop yet, so I steadied myself on Chigger's shoulder and kept walking, using just the toes of my right foot, my eyes teared up from the pain.

Chigger looked down and a perplexed look came over his face. "Clutie? You gonna get you a peg leg like Uncle Beetle, and put you a sword blade in it for fights?"

"I hope not," I said, and hopped on one foot for a second, groping at my heel and trying to find the tip of whatever it was I'd stepped on. There was the nub of something sticking out, although I couldn't get enough grip on it to slide it free. My heel was wet; when I brought up my hand, it was all sticky and covered in blood. It was not the best augur for the beginning of a cross-country walk, but I tried not to let myself get downhearted.

Chigger was still staring, real interested-like. "My knife's sharp," he said. "If'n you want, I could cut that bad foot right off for you."

I went back to hobbling. I wanted to find a place to sit, where I could strike a match and have a good look-see. Also, to get Chigger settled down so he could tell me what he'd done with the things I'd asked him to bring.

Chigger tugged at my sleeve. He had his knife out and aimed at my foot. "You want I should cut it off, Clutie?"

I said, "I don't believe we need to amputate quite yet, Chigger, but I thank you for the offer."

He folded up his knife, kind of disappointed. Then he brightened. "Clutie? If you gets yourself a peg leg, you could have my knife blade to stick in it."

I said, "Thanks," and sank down in a heap on the trunk of a fallen tree. I propped my ankle on my knee. Despite the pain, I was pleased that the wound was bleeding so much, for the blood would clean it out and maybe I would not get the lockjaw. "I think we had better stop while I see to my foot and reconnoiter, Chigger."

"OK." He plopped down next to me and peered at the bottom of my foot. "Blood," he said.

"Chigger, I want you to think hard about something."

"OK."

"Remember my quilt I told you to get for me? The one up the tree by my cave?"

He nodded. "I followed you there. I went a lot. I didn't tell nobody 'cause it looked secret."

I said, "That's real good, Chigger. Did you remember to go up there and get my things, like I asked you?"

His face twisted up, like he was thinking real hard. Finally he said, "What things?"

Honest-to-Jim!

There was nothing for it but to go back to the farm. I was in no shape to walk to the Golden West, and we had no supplies. I suppose we would have been all right if the Suggses hadn't requisitioned my pistol. I could have shot game, at least, until I'd used up the powder and lead. If Chigger had remembered my quilt bag, we would have been all right, too, for besides my quilt there were all manner of handy things in it. But we had neither, so that was that.

The next day we did not make very good time. I had pulled a thick splinter of green wood out of my heel, but I could still feel something grinding around in there. I had no needle to dig for it, and also no pork rind to cover the wound to pull out poison and prevent lockjaw. I did not even have a green penny to bind to it.

In the end, I had settled for packing the hole with spider webs, saying a spell to ward off festerment, and binding my heel with the tail of my shirt. Chigger cut it off for me, but, being Chigger, he did not do such a good job. What was left of my shirt in back did not even go down to my belt, and I could only tuck in the front part.

I guess we made an odd-looking pair—odder than usual, I mean—as we trudged toward home: Chigger singing almost nonstop the whole time, and me limping along beside him with the help of a make-do walking stick. I doubt we made even ten miles.

On the next morning, it rained.

We went right along in it, me limping and him singing and remarking upon the shapes the thunderheads made as they rolled overhead. By noon it had stopped and the sky had gone solid gray and the air was muggy and thick. Me and Chigger just kept on trudging northeast through the afternoon, counting cows and slapping bugs to pass the time.

Also to distract us from our empty bellies, since Chigger had picked up my poke sideways and dumped the contents into a puddle. Our food, of which we had precious little, was ruined. It didn't do my borrowed copy of *Ivanhoe* much good either.

"Was them folks nice to you, Clutie?" Chigger asked, runny nose pressed to his rain-damp sleeve. "Was they nice?" It was the sixth or eighth time he'd asked since noon.

"They were nicer than some," I replied again. "Worse than some, too." I tried not to think about the sticky mud squishing warm between my toes and into my heel bandages with every step, or those pesky little gravels that kept rising up to peck the bottoms of my feet. Two days is a long time to be shank's mare with no shoes when you're not used to it. Maybe even if you are.

Chigger rubbed his nose again. "Is your feet hurtin' you, Clutie?"

I said, "I'm gettin' some stone cuts." I was wishing Granny Wren hadn't packed away all the underdrawers for the summer. Right then I would have given about anything for a nice heavy pair to rip up and wrap round my feet.

I said, "Mayhaps tomorrow I'll cut off the tail of *your* shirt for another bandage."

He ignored that part. "Don't know why you tooked 'em off," he said, and made a show of stomping in a little puddle. "I never takes my boots off. Not even for washin'. I's growin' out my toenails for sport."

He rubbed his freckledy nose on his sleeve again and grinned big, He pointed ahead to a hilly pasture. "More cows! One, two, three . . . three . . . five! How many's that cipher to, Clutie?"

"Four. Makes eighty-two, all told. And I didn't take 'em off because I wanted to. I told you." He raised his cuff to his drippy nose again, and I said, "Crimeny, Chigger John, use your kerchief."

I watched out of the corner of my eye while he slapped at his pockets. A ball of twine, his pocket knife, a buckeye, the lucky bones from a crawdad, and a little dead frog came out. By its odor and color, I figured the frog to have been dead for a little too long.

"Ain't got no snot rag," Chigger muttered, sniffling. He shoved everything but the frog back in his pockets, then ran grimy fingers through his hair.

It was still as silky and full of ringlets as when he had been a baby, and had not gone to that brittle, cowlicky orange like the other Jukeses. Instead, it had gradually darkened from a soft reddish gold to a deep sorrel that changed with the light. Right then, between the dirty parts and the wet parts and the sun-bleached parts, it was two dozen shades of unbridled auburn. When the light hit him right, his head looked to be on fire.

"Don't say snot rag, say handkerchief." I leaned on my

walking stick and dug into a pocket to find him mine. He honked into it, then held it out.

I said, "No, you can keep it."

"The Bug Boys say snot rag."

"The Bug Boys are in jail half the time, too."

" 'Cause they say snot rag?"

"No, because they . . . Oh, never mind."

Chigger frowned. "I'm hungry, Clutie." He stuck the frog under his armpit, then rubbed at his stomach. "My belly's quit growlin'. Hurts."

"Best throw that smelly old frog away, Chigger John."

He paid me no mind. He was staring straight up, into a sky the color of metal. A little blue had broken through here and there, but not enough to make me hopeful. I wondered how long it would be before my family ran across somebody else to trade me to, somebody who could give me a head start west. I wondered if Chigger would remember my quilt bag the next time.

"Stopped rainin'," he said, blue eyes blinking. "No more sheepses in the sky." There was a shadow over the land as far as I could see.

"Stopped about an hour ago." I slapped at a bug.

" 'Skeeters is bad this year," said Chigger, without looking.

I said, "Throw the frog away, all right?"

"We could eat it. I'm awful hungry, Clutie."

"That thing's too dead to skin. You'd just puke it up."

"OK. Don't want no puke dogs." He kept his face lifted to the sky, the kerchief balled in one hand and the dead frog swinging in the other. "Was these'uns nice to you, Clutie? I would'a killed 'em if they wasn't nice to you." He scrunched up his face to look tough, the way Uncle Beetle did when he was sozzled and talking about how the Yankees shot his leg off in the war. On Beetle that face was a menace, but on Chigger it was endearing.

Seemed a real shame that one day he'd turn into a fully-growed Jukes man and start sucking eggs and lifting his leg on every bush and fence post in sight.

But right then, he was kind of cute, talking murder and all.

"You would'a killed 'em?" I pressed my mouth tight, so as not to smile.

He nodded, serious as a preacher. "Deader'n dirt," he said. "Deader'n hammers. Deader'n a dead frog."

I stopped walking and put my hand on my hips. "Chigger John Jukes, I expect you are about the bloodthirstiest twelve-year-old on the broad green face of the Earth."

He stopped, too, and turned round to face me. "Yes'm, I reckon I is." He smiled real proud. He did love a compliment.

"Now, throw the frog away, Chigger. I mean it. It's got a stench."

"Aw, Clutie . . ." He stared at his frog for a second, real sad, and was just about to fling it when he froze. Frog dangling from his fingers, he pointed past my shoulder. "Riders!" he said, then grabbed up my hand and dived for the ditch.

ten

Me and Chigger John most always had to make for a ditch or a tree line or a bramble or some such on those treks home. The backroads could be a dangerous location for travelers in those days, plus we were always scared that whatever folks I'd run off from would be following, and mad.

On this occasion, we landed backside-first and skidded down into wet, waist-high weeds and thick black Missouri mud, and while Chigger parted the greenery and peered down the pike to see what sort of devilment was riding toward us, I seized the opportunity to ease that putrid frog from his fingers and toss it away. He was so intent on the approaching travelers that he didn't notice.

"Horsebackers," he whispered finally. "Two." By then I could hear the sucking sounds of hooves on the road.

"Got a wagon or a big hog with 'em?"

He squinted. "No."

"Then it's not the Suggses. Get your head down, Chigger John."

He crouched in the weeds beside me, then looked at his hand, the one that had been holding the frog. His eyebrows knitted up. "I believe I lost somethin', Clutie," he said, real perplexed.

"Nothin' important. Now, hush."

I ducked low and put my hands atop Chigger's head, in case he forgot he was supposed to be hid and tried to jump up, and also to hide what I could of that signal-fire hair.

The hoof sounds came closer, and then I could hear the riders' saddle leather creaking, too. And just before the sounds came even with where we were hid, they stopped.

There was a real nervous silence, during which both me and Chigger held our breaths. And then, finally, a man's voice said, "Goodness gracious." He didn't sound murderous, but you never could tell. "Has this part of Missouri raised up such a bumper crop of young'uns that they're throwing the extras away in ditches?"

The second man chuckled.

Right then, I would have given just about anything to have back my bootknife or gun, either one. I tried to decide whether to stand up and bluff it out, or just grab Chigger and run.

Above us, on the road, the first man spoke again. "You young'uns climb on up out of there, now. Don't make me send my friend down after you." .

Beside me in the wet weeds, Chigger whispered, "You reckon they've see'd us, Clutie?"

I whispered, "I suspect they have, Chigger John," then louder, "Don't shoot, mister. We're coming out."

Chigger scrambled up ahead of me and gave me a tug when I slipped on the lip of the ditch's slope. I ended up on the road, all right, but sitting on my backside and staring right at pair of mud-speckled horse knees.

Chigger still had a tight grip on my hand. He also had a big smile plastered to his face. He pointed up at one of the riders, who I couldn't see yet because of practically being under his bay horse, and said, "Look, Clutie! Angels!"

Well, he burst straight into song, and was about three lines into a shape note hymn before I got my stick under me good enough to regain my feet. When I lifted my eyes to the first rider, whose horse was nosing me so hard as to about knock me over again, the face that looked back down into mine was a welcome sight indeed.

"Why, is that Miss Clutie Mae, all grown up?" he said after a moment, leaning a forearm on his saddle horn. "That's right, isn't it, little sis? Wig Jukes's niece?"

Well, ten armed brigands couldn't have kept the smile from blooming on my face. "Yessir, Frank. I mean Mr. James. It's me." Chigger was still lost in song, and I settled my hand across his mouth. He kept right on singing, but at least it was muffled some. "Maybe you recollect my cousin, Chigger John?"

"Frank is fine," he said, still slouched over in his saddle. "And yes, I remember this boy. Both of you have grown a bit taller. Me, I've just got older." He sat up straight then, and motioned to his companion. "This here's Joaquin. Joaquin, I believe you've heard Jesse and me speak of the Jukes family."

"*Sí*," said the other man. "This is the little girl you told me of? If so, you did not do her justice."

Up till right then I'd only had eyes for Frank, but when that other man started to talk, I couldn't help but stare at him. I had never in my life heard such a voice, all deep and dark and rumbly and foreign. It was at the same time soft and hard, sweet and kind of scary, too, and it made my tailbone go all tingly.

And then, just like somebody had slapped me, I recognized him. It was that sudden. I blurted, "You're the Spanish Kid!"

He swept the black hat off his head and held it out at arm's length. His hair was long and dark brown, near the color of mine, and it was tied at the nape into a horsetail that bobbled over his shoulder when he bowed his head.

I felt my mouth drop open, and I couldn't seem to get it closed.

"At your service," he said. His eyes were light brown, the color of bark tea, and fringed thick with dark lashes.

Just then Chigger kicked me in the leg, and I let go of his mouth. I guess maybe I had been squeezing his head a little hard.

"What are you youngsters doing out here?" Frank asked. "Your Uncle Beetle still pulling that old dodge with you, missy?"

"No, sir," I said. I was having a hard time of it not to stare at the Spanish Kid, and made a real strong effort to keep my eyes on Frank. "Uncle Glow and the rest of the Bug Boys did it this time. Beetle's in jail on account of his horse bit him in the knee while he was holding up a coach. He's due out any day now.''

"Can't imagine you're much lookin' forward to that," he replied, kind of dry.

Out of the corner of my eye, I saw Chigger walk right up to the Spanish Kid's chestnut and tug his stirrup. "Can Clutie ride your horse, mister?" he said, his neck craned up. "Her feet's hurtin' her somethin' fierce."

I felt the red fair shoot up over my face. I said, "Chigger John!" and hauled him back by his collar.

Frank looked down at my bare and muddy feet, then back up into my eyes. "How'd you come to be out here unshod, Miss Clutie?"

Well, I told him about the Suggses and Bertha the sow and how I'd lost my boots and knife and pistol and such, and when I got done, he pointed a finger at Chigger. "Joaquin, give the songbird a boost up on that oater of yours." Then he kicked free a stirrup and held out his hand to me. "Hop on up, little sis. I reckon we can take you down the road a piece."

We rode the rest of the day while Chigger sang, and the Spanish Kid stared at me practically the whole time. I was fair embarrassed. I could feel his eyeballs on me, and I knew he was mocking me because I was big and lumpy and was dressed like white trash. Worse—white trash with no boots and a ripped shirt and mud on my face.

Not that his features gave him away. Not when I dared to take a sideways glance at him, anyhow. No, he was real proper and serious. That made it worse.

They made their camp along a creek with woods all around, a place I had camped myself, once or twice before. The sun was still up, but Frank insisted he was going to see to my foot, and said he needed the light.

While the Spanish Kid tended the horses and Chigger waded at the edge of the creek—looking for a new frog, I guess—Frank brought out a long needle he kept for mending tack and set into digging for the chunk of splinter still lodged in my heel.

I had a hard time of it not to holler, it stung so bad. I bit down on a stick and closed my eyes tight and tried not to think about the hurt, but by the time he said "Got it!" the tears were fair rolling down my cheeks.

"Wasn't much left in there," he was saying as I opened my eyes. He held out a little bit of bloody wood in his fingers. "Don't take much to hurt like sin, though."

He was about to say something else when Chigger gave a loud yelp. Frank whipped round and I sat up, and there was Chigger John, legs pumping air as he dangled off the ground at the end of the Spanish Kid's fist, which was clamped around Chigger's arm. Chigger had hold of my walking stick, and he was swinging it wild.

Frank got to his feet quick, and I shouted, "Hey!"

The Spanish Kid, calm as you please, said, "Drop your weapon, *muchacho,* if you wish to see the ground again."

Well, Chigger wouldn't drop it, and Frank had to go wrest it away. The minute the Spanish Kid let Chigger down, he ran to me. I thought it was going to be for a hug, but instead he planted himself between me and the men and shouted at Frank, "Don't you hurt my Clutie! I seen you! You was makin' her cry!"

The Spanish Kid smiled, just a little, and had the nerve to look even more handsome. "He was going to break that branch over your skull, Frank."

"Lord a'mercy," said Frank, shaking his head. "I didn't even hear him comin' up."

Everything calmed down a good bit after I explained to Chigger that Frank had only been doctoring me, and explained to Frank and the Spanish Kid about how Chigger was. I did that last part after I'd sent Chigger down to the creek for water.

Frank gave me two pairs of his own personal extra socks, which I put on after I'd washed my feet real good and stuffed the hole with more spiderwebs, and then we had a fine supper of fried chicken and ham and corn fritters that Frank had in his pack, and some good coffee that I made.

The first time I met Frank James, he had given me a packet

of freshly fried-up chicken for the road. I guessed he was so popular that all he had to do was stop by a farm and they'd run straight out and kill a hen.

It was night by then. Chigger John fell asleep about half-way though the meal, and as me and Frank and the Spanish Kid sat around the little cook fire, we kept our voices low so as not to wake him. Well, me and Frank, anyhow.

"So you lost your pistol, too?" Frank was saying.

"Yessir, Uncle Wig's Navy. He lets me use his firearms on account of I bring in about all the meat."

Frank raised a brow. "You hunt with a pistol?"

"No, sir, with a rifle. I am a good shot, too. One slug." I snapped my fingers.

"Goodness gracious," he said with a little sideways smile at Joaquin. "I believe I'd like to see that."

My face went all hot. I said, "You're makin' sport of me, aren't you?" When he didn't deny it, I said, "Well, it's the truth! Wig says I've got the gift, like Grandpappy Viper. You just set up some targets and give me the loan of your long gun, and I'll show you!"

Frank chuckled and patted my knee. "Don't go giving yourself the vapors, little sis. Mayhap in the morning."

The Spanish Kid was not saying much, which was just as well. I could hardly look at him without my stomach going all a-flutter. This was not only because he was so handsome in real life, but because I was secretly afraid that somehow he knew about me staring at his poster down at our barn and making up romantic stories about him.

"We have got a place to be in two days," Frank was saying as he poked the fire. Out of the corner of my eye, I watched the Spanish Kid roll a cigarette. "No offense to you personally, Miss Clutie," Frank went on, "but I don't believe I wish to pay a social call upon your family. But Joaquin and I will be within about five miles of your place by tomorrow mid-afternoon. Think you and your little watchdog, here, can hoof it that far?"

I nodded, glad the subject had turned away from firearms. "Thank you, Frank. You've been real good to me and Chigger."

He poked the fire again, then drained his coffee cup. "You don't look any too joyous about it. Would you be happier if we were hauling you in the other direction?"

That just goes to show you that Frank James was not called a great man for nothing. I told him about my escape plan, and how Chigger had forgot the quilt sack, and how now, especially after losing my boots and weaponry, we had no choice but to go back.

"I plan to try again, though," I said at the end. "I've got my eighth-grade certificate. I'm thinking that maybe even without teacher's college I could get a schoolmarming job someplace out in the West. California, maybe."

"Good for you," said Frank. "If I were you, I'd do it quick, before your Uncle Beetle gets home. He is one sour piece of business. I believe it's only your granny holding him back, and she's no spring chicken."

He settled down on his blanket, and just before he eased his hat down over his eyes, he said, "Get out of there soon as you can, Miss Clutie, and take that little ring-tailed tooter of a songbird with you. Don't reckon you'll come to much harm with him on the prowl."

He pulled the hat the rest of the way over his face and crossed his arms over his chest. Muffled, I heard him mutter, "Didn't even hear him sneakin' up!"

It wasn't more than a minute or two before he was asleep, his chest rising and falling regular. That left me sitting across the fire from the Spanish Kid, with nothing to distract us except the crickets and the frogs and the sound of the creek. I looked up from the flames, found him staring at me, and looked back to the fire real quick. All the little hairs on the back of my neck were prickled and I felt real odd in my spine.

When he stood, I jerked a bit. I hoped he hadn't noticed. Without a word, he scuffed dirt into the fire until it was nothing but a few embers glowing in the middle. And then he walked around it and sat down right next to me, practically touching. Just like that, I went stiff as a board.

"Clutie. That is a strange name," he said real soft. I swallowed hard. I couldn't make myself look at him for fear I'd do something real unacceptable. I wished Frank would wake up and talk about guns again.

"I-it's for Chrysanthemum," I stuttered finally.

"Chrysanthemum," he repeated.

I had always hated that name, but he said it so beautiful, with the R rolled and the syllables accented all melodic, that it came out poetry. I could have listened to him say my name all night long and never got bored.

There was a silence again. He was sitting awful close, and he was a big man. Earlier, I had noticed that he towered over Frank James, who was maybe five-foot-six, and two inches shorter than me now that I had got my full height. I guessed The Spanish Kid at maybe six-foot-two, and wondered where the top of my head would hit him if we stood close. I had always felt lumpy and awkward around my family, but next to the Spanish Kid I felt almost delicate. It was a feeling I admired.

The way he'd made music out of the word "Chrysanthemum" was still just hanging there in the air, and I decided that I had best ignore my trepidations and say something lest he think me rude. For some reason, I wanted him to only have good thoughts about me.

Keeping my gaze glued to what was left of the fire, I said, "Why does Frank call you Wa-keen? It doesn't sound a very Spanish name for somebody called the Spanish Kid." The only Spanish names I knew were conquistadors', like Cortez or Balboa or Pizarro, from Miss Hanker's classroom. Well, Pancho and Juan and Manuel, too, but those were Mexico names.

He pointed at my foot. "It must hurt. Drink this."

He handed me a slim silver flask. I took it, my hands feeling numb, and stared at it kind of blank.

"Go ahead," he said, and touched the back of my hand with his finger. Gooseflesh shot right up my arm, across my shoulder, and down my backbone to my sitting parts.

I may have let out a little gasp, but if I did he did not notice. At least he pretended not to. He said, "Drink. It is not like that panther piss your family makes. Frank has told me. No, this is brandy. Good brandy.''

I couldn't move. He took the flask back and unstoppered it, and then put it in my hands again. "Take a sip, Chrysanthemum," he said low, over the soft burble of the creek and the frog song. "Drink, and I will tell you my name."

I drank. It tasted warm and sweetish, almost thick in my mouth and down my throat, but it was good.

"Again," he whispered.

I took another swallow.

He eased the flask from my fingers and said, "Better. It is a shame to drink this brandy without first enjoying the sight of it through crystal. It is red and deep, like the liquid hearts of rubies."

I was in a terrible state. He was sitting so close that I could feel his breath on my ear. The brandy seemed to be swirling inside me, relentless, like a slowed-down but iron-minded cyclone. If I could have moved, I would have thrown myself into that cold creek water just so as to think clear again. But I couldn't move. It was about all I could do to breathe.

"My name," he said at last, "is Joaquin Gabriel Mondragon Delacroix. The Delacroix is not Spanish. It is French. I am half-Spanish, though. My mother was of the Mondragon family, of the purest Castillian lines, and her father held a fabulous grant of lands in California, handed to him from his father, and his father before him. This rancho is no more. The gringos took it away through treachery and deceit and the spilling of much blood, but this is nothing to me."

Well, he sure had my attention. I almost forgot to be nervous. I said, "Was there a hacienda? With speckled cattle and orchards? Don't you want it back again?"

His smile was odd, sort of amused and sad, all at once. He touched my hair, right at my temple, and those goosebumps were back again. They nearly lifted the scalp right off my head.

He said, "*Sí, querida.* There was a grand hacienda with a ballroom and balconies and many servants, and a fountain in the courtyard. And herds of cattle, and orchards, and the finest vineyards. But I have only been told of these things. I never lived there."

He stroked my temple with his knuckles. "Do you always wear your hair in this braid down your back? Your hair is beautiful. It should be loose, to fall about your shoulders like a cloak."

That just about did it for me. I almost stammered that I had made a quilt out of deerskin, once, and how did he feel about marrying me, and only got myself stopped just in time.

Instead, I swallowed hard and said, "Then why's your last name French?" It struck me what a fortunate thing it was that Chigger was sound asleep, or he would have been asking all kinds of questions about how they trained the puke dogs over in Paris.

He opened the silver flask again and took a sip of brandy for himself. "My paternal grandfather, Victor Delacroix," he began, "was not wealthy, but he was a scholar, a man of culture. When he was in his fortieth year, he fell deeply in love with the daughter of a prominent family. Her name was Gabrielle, and she was the most beautiful Jewess in Marseilles, perhaps in all of France. Despite the warnings of his family and the indignation of hers, he turned his back upon the church and she upon her heritage, and they eloped."

All of a sudden I realized I was looking right square at him, that's how good he told this story. His face was turned to me, but his eyes were not. They seemed to be searching the darkness beyond my shoulder.

"Ten months later," he continued softly, "a son was born to them—my father. But despite Gabrielle's radiant beauty and strong will, her body could not bear the strain. She died soon after the birth. It is from her, my beautiful grandmother Gabrielle, that I received my first middle name of Gabriel."

He paused for a moment to dig for his tobacco pouch. Whether because of the brandy, or maybe because I was being so soothed by his voice, all silky and deep, I had begun to relax a little.

I said, "You are about as good a storyteller as my Granny Wren. She says out long tales of our family, too, and how

we came to be in this country. How did you come to America
if your people are French?''

He gave a last lick to the smoke he had just rolled, and
stuck it in his mouth. Lucky for me, he was still looking
away. It gave me a chance to study his face, all hard planes
and high cheekbones and strong jaw. When he started in
talking again, it almost startled me.

''When my father, whose name was Jean-Pierre, was a
young child,'' he said, striking a match, ''Grandfather
brought him to America, to New York City. They did not
get along, my father and his father, and when Jean-Pierre
was fifteen he ran away to the West to seek his fortune. He
was a trapper and a guide. For ten years he was a wanderer.
His travels one day took him to California, where he became
a guest at the home of Don Ramon Mondragon, and where
he met and was much taken with the youngest daughter of
the house, Isabella.''

Well, it was sounding more and more like a novel to me,
it was that romantic, and I said so.

He gave that funny half smile again, and his eyes met
mine. ''Easier to read than to live, I suspect,'' he said. ''But
to make this tearful saga short, Don Ramon would not hear
of a marriage. My father was not Castillian, let alone Spanish, and half a Jew on top of that. So he and Isabella Mondragon eloped. History repeats itself, no? My second middle
name, Mondragon, is for my mother's people. The Delacroix,
of course, was my father's. So there you have all of my
name.''

I stared at him for a second, and then all I could think of
to say was, ''What about the other? The Wa-keen one.''

''Joaquin,'' he repeated. ''I would like to think I was
named for Joaquin Murieta, *El Patrio,* but the timing, it is
wrong. No, I was named for my mother's brother, who died
in infancy.''

I didn't know who that Murieta fella was, but it didn't
seem the time to ask. ''But what happened next? Did they
live happily ever after? Your ma and pa, I mean.''

He stubbed out his smoke. ''Does anyone, *querida*?''

He didn't look like he was going to tell the rest, even

though there looked to be a good bit more of it, but I decided not to press him. Besides, I was getting that nervous feeling in my bones again. I said, "Then what do you like to be called?"

He opened the flask again and pressed it into my hands. "One more sip, little one, and then you go to sleep."

I raised the flask to my lips. I was getting to admire the taste.

"Any of my names," he said. "Call me what you like. I will answer also to the Spanish Kid, although I do not favor it. I will answer also to *El Dragón,* which is what certain parties, farther west of here, have christened me without my permission. Whatever you would choose, Chrysanthemum, that would I answer to."

The goosebumps were back, and everywhere. I stuttered, "W-what did your mama call you?"

He raised his hand and touched the flat of his thumb to my jaw, just under my ear. "Joaquin," he said. "When I was small, Joaquinito." He ran that thumb right down my jaw, real slow, to the tip of my chin, and then just held it there. "How old are you, *querida*?"

"S-seventeen. Almost." My mouth had all of a sudden gone dry.

"You must do what Frank told you." His thumb was still under my chin, and his face was dead serious. You couldn't have got my eyes away from his with a crowbar.

"What Frank told me?"

"You must take yourself and this boy away from the people you live with. Frank has told me about them, about these uncles of yours, these Bug Boys. I know they are your family. But sometimes family can be poison. You are a flower, *querida*. You must go where you can bloom."

He took his thumb away from my chin, his fingertips touching the side of my throat in the process. Maybe the brandy had something to do with it, but I felt like I was going to melt away.

"And now, Chrysanthemum," he whispered, "what name would you have me answer to?"

"Joaquin." I tried to say it like he did, all breathy, although I was in such a state I was real surprised the word actually came out.

He gave his head a small nod. "*Bueno*." And then, although I could scarce believe it was happening, he leaned right over and kissed me full on the lips, not sloppy and wet and hard like Spider, but real soft and warm and slow, and without grabbing me, although to tell the truth I was sort of wishing he would.

Then he drew back and kissed me again, this time on the forehead, and whispered, "Sleep well, *querida*."

I could not get my breath. I watched him rise, all long slim legs and wide shoulders and narrow hips, the gunbelt riding them just so. From where I was on the ground, he seemed about a Jukes-and-a-half high. Without looking back at me, he sauntered down to where the horses were tethered.

I had just stretched out beside Chigger—and was trying to force my brandy-fuddled brain to figure just exactly what had transpired between me and the Spanish Kid—when Frank stirred on his blanket.

"That dang Mex," he muttered, kind of grumpy, from beneath the hat that still covered his face. "Half the time you can't get him to talk. The other half you can't get him to shut the hell up. Lord, but he does go on. You get yourself to sleep now, little sis."

eleven

The next day we made good time, although the ride was some uncomfortable for me. Part of me had wanted almost sinful bad to ride up behind the Spanish Kid, but I was relieved when he held his hand down to Chigger. I guess I don't know what I might have done if I'd had to ride most all day so close to him, with my arms tight about his waist like Chigger's were. So I rode behind Frank, staring at the back of Joaquin's head if he was in front, and wondering, when we took the lead, if he was staring at me.

Right off, Chigger was real confused about all the Spanish Kid's names. "The Spanish Kid" had locked into his brain as the moniker to go with that face, and whenever me or Frank called him Joaquin, Chigger would say, "Who you talkin' to, Frank?" or "Who's that, Clutie?" For his part, Chigger had decided to call him Mr. Kid, and every once in a while, I'd hear him spout, "Mr. Kid, do you got a candy?"

Chigger's puzzlement did not stop him from singing, though. That day he chose hymns, mostly, and he kept us entertained, off and on, for a goodly part of the morning. The first time he started up, I hushed him, but Frank said to leave him be.

"I never heard such a thing in or out of a church," he said. "It's enough to make a grown man weep."

Joaquin Gabriel Mondragon Delacroix said practically nothing, which was, I guess, both good and bad. Good, because after the kiss he'd given me the night before, I would not have known how to carry on a normal conversation with him. Bad, because the sound of his voice had somehow threaded itself into my innards, and I pined to hear it again, and as much as possible. I spent most of the day rolling that fancy name of his around in my head, and remembering the music he'd made when he said mine.

At around two o'clock, and not more than an hour after resting the horses, they whoaed up again.

When I asked why we were stopping, Frank said, "Why, sis, I had about clean forgot that you were going to give us a demonstration of your deadly marksmanship! Hop down."

He was teasing me again. As much as I admired Frank, it made me kind of mad. I slid down off the horse and he dismounted directly after.

Joaquin looked disgusted. "Frank, what is the point of this?"

"Well, I just wanna see, that's all. Mayhap, if she's as good as she says, we could use her. Always got an opening for a crack shot." He slid his rifle from the boot and handed it to me. He was grinning by this time. "Go ahead, little sis. Take it."

I did. I was getting madder by the minute. I heard Joaquin let out an exasperated sigh, but I did not look round. "What do you want me to shoot at?"

He pursed his lips. "Forest's full of trees. How about that dead oak over yonder? The tall one. Joaquin, a dollar a shot?"

Joaquin's saddle creaked as he dismounted. Chigger John was already down and all excited. He said, "Clutie shoots good!"

Joaquin said, "You wager that she hits or misses?"

"Misses. A dollar a shot."

There was a silence, and then Joaquin said, "Ten dollars. That she hits."

I could not look at him. All of a sudden I was sure I could not hit an elephant at five paces with a handful of beans.

After a pause, Frank said, "All right. All right, you're on." To me, he said, "Five shots, little sis. Wouldn't want to clean Joaquin out. That big old branch to the left, up on top. See where it stick up, like a devil's pitchfork? See can you hit that."

I brought up the rifle, looking first, out of the corner of

my eye, at Joaquin. He stared at me, real serious, then looked up at the tree.

I said, "One shot first, to check the sights?"

Frank said, "Shoots true. No need."

I hoped he wasn't fibbing.

He wasn't. The first shot took the tip, and the next four cut it down, about three inches at a time. I could have cut it closer, but I did not know how good their eyes were and I wanted to make sure they saw. I handed back the rifle. I said, "I believe you owe Joaquin fifty dollars."

"Clutie shot the tree!" said Chigger. "My Clutie shoots good!"

Joaquin was laughing, and oh, it was a pretty sight! Frank looked fair angry, but then he started laughing, too. "I do believe I have been skunked!" he said, and reached into his pocket.

He peeled off fifty dollars and gave it to Joaquin—who bowed low and said "*Gracias,* Chrysanthemum"—and then Frank pounded me on my back, real friendly.

"By Christ, I never seen the like!" was all he could say.

We rode on another couple of hours before Frank called a halt again. We were close to home, and I knew it was time to make our good-byes. Chigger and me slithered to the ground and said our thanks.

As he handed me down my poke, Frank said, "If I were you, Miss Sharpshooter Clutie, I'd sneak down in there and get my things and sneak right back out again. I feel bad I can't do more to help you, but I stuck something in your poke that might ease your journey. God bless you both."

He reined his horse away, moving down the road at a jog. Joaquin paused a moment. His eyes locked onto mine. Real solemn, he said, "*Adios,* Chrysanthemum. *Vaya con Dios.*" Then he winked, touched the brim of his hat, and wheeled his horse away, pushing it into a lope that caught Frank up in no time, and left me and Chigger standing all alone in the road.

I tell you what, I just about cried.

• • •

Me and Chigger did not go straight down to the farm.

Instead, we hiked out through the woods to my cave. I hauled the quilt bag down from its tree. There were about ten or twelve buckeyes in there, and I said a spell over each one. I had already done that, of course, but I figured it couldn't hurt to get a little extra magic on them. Then I spread out my quilt for us to sit on.

I had kept some decent-sized scraps of deerskin, and after determining that I had just about enough, I borrowed Chigger's pocketknife and began trimming what I would need to lace together some moccasins. They would be slapdash and not at all fancy, but they would do until I could find myself some boots. Even after the removal of the last of the splinter, and even with two pairs of Frank James's socks to protect them, my feet were still terrible sore. My heel was the worst, and had started to bleed again.

By the time it was coming dark, I had the first one put together and on my bad foot, and was just cutting the laces for the second.

"I's hungry, Clutie," Chigger said. He had been real good not to bother me, having gone down to the creek to look for frogs. But he was back again, his face pressed flat against the piecework. I was hungry, too, and opened up my poke. I figured when Frank said he'd put something in there to ease our journey, it was most likely another batch of chicken.

It wasn't, though. What it was, was a fat roll of bills, genuine U.S. currency, that totaled at two hundred and thirty-four dollars. I reckoned there might have been more if I hadn't lost that fifty dollars for him. I must have sat there for a good minute, just staring at it, before Chigger yanked on my sleeve and said, louder this time, "I'm *hungry,* Clutie!"

I gave him a chunk of the jerky I always kept in my quilt bag, and while he gnawed on it, I fished out one of the stumpy candles I kept in there. I lit it, grabbed a piece of jerky for myself, and then I cut and pieced together one real long deerskin lace. I re-rolled the bills, passed the lace through the hole in the middle, then tied the lace around my neck with the bills dangling down inside my shirt, just below the little gold heart Miss Hanker had given me.

"What you got there, Clutie?" Chigger said. He took his jerky real serious, and had been engrossed in that. "What'd you drop down your front?"

I picked up the piece of moccasin again and said, "Our future, Chigger John."

We went down to the farm at about midnight, me lugging the big oilcloth sack with my quilt and Agnes Ann's dress and my cave supplies, Chigger toting my poke. It was funny about that dress. I loved it, all robin's egg blue and ruffledy and darted and fine-stitched, but as many times as I had taken it out and admired it, I had never once put it on. I did not even know if it would fit me. But I wasn't going to leave it behind.

I had done quite a bit of thinking about what was, and was not, important for us to take. I would have liked a clean shirt without the back of it cut out, but that would have been too hard to sneak, since my clothes were in an old bureau right next to Granny Wren's cot. Besides, now that we had Frank James's money, me and Chigger could stop somewhere along the way and get an extra set of clothes.

We would not have had to bother with the cabin at all, except that it had dawned on me that if I wanted to teach school someday, I would need my certificate. And it was in the cabin, in the Bible.

I figured Chigger to be prime for the job, him being so quiet and stealthy and such. I explained his task to him three times, and real slow, and made him repeat it each time until I was sure he had locked it into his brain.

"The folded-up paper in the Bible," I said a fourth time for good measure. "And then you come straight back up here to me." We were just up the slope from the clearing, a few yards back into the trees. There was most of a full moon, and I could see the cabin and the barn and the berry bramble and such real clear.

"Straight back up to you," Chigger repeated, all serious.

"Good boy. Now, go on!"

I watched him creep down into the open, past the bramble,

and down to the cabin, and then he turned the corner and I lost sight of him.

I crossed about all my fingers and toes and said, "Mercy on him who creeps by night, Have mercy on the creeper," about fifty times with my eyelids clamped shut, and it seemed like forever before I felt an elbow poking me in the ribs.

"I done it," said Chigger, beaming. He held out his hand, in which was not just my certificate, but the whole dad-gum Bible.

"Honest-to-Jim, Chigger! You go stealing a Bible and we won't have to worry about the Bug Boys, for the Lord'll strike us down for certain sure!"

His face kind of crinkled up, and real quick, I added, "It's all right. You did good. I'll take out my paper." I stuck it in my poke. "And we'll put this back." He grabbed for it, but I held on. "Wait a minute. I'll do it. I'm just going to leave it on the porch. You wait here for me, Chigger, understand? It'll be a while, because I have to go to the barn, too."

His eyebrows shot straight up. "The Bug Boys is in there!"

I patted his head. "I know. But I been thinking. We can't just leave old Johnnycake. Beetle'll murder him for sure when he gets back. We're going to take him with us."

"But Clutie!"

"I think I can do it, Chigger. I can't be as quiet as you, but they'll more'n likely be donked. You stay right here and guard these things. Pretty soon I'll come walking up this slope with Johnnycake, and then we'll all go west."

"West," he said, and grinned. "OK."

I crept down the slope and past the bramble, slid the Bible onto the porch with no trouble, and limped my way down to the barn. The door creaked a little on its old leather hinges as I eased it open.

The Bug Boys were snoring up a storm. I stood there for a few seconds, letting my eyes get used to the dark and my nose to the stench of the still—let me tell you, it like to tore your face off.

Quiet, I made my way toward the back stall. Uncle Glow was passed out across a couple of hay bales, a jug beside him in the straw. All I could see of Spider was his tattooed arm, sticking out of the shadows that lay over the pile of straw he'd picked for his bed. He was snoring real regular, though.

Poor Johnnycake. You could have used his ribs for a washboard, they stuck out that much. I patted his scrawny neck and told him to be quiet. In reply, he bit me in the shoulder, although not hard.

Now, I knew for sure that old Johnnycake was in no shape to carry a rider. I did not even know for certain that he'd be able to walk good, having stood for a whole year in that cross-tie stall with no exercise. But I figured that maybe someday he'd make a decent mount again, and that is why I stole Beetle's saddle.

I cinched it up, hung his bridle over the saddle horn along with an extra coil of rope—you can never have too much rope—and then I untied Johnnycake's lead and gave a backwards tug on his halter.

"Back," I whispered into his furry ear. "Back up, you old fool."

He cow-kicked once and tried to nip me in the leg, but then he did what he was told, and backed out of the stall. He seemed a little confused to be standing in a whole new place after so long, but after a lot more tugging, this time toward the barn doors, I got him moving again, and then me and Johnnycake were outside in the moonlight, and the next thing to free.

But there was one more thing I wanted to do before we waved good-bye to Jukes Holler forever. I tethered Johnnycake to the corral fence, just in case he decided to move on his own, and crept back to the open barn door. Careful as I could, I peeled back Green Liver Bob's poster and freed the Spanish Kid's. I took it down without making one tear, and folded it real precise.

I was just sticking it into my pants pocket when a bony hand clamped on my shoulder and spun me about.

"What you doin' with Uncle Beetle's nag?" snarled Spider. He let go of my shoulder, than gave it a shove. It knocked me back a few feet. He was shirtless, and his britches were held up by one suspender. He'd thrown a gunbelt over his shoulder, and his brand new Colt Peacemaker dangled from his hand. His brow wrinkled up some. He didn't look quite all the way awake. "When'd you get home, anyways?"

"I'm just giving Johnnycake some air," I said. It wasn't real clever, but it was the first thing I thought of. "Beetle'll want to ride him when he gets home. I thought I might could start to get him in shape. You worthless lot have just let him stand."

"I'll air my own horse, Little Miss Midnight Sneak." It was Uncle Beetle's voice, and all of a sudden I felt like all the blood in my body was draining out, fast, through my toes.

He must have been sleeping up in the loft. He stepped out of the barn and into the moonlight. He was dressed pretty much like Spider, with no shirt, just his pants and suspenders, except instead of toting a pistol and gunbelt, he was carrying a shotgun.

"Thought maybe we had us a thief," he said. "Looks like I was right." He walked over to the corral and leaned against a post, just past the reach of Johnnycake's teeth. "Why's you skulking in the night, Clutie? Was you gonna make off with this bag'a bones? Was you gonna try to thieve a horse off me? Off *me*?"

I said, "Uncle Beetle, I—"

He paid me no mind. He brought up that shotgun and aimed both barrels straight at Johnnycake's bony forehead. "Should'a did this first thing this afternoon when I come home," he said. There came two soft clicks, one for the cock of each hammer. "Might's well—"

Uncle Beetle never finished the sentence, because just then there was a big dull metal sound, like the muffled thud of a gong. Uncle Beetle dropped straight down to his knees, and then the ground. It was a pure-dee miracle that shotgun didn't go off. Above him, Chigger clung to the fence post. Granny

Wren's favorite iron skillet was in his hand, and he was smiling big.

He said, "I thought maybe we'd be needin' it if we was to fry up some fish."

I was about to ask him what in tarnation had possessed him to go back to the cabin, when Spider reminded me of his presence by poking the nose of his Colt into my middle.

"Christ a'mighty, you killed Uncle Beetle!" he hollered. He was looking pretty awake by then. "Glow!" he called. "Glow! Wake up and get your butt out here!"

"Shut up, Spider!" I hissed, and pushed the gun away.

He pushed back, and before I knew it we were tussling on the ground, slapping and punching and fighting over that shiny new gun. Now, if we'd been standing up and I'd had room to pull back, I probably could have knocked Spider out cold—or close to it—with one punch. But in up-close fighting he was wiry and strong and quick, and right then he was twisting and turning something fierce, not to mention cussing to beat the band.

Then the gun went off. I felt the heat of it sear my middle and I rolled off Spider fast, sure I'd been shot. My hands went to the burning place. Smoke rose from my shirt. I batted at it, and my hands came away dark. I cried, "You've shot me, you fool!"

From the corral fence, Chigger wailed, "Clutie, Clutie!"

Then I took another look at my hands. The darkness on them was dry, not wet. Ashes from my shirt. Gunpowder. I sat up. Spider didn't though. He lay flopped on the ground like a busted rag poppet, and there was blood all over his thin white chest.

Up at the cabin, a light bloomed in the window, and I knew Granny and the others were up and would be upon us in no time. Johnnycake was moving so slow and lame there was no way to get him up into the trees without them seeing. So I yelled to Chigger, "Hide! Hide till I call you!" He jumped down off the fence, skillet in hand, and disappeared into the night.

I swept up Spider's pistol and gunbelt, and was about to

take off when Uncle Glow staggered out of the barn, lugging his old twenty-two.

"What's this?" he slurred, twisting his head from side to side so that his braid whipped out in arcs and I thought he might lose that Johnny Reb cap. "What's—" Right then he saw Spider.

"Who has did this? Who's did this, Clutie?"

"Yankees," I said, which was likely the only true stroke of genius I'd had all night. I heard shouting from up at the cabin, and knew I didn't have long.

His eyebrows shot up. "Yankees!"

"Five or six bluecoats. They're back, Uncle Glow, and they got Beetle and Spider. They took off yonder, said they were going to torch the west sixty for the glory of U.S. Grant!"

"Torch it?" he hollered, and waved his rifle over his head. "Yankees gonna fire our woods? Like hell they is!"

And just like that, he was off and loping in a wobbly line toward the west sixty to prevent further calamity.

I didn't hesitate, either. I shoved Spider's gun into its holster, slung the whole business over my shoulder, and ducked around the corner.

I had only just hunkered down in the hollyhock patch when Granny Wren and Gnat, followed close by Mama and trailed by Violet, came down the slope, lanterns bobbling before them. I heard Mama cry out, "Spider!" before she set in to weeping. She broke into a run, as did the others— except for Violet, who was too swole with child to do more than clomp along—and then they were too close and, the angle being wrong, I couldn't see them anymore.

Under my breath, I chanted:

> "Wind to the race,
>   Storm to the chase,
>   Clouds clabber overhead,
>   Hide my face!"

I'll be danged if right then the thunder didn't rumble! Mama's weeping grew into a wail and Granny Wren growled, "Shut up, Tulip! Shut up and help me."

Violet, sucking her thumb and dragging a poppet, waddled over and eased herself down on a stump about thirty feet away from me.

And then Gnat called out, "It's Beetle! They's got Beetle, too! Who's did this, Granny? Where's Glow?"

Violet's face widened with a big smile. She stared right at where I was crouched in the bushes, and then she waved.

Well, if I had been in the clutches of cold panic before, that wave turned me into the next thing to a block of ice. I could not breathe.

Across the yard, Violet's smile went into a little frown. I could see this real plain, because just then lightning lit up the sky. She waved at me again, harder this time. I guess chants don't work on folks who don't understand them.

To this day I don't know how I did it, but somehow I managed to lift up my arm and wave back at her. I think I might even have smiled some.

In either case, it appeared to pacify her, and she set right into ignoring me and rocking her poppet.

It seemed like forever before they dragged Spider and Beetle, one at a time, up the slope to the cabin. The thunder was booming by that time, though there was no rain yet— and I had already consigned that "clouds clabber up" spell to extra-special grade. There was wailing a-plenty, and I supposed they were hauling them up there to clean and dress them for burying. I can't say I felt bad about it, at least right then. I was too scared of them, and too impressed with my own magic.

Even after I heard the last *bumpety-thump* of Beetle's boots dragging up the porch steps between the thunderclaps, I was afraid to peek out. Nobody had mentioned Johnnycake, though he was tied to the corral and big as life, and I was certain Granny Wren would send Gnat down to put him away or clobber him or something. But nobody came, and after a few more minutes I heard Chigger, giving out that eerie Indian whistle of his.

I stood up slow and creaky, my knees having near locked

up. *"Chigger!"* I hissed as I stepped from the hollyhocks.

"I's here, Clutie."

I just about leapt out of my skin, for he'd come up directly behind without my hearing.

"Don't *do* that!" I whispered, hand to my heart.

That iron skillet he'd banged Beetle with was still in his hand, and there was a burlap sack in the other. Puzzlement furrowed his brow. "Do what?"

"Never mind. Let's just go."

The lamplight glowed bright from the windows up the hill. As Chigger and me untied Johnnycake and began to slowly lead him out of the yard and up toward the tree line, I could hear weeping and shouts coming from the cabin. I made out Granny Wren hollering, "Shut up, Tulip," and then it just turned into noise, all blurry, half-drowned by claps of thunder.

I attempted to take my mind off it. "What you got in here?" I called to Chigger once we made the woods, for the wind was whipping up fierce. I had already secured my poke and quilt bag to Johnnycake's saddle, and was just lifting Chigger's burlap bag up to do the same with it. It weighed nigh on a ton. He had put the skillet in there, too.

"What?"

I tied the end of it round the saddle horn. All around us the branches lashed. The storm was coming in fast. "What'd you swipe?"

"Can I sit on Johnnycake?"

We started back into the wild, wind-hungry woods, Johnnycake wobbling behind us. The shouts from the cabin were lost in the storm. "No, Chigger. He's real sore."

"How come he's mad?"

"Not that kind of sore. He's been standing so long his muscles don't work right. I reckon his feet hurt, too."

"Did he step on a stick, too, Clutie? Maybe Frank will give him some socks. Are we goin' to see Frank and Mr. Kid again?" The skies opened up just then, and it began to rain with a vengeance.

"No, Chigger." I had to shout it over the wind.

"No, *which*?"

"No to all of it."

As we went past the last vantage point from which we could see the farm, I paused and looked down through the trees at our cabin, its windows glowing yellow against the storm and the dark, sound lost in a howling wind.

"Good-bye, Mama," I whispered as I turned away, rain running in rivers from my hat, rain everywhere.

I never looked back.

twelve

I expected that it wouldn't be too long before Uncle Glow figured out there were no Yankees after his still; not much longer after that before he went and told Granny I'd been there. It was a pretty sure bet that sometime before the dawn, one or another of the Jukeses would think to set Beetle's hounds on me.

For that reason, I led Johnnycake and Chigger out through the sodden woods on an angle to meet the Little Shy Creek, a place upwater from the crook of it that ran past my cave. By the time we reached it, the rain had stopped. Poor Johnnycake was moving more creaky than ever, and I was not doing so well myself, in spite of the extra deerskin pieces I had set into the soles of my moccasins.

We could not rest, though. By my reckoning, we had maybe two hours before the dawn, and it was important to put as much distance between me and the Jukeses as possible. So we all waded down into the Little Shy, me and Chigger and Johnnycake. Even swollen with rain, the water was shallow, coming about halfway to the buckskin's knees, but it was cold, the Little Shy being spring-fed.

This was a good thing for Johnnycake, since his muscles and feet were real tender to start with, and I had just made him walk a goodly ways over uncertain turf, burdened with a saddle and my quilt bag and poke, not to mention Lord-knew-what in that burlap sack of Chigger's.

The cold water felt good to me, too, except that every once in a while I would accidentally step my heel down just so on a stone. It would be about all I could do not to let out a yelp.

I was thinking a lot about that spell, too. I had never seen one to work so fast, and I was fair afraid to use it again except in dire emergency.

Chigger sloshed along real happy, although several times I had to caution him to keep off the banks.

"We've got to stay in the center to throw off the hounds," I told him again and again.

"Puke dogs?" he'd say every time, hands clasped before him in panic.

"No. Beetle's hounds. You don't want them catching you after the way you killed Beetle with that skillet."

"I did?"

Sunrise came and went, and by midday we had just about walked ourselves out of creek. We were close to the source, and the Little Shy was only a couple inches deep and maybe three feet at its widest. We were also in the middle of what looked to be somebody's cow pasture.

"All right, Chigger," I said. He was still walking, but half-asleep. I wasn't doing much better. "Let's find us a place to hide away for a while and get some shut-eye."

We cut up to the north. We did not make very good time. What with Johnnycake being so muscle sore to begin with and now having added stone bruises to it, he would pause about every other step and hold up first one leg, then the other. I kept up a stream of chatter, as much to keep us awake and moving as anything.

I mostly talked about California, I think, and how we would find a nice place to live, all lush and grassy and maybe with an orchard, and how Chigger would grow up straight and tall, and how Johnnycake would get fat and glossy and never feel a whip again, and about how I would be a school-teacher and wear dresses and be able to talk to anybody, just like equals.

Late in the afternoon we found a goodly stand of timber and made our way back into it to a small clearing. It was a good thing, for I had nearly talked myself hoarse. The minute I slid the saddle off him, Johnnycake groaned and sank right down to the ground. That scared me. Except for a roll to scratch their backs, horses hardly ever lie down unless they are real sick. But instead of flopping over on his side and ceasing to breathe, he stayed on his belly with his knees bent, and started in to graze on the clump of grass before him.

Chigger was even more tuckered than I'd thought, too. When I turned round, he was stretched out in a patch of sunshine and clover, sound asleep.

I used the long rope I'd swiped to tether Johnnycake to the closest strong tree, although he was so weak that a sapling would likely have held him even if he'd bolted. Then I walked round the clearing tearing up handfuls of long spring grass and thick clover until I had an armload. I dropped that in front of Johnnycake, who thanked me by ripping my sleeve with his teeth, and then I went to the middle of the clearing.

I turned three times in a circle, clasped my hands behind my back, squished my eyes shut, and said a chant for journeying.

> "Toenail farthest from the heart,
> Soonest come will last depart,
> Dog chase tail,
> Rope chase pail,
> Jesus keep me safe to start."

I spat to the east and the west to seal it, and then I flopped on the ground beside Chigger John and went straight to sleep.

"Clutie!"

I cracked open one eye. It was almost dark, and it took me a second to remember where I was, and to figure out that the sun was just rising, not going to bed, and that I had slept like the dead near the whole night through. Chigger was pushing at my shoulder, pounding on it. "Clutie!"

I pushed his hand away. "What?" Before the word was clear out of my mouth, I knew the answer. I was on my feet and moving before I had the other eye open.

"It's Johnnycake!" Chigger said, jogging after me through the long, wet, shadowy grass.

"I know. I hear him."

A colicky horse makes a sound so terrible it hurts you to hear it, all deep and agonized and groaning. He was down on his side in the grass about twenty feet from where I'd left him, and he was moaning and snaking his head around to nip at his swollen flank, and swinging his legs in the air as he tried to roll onto his back. I grabbed his halter right away and started tugging.

"Get up!" I shouted at him. "Get up, you bag of bones!"

He swung his head back toward his side again, and the halter was ripped from my hands. This time I grabbed his lead rope and yanked hard on it. "Get up, I say!" I kicked him in the shoulder. "Take your feet!"

"Clutie, no!" cried Chigger. "Don't hurt him!"

I gave another pull on the rope. "He's sick, Chigger. If he doesn't get up, he'll die. Get back there and boot him in the rump!"

Between Chigger kicking the back end and me tugging on the front, Johnnycake finally struggled to his feet. Belly distended, he was drenched in sweat and still making those moaning, huffing sounds, but I got him to walk a few steps.

"Easy, easy," I said, and rubbed his forehead. My hand came away sopping and furry. I put all my weight on the rope to make him take another step.

"Is he OK now, Clutie?" Chigger asked. Dawn was coming fast, but it was still shadowy because of the trees around the clearing.

"I don't know. How long you been up, Chigger John? Did you untie him? Was he sick when you woke?"

"He was real hungry, Clutie. I gave him some dinner."

Just like that, all the hair on my arms stood up. I said, "When?" He looked blank and I shouted, "When!"

Chigger's lip quivered. "L-last night. Don't be yellin' at me, Clutie."

"I'm sorry, but it's important. Think, Chigger. What'd you feed him? I didn't bring any grain."

"I did!" Just like that, he was bursting with pride. "I brung a whole half a bag. I give it to you."

"But that bag was lumpy! Even without the skillet, it was lumpy!"

He shrugged. "They was a coffeepot in there, too." He pointed over to where we'd piled our things. There was the empty bag, Granny's coffeepot sideways atop it. "You makes good coffee, Clutie."

I had wondered what he had in that heavy old sack, but we'd been in such a hurry that I hadn't looked, and I knew right then that if Johnnycake died, it'd be my fault for not checking the bag, and for not watching Chigger more closely.

I pulled on the lead rope again, and Johnnycake took another faltering step. He was sweating worse, and swinging his head low and from side to side. My voice breaking, I said, "How . . . how much did he eat?"

"Nigh on all of it. He were right famished. But when I woked up this mornin' he were sickly. You reckon it were bad feed, Clutie? Why's he tryin' to bite hisself like that?"

Right then, Johnnycake went down again with a loud, drawn-out groan. I dropped on my knees in the dewy weeds beside his head, whispering, "Dear Jesus, please help me. Please help this poor critter." Johnnycake twisted his neck and tried to roll again. I yanked the rope and grabbed his foreleg, shouted, "Stop that, goldern you!" and about got knocked over when a hoof glanced against my arm.

Chigger put his hand on my head. "Clutie? Did I do bad? I'm hungry. Are we gonna eat breakfast pretty soon?"

I scraped sweat off Johnnycake's neck with the side of my hand, and he bit me in the thigh—not hard, just a halfhearted pinch. The sun broke through the trees just then. It burnt against my forehead, my eyes. "You shouldn't have given him so much, Chigger. He's got the colic and he's hurting. Chigger, I want you to think hard, all right?"

He nodded, his features all puckered with regret. "I didn't mean to make him sickly, Clutie."

"I know. Now think. Think with purpose. Did he roll?"

"Who?"

"Johnnycake!" I got back on my feet, rubbed at my horse-bit leg, and started tugging at the lead rope again. "After he got sick and lay down in the grass, did he roll?'' I already knew the answer, but I hoped I was wrong.

Chigger brightened a little. ''He rolled a goodly bit, Clutie. Will he get better now?''

Johnnycake groaned again. His eyes were ringed with white. I took the free end of the lead rope and smacked his shoulder as hard as I could. ''Get up!'' I shouted. ''Get up and walk, you no-account bang-tail!''

But he wouldn't, not even after me and Chigger pushed and beat and pulled on him for ten more minutes. And I knew it was too late. I guess I'd known that from the first time he tried to get over on his back. He'd been sick all night, and he'd rolled, and he'd for certain sure twisted his gut doing it, and I could not imagine the agonies he was surely feeling.

At last I got to my feet and went and found the Colt pistol I had taken off Spider. I stood over Johnnycake, tears streaming down my face, sweat pouring off his.

Over his groans, I said, ''Horse, I am sorry. I am sorry deep in my heart for all the wrongs my family has done to you. I'm sorry for the whippings and beatings. I'm sorry that even when one of us tried to help you, it ended up torture.''

Chigger put his hand on my arm. ''Clutie?''

I said, ''Turn away, Chigger John.''

He did, and then I shot Johnnycake through the head.

I couldn't cry any more for Johnnycake. I couldn't cry in the first place for Spider, and I surely couldn't shed a tear for Beetle. It seemed like I was wrung dry of tears, and although I walked on in terrible sorrow—mostly for Johnnycake—I did it dry-eyed.

I chanted pretty much nonstop for the first whole day of travel, till I was sick of it and hoarse to boot. Spells to quicken our journey, to blind Granny Wren to our whereabouts, to keep us safe. I figured once we got to Kansas, we'd be in the clear. Granny Wren was a Missouri witch. Well, maybe Arkansas, too, but I didn't figure she'd have much magic in Kansas.

I kept my ears open for the pursuit of baying hounds for

the next days, but we never heard any. Maybe Glow hadn't thought to come after us with them, or maybe having been used only on varmints, Beetle's dogs would not follow a human scent. I had left the saddle lay. Maybe they had found it and settled for that. Maybe one of those spells I had laid on had worked after all. It didn't matter much either way to me, so long as we were free.

Between both of us mourning Johnnycake and my foot still hurting, we did not exactly keep a lively pace. But eventually we crossed the Missouri, north to south, and made our way into the metropolis of Kansas City.

I tell you what, it was a some kind of town. There were all kinds of people coming and going every which way, on horseback and in buggies and in wagons and on foot, and they were none of them very quiet about it. Chigger John got kind of scared, not so much by the street traffic as by all the buildings.

I gave his fingers a little squeeze, and we walked on, right into the heart of the town. I asked a lady in a yellow dress for directions to the depot, but she stuck her nose up in the air and shifted her parasol, real haughty, and kept on walking like she hadn't seen us.

"Why's she mad?" Chigger asked.

"I don't think she's mad," I replied. "I guess we look fair ratty. Especially me, with this big old powder burn on the front of my shirt and the back cut off. Not to mention all these rips." I did not say it was Johnnycake that had made them. I didn't want to remind Chigger.

"I guess maybe if I was as fancy as her," I went on, "I wouldn't talk to the likes of us, either, Chigger, for I do believe we are a sight. We might ought to find us a mercantile and get some clothes. And some boots. And we both need a bath."

Chigger's mouth twisted into a grimace. "Not me. I's fine."

"Fine for a hog, maybe."

Pretty soon we sighted a mercantile. The man there made me show him my money before he would even let us in the door, and he watched us close like he thought we were going to steal something, or maybe touch his yard goods and contaminate them. But I bought us some new duds, and he did not seem loath to take our cash.

I put on my new socks and boots right away, which was sure a comfort to my sore foot, but the rest we left in their paper wrappings until we could have a bath. I also bought a box of ready-made ammunition for Spider's Peacemaker, and, although it was not necessary, I got myself a couple big thick pads of paper and some pencils, so I maybe could do a little sketching along the way.

The man at the mercantile gave us directions to the depot and they sounded simple enough, but after a while, what with the crowds and such, me and Chigger got lost. The reason for this was that Chigger had gradually lost his fear of the people and buildings, and worked himself into a sort of carnival frame of mind.

"Lookee lookee, Clutie!" he'd cry about every two minutes, and then dart off into the crowd toward a fancy window display or a big cart horse or a dog or whatever it was that had struck his fancy, and then I would have to go chase him down.

Normally, I was pretty good at keeping up with Chigger John. But being burdened with probably forty pounds of quilts and supplies and coffeepots and such kept me from skittering after him at my usual speed.

And there was a scary moment, when Chigger all of a sudden cried, "Beetle! Uncle Beetle!" and dived into an alley, all shaky and scared. I knew how he felt, for I ducked in there right on his heels, dropped my parcels, and pressed him to the wall, my heart a-thump.

That was until I sighted the fella that had spooked Chigger John. He had orange hair, all right, but he was a good half head taller than Beetle and wore glasses to boot.

After I got my breath back, I said, "Chigger, that's not Beetle. Beetle's dead, back home. He can't bother us anymore. You better not scare me like that again."

He mulled this over, serious-like. Then he said, "Beetle's dead?"

I did ask a few other folks for directions, but it seemed

like everybody told me a different way to go. After a while we were real turned around, and found ourselves in a part of town that didn't seem so nice. It was near dark, too. I could tell Chigger was scared again, because he stopped galloping off. He stuck close, and started making these funny humming sounds under his breath.

"Sing us a song, Chigger," I said, for I knew it would give both our spirits a lift. He started right into "The Seven Kings' Daughters," which is a ballad about this gal who steals a couple of her daddy's horses to run off with a fella, except that when they get to the ocean he tells her he's already drowned six gals and she's to be the next. It was one of my favorites, although, on account of being nervous, Chigger was singing it faster than usual.

Where me and Chigger were walking, there were all these narrow alleys lined with teensy shacks. Men came and went from their doors, and low women in their underwear stood or sat out front of some of them. When me and Chigger went by, Chigger singing high and clear, some of the women called us names or threw things or did lewd movements of their bodies. I did not ask any of them for directions. I just looked straight ahead and kept on walking.

By the time Chigger got up to the part in the song where the girl gets mad and hauls off and throws her lover over the ocean cliff instead of the other way round, it was nearly dark except for the lantern light coming from the cribs.

By the time he came to the last verses, where the girl sneaks back into her daddy's house and makes a deal with the pet parrot not to tell on her, we were passing the third and last row of those little shacks. And just as Chigger sang the very last line, just as we were about to step out into the open street, I heard somebody call out, "Jukes!"

Well, if it had been a man's voice, I would have dropped my burdens and grabbed Chigger's arm and taken off running. But the voice was female, and something about it stopped me dead in my tracks.

"That red-haired singer-boy a Jukes?" said the lady, this time from closer.

I turned around. She was dressed in a ripped chemise and

high-topped shoes and a garter and rouge and not much else. Orange-headed, and not five feet tall, she had wobbly eyes like blue ice, and I knew right then that she had to be one of my long-lost aunts. She walked right up to me—well, more like staggered, for she was fair lit up—and pointed at Chigger John. "He a Jukes?" she repeated.

"Yes, he is," I allowed. "Me, too."

She cocked her hands on her hips and stared me up and down. "Don't look Jukes," she said. Her words were kind of slurry. She had a tic going at her right eye, too.

"Tulip Jukes is my mama," I said. I was fair exhausted, and took the opportunity to settle all those packs to the ground. I felt about a foot taller to be rid of them.

She stared at me for a second. "Nope, you dasn't look Jukes a-tall. Tulip must'a ran off to have you." Her eye ticced four times, fast. "She turn to whorin'?"

I stood up a little straighter. "No such thing," I said. "She wed a button salesman."

She just stared at me.

"Some of his folks were from Hungary," I added, like I had to make some excuse for being brown-headed and such. "That's over in Europe."

She made a little *humph* sound, then jabbed a thumb up at Chigger. "This boy be your'n?"

That got me kind of annoyed. I knew I was dirty and scuffed up, but I didn't think I looked grown enough to have a boy as old as Chigger. I was about to say he was my cousin when Chigger piped up, "Clutie's mine. She's my Clutie."

She gave out with a chopped-off laugh. "They's marryin' 'em off younger and younger back home, ain't they?"

I think I blushed—at least, I felt my face go hot—and I said, "He's my cousin, but not the marryin' kind. I take care of him." Chigger looked kind of hurt, so I added quick, "And he takes care of me."

Chigger brightened a little, but the woman gave a snort, like I had just made the whole situation a lot less interesting.

I said, "Would you be Carnation or Myrtle?"

She said, "I expect I'd be your Aunt Myrtle Marie. What'd this boy say your name was?"

"Clutie. For Chrysanthemum. Is Aunt Carnation here with you?" The second that question came out of my mouth, I had a real odd feeling, all fraught with dread, but by then I had asked it and it was too late.

"She be here," said Aunt Myrtle. "Well, not *right* here. She's found a cozy roost a few blocks over." Myrtle had reached down to run her hands over our bundles, like maybe she was thinking about swiping them. I gave her a scowly look and she took her hand away, but I couldn't be too mad at her. She was a Jukes after all, and I don't guess a person can fight their nature.

I said, "Does she fare well?"

Aunt Myrtle scrunched up her little orange Jukes brows, her lips a-twitch and her eye ticcing. It was almost like being home again.

"I said she were cozy, ain't I?" she grumbled. "She got herself a sugar man what keeps her in style over to the Wigwam Hotel, but do you think she'd help her own dear sister outta these scroffuloed cribs?"

She looked to be on the verge of a tangent, so real quick I said, "Mayhap we could visit and give her our regards? Besides, if it's a hotel, maybe me and Chigger should stop there for the night if the cost isn't dear." The truth be told, I was nervous about the money part, but more nervous about being out on the street in the dark in a town like Kansas City.

"You say Chigger? This boy be Chigger John out of Carnation Jane?" She was looking at him in a whole new way. I didn't answer, but she said soft, "Yessir, I believe it. I do believe he is." She looked him up and down again, and then she said, "If we's goin' to the Wigwam, I'd best put on more clothes."

Aunt Myrtle ran off at the mouth nonstop the whole way to the hotel. She said that when her and Carnation got a big enough stake saved up, they were going to head north.

"Chicagee's the place," she said, and it took me a second to think where she meant.

"Oh," I said. "Chicago."

She stopped walking and propped hands on her hips. "You know," she said, "when I see'd this boy's red hair and heared him singin', I would'a bet cash money he were a Jukes. Why, for a second, I thought sure it were the ghost of my poor dead brother, Bumble. When Bumble were a boy, he had him a voice just that way—so purty it made your flesh curdle—and he used to sing that selfsame song. But you? I still ain't so sure. You don't look nothin' like a Jukes and you dasn't talk like one, neither. You sure you ain't just yankin' my leg?"

"I've been to school," I said, maybe a little too proud. "I've got my eighth-grade certificate."

"Clutie reads books all the time!" Chigger added with extra enthusiasm. "She's got her a book right now. It's called *Iva Hoe*."

Chigger never could remember titles too good, but I guess it did not matter, for Aunt Myrtle did not prove to have much interest in literature. Her eye gave a couple of tics, and then she said, "Don't know why nobody'd wanna read no book about farmin'."

She also warned us not to call Aunt Carnation by her true name unless we were given leave to.

"She goes by Carrie now," Myrtle said, "on account of she wearied of the joke."

"I likes me a joke," Chigger said.

Myrtle gave a sniff. "Well, she don't. She changed it when we was working over to Independence, and all them boys would come in gangs and sit out on the stoop to wait their turns, and ever' time one'd stumble out, all the others'd say, 'Where in Carnation have you been?' and then they'd all laugh like they was real clever and hadn't nobody ever thunk to say that before. So now she goes by Carrie."

Pretty soon we were standing in the dark and tiny lobby of the Wigwam Hotel and I was paying out three dollars for a room for Chigger and me. I thought the cost was a little steep since we only intended to stay for one night, but I supposed prices for everything were high in the city.

Aunt Myrtle went on ahead to Aunt Carnation's room. Me and Chigger locked all our bags and parcels in ours, which was about eight feet square with naught but two narrow cots, a battered lantern on a wobbly table, and no window, and then we went on down the hall and knocked on the door of number 17.

thirteen

"Well, get in here," Aunt Myrtle called. "Took you long enough."

Aunt Carnation's room was about triple the size of mine and Chigger's, and had a real, honest-to-Jim bed and a rug, and a cushioned chair beside a little table. There was also a mirror-crowned, marble-topped chifforobe and two windows with curtains. The curtains were frayed and didn't look real clean, and there were some holes in the bedspread, but compared to home it seemed pretty high-tone.

There was a man stretched out under the covers. I couldn't see much of him except the back of his head. He had dark blond hair, longish, and he was not snoring. He was alive, though, for I could see the rise and fall of his breathing.

The one who I took to be Aunt Carnation was at the window with her back to us. Aunt Myrtle was down on the floor, her backside stuck in the air and her head under the bed.

I said, "Have you lost an earbob?"

Chigger pointed to the bed and said, "Who's that?"

Aunt Myrtle scrambled to her feet and gave her shirts a shake. "You was right, Carrie," she said, real annoyed. "Ain't nothin' there."

"Told you, didn't I?" replied the other women. "Been lookin' for his stash for three days. Can't find it nowhere." She was just as teensy and orange-headed as Myrtle. She turned round to face us. "That man is my friend. His name is Mr. Jones." She looked at me. "And I guess I'm your Aunt Carrie." She glanced at Chigger, but she didn't say anything to him.

"How do," I said, real soft.

Carnation waved her hand, upon which there were several rings, all sparkly. "Don't need to whisper. Cain't nothin' wake him when he's took on a snootful. Had a snootful, more or less, ever since I knowed him. Don't even get sober enough to diddle me." She appeared a little disgusted. "Just go and get him booze and more booze and clean it up when he pukes, that's all I does."

At the word "puke," Chigger opened his mouth, and I clamped my hand over it. I was not in the mood to explain all about the puke dogs right then.

"Well, I suppose I shouldn't complain." Carnation went on. She pointed at the chair. "Suppose you might's well sit down."

The chair was blue plush and extra wide, and both me and Chigger fit into it. Aunt Myrtle and Aunt Carnation both sat on the foot of the bed. Carnation brought a flask out from a drawer, and the two of them passed it back and forth, taking sips. They did not offer it to me.

It was strange, meeting Chigger's real, true, blood mama like that, when I had been the next thing to his mama for his whole life. I suppose that if Chigger'd had much more in the way of brain power, it might have turned into a real emotional scene. As it was, he just yawned.

"So you is Tulip's gal," Carnation said. Her dress was deep electric-blue and low-cut and shiny and showed a wide sweep of freckledy shoulder and bosom. She did not even have a shawl, and it was a wonder to me that she had not caught the double pneumonias if she went round rigged like that all the time.

It was a real pretty dress, though. Sitting next to Myrtle in her patched frock, Carnation looked almost like a fairy princess if a person didn't pay too close attention to her face. "Reckon Tulip was maybe eleven or twelve the last we see'd her," she said. "You doesn't favor her much."

I said, "I guess I look more like my daddy's folks."

Myrtle knocked back the flask with one hand and fingered the shiny fabric of her sister's skirts with the other, like she wished she could swipe it right off her. "She says they was Hungary people," she said, kind of absent.

"Why didn't they eat somethin', then?" Carnation quipped, and even though I didn't think it was very funny, both of them set to laughing. They laughed real odd, like a couple of young jenny mules braying in two-part harmony.

The man on the bed rolled over and grumbled, jostling Carnation and Myrtle, and Carnation slapped one hand over her own mouth and the other over Myrtle's until he settled down again.

"Oh, Carrie," said Myrtle, smoothing her tattered skirts and still grinning after Carnation took her hand away, "you is a caution."

I brought them up to date on the news from home, although it turned out they already knew quite a bit of it. He had never said as much to us, but over the years Uncle Wig had kept in touch with Myrtle and Carnation, off and on, so that there were not a whole lot of cracks left for me to fill in.

"We heared you had married Spider," said Myrtle, and tilted the flask again. "Glow's oldest boy."

"Yes'm. He sort of got shot."

They both nodded, kind of solemn. I supposed they thought it had happened during a robbery or something, and I was not inclined to advise them otherwise.

"Well, I reckon that's enough small talk," Carnation said, leaning forward and looking straight at Chigger John. He was so worn out that he had gone to sleep next to me in the chair, his head on my shoulder. She stared at him for maybe a whole minute, and then she turned back to me. "You come to dump this boy off on me?"

"No such thing," I replied, maybe a little testy. "We didn't even know you were in Kansas City. We are just passing through on our way west."

Myrtle arched a brow. "You run off, then?"

"You could say that."

Carnation was back to staring at Chigger John. Myrtle said, "You goin' into the trade, like me 'n' Carrie?" She kind of pulled herself up, like she didn't want me tramping on her turf.

"No. More like Uncle Weevil."

Now, at home we were not allowed to talk about Weevil in front of Granny Wren and Mama, on account of he had run off, long before the war, at the age of fourteen—first stealing his daddy's horse, plus eight dollars cash money—and gone to the far west, which was, to Granny Wren's and Mama's way of thinking, the same as perdition.

I am not sure they had the right to be so offended as they put on, as I once heard somebody in town say as how there were already so many Jukeses in hell that you could see their feet sticking out the windows.

"We're just goin' to be goin'," I added.

Myrtle laughed. "I'll lay money your granny's still pitchin' a fit, you kitin' off like ol' Weevil! You should'a thieved a horse off'n 'em, too, would'a made it more perfect. Ain't that a hoot, Carrie?" She poked Carnation in the ribs and got her elbow slapped away.

I got a chill when she said that thing about stealing a horse, first because it was reminder of poor Johnnycake's grisly death, and second because it reminded me that I had stolen him. But I kept my mouth shut.

"He's an awful purty child," Carnation said, soft. She had eyes for nothing but Chigger. "He still that purty when he's awake?"

That sick feeling was back in my stomach. I said, "I'm taking him to California with me. He's kind of slow in the head." I put my arm around his slim shoulders and, still sleeping, he cozied against me.

Myrtle Marie stood up. Her eye was twitching again. "Carrie," she said, kind of mean, "don't you go gettin' soft on me. You already give that boy up once."

Carnation's face kind of wadded up, and she began to sniffle. "He's all I got left'a my Big Joe." She took the flask from Myrtle Marie and had herself a gulp. "Poor Big Joe."

Myrtle traded Carnation a crumpled hankie for the flask. "You never did like Big Joe when he were alive, Carrie," she said. "Always batted you around, as I recollect. And you tried to set him afire that once."

Carnation daubed at her tears. "Only for a joke, Myrtle.

I would'a put the flames out myself if he hadn't'a woke up and blacked my eye first. Oh, but he were a handsome man. Strong, too. He could pick him up a live, full-burdened mule and tote it half a block before he staggered.''

I said, ''You mean you knew all the time who Chigger's daddy was?''

Carnation set in to full-blown weeping right about then, so Myrtle answered for her. ''Not the whole time. Not till he got borned and we see'd that little strawberry mark behind his knee. He still got that? Just like Big Joe's.''

Well, Chigger John did in fact still have the mark. I said, ''Big Joe who? Did he have a last name? Where did he come from? Who were his people?'' I thought Chigger had a right to know everything about his own. Not direct from Myrtle and Carnation, maybe. I figured to tell him later.

''Big Joe O'Cain,'' sobbed Carnation. ''Oh, he were a handsome man, even with that one eye gone. And kind? Oh, he were good to me!''

Myrtle shook her head. ''Now that he's croaked,'' she confided, ''Carrie's got Big Joe rigged up like he were Christ Jesus hisself.'' She wrenched the flask out of Carnation's fingers and tipped it to her lips. ''I'll allow he were fancy lookin', though,'' she added, wiping her mouth. ''Big tall feller, redheaded. Mostly Irish and part Mandan Indian, and he worked for the railroad till he got knifed through the lungs at a poker game.'' She pointed at Chigger. ''How slow in the head is he?''

''Fair sloggy. Has to have nigh on everything done for him.'' I felt bad to say it, for I loved Chigger, and there were some things he did real good. But I was afraid if I talked him up they might decide to keep him. Carnation was his mama, after all, and had every right.

Myrtle shook her head. ''Cain't say I's surprised after all Carrie done to lose him. Potions, buttonhooks, knittin' needles . . . well, you know. Miracle he ain't got a tail like a fish.''

Just then, the man in the bed sat up. I gave a little jump, for with all Myrtle's talk and Carnation's weeping, I had forgotten he was there.

"Miss Carrie!" he bellowed, all grand and thunderous, even if his voice was cottony with slumber and drink. "Who are all these persons in my chamber?"

Carnation rubbed at her eyes, hopped right, up and scurried to his side, her purple skirts flashing. "It's all right, Mr. Jones honey," she soothed, her fingers on his wide brow. "It's just family."

"No family of mine, fair Carrie," he said, staring straight at me. Then his eyes flicked over to Chigger. "There is a child in this room," he announced, like maybe he thought the rest of us were unaware of it, and he was just letting us know.

Now that he was sitting up and the covers had fallen away, I saw that he was actually kind of a nice-looking man. Fortyish and big boned, he had dark blue eyes and longish sand-colored hair and a pleasant face. But for his nose and cheeks being so ruddy from drink, you could have called him handsome.

"Hello, mister," said Chigger from under the crook of my arm. I was surprised he had come awake.

"Young man," said Mr. Jones, "I believe you are far too tender to be keeping company with these seasoned women."

Chigger didn't answer, just tipped his head to the side. To Myrtle and Carnation, I said, "I reckon me and Chigger had best go now. I need to be ordering us up a couple of baths." That was part of the truth—the other part was that I had spent too much of my growing up with drunks, all of them mean, to want to stay any longer. Mr. Jones seemed nice, but you never could tell.

I stood up and brought Chigger along with me.

Carnation waved us back down. "Mr. Jones, honey?" she said. "Why dasn't you tell your Carrie where you's got your money put by? I'll sent Myrtle out for whiskey so's we can all have us a party."

Mr. Jones tilted his head back and stared down his nose at her. Even as drunk as he was, you could tell he was real smart just by looking at him. Something about his eyes, I guess. He said, "Madam, how many times must I tell you that my name is not Jones, it is Burke-Jones. Burke-hyphen-Jones.''

"Whatever you say, honey," Carrie said soothingly, "although I never heard of no middle name of Hyphen."

Behind Burke-Jones's back, Myrtle paused her search through the bureau drawers to muffle a giggle. She circled one finger at her temple, as if to say that Mr. Burke-Jones was unsettled in the brain.

I said, "I don't believe Hyphen is his name, Aunt Carrie. It's a little mark between Burke and Jones, when you write it out. He's got two last names."

Myrtle snorted. "And here you said you went to school, you big liar. That's the stupidest thing I ever heared."

"Ah," said Mr. Burke-Jones. "There is a scholar among us." Then he belched, real loud.

"Where's that money, sugar-pie?" asked Carrie, her face close to his.

"Where you'll never find it, my treacherous dove. All of you, take yourselves into the passage."

I guess this must have been a real common thing for him to ask, because just like that, Carnation and Myrtle trooped out into the hall like trained monkeys. Me and Chigger went right along with them.

"You lazy whore," Myrtle whispered to Carnation once we were all out in the murky hall and had closed the door behind us, "I dasn't know why you ain't found his trove. Ever' time I comes up here, it's always 'Out into the passage!' and when we goes back in he's got another gold eagle." She squatted down and squinted through the keyhole.

"Only place I ain't looked yet is up his butt," Carnation said, "and I got no plans to search there." She whispered it behind her hand, but I have got good ears. I pretended not to hear, though, made myself busy combing Chigger's hair with my fingers.

"I can't see diddly-damn," Myrtle muttered, pressing her eye closer to the door. "I believe he's hung a hat over the knob!"

Chigger paid them no mind. He pushed my hand away,

rubbed his eye with a grubby fist, and said, "I got me a hunger, Clutie."

I said, "First a bath, then dinner." I didn't say it soft. I hoped to impress upon the aunts that me and Chigger had important things to attend to and would not have much more time for family reunions. I figured we had best get shed of them before they decided to murder that nice old drunk for his poke. Or worse, take Chigger John away from me.

Aunt Myrtle had sunk down on her knees to peer through the keyhole, but Aunt Carnation said, "You young'uns got cash for a bath and eats?"

Before I could slap my hand over his mouth, Chigger said, "We's rich!"

Myrtle's head jerked up so fast she crashed it into the doorknob.

"Rich?" said Carnation, brows hiked.

I waved my hand over him, like to say he was off his head.

"Frank give us thousands of hundreds," Chigger added.

That time I got my hand wrapped over his mouth before he could spout any more. I laughed, real carefree. "It's a game we played on the road to pass the time. Well, we'd best go see about a bath now. It's been right nice meeting you both."

"Mmm-mmm," said Chigger, beneath my hand.

I turned to leave, taking Chigger with me, but Carnation caught us up. She pried my fingers off Chigger's mouth.

"On a string round Clutie's neck!" he blurted, and then looked proud for remembering. Right about then I could almost feel that roll of bills burning a hole in my chest.

"Why, ain't that nice!" Carnation said, real pleasant. "Your mama's glad to hear you and Clutie has got yourselves some travelin' cash."

Chigger cocked his head. "Mama?"

Myrtle hissed, "Carrie, don't you do it!"

"Me, boy," Carnation said, her voice all of a sudden soft and wobbly. She held him real still and looked right into his eyes. "I's your mama."

I couldn't breathe.

Chigger's face was dead serious. "You ain't my mama," he said after a second. "My mama's a two-bit bitch-whore with puss-drippin' sores and I'll never see her no more. Spider said."

I got my breath back in a big whoosh, but boy, was I mad at Spider, even if he was dead. He must have said those loathsome words to Chigger a lot of times for Chigger to just reel them out like that.

Carnation's face was real still, her mouth in a stony little line. She stood up and straightened her skirts. "That's right, boy," she said finally, and the way she said it made me feel true sorrow for her.

Not enough to stick around and talk about it, though.

I grabbed Chigger by the shoulder and headed him down the hall just as, from the other side of his door, Mr. Burke-Jones hollered, "You may rejoin me, my flame-haired beauties."

I waved one last time as Myrtle, mumbling "Where the Holy Christ is he squirrelin' it?" and still rubbing her head, shoved Carnation into Mr. Burke's room.

We paid for one bath and shared it, Chigger going first, and hollering like the tortured when I scrubbed behind his ears. Then we put on our store-bought clothes and had ourselves a real fine supper of roast beef with all the fixings and hot cherry pie in the Wigwam's little café. It was a good thing I made Chigger tuck an extra napkin into his collar, or that new shirt of his would have been solid cherry-red, he was that enthusiastic about his dessert.

We were both awful tired, and went straight to our room. It was all Chigger could do to crawl out of his duds before he fell asleep, but I was nervous. I sure wished he hadn't blabbered to the aunts about our bankroll. They were Jukeses, after all, and larceny came as natural to them as sunbathing did to a barn cat. Of course, they were pretty well occupied with that nice Mr. Burke-Jones, what with getting him drunker and trying to rob him and all, but I figured to stay on the safe side.

I therefore divvied out what was left of our stake money

and hid it in little bits all over our room. One packet got rolled up inside my deerskin quilt, another I stuck down in the toe of one of my new boots. Forty dollars went under the mattress, another forty inside the empty pitcher on the nightstand, twenty inside my new tablet of drawing paper, and so on until it was all parceled out but for thirty-two dollars. That, I rolled back up and strung on the thong about my neck, my logic being that if one of the aunts looked there first, maybe she'd think it was all we had and go away.

Then I dug out Spider's shiny new Peacemaker pistol— my pistol now—and hugged it to my chest. I blew out the candle and settled back on the narrow mattress beside Chigger, who was already snoring in soft little cat purrs.

I did not fall right to sleep, though. I got to thinking how maybe it wasn't such a good idea to go to bed with a loaded gun, and how maybe it would go off and I would accidentally shoot Chigger or myself, and how I had already shot and murdered my own husband, even if he was cheap Jukes trash, even if I didn't really mean to do it. Finally, I slid that pistol underneath the cot, said a rhyme for general protection, and spat once to the left and once to the right. I guessed that we would just take our chances with Myrtle and Carnation.

fourteen

Considering the Jukesness of the situation, I was genuinely surprised to wake the next morning and find we had not been robbed of one cent. I guessed that the aunts had found some charity in their hearts after all. Or they had spent the whole night turning over Mr. Burke-Jones's room and had forgot about us.

Either way, it was a relief that they had not crept in to club us senseless and steal us blind, so I was feeling real chipper as I gathered all the money again. I rolled it up and threaded it back on my neck thong. All, that is, save for forty dollars that I stuck down my boot and a few coins, which went into my back pocket.

"The birds are awake, Chigger John," I said, shaking him gentle, "and so should you be, too."

He yawned and rubbed his eyes. "I don't hear no birds, Clutie. Still dark!"

"That's 'cause we've got no window. The birds are singing someplace, I guarantee it."

Ten minutes later we were out in the hall, faces washed, ready to find the depot. On our way out, we had to pass Mr. Burke-Jones's room. His door stood wide, and the man himself was stretched out on the floor in his butternuts, moaning.

It did not seem like a time to stand upon the formalities. We went right in. I dropped my bundles and bent down to him.

"Mister?" I patted his cheeks and felt his head. He was breathing fine but he was not clear conscious, and there was a big goose egg on the back of his skull. I bade Chigger bring me the pitcher from the washstand, and then I dumped the contents over Mr. Burke-Jones's head.

Just like that, he came to and sat up and shook his head like a dog fresh from the creek, spattering water all over my front and half the room. Then he just sat there, kind of glassy-eyed, like he didn't know me or Chigger were there at all.

"Good morning, mister," Chigger said. "The birdies is singin' someplace."

Real plain, he said, "Bugger the birdies." And then slow, he twisted his face up until he was looking at Chigger. "And who might you be, child?"

I said, "We were here last night, Mr. Burke-Jones."

He gave a little start, then turned toward me. "And where did you come from?" Just then, a drop of water ran down his nose and dripped off the end, spattering his hand. He wiped it away, and then looked at his soggy butternuts. "Are you responsible for this, young woman?"

I got to my feet. "I thought you were dead, Mr. Burke-Jones. I was only trying to help."

He tried to hoist himself up off the floor, and when he faltered, Chigger went to help him. Chigger was real good-hearted that way.

"Help?" Mr. Burke-Jones said to me. "And in your experience, does drenching resurrect the dead?" He was sitting on the edge of the bed by then. He gave a kick to the pitcher I'd doused him with. He missed.

I said, "Well, if you're all right, we have a train to catch. Give our regards to Myrtle Marie and Carna—I mean, to Carrie."

I had started picking up my bundles again, when the man said, "I remember you. You know about hyphens."

"That's me. Chigger, pick up Mr. Burke-Jones's pitcher and put it back on the stand."

Mr. Burke-Jones was looking at me real strange.

I said, "What?" I might have said it a little crankier than I planned. All those parcels were heavy, and besides, I was antsy to find the train depot.

"I don't believe you were in on it," he said.

Behind him, Chigger eased the pitcher back into place and then looked to me to see if he'd done it right. I said, "That's fine, Chigger, that's good." Then, to Mr. Burke-Jones, "In on what?" Not that I didn't have my suspicions.

"The crime." He said it real dramatic, with one brow arched, then added, "Although it was not much of one. At least I trust not."

"Look here, Mr. Burke-Jones," I said, "if my aunts have done you dirt, I'm sorry, but it's nothing to do with me. Serves you right for consorting with low women, especially the kind named Jukes. You're lucky you still have your scalp."

He seemed to study me for a minute, and then he said, "How jaded you are for one so young. And do call me Prometheus." Then he turned to Chigger. "Boy," he pronounced, real commanding, "run your hand back behind that chifforobe and tell me what you find."

"His name's Chigger, not Boy," I said, and let the bundles slide back to the floor. It didn't look like we'd be racing out the door anytime soon. "And what kind of name is Prometheus?"

"In mythology, Prometheus was—"

"I know who he was."

"He stole fire from the gods," he went on, ignoring me, "and brought art and science to man. In my own humble way, I have tried to do the same." He rubbed at the back of his head, where the lump was, and winced. "Generally speaking, this is the sort of thanks I get."

"I know about Prometheus and fire and such," I said quick, before he could interrupt me again. "I've been to school. Prometheus also got chained to a rock and an eagle pecked out his liver." I pointed to the empty whiskey bottles on his night table and added, "I guess you are following through with the whole thing." Maybe it was a mean thing to say, but I said it anyway.

He didn't seem to mind if it was mean, though. He hoisted up a brow and said, "Ah. Hyphens and mythology. I should have known. A scholar."

He said it kind of sarcastic, but I guessed it made us even.

I said, "What I meant, back before you started telling me about mythology, was that Prometheus doesn't seem very American. Also, it's even longer to say than Burke-Jones."

"And your name? Since we're so swiftly becoming intimates."

I felt my face go a little warm, but I said right out, "It's Clutie. Clutie Mae Chestnut. The Clutie is for Chrysanthemum."

He pursed up his lips for a second, then said, "One might observe that Clutie Mae seems *wholly* American."

I wasn't quite sure I liked what he meant by that, but I didn't remark on it, for just then Chigger skipped over to the bed and handed Prometheus Burke-Jones a long piece of sticky tape. It kind of startled me. I guess I had got so interested in conversing that I'd clean forgot about Chigger.

Prometheus took the tape and let it dangle from his fingers. "Thank you, young man. Chigger. This was all?"

Chigger John nodded. "And a dead spider. A big'un. You want I should get it for you?"

I think I went a little red in the face at the phrase "dead spider," for it reminded me of my late husband and the unfortunate manner of his death. Prometheus did not notice, though, as he was busy grabbing Chigger's arm before he could race off to fetch it. "No, thank you, son. This will suffice."

Chigger cocked his head. "What?"

Prometheus did not reply, as he was busy trying to stand up. I suspected his wobbles arose more from the blow to his head than from drink, and so I went to help him.

"Thank you, Miss Chestnut," he said.

"You bet, Prometheus," I replied. "Where are we going?"

He pointed to the foot of the bed, and after we managed the two steps it took to get us there, he bent to try and lift the frame. He would have fallen down if I hadn't caught him. Finally I got him to the chair and he gave me instructions to lift up the corner and look up inside the hollow leg of the bedframe.

There sure was a lot of money in there. I did not count it,

for it was in three small leather pouches, but the one that he spilled out into his palm was full of twenty-dollar gold pieces. He gave out with a laugh—one big bark—at the sight of the coins, and then he stuck all three pouches inside the front of his butternuts.

I said, "If my aunts are coming back, I'd sure hide those again if I was you."

"Were," he replied, kind of absent. "If I *were* you."

"Oh, never mind. Chigger, hand me that package." I was loaded up again in less than a minute, during which time nobody said anything. "Good luck to you, mister," I said from the hallway.

He looked up, kind of bored. "Thank you, my dear, although I very much doubt it will help."

The desk clerk gave us real clear directions to the depot and even drew us a little map, and after a quick hotel breakfast of biscuits and ham and fried potatoes, we set out for the station.

Chigger was in high spirits, skipping round and round me in circles and singing "Don't Be Kicking My Dog Around If You Want to See Tomorrow." Me, I was so busy trying not to trip over him and wondering what it would be like to ride on a train, that when somebody grabbed my arm and yanked me into an alley, I was so surprised I didn't even manage to yell out.

I heard Chigger holler, though, just as something awful hard slammed me alongside the head. And in that slice of a second before I passed out, I got a blurry glimpse of orange Jukes hair.

"Clutie? Oh, Clutie, don't be dead, please don't be dead!"

My eyes came open slow, and even then I could not see very well. My head felt like mules had stomped it. "Chigger?" I whispered. It came out all croaky. "Chigger!" His face was blurry to my eyes, but I could not mistake the blood all down one side of it. I sat up quicker than I should, for it felt like somebody had knifed me through the skull and I nearly blacked out again. "Has Beetle got us?" I whispered. "Has he come to drag us down to hell with him?"

"Oh, don't be a-dyin'," Chigger wailed, and clutched my aching head so hard against his chest that he nearly smothered me.

"Not going to die," I said, once I got my face away from him. My thinking was a tad clearer by then, too, and I realized we were still in that alley, and that our assailants, long gone, were no ghosts. I said, "Let me see your head, Chigger."

It was not so bad as it had looked at first. This is because scalp wounds, even small ones, bleed a lot. I guess I was not so surprised that my aunts would drygulch me and steal my money, but I was shocked that they would clobber a child like Chigger John over the head and then just leave him lay to bleed.

I got him cleaned up as good as I could, and only then did I feel for my money roll. Just like I suspected, it was gone. We had been dragged far back from the street and into the shadows. Our bundles had been opened up and gone through and left scattered like so much trash, but I guess Myrtle and Carnation hadn't fancied any of our meager possessions, for there was nothing else missing.

They had got my boot money, though. I was in my stocking feet, both my boots having been tugged off and left in the pile of our jumbled possessions. Chigger brought them over to me. They had even got the few coins from my pocket.

"Don't cry, Clutie," he said.

Right then my tears went from drizzle to full-blown torrent. There was no getting our cash back. Myrtle and Carnation were good Jukeses, which meant they were long gone, probably to Chicago like Myrtle had talked about. I realized they were most likely riding a train in stately luxury on our stake money, and that got me weeping all the harder.

Chigger took my face in his hands. By then he was bawling, too. "Does you want a candy, Clutie? Please don't be cryin'."

"I guess I can't help it," I sniffed. "All our money is thieved, and now we can't ride the train west."

He rubbed my face with his sleeve, a little too rough, and

sniffled, ''I likes me a good long walk, Clutie.''

I hugged him awful tight.

Maybe it was God's way of punishing me for murdering Spider. That's what I was thinking as Chigger helped me put our parcels back together. He was a cat killer and a son of a bitch, and to my mind hadn't been worth what you'd call large-scale retribution. But I guess no wrong, no matter how justified, goes unpunished. And it was kind of poetic when you thought about it, a couple of other Jukeses having been the instrument and all.

I supposed I was due some discipline, for to tell the truth I felt ten times worse for having shot poor old Johnnycake than for shooting Spider. I just wished it hadn't been at Chigger's expense. Of course, he had banged Uncle Beetle over the skull with that iron skillet and killed him, too, but Chigger was so simple-that I didn't figure the Lord would be mean enough to hold it against him.

Although my new plan was to follow along the rails as far to the West as they ran, we did not go all the way to the depot. I knew just the sight of all those trains and tracks and happy travelers would make me too sad. Instead, we walked through Kansas City in a generally western direction until we were clear of it, then cut over until we ran into some tracks.

I put on Spider's gunbelt—at least the aunts had not stolen that—case of snakes and such, and told Chigger John for the seventh time to leave his hat on, or I would not be responsible for his sunburn. A couple times trains came roaring down the track like dragons—sometimes east, sometimes west—and we had to get back and duck our heads lest we be stung by flying cinders.

We walked without rest until well into late afternoon, at which time I shot and gutted a rabbit. I am not so good with a pistol as a rifle, but almost. Chigger carried the rabbit along, swinging it in one hand, singing as he went.

About the time it started to get dusky and I started to think about making camp, we came upon a tank—the kind up on stilts where the trains take on water for their boilers. And not much past that, a stand of juniper and a spring. The edge of it was about fifty yards up from the tracks to the north, and ripe for a stopping place. We made for it.

I was glad to lay down my burdens and get off my sore heel, and sent Chigger off to find some kindling while I skinned the hare and enjoyed the scent of the junipers. It reminded me of certain parts of our woods back home, and while I can say I was not overwhelmed by nostalgia, it did bring a tear to my eye. I had just finished up the rabbit and was wiping my hands on my britches when I heard Chigger call out, "Clutie! Clutie, come quick!"

Pistol in one hand and rabbit in the other, I wove through the scrubby juniper toward his voice. I found him right off, kneeling in the deepening shadows next to something dark.

"It's a man!" he said, just as I made out the shape myself. "It's Mr. Hyphen!"

For a second I could not fathom his meaning, but just then the man groaned and rolled toward me and I saw his face. I handed Chigger the rabbit, whispered, "Don't go dragging that in the dirt," reholstered the pistol, and then I patted Mr. Prometheus Burke-Jones's cheek.

"Another round on me, my good man!" he announced without opening his eyes, but so loud and clear that both me and Chigger jumped back.

The next time I didn't just pat his cheek, I smacked it. His eyes flew open and he grabbed my wrist. "Madam!" he said, real stern. "There is no need for violence."

Chigger hollered, "You let my Clutie go!" and made to smack him with the skinned rabbit, but I stopped him.

I pulled my arm free. "Mr. Burke-Jones, do you remember me? What are you doin' out here in the lonesome Kansas bushes?"

He sat up slow. "What? Oh. Miss Chestnut. Call me Prometheus. To the second query . . . I seem to recall the train stopping, and the overwhelming scent of gin in the air . . ." He stuck his nose back in the closest juniper bush and inhaled deeply with an "Ah, yes!" before he sighed, "Defrauded by the fragrance of nature. I don't suppose you'd have a drop of—"

"No, we wouldn't." I grabbed him under the arm and helped him up. He was a good bit taller than I remembered, six-foot-three or maybe-four, and when he got stood all the way up, his armpit hooked right over my shoulder without his having to stand on tiptoe or hike up his arm the least little bit. He had on a black banker's suit, and even though it was dirty from him lying on the ground, you could tell it must have cost him some money.

I said, "This is the first time I have ever seen you with clothes on. And shaved. You are not a bad-looking man for a drunkard."

"I would fare better with a drink. A sherry? A drop of bourbon? Surely you carry something for medicinal purposes?"

Just then Chigger hopped in front of us. "We got us a rabbit, Mr. Hyphen, and it's already skun," he piped, holding it high, all purply pink in the sunset light.

"Hardly similar," Prometheus said as we started back. "Hardly the same thing at all."

Fate is a real funny thing. All that day, as we'd walked along, I'd been doing a lot of thinking. To be sure, much of it had been about the aunts and the Bug Boys, and about how in the blue thunder we were going to make it all the way to California with no supplies and no money. But my mind had also been drawn to thoughts of my friend Joaquin, the Spanish Kid.

I admit that despite the warm Kansas sun, I had busted out in shivers two or three times, just thinking about the way his voice was, all rumbly and foreign, and the way he looked. Mostly the way it had felt when he kissed me. And it did not seem fair to me that if we were going to stumble head-long over some fellow we already knew, that it should be Mr. Prometheus Burke-Jones and not the Spanish Kid.

I guessed there was nothing to be done about it, though. I mean, it wasn't exactly like I could trade him back to God for the company I wanted more. So I built a little fire and Chigger roasted up the rabbit on a spit. I thought it was pretty good, although Prometheus threw his part up directly.

Chigger launched straight into hysterics over the puke

dogs. "Calm down!" I said once I had him in a headlock. "We're in Kansas now, Chigger. Puke dogs are illegal in Kansas."

He stopped struggling and rolled his eyes back and forth beneath scrunched brows. "Is you *sure,* Clutie?"

"Positive. A person cannot bring a puke dog over the Kansas border without getting himself thrown into the hoosegow and that puke dog impounded and sent back to Paris, France."

"OK." He looked a good bit relieved. For my part, I was wishing I had never come up with that dumb story in the first place.

Right about then, Prometheus staggered back from the bushes, wiping at his mouth. I remembered what Myrtle and Carnation had said about having to clean up after him all the time, and after he sat back down at the fire, I said, "You're prone to vomit, Prometheus. Have you seen a doctor? Maybe you have got a stomach tumor."

He rubbed at his forehead. "At the moment, a tumor would seem the lesser evil."

Beside him, Chigger lifted the spit from the fire and swung it, the last of the carcass dangling, in front of our new friend's face. "They's more rabbit, Mr. Hyphen. Grab 'er now, or she's mine."

Prometheus moaned and covered his face with his hands.

I said, "You go ahead, Chigger John. I think he's full." Then, to Prometheus, I said, "Whereabouts were you headed before you fell off the train?"

He splayed open one hand to peek out between two fingers. "I did not *fall*. I purposely detrained."

I was about to remark that it seemed a foolish thing to argue, when we heard the distant rumble of a locomotive. We all three just sat there, watching down the tracks. It came from the west, headed for Kansas City, I supposed, and went past us with a serious roar and rush, its windows, golden with lantern light, winking with the speed of its passing.

"Colorado," Prometheus said after it has passed by and all but disappeared into the night. "I suppose there is nothing to do but to walk to the next station and board another conveyance there?''

''Maybe for you,'' I said. ''But the aunts robbed me and Chigger of our travel money. I guess we are walking to California now.''

Across the fire, Chigger licked the last of the rabbit from his fingers. ''I likes me a good walk, don't I, Clutie?''

''That's right, Chigger.''

He gave Prometheus a serious look. ''You's safe, Mr. Hyphen. They's no puke dogs allowed in Kansas. They's all been sent back to France.''

fifteen

I guess we were all pretty tuckered. Chigger dropped off to sleep about five minutes after he finished his supper, and Prometheus Burke-Jones was not awake much longer. I waited a bit, though, sipping slow on the last of the dinner coffee and staring at Prometheus and thinking about whether or not I should steal his money if he still had it.

The Chestnut part of me said he was nothing but a harmless old drunk who had never tried to handle me, and who had been decent to both me and Chigger. Who had, in fact, done nothing much besides talk fancy or puke or snore the whole time I'd known him.

None of that mattered to my Jukes side, of course. The only thing that counted to my Jukes part was that somewhere, hid in his clothes, were those three small pouches filled with gold eagles.

I told myself that he had already been robbed once by Jukeses and did not deserve it a second time, and that what he needed most was somebody to get him off the liquor and nurse him back to a hearty condition. But hadn't he fallen off a train in the middle of nowhere? Mightn't he have died in the wilderness without me and Chigger coming along to save him?

Didn't he owe us something for that?

Well, you can see how it was. It was either wash out his socks and make him soup, or else shoot him through the head and roll the corpse. What I ended up doing was someplace in the middle.

He was real easy to rob. He did not rouse as I went through his pockets except for one time when he said "butterfly'' and went back to snoring. I found his wallet right off, but the gold pouches were tougher, being ensconced in secret pockets sewn into the inside back of his suitcoat.

I dropped the pouches into my shirt pocket, then sat down beside the fire and commenced to go through his wallet. There was not much money in it, just four dollars, but there were a lot of papers. Telegrams, mostly, and some of them were old and crumbly.

The newest was dated just two weeks back and had been sent from clear over in England. It said: ''SORRY TO IN-FORM YOU BUSBY TRIPLETS PERISHED WEDNES-DAY LAST IN TRAGIC TOPIARY ACCIDENT STOP HEARTFELT SYMPATHIES STOP TRUST YOU ARE HALE,'' and it was signed ''ANDREW FITZPUGH, ESQ.''

Well, that stopped me. I didn't know what a topiary was, but I decided it must be a fearsome thing indeed to take out three whole people.

While Prometheus Burke-Jones, his pockets sucked dry, snored soft beside me in the firelight, I went through all his telegrams, one by one. Each told of the demise of some relative or other. Uncle Apollo had been trampled while fox-hunting, Cousin Jason got himself lost at sea, Great Uncle Achilles had choked to death on a partridge bone, and so on, until I had near a dozen dead men there in my lap, told about in those telegrams. The oldest one was dated 1865, just after the war, and they were all from London, all signed by Andrew Fitzpugh.

His discharge paper was in there, too, and considering the wreck of a man I had stolen it from, I could scarce believe what it said—that Prometheus Burke-Jones had been honorably discharged from the Army of the Republic at the rank of colonel.

I sat there for a long time, that paper in my hand, trying to see the slumbering wreck beside me as a slicked-up military man wearing pressed Union blue and shiny brass buttons and waving a baton and giving orders. Try as I might, I just couldn't picture it.

But I got to feeling bad about having robbed somebody who had lost so many kinfolk. I guess it was my Chestnut side getting the better of me again. Finally I folded up all his papers the way they had been and returned them to his wallet, and then I put it—and the gold pouches—right back where I'd found them.

Not before I slid out five double-eagles, though, which I sewed, one by one, into the hems of my trousers.

I woke to the smell of coffee and the slanting light of morning. The first thing I saw was that I was alone in the camp, and I sat up quick. I scrambled to my feet, looking for Chigger John in the long shadows and fearing the worst, when the tail end of a song, followed by a cry of laughter, came to my ears.

I found Mr. Prometheus Burke-Jones fetching water from down by the spring hole and Chigger John up a cottonwood, dangling by one hand and laughing to beat the band.

"Hi, Clutie! Lookee! I's a flyin' kite!"

My hand went straight to my heart. "Chigger John! Get down out of there!" He was at least twenty feet up.

"Whee!"

"You'd best come on down, my lad," said Prometheus. He was over to my right, just standing up and corking off my canteen. He seemed a whole lot more hale than he had a right to be.

"Whoop in the air!" Chigger called, dropping himself from branch to branch like a monkey, then onto the sun-speckled bottom-most branch, then into the cool purple shadows of the ground. He landed on his hands and knees, and for a minute I could hardly make him out.

"Did you see?" came his voice, from the shadows.

"I saw you, Chigger. Just what are you doing out here, Prometheus? Training boys for the circus?"

"Gracious! I should say not!" he said with a bow, or maybe he was just picking up the canteen. "No such thing at all."

He started up the little rise toward me, Chigger dancing after him through the brush.

"I have come," he said once he neared me and we had started to walk together toward camp, "to see Master Chigger in an entirely different light. He's entirely . . . carefree, isn't he?''

''That's a nice way to put it,'' I said, feeling grouchy. ''About dang time, too. A body'd have to be drunker than two judges not to notice.'' I thought on it a minute, and added, ''But then, I reckon you were.''

Prometheus said, ''Think nothing of it. I certainly won't.'' He brushed some dust off his knees and then sat down, for by then we had reached our camp.

Chigger sat down beside him. ''Did you see, Clutie? Did you see?''

''I saw, Chigger. You make this coffee, Prometheus?'' I had just taken my first cup and eyed it. I may not be able to cook much of anything, but if I do say so, coffee is my best thing. Even Beetle would drink my coffee before Granny's, no lie.

''Go ahead and taste it,'' he said. ''I guarantee it isn't poison.''

I said, ''You first.''

He hiked up one eyebrow kind of haughty, or maybe amused—it was hard to tell with him—and took a big swig. ''Ambrosia!'' he exclaimed, then, ''Of course it would be better with a touch of bourbon. Everything is.'' He was starting to get on my nerves. ''Your turn.''

Well, it was the best coffee I ever tasted, bar none. I said, ''It's all right, I guess,'' drained my cup, and tried to look nonchalant while I poured out another. ''What is the next stop on this train track?''

''We are,'' Prometheus said. He slapped his coat pockets, then his vest.

''What do you mean 'We are'?''

Chigger had taken a fancy to a rock, which he was busy shining on his trouser leg. ''Mr. Hyphen says if'n we waits by the tank, a train'll take us.'' He spat on his rock and, without looking up from it, added, ''Blue!''

I looked back at Prometheus. ''Well, that's fine for folks with money, but—''

''Botheration!'' said Prometheus. He was on his feet and holding up his coattails, having found his pants pockets empty, too. "I believe I've left my tobacco behind as well! This will not do, it will not do at all!"

Chigger looked up from his rock to me. "Should I go to singin', Clutie?"

"No, Chigger. I believe we'd best be moving before we burn away the day. We'll leave Prometheus here to pocket patting and train hopping." In truth, I was wanting to get clear of there before Prometheus came up short on a money count. "Get your things."

I started to gather my possessions.

Prometheus looked up from his pockets. "What, may ask, are you doing?"

I lugged the quilt bag over my shoulder. It seemed like everything had gotten heavier overnight. I reckoned it'd wear off, though. "Getting ready to go. And you'd better look lively, yourself. Your train is bearing down on the horizon." I pointed. Sure enough, there to the east, a thin plume of smoke marked it black against a gold-and-pink sky.

Prometheus forgot all about slapping his pockets. He stood for a moment, shading his eyes, staring out. For a minute there, he looked real commanding: his banker's suit all gilded with the morning light, one hand raised to his eyes, his hat in the other. For just that time, I could see him as a colonel, like in his discharge papers. I could picture it easy.

It didn't last long, maybe a half a minute, but it sure made an impression on me.

Then just like that, he turned and it was gone. "Chigger," he said, "get some of those packages for your . . . Clutie." He started picking them up, too.

"Wait a minute! We're going different—"

"No, we're not." He slung my traveling poke over his arm. "Far be it from me to leave a damsel in distress in the hinterland."

"But—"

"Chigger, lad, give us a song!" he commanded, and Chigger burst right in to "Boil That Owl in Deep Hot Fat and Save the Thighs for Me" like he was trying raise the dead.

"Best take off the gunbelt and throw it in your sack," shouted Prometheus over Chigger's song.

Not two minutes later, we were running to meet the train.

• • •

Once it came to a halt with a hiss and a roar and a big enough billow of steam that I could not see for a minute, Prometheus had a few words with a conductor and then led us down a ways, to a passenger car. "Watch your step, young Master Chigger," he said, and just like that, we were on the train and moving.

Honest-to-Jim, it was like nothing else in the world. The roll of big iron wheels on the track below, the sway of the cars up top, and my oh my, did the landscape just speed by! I reckoned I could have spent the rest of my life as a professional train rider, if only it paid.

We stowed all our gear on one of the seats and after Prometheus asked one of the conductors to mind it for us, he said to follow him. Having been raised a Jukes and all, and therefore not being overly trusting, I was loathe to leave our things behind. I would have been happy just to sit and watch the landscape tear past the windows and look at the people in their fancy clothes—and Lord, there was a woman in a hat that they must have killed six birds for—but Prometheus insisted.

Finally, and against my better judgment, I allowed myself to be dragged back through the car, then through another car, and to a place that passed all wonderment.

It was like a restaurant, with tables and chairs all set in rows along the sides, and white-suited waiters carrying trays with silver thingamabobs on them. I guess it was about quarter full, and fancy ladies and smart gents sat at the tables, eating and smoking and laughing. Prometheus steered us toward a table and sat us down, which was just as well, for I was too dumbstruck to see where I was going. I stared at the curtains in the windows—blue gingham, they were—and was just reaching out to touch them when a waiter came over and said something to me.

I snatched my hand back, thinking maybe he was going to give me a rap, but instead he smiled wide and handed me a menu.

I had barely got it open when Prometheus snatched it away with a flourish and handed it back to the waiter. "That won't be necessary, my good man," he said. "I believe we'll all have flapjacks and syrup. Bacon, sausage, three eggs on the side. Sunny-side up agreeable with you two?"

Me and Chigger just looked at each other, then back at him.

Prometheus went on talking like it was nothing out of the ordinary. "Sunny-side up it is. The young lady and I will take coffee, and a large milk for the young man, and I will also take a fifth of gin. And a small box of your finest panatelas. The gin and panatelas now, please."

Chigger whispered to me, "Clutie, ain't he gonna get us some grits?"

I whispered back, "Don't look a gift horse in the mouth."

I had decided that the dining car was so fancy, I didn't mind if the parcels we had left up front did get stolen. The tablecloths matched the curtains. There was a silver bud vase on the table with a pink rosebud in it, and silver shakers and flatware and napkin rings, just like in books. And it all of a sudden dawned on me that it was just the way I'd dreamed about fixing up the cabin when I got to be the head Jukes, only nicer in most every way.

It got me misty, thinking first about home and how stupid I'd been not to think of the silver doo-bobs, and second, how much nicer things were in the real world then I had ever imagined.

When I looked up again, Prometheus already had the gin at his elbow and was just lighting his cheroot. "I hope you don't mind, Miss Clutie," he said, shaking out the match. He poured out a big splash of gin into his tumbler and took a swig.

Chigger opened his mouth to say something, probably to complain again about no grits, but an elbow from me put the squash on that.

"Well, now," said Prom, settling back into his chair, cigar cocked up in one hand, "that's better. So tell me, Miss Clutie, what's a woman of the world such as yourself doing on the trail west?"

I don't know why, but something about his attitude just plain ticked me off. I blurted, "First off, Prometheus, I am not a 'miss.' I am a Jukes by marriage, and a widow woman.''

I guess I said this just to show off, or maybe to tell him it was "hands off." You know how it is when you say something stupid—you've got about sixty different excuses for saying it, each one lamer than the next.

Prometheus didn't give me any time to backpedal. He leaned toward me, across the table. "Oh, a widow! My condolences. And might I ask how long since the tragic event?''

I could tell he was stringing me along and not taking me the least bit serious, but I decided to brave it out. I squared up my shoulders. "I expect about a week. Give or take. Isn't it about a week, Chigger?''

"Reckon," he said. He was kind of distracted, as the waiter was just walking up the aisle with our flapjacks. He looked like Uncle Beetle's hounds come feeding time, all drooly.

I said, "Close your mouth, Chigger John.''

The waiter slid steaming plates of flapjacks, five high, and sausage and bacon and eggs in front of us. Chigger picked up his fork and confided, just before he dived in, "I do avow, Clutie, I thinks I could maybe make do without the grits.''

Prometheus Burke-Jones knew better than to interrupt two dangerous cutthroats who haven't eaten naught but a rabbit in twenty-four hours. I was glad for it. I hoped his mind would be swept clean of my revelation, for I had no intention of confessing to the crime of murder, and I hated to make up another whopper. So I ate and Chigger ate, and Prometheus pushed his food around and drank, and by the time we finished our breakfast, full as ticks and ready to pop, Prometheus was half-donked and past the point of knowing what a question was, let alone asking one.

He paid for our food—and that part gave me a true scare, for I was suddenly certain that he would discover the theft and regain his senses long enough to have me thrown from the moving train. But he must have transferred some money to his wallet before I got up, for he parceled out the bill and a tip for the waiter like he was Midas himself.

"And that's for you, my man!" he said, all grand and

sweeping, when he handed the waiter his tip. "And now," he said, rising too fast, then falling back upon Chigger's shoulder with a sway, "I believe we should retire to our car for a little mid-morning . . . a little mid-morning . . ."

"Nap, sir?" ventured the waiter.

"Siesta!" cried Prometheus, punctuating the air with his uncorked gin bottle. Part of it sloshed out onto his cuff and the floor, but he didn't notice. "Onward, young Chigger!"

Well, I tell you what: I had seen a lot of drunkards before, but none of such outstanding cheerfulness as Prometheus Burke-Jones. Any of the Bug Boys would have beat three mules and torched the church if they'd drunk so much in so little a time, but he was singing along with Chigger and falling down every ten feet and sweeping his hat off to apologize to whoever he'd tripped over, and he was so dang nice none of them got mad. Well, almost none.

Holding my breath on the platforms, I followed him and Chigger back up through the train. And just like he had promised, our belongings were still in the same place with no things taken. I knew, too, because I went through everything.

Prometheus went to sleep straight off, Chigger close behind, dozing under the crook of Prometheus's arm. I sat there for a while, torn between watching the prairie roll by—there were hardly any trees now—and watching them sleep. I don't believe I had ever seen Chigger cleave to another human, save myself, like he had to Prometheus Burke-Jones. There he was, all sprawled and cozy like a tom-kitten with its mama. I half expected him to purr and Prometheus, half-asleep, to lick his forehead.

Well, there was no accounting for taste. Mr. Prometheus Burke-Jones was a drunk, not to mention a mark I'd already cleaned. Well, lightened. Chigger's sentiments aside, we needed to be shed of him at our earliest convenience, which meant maybe as soon as the train stopped. He did not look much like a man headed for west of Kansas—he was too fancified and citified for that—so I figured maybe the next stop, or the one after that. For sure he'd get off before we reached the border, and when he did we'd give him the slip.

The steady rhythm of the telegraph poles got to me after a while, and I, too, went to sleep. I'm not sure how long I slept, but I sure woke up in a hurry.

"Great day in the morning!" Prometheus shouted.

He was climbing over me, or maybe he had been thrown atop me, since the air was filled with the scream and stench of iron on iron as well as Prometheus's knees. Somebody was playing hell on the hand brake and it was not at a station, that was for sure. Gunplay filled the air, and Chigger was crying, "Bug Boys! Bug Boys is robbin' the train!"

Somewhere, a lady screamed, "Villains! Thieves!" and the car went to tumult.

I struck out with my fists—mostly to get Prometheus off of me—and by that time I was awake. What had seemed at first a barrage of shots was only two or three, and that the train was indeed stopping. I yelled at Chigger to be quiet. I yelled to Prometheus to kindly take his elbow out of my face. I stopped yelling as the train stopped, throwing me back against the seat, hard, and throwing Prometheus in my lap again—Chigger, too—and half my parcels on the floor.

I crawled out from under them, losing my hat in the process—or maybe I had lost that earlier—onto the aisle floor, and straight into the fancy tooled boots of a man with a gun.

Now, I believe I have said that I was a fighter, so you will not think it odd that the first thing that sprang to my mind was to butt my shoulder into his knees as hard as I could.

He toppled, all right, and as he did his gun went off and a lady screamed. I thought maybe he had shot her. But it was not a Jukes trait to be concerned for other folks, and right then I was all Jukes. I had him flat on his back and I went for his throat.

I had him about choked clear to death when somebody grabbed my shoulder and yanked me off him, and smacked me across the face two or three times, hard. I was kind of dizzy then, but I remember boots running in the aisle and men shouting and then it got quiet. My head was still ringing and somebody had me by the collar. I gave my head a shake to clear it and get my bearings, and then I looked over toward Prometheus.

He was sitting still in the middle of the wreckage my parcels, his eyes on me and his arms wrapped around Chigger, a hand over Chigger's mouth. Chigger John looked like he was about half a fuse away from exploding, but I gave him a look that said *No you don't*. He had been wrong about it being the Bug Boys—I had known that as soon as I saw those fancy boots—but he was not wrong about there being a robbery.

There were two men in our car, although I couldn't tell how many all together, and they had about cleaned out the passengers by that time. The one that had me by the scruff of the neck was a big man with dirty fists and a rough face. He had one pistol drawn, and every once in a while he gave me a shake.

The one I had attacked had got a bloody nose from the scuffle. He was about five seats up the aisle from where we stood, and he was relieving a gentleman passenger of his pocket watch and his wife of her rings. Only the lowest kind of thief will steal from a woman. I know, because the Bug Boys did it all the time. And it looked like this fella had been doing a lot of it, because when he stuffed the rings in his pockets, they rattled.

Fancy Boots finished plucking his pigeons and turned away, but not before he gave the gentleman a lick upside the head with his pistol butt. The man crumpled in his seat, and as his wife caught him, Dirty Fists said, too close to my ear for comfort, "Give him one fer me!"

Fancy Boots laughed, giggled really, and raised his pistol to give another blow. But he did not strike, for I seized the opportunity to sink my teeth directly into the fleshy part of Dirty Fists's gun hand.

It did not taste too good, but it made a satisfying sound.

Well, he had to let go of my collar, what with my teeth being in his other hand, and he commenced to strike me about the head and shoulders, all the while hollering like a scorched sow. His gun went flying. For the blink that I was turned that way, I saw Prometheus lunge for it and miss.

Then something cracked me hard in the head.

I went all limp and dizzy then, and the next thing I recall was someone dragging me up on my feet. I couldn't see much, for my eyes had gone all blurry, but there was the sound of another blow being struck as I rose, and then Chigger crying, "Clutie, Clutie!"

"She's give me the hydrophobics!" a voice said. Dirty Fist, I reckoned. "I'm bleeding to death, I tell you!"

Prometheus was next. "Unhand her, you brigands! Unhand her or suffer the—"

There was the sound of a slap, and he stopped, and I feared the worst. But the worst had yet to come, because the second he stopped, Chigger charged.

Whoever had my hands let go, and I dropped to the floor, rubbing my eyes, trying to clear my vision. There were shouts of "Get him off!" and "Christ Jesus!" and I finally got my eyeballs down to three and four of everything in time to see Chigger—all three of him—fall to the floor, unconscious, his head bloodied. He fell atop the body of Prometheus Burke-Jones. I thought I saw Prometheus's chest rise and fall. Just then the train lurched forward, and I heard someone call out, "Hurry up!"

Dirty Fist growled, "I ain't done with this one," and dragged me up by the hair. I don't mean to sound like a weak female, but he had me pretty tuckered out by then and it was all I could do to shove my elbow back into his ribs.

"God*damn*it!" he said, and picked me clean up of the floor.

Fancy Boots was pushing us toward the rear door of the compartment. "Bring her, bring her, just get off the damned train!"

I went through to the platform, back first, and just as I realized what was happening, just as I strove to get my balance so I could really give him what for, somebody threw me off the train.

sixteen

I woke up on my belly at a hard gallop, and puking out my guts, or very near to. Bacon and flapjacks, sausage and eggs: they were left behind, a spotty trail through the weeds. It occurred to me practically simultaneous that I was sure glad Chigger wasn't here to carry on about the puke dogs, and that I wished they were real.

I didn't have a chance to mull this over for more than half a second, though, for I had thrown up all I had, and the horse's rump over which I was slung was about to make mincemeat of my aching belly. Plus which, all I could think was that I was getting farther and farther away from Chigger John with every step that bangtail took.

There were about eight riders in our group—at least eight that I could see—and a second bunch in the distance, pacing us. We were fast falling behind.

I knew I was tied on, for naught but a fool would dump a body crost a horse and expect it to stay on for more than two strides at a gallop, but whoever had tied me on there had been the next thing to it. All in all, I reckoned it was a miracle my arms weren't busted to crumble, for they had been left to dangle down and interfere with the horse's rear locomotion. I congratulated myself that, even unconscious, I had owned the sense to keep them out of his way, and then I started working on getting myself loose.

It sure didn't take much. Whatever knot he had used to tie me must have been worked most of the way free, because all I did was to shift to one side and crank my weight on one hip, and I felt it give.

My head swung back over the horse's rump with me on

my side and nothing to grab, and that horse galloping full
tilt, never breaking stride, and my head slowly slipping
down, down, down, toward those pistoning hocks. I said,
"Chigger, I'm sorry!" although the wind snatched it from
my lips. Then I closed my eyes and prepared to die.

There was a jolt and a thud and a sudden stillness. I could
not breathe, and I knew any second an angel was going to
call my name. Of course, as soon as he found out that I was
a Jukes in life he wasn't going to be so nice, but there was
naught to be done about it now.

But nothing happened. No angel came. I opened one eye.
Then two. And all of a sudden I took in a big *whoosh!* of
air.

I got to my knees, alive after all, and stared ahead. All
that was left of the robbers were a couple dust clouds moving
fast toward the horizon. Still breathing hard, I stood up and
had a look around. There was not a tree in sight, nor a house,
nor any sign of civilization. Just yellow grassland, rolling on
and on, out of sight. I felt like I was in the middle of an
ocean of grass, with no food, no water, and no one to save
me.

There was part of a cord looped round my waist, and I
pulled it free. It had been cut. And all of a sudden I got mad.
I hadn't fallen off—they had cut me adrift in the smack-dab
center of nowhere and left me to die.

"Hey!" I shouted to those dwindling puffs of dust. "Hey!
Come back! I got five double-eagles sewn in my hems, and
they're all yours!"

I might as well have said it to a tree.

A person has to do something to save themselves. What I
did was start to walk. I was limping a little, for my foot still
hurt, although since I'd twisted the opposite ankle when I
fell off the horse, it evened out some. My ribs were achy,
too, but all things considered, I made a good pace. I tried to
go back in the direction we'd come from. This was easy at
first, since the horses' legs had made a swish through the
weeds and grass that any fool could make out at a distance,

but after an hour or two it had righted itself and I was walking blind.

There were birds all around me. Meadowlarks and bluebirds, finches and sparrows, and every once in a while a big old hawk circling overhead. I thought it was the red-tailed kind. What beat me was how those birds could be so happy when there was not a tree in sight, let alone a pond or a pool.

For my part, I was parched. There is nothing that can make a person thirstier—or leave a worse taste in the mouth—than throwing up a whole load of flapjacks and then having nothing to wash the taste out with. After a while, that taste begins to fester.

Noon was gone by the time I started, and before long it was almost dark and my situation had not brightened. Night fell, and so did I. It felt so good to sleep that I didn't notice the thirst, but when I woke again it was gnawing at me.

I started walking again. I was limping less, but I guess I has lost track of where I was going. Not that I had my finger on it in the first place. I remember I walked through a place where buffalo bones lay thick as autumn leaves. I tripped over them for near a mile.

Toward the end of the second day I could have been walking in circles for all I knew. I was so thirsty I could hardly croak a word, but I said out the chant for calling up storms and hiding a person, and prepared to catch as much rain as I could in my mouth.

Nothing happened. I guessed Kansas skies were more stubborn than those back home. I tried again.

> "Wind to the race,
> Storm to the chase,
> Clouds clabber overhead,
> Hide my face!"

Still nothing. I tried a third time, three being the charm for even the most stubborn bewitchments, but nothing happened. I finally decided it was a Missouri charm, pure and simple, and would not work in Kansas for anybody.

I kept walking. I remember talking to Chigger John for a bit, and cussing out Spider. I guess then I really must have flipped my bonnet, because I think I was talking to the Spanish Kid. He was showing me around the old family hacienda and the orchards and such.

"And here's where we will hang your fine deerskin quilt, *querida,*" he said, and kissed my hand. "It is fortunate indeed that you do not have red hair. Will you do me the great honor to be my wife?"

I guess I spent some time up in the old oak in my secret place, too, for I recall thinking I was staring out across the miles with my spyglass. I looked out toward Agnes Ann Roebuck's place, and there was Agnes Anne, naked as a jaybird and dancing with Frank James.

The mind can play funny tricks sometimes. There were some other things, too, but they were too silly and I do not remember them too good, which is just as well as far as I'm concerned. The main thing was that I passed out not long before sunset.

I woke sometime in the night to the howl of a wolf, but someone put their hands on my shoulders and eased me back down without a word.

I did not fight.

I went back to sleep.

Morning snuck up on me like spring sneaks up on a bear. One minute it was night and I was sound asleep, and the next it was full-blown day and I was wide awake and ravenous. Also, I was not alone.

Someone had made a camp, and I was stretched out next to a dead fire, and there were blankets on me. There was a canteen, and I opened it and drank. My thirst was not so deep as I had imagined, and I guessed that whoever had found me had given me water the night before. When I went to stand up, to scout the countryside for my savior, my legs proved the enemy. I sat down fast, not entirely of my own accord, and waited.

I must have dozed off again, because one minute I was all alone in the middle of nowhere, and the next somebody was making a lot of noise getting off a horse. Quick, I grabbed a rock and held it behind my back just in case, and opened my mouth to say my thanks. But I never got any farther than "I want to . . ." because my rescuer was not unknown to me.

"If you do not close your mouth, a fly will go in, *querida,*" he said.

I closed my mouth, slow, but I could not think of a blasted thing to say. To think, of all people, I should run into the Spanish Kid in such a godforsaken place as Kansas! Now, what kind of odds do you suppose those were?

Just like he could read my mind, he said, "It is not so strange, you know." He was bent over, busy getting the fire started again, so he was not looking at me.

I made a sound that was supposed to come out "What's that?" but instead came out like a croak. He made no sign if he thought it was funny, for which I was eternally grateful.

"When we met up and Graham talked about the girl on the train, and how he had cut her loose on the prairie—"

I found my tongue. "You mean you were one of those half-baked cutthroats? Those kidnapping polecats?"

The fire was started, and he sat back on his haunches and began cleaning the first of two partridges. "*Sí,*" he said, and tossed me the other partridge. "The faster these are cleaned, the sooner you eat, Chrysanthemum."

I shut up and cleaned my bird and kept my eyes on my work, thinking the whole time that God works in mysterious ways indeed, and it might be the better part of valor to just get out of His way and let Him do it.

Joaquin did not speak again until the birds were almost ready, and I was too flabbergasted—and tired—to say anything. But then, just like Frank James had said, he started talking and there was room in the world for no one but him.

Well, Frank had just said you couldn't shut him up. I added on the other.

"So, Chrysanthemum," he said, leaning back, my name like music on his lips. "What brings you to my West?" He said "my West" like he was the solitary proprietor.

"California." I managed to say it without stuttering,

which I thought was pretty good considering how nervous he was making me. I didn't press my luck with saying more.

He mulled this over. "You have run away from the Bug Boys?"

I nodded.

"But you have left your cousin, the boy with the beautiful songs, on the train?"

I nodded again.

"You are wishing you were back with him, yes?"

That time I managed to say, "Yes."

He handed me one of the spits, a partridge on it, and took one for himself. "Then I will take you to him," he said. "Be careful. That is hot."

Well, according to Joaquin, I had walked my way near to Indian Territory, and spent a day longer that I thought on foot. He said my tracks had wandered practically all over hell and gone, and that by the time he reached me he didn't know if I would live or die, I had gone without water so long. He had nursed me for two days and a night, with me feverish and out of my head most of the time.

"That's a lot longer that I thought," I said, my eyes on his hair, which was in a long horsetail down his back. We were riding northwest atop his big chestnut horse. I had my arms around him, careful not to hug too tight and therefore give my emotions away, but unable to keep from pressing my cheek to his back every once in a while.

"That is the way with sickness," he said.

"Did I . . . Did I say anything, um, funny?" I was so scared to death I'd spoken of Spanish men and romances, my face went all hot. I was glad I was behind, so he couldn't see.

But all he said was "I did not laugh, Chrysanthemum."

We had not been riding long when we crossed railroad tracks, but he said they were the wrong ones. "These are for the southern route, *querida*. You came from the northern."

When I started to argue with him—northern route meaning Oregon to me—he held out his hand, the first two fingers extended. "No, like this," he said. "The Atchison, Topeka and Santa Fe here . . .'' He wiggled the middle finger, that being on the bottom. ''And the Kansas-Pacific here.'' He wiggled the index finger, that being on the top. ''Both go west. To Colorado. The railroad, she splits. *Es verdad,* my flower?''

He smiled at me so beautiful that I nigh on fainted.

I swallowed hard, said ''Yes, Joaquin,'' and went back to staring at his braid. He had my innards in a genuine uproar by them.

We went slow, for riding double is a strain on a horse. But we walked steady—him talking all the time and me with my cheek pressed to his back so I could feel the rumble of his words all through me—and by midday we had walked our way to the banks of a little creek with cottonwoods and willows all around so that the light came down through them, all filtered. There were boulders scattered here and there through the stream, and the water was so clear that you could see every pebble and stone on its bottom. A big covey of quail flew up when we rode in, and their wings sparkled against the sun like magic.

''I think we rest the horse, *querida,* and ourselves as well.''

I took his arm and slithered down, holding my breath the whole time. Not because I was afraid I'd fall, but because I was sliding right down his leg. I tell you, I was so maddened by lust that I could have qualified for an asylum. I dug my nails into my palms to distract my mind.

He dismounted, so graceful as to bring tears of admiration to your eyes, and said, ''Go now and sit. I will take care of Peligroso.''

This was the first time I had ever heard him say the horse's name. I said, ''Peligroso? What's that mean?''

He smiled at me, and I very near melted down into my boots. The fingernails in my palms weren't helping. ''It means 'dangerous.' '' Then he went back to stripping the horse like nothing had happened.

I sat down in a heap. In all honesty, I didn't think I could stand much more of this. All my married life I had never felt the want in any way, shape, or form. Course, considering who I was married to, that was understandable. But to be widowed a week and a half and all of a sudden be driven nearly all the way crazy by the mere presence of a man? It didn't seem Christian.

Besides, he probably didn't feel the same way about me. He probably rescued somebody about once a week. Probably called every female he met *querida*. Probably kissed them all, too.

That last part gave me a shiver. I guess I had not let myself think about that kiss on purpose, but now that it was there, I hugged my knees and closed my eyes tight, like I could make it all go away.

I was therefore surprised when I felt the warmth of a body next to me a fraction of a second before an arm circled by shoulders.

"Chrysanthemum?"

It poured out slow, like half-cooled taffy, and wound around my insides. I scrunched my eyes tighter and put my hands over my ears.

Bigger hands eased them away. "Chrysanthemum? What is wrong?" I felt him open my hand. "Ah! *Querida,* why have you done this?"

Slow, I opened my eyes. He was hatless, his face inches from him. His horse tail had fallen over his shoulder. Soulful brown eyes searched mine. He said, "While you are sick, you talk." He kissed my palm. "You talk about us. About you and me. And love."

I was a goner, and I knew it.

So faint even I could scarce make out the words, I said, "I want you."

For a long minute he stared at me, his expression unchanging. And at long last, he said, "Then I shall be yours."

It was, like Uncle Wig used to say, a real eye-opening experience.

Afterwards, when the loving was done and the sun was going down in a glory of orange to the west, I lay in Joaquin's arms wishing I was a cat so I could purr. He had blown the lid off anything I had thought before about loving between two people. Not just blown the lid off, but pure annihilated it.

I didn't know a body could feel like that, like skyrockets and Christmas mornings in books and tender shoots of grass, all at once and ten times over.

He was playing with my hair, rolling a wisp of it up on his finger. I wondered, all sleepy and content and full of myself, if he just went around ruining women for other men. Maybe it was a hobby with him.

I didn't care. I figured that if nothing else ever came of it, one afternoon with him was worth putting up with a hundred with Spider Jukes, with Mr. Foot thrown in to boot. Of course, this did not stop me from daydreaming that he would ask me to marry him, and that he would take me and Chigger John to live with him in his hacienda in California. I knew he didn't have the hacienda, of course, but a fact like that doesn't figure into a daydream.

"Querida?" His breath came soft on my ear.

"Mmm?" I rolled over a little so I could look into his face. Oh, he was handsome. It seemed every time I turned away and then looked at him again, he got prettier. Brown naked skin, broad chest, strong arms to hold me, hands to please me; with those soft brown eyes and his hair all gone to a tumble, he was so beautiful it took my breath away.

"Querida, my leg is asleep."

I slithered off him and began putting my clothes back on. I had just realized that we were bare-ass naked in the dirt, and that my clothes were scattered all over the place, and I was embarrassed. I dressed in a flurry, and I was just tucking in my shirt when a hand touched my shoulder.

I turned to face him and it took me a second to register that he wore only his boots. The rest of him was as naked as a jaybird. And proud as a peacock, if you get my meaning.

"There will be plenty of time in the morning for this, Chrysanthemum," he said, fingering my shirt. "But tonight is for us, and for love. Come, I have made a bed for us."

Well, he took my hand and I stumbled after him, and then he sat me down in some blankets he'd rigged out, and then he told me to wait. I watched while he tended the horse and fixed the fire and made some coffee and beans—and let me tell you, it was a sight I won't soon forget—and then he sat beside me with a plate of beans in one hand and a cup of coffee in the other.

He put them down on the ground and looked into my eyes so hard and long that I had to look away, and all of a sudden, all I could think was that he was going to leave me, sooner or later.

Leave it to a Jukes.

"These are for you," he said.

"Thanks," I mumbled.

"There is whiskey in the coffee."

"OK."

"Chrysanthemum. Look at me."

I didn't, so he took hold of my jaw, gentle, and turned it for me.

"The night is young. The stars are just beginning to wake. And you are so beautiful."

Just like that, I went all to mush again. I drank my bourbon-laced coffee and ate my chuck and forgot my fears, and shucked my clothes and made love with him again, this time under a million stars. We danced beneath a three-quarter moon while he hummed old Spanish songs and we made love again. And when I fell asleep in his arms, I dreamt of haciendas and fine Spanish lace.

I woke first, and scrambled down to the creek for a wash. My hair was almost dry and I had breakfast started—well, coffee—when Joaquin woke up.

"Good morning, my dove," he said, giving me a big bear hug and a kiss before he walked down to the creek, still naked, and took a long piss into the stream. I was kind of embarrassed. I had never heard my male kin pee for so long even when they had been drinking, and every time he stopped, he'd start up again. But pretty soon he stopped for good. When he came up behind me, he had his pants on, and he was just shrugging into his shirt.

"Ah, coffee," he said, smiling, and poured himself a cup.

"I can't fix anything else good," I said, "so I didn't try.

But I could shoot some game if you give me the loan of your rifle.''

He said, ''That I do not doubt.'' Then he drank his coffee down in one gulp and finished tucking in his shirt. ''I will fix breakfast,'' he said. ''And while I do this, you will tell me a story of your growing up, and your family.''

I said, ''Well, I could tell you about the time Uncle Beetle was sozzled and mistook the boar for a settee.''

He shook his head no.

''How about the time that Uncle Glow got the—''

He shook his head again, and said, ''No, Chrysanthemum. About *you.*''

I sat down on a rock and stared at my hands. ''I can't think of anything good,'' I said.

''Then tell me something bad.''

I looked up at him. He was watching my face. I said, ''All right. How about one that happened to me during the war?''

''Good. And while you talk, I will make the breakfast.'' He started poking around in his saddlebags.

''This happened when all the men were off fighting Yankees,'' I began. ''Just me and Mama and Granny Wren were there. Well, and Violet and Chigger, too, but they were real little. And Nit and Gnat, but they were off somewhere.''

Joaquin looked up. ''About *you,* Chrysanthemum.''

I sighed. ''Anyway, this Jayhawker, a deserter, came to the cabin. He just walked right up—that will tell you how bold he was—and stuck a pistol to my head and said he wanted a meal or else.''

Joaquin had stopped, a paper-wrapped parcel in his hand. ''He put a gun to your head? How old were you?''

''Five.''

''Five?''

I couldn't figure out why he was so dumbfounded. I had picked a pretty tame story to tell him, and I hadn't even got to the good part yet. Or bad part, depending on how you looked at it.

''Anyway, Granny Wren was real nice to him and cooked him dinner. Treated him like one of her own sons. Course, it wouldn't have been out of line for one of them to stick a pistol under my jaw either, now that I come to think of it.''

Joaquin had sat down, the parcel in his hand. I could see it was bacon in there. He said, ''Your grandmother, she made him dinner?''

I said, ''Do you want me to tell this story?''

He nodded a small bow. ''*Perdone mí,* Chrysanthemum. Proceed.''

I started in again. ''Anyway, Granny Wren didn't bat an eye. She fed him supper while she made and baked a sweet-tater pie, and sent the pie and her blessing with him when he took off through the woods. He still had me with him, on account of I was his hostage.

''We went and we went. I was more scared by the minute, I can tell you. I was so scared that I even stopped talking. Course, he'd taken to thumping me on the head with his big old pistol every time I opened my mouth. Anyhow, we walked out through where the woods were old and dark, up through places I knew, and then to a place I didn't recognize. I remember there was a big old larch that had fallen, and he told me to squat myself on it.''

I looked over at Joaquin. He was rapt.

''I sat down, and then he told me to give over the pie. I'd been carrying it in a towel on account of it was hot, just out of the oven. It had cooled by then, though.

''I gave it over and he unwrapped it and scooped himself up a big handful. It was real disgusting, and I say that as a person who's eaten a lot of meals across the table from the Bug Boys. It was right smack on the tip of the non-Jukes half of my tongue to tell him *Don't eat that pie, mister—*''

''But why should he not eat the pie?'' Joaquin asked.

I said, ''Do I ask interrupting questions while you are story-telling?''

He said, ''*Sí.* Yes, you do.'' Then he smiled. ''Go on.''

''So I was going to tell him not to eat it. But I guess I must have made a face first, because he growled, 'You say one more word, and I will shoot you through the ear like a lame horse.' ''

Joaquin cursed under his breath, but not so loud that I stopped talking.

"He started shoving handfuls of that sweet-tater pie in his face. He didn't offer me any. I sure as shooting didn't want it. Not after I'd seen what Granny put in there."

Joaquin opened his mouth, but I shot him a look and he closed it.

"He doubled over about a minute later, clutching at his gut, and smeared orange pie goo on his shirt. 'Poisoned me! Poisoned!' he cried, and brought up the pistol."

"What?" said Joaquin. I ignored him.

"He didn't shoot me, though, for right then another cramp took him. I dived over the log and crouched down, shaking.

"It didn't take long. I waited, all hunkered up, with my fingers in my ears. He was moaning bad. After maybe two minutes it stopped. I came up slow, and by the time I peeked over the edge of the log, he was cold as a frog. I crawled the rest of the way up and straddled the log and just sat there, looking at him, all peaceful and still on the green forest floor, with a ladybug wandering along his eyebrow. I remember the ladybug especially."

"Poisoned?" Joaquin said.

I ignored him. "About ten minutes later, there came a rustling in the undergrowth and I hid myself again. But it was only Granny Wren and Mama, and Mama had a shovel. Right away my tongue loosened up. I guess I was babbling, because Granny Wren said, 'Hush up, Clutie,' all gruff. She gave the body a kick. She said—and I remember this clear— 'If t'weren't for you, I could'a just slit this piece'a Jay-hawkin' trash and wouldn't't'a had to ruin my pie and waste the last mite of our honey, ner trudge all the way into the piney deep after you.'"

"Poisoned?" Joaquin said again. He was a good audience, but he had a one-track mind. "But how? Where did she find the poison?"

I shrugged. "The high cupboards. Her pockets. Thin air. She was a witchwoman. I reckon it was all over the house."

"*Madre de Dios.*"

"Mama and Granny took turns digging till they made a shallow grave, then they pitched him in and buried him. Oh, and Granny Wren rolled the body. She got his pistol and a smidge of gunpowder, but no lead. And a pocket watch. And I had to sleep in the smokehouse for two days as punishment. The end.''

"Chrysanthemum?"

"Yes?"

"I think I will tell the stories for a while."

seventeen

Long about midday we stopped for lunch again—just
lunch this time, with no hanky panky—and by sunset
and dinner we had made good time toward the rail
lines. "I think by this time tomorrow you will be maybe
back with your Chigger John," Joaquin said. He was stirring
the fire. "Or at least with a search party. They will be looking. I think by noon tomorrow I will leave you."

"Why?" I blurted. "Why can't you come with us?"

Aside from the lovey-dovey part—for which I was growing more itchy by the minute—I would miss his company.
All day long as we traveled that inhospitable country, we
had traded stories about our lives and growing up. It was a
while before Joaquin let me tell another, though.

He told me about how his mama left him and his daddy
when he was five and went back to her family, and then how
his papa ran to save him from the Mondragons. They were
trying to get him back, and did, but they killed his daddy in
the process. Joaquin saw it, and it was pretty gruesome. It
was a lot worse than my pie story, if you ask me.

Anyway, his grandpappy Mondragon died about that
time—Joaquin said it was divine retribution for having killed
his daddy so cruel—and they lost their big estates and had
to go to Mexico to live. Ever since he had been old enough
to be on his own, he had been after the men his grandpappy
hired to kill his daddy, and along the way, he'd had exciting
adventures.

He said as how he fought the Comanches in Texas, and
about the time he was hanged in Alamagordo, New Mexico,
for thieving a horse, but got saved at the last minute. He

showed me the scar. It was pretty faint, and I think I can be excused for not noticing it the night before, being otherwise occupied.

All of that took a lot of telling, especially when you figure that I told him a lot about me, too. You can sure learn a lot about a person when you're traveling double on horseback, especially when that person is as prone to gab as was Joaquin. Well, me too. I guess I told more than my share. And it should be said to his credit that he did not yawn during my speaking, and appeared to be interested in even the lowliest thing I had to say, so long as it did not include poisoned pies.

I got so lulled by this—his being so accepting and all— that I even told him about Mr. Foot, and I had sworn never to say that out to anybody. I realized what I was doing about halfway through and tried to cover up, but he stopped the horse and said, ''Go on, Chrysanthemum,'' real serious-like.

I finished the tale in a tremble, afraid he'd shove me off the horse and gallop straight to Mexico, but he didn't. Nothing of the kind. He got down off that horse and pulled me with him, and then he put his arms around me and said, ''Poor *querida,* poor darling. Just a baby.''

Saying it out—about Mr. Foot and everything—brought it all up to the surface again. He smoothed my hair, and wiped my tears, and added, ''This brother of his. You say his name, it is Lester?''

I nodded.

''Lester Foot. I could find him. I could kill him.''

I said, ''Joaquin, that won't do any good.''

''But if he is as his brother? What if he has a young girl, a slave for his sick pleasures? I could shoot him, and I would say, as I held the gun to his head, 'This is for my Chrysanthemum, for she suffered greatly at the hands of your brother Ezra, who was scum like you.' And then I would set his woman free, like Frank did for you. This pleases you?''

It was an awful pretty picture, and I hadn't thought about it like that. I guess that's just what Mrs. Foot had been, a slave, and what I would have been if I hadn't got my hands on that knife.

I said, "OK. You can kill him if you happen to be in Mexico and you happen to run across him, and he happens to have a slave woman for the fulfillment of his perverse pleasures."

That seemed to brighten him up. Me, too. Just thinking about Joaquin riding to the rescue of some poor girl, even if it was imaginary, made me feel all proud.

But now he that he was talking about dropping me off like so much excess baggage, I was kind of hurt. "Why can't you come with me and Chigger to California?"

He looked at me, a sadness in his eyes. "Because I am an outlaw, *querida*. I am wanted in Missouri and Kansas and California. New Mexico Territory, too, as well as Texas."

"Outlaw? Why, that never stopped my uncles. Some of them were drinking buddies with the law, and—"

"Say no more. Your uncles were . . . a case *especial,* Chrysanthemum. It is not so for me. In Kansas alone I am wanted for murder. It is simple: If I am caught, I hang."

I couldn't say anything. He had said it so final that I just let the subject drop. But I couldn't help feeling an inner sadness for what might have been, and started stripping the horse so that my back would be turned and my tears wouldn't show.

"Chrysanthemum?" came his voice from the other side of the fire.

I kept my face toward the horse, slid the saddle from his back. "Yes?"

There was the snap of a stick in the little blaze. "I am not wanted in Colorado."

It was a good long time before we got round to fixing dinner.

The next morning Joaquin spent telling me all about something called "rendezvous," which his papa had taken him to before he got killed by the Mondragons and Joaquin went to live with them. It was a real exciting thing. Trappers—and Indians, too—would come from all over the land to meet up and carouse and trade and have a high old time. Joaquin had been just a little tyke when he went, but he said he would never forget it.

"I spoke only French, then. You would not believe it now, I speak such good English, no?"

"I think you speak real good, but for a Spanish man," I said. "I would never know that you were French."

He stopped the horse and twisted round to look at me. "You think I have an accent?"

"Yes."

He looked at me for a couple of seconds, and then he turned round and started the horse up, and I could hear him mumbling in Spanish or maybe it was French, and then he whoaed the horse up again. He was just turning to say something to me when a rider burst over the top of a rise bearing straight at us, followed directly by three whooping Indian braves.

Joaquin yelled at me to hold on and kicked Peligroso into a gallop. He did not need to yell. I was stuck to him like glue.

He headed for a little rise not far away. The other rider followed our lead and no more had we dived off the horse and crawled under bushes than his bay flew over our heads. He hit the dirt a second after.

Joaquin had his pistol out and already had taken a few potshots at the Indians, who had backed out of range while they figured out what to do next.

"What in the blue blazes did you do to make those Indians so mad, mister?" I had never seen a genuine live Indian in my whole life, and I was annoyed that some total stranger had ruined my first introduction.

"What?" said the man. He was digging in his saddlebags for ammunition. His eyes were white all around and he was sweating terrible, though it was not all that hot.

"I said, how come you have got the Noble Savage so stirred up against you?"

The man looked up from his box of cartridges. "Are you crazy?"

"Chrysanthemum," said Joaquin, "get—"

A bullet spatted into the dirt overhead.

"—down," he finished up.

"Thank you, Joaquin," I said. It was hard saying anything, what with the stranger scrambling up the hill to fire and Joaquin holding my head down with the hand he wasn't shooting with. "But would somebody just tell me—"

Joaquin put his hand over my mouth. "Who are they?" He was looking at the stranger, who was dressed rough and didn't look to have had a bath in a long time.

"Kiowa," he said. He reloaded his rifle. "Can you see them? Can you see anything?" When he spoke, I saw that he had a tooth missing in front, too.

Joaquin looked at him real disgusted. "Of this I am aware. But what Kiowa? Who?"

The man looked at us like we were a pair of loonies straight from the bin. "I don't know, dammit! I was just goin' along, mindin' my own business, when all of a sudden—"

Another bullet splatted into the dirt about a foot from Joaquin's head. He ducked, and then he let go of my mouth. I opened it straight off, saying, "I read about the Kiowa in a book, and I didn't think they were . . . were . . ." But the way he looked at me made me close it right up again.

Then he did an amazing thing. He started talking—yelling, really—at those Indians. I could not understand a single word he said or that they answered back. And neither, it seemed, could the stranger. He just sat there, hugging his rifle, looking from Joaquin to me and back again, looking more worried by the minute.

At last the palaver was finished. Joaquin just sat there a minute, looking at the stranger, and then he said, "Chrysanthemum, catch Peligroso."

I didn't move. I thought he'd gone crazy.

"Chrysanthemum!"

He said it so commanding that I was halfway down to the horse before I knew what I was doing. By the time I caught it and started leading it up the slope, Joaquin's gun was aimed at the stranger and they were having words.

"They ain't but a pack of liars!" said the stranger. "How can you believe—"

"By the hair on your saddle, amigo. This is not my fight." Then he backed down the slope to me and got on, never lowering his gun.

"What are we doing?" I said as I climbed up behind him. He paid me no nevermind. "*Vaya con Dios, señor*," he said, and then he lashed that chestnut into a hard lope.

I thought for certain that we would be shot as soon as we broke through to the clear. Noble Savage or not, those boys were het up. But nobody shot at us as we breached the clear. Nobody shot at us at all.

We didn't keep to a canter for long—just as well, for I had used up nearly all the bounce in my backside—and slowed to a jog, then a walk. We could hear faint gunshots behind us for a while, and then they stopped. Then we didn't hear any more.

Finally we stopped beside a tiny creek to rest the horse. He had not spoken since we left the battle and neither had I. Without a word I slid off. Without a word he led Peligroso to water. By the time he led the horse back, I couldn't stand it anymore.

"Who in tarnation do you think you are, leaving that man there to die?"

He stood for a minute looking at me, then pulled the saddle off his horse. "It was not my fight." He put the saddle down.

"But—"

"You yourself questioned this when we first rode in."

"But that didn't make me—"

"The Kiowa said he was a bad man, *muy malo*. They said he had taken many Kiowa scalps."

"But—"

"*Silencio!*" he barked, and the way he looked right then gave me a chill. "They said he had taken these scalps from women and children. I looked at his saddle. Did you? Five or six scalps, some very small. Would you wish to die to save the life of a man such as this?"

I couldn't say anything, I felt that small, and I sat right down on a rock and put my face in my hands.

"Do not cry, Chrysanthemum," he said soft. He had come

over and knelt beside me. "Do you think I would let you die for a man like that? Do you think your life means so little? *Dios mio!*"

I rubbed my nose on my sleeve. I said, "I have got a quilt. I made it from deerskin. And a dress. It's blue. It's in my bag. I wish I could have worn it for you to see."

He smiled, his bark-tea eyes all crinkled up in that tanned Spanish face. "All in good time, *querida.* There will be many beautiful dresses, and many beautiful quilts."

By late afternoon we sighted a posse from the top of a rocky hill. I knew that the time had come for me and Joaquin to say our good-byes, but that did not make it any easier.

Finally he peeled me off him and said, "Chrysanthemum, it is time. I will wait until I see you safe. And here." He dug in his pocket for a second, came up with a pocket watch, and folded it into my hand. "For you to keep," he said.

I bit my lip and made a fist around that watch. I was already crying, but this just made it worse. I swan, if it had not been for Chigger John I would have been off with Joaquin in a minute, and I would not have given two snaps for the consequences.

"I have nothing for you," I sniffed.

"Yes, you do," he whispered, and before I knew it he had produced a little pocketknife and was cutting a lock of my hair. "Go to Colorado. Go with the train, to where it ends. I have business elsewhere, but I will come. I will find you. When we meet again, I will put this in the watch," he said, holding up a little loop of brown hair. "Now, go."

I got maybe ten feet down the hill before I turned back and ran to him and pressed my lucky buckeye into his hand, and kissed him hard, hard enough to last.

Then just as quick I was running away from him, down the slope, and I heard men call out, "Over there! She's found! Over there!"

I stuck to my story, just like me and Joaquin had worked out, about how the gang had dumped me and then I had wandered aimless through the grasslands for days. I said I had found water, and showed them a canteen that I had filled—supposedly taken from the train robbers, but really a gift from Joaquin.

Well, I suppose that really made it from the train robbers, so that part wasn't a lie.

With me missing Joaquin like crazy but never letting on—and touching that watch in my pocket every few minutes for luck—we traveled on into Abilene. It was late at night when we rode in, and chilly, and one of the men tried to loan me his jacket. But I said, "Then that would just make you cold instead of me." I didn't need his coat. I had the Spanish Kid's steadfast admiration and undying affection to keep me warm from the inside out.

We had barely got into town—and I was about to remark to one of the men that I had expected to smell a lot more cow, Abilene being the Queen of the Cow Towns and all—when I heard, "Clutie! Clutie, you's back!" and looked up to see Chigger John hanging out of a second-floor hotel window and waving to beat the band.

With a quick "Thanks, mister" to the fella that had let me ride double, I was off that horse and across the street right about the same time as Chigger tumbled out the front door of the hotel.

"Oh, Clutie, you ain't b-buzzard b-bait!" he sobbed. He was shaking so hard that he couldn't do anything else but bawl, and I knew then that I had done right to come back to him. I was all he had.

At least, I thought I was all Chigger had. Once we had dried up the most of our tears, it struck me that there was something different about him. I said, "Step back into the light, Chigger. Let me take a gander at you."

Well, he did, and I dang near fainted.

"Chigger, what have you done? Who's got you rigged out like that?"

"Mr. Hyphen," he answered with a grin, wiping his hands over a black velvet jacket. "He got 'em special. He says I'm a pip! You want he should get you some, too, Clutie? You wanna be a pip?"

"I don't think so. Just where is Prometheus?"

"Here I am, Miss Clutie," came a voice from the doorway. "Or should I say Mrs. Jukes?" There was a great big grin plastered over his face and a fog of whiskey over his demeanor. "I am delighted beyond . . . beyond . . ." He seemed to get stuck there, but saved it by bowing low with a sweep of his hat. "Delighted to find you have been returned unharmed. You are unharmed, I take it?"

"Without a scratch," I said, "but we can talk about it in the morning. Right now I want some sleep."

"Nonsense!" said Prometheus. He sure was happy. He stuck his thumbs in the armholes of his waistcoat. "You shall regale us with the fruits of your . . . with the exploits of . . . with the, uh . . ." He stopped to hiccup. "Tell us over dinner!"

They opened the kitchen special, and over a big steak and potatoes and onions—and it was pretty good, too—he made me tell him the story of my time on the plains. I couldn't say much, not wanting to give Joaquin away and all. And he was so far into his cups that he didn't care, anyway, so I guess it was pretty boring.

Mostly I stared at Chigger. Prometheus had him rigged out like Little Lord Whosis in these short pants and a ruffled shirt and a little velvet jacket and white stockings and shiny shoes. He was more fancied up than a two-dollar whore, and I couldn't imagine how Prometheus had managed to get him to put the clothes on, let alone like them.

I pointed at Chigger with my fork. "Where'd you come by the duds?" I asked.

Prometheus opened his mouth, but Chigger beat him to it. "At the store! The man said he had 'em a spell, and ain't nobody bought 'em, and ain't I the lucky boy!"

As I pushed my plate away, Prometheus started, "Actually . . ."

I headed him off. "Yes, you sure are the lucky boy. But we're going west tomorrow, and you are not wearing those clothes."

"But Clutie!"

"No."

•   •   •

I had been having a dream. In it, Johnnycake was sick and moaning again, and I was shaking and crying and trying to level the gun at his head. Then all of a sudden he turned into Spider, writhing on the ground with one hand up. He cried, "Clutie, no!" And my shaking hand turned to steel, and I shot him.

That was what woke me up, I guess. I was in a sweat. I guess I had expected that if I was going to dream, it would be nice ones about the Spanish Kid, not nightmares about killing my horse. Or my husband.

I had been more tired than I thought, for it was nigh on ten o'clock in the morning, and Chigger was not to be found. Neither was his fancy outfit. Feeling like I had been rode hard and put up wet, I dragged myself up out of bed and dressed, took another buckeye from my quilt bag and stuck it in my pocket, and then I went looking.

I found him and Prometheus down to the station, just coming out of the depot. They were a pair to draw to, Prometheus all sharp in his black banker's suit with a carnation stuck in his lapel, and Chigger John rigged out in black velvet and silk stockings. There was a black hat that matched, with two long ribbons down the back. Between the two of them, they looked like they'd just come from paying a call on the Queen.

"Ah, good morning, fair Clutie!" Prometheus said as they walked down the depot steps and came toward me. "I have wonderful tidings!"

"Nothing's going to sound good to me till Chigger gets rid of those clothes."

Chigger ducked behind Prometheus. I guess I sounded pretty cranky. Prometheus paid me no mind, though. He just kept on talking.

"I have arranged for a car—a private car—to take us as far as Ellsworth. How does that sound to you?"

"It sounds fine on the face of it," I said, trying to peek around him to give Chigger the eye. "Why Ellsworth? And what's a private car?"

Prometheus raised a brow. "My, we *are* the rustic, aren't we?"

I wasn't quite sure what he meant by that, so I ignored it. "Chigger, come out from behind there and change your clothes. Probably half the town is laughing at you right now."

He stuck his head around Prometheus long enough to say, "Don't wanna change! I likes 'em!" and then ducked back behind.

Prometheus said, "You know, a funny thing happened when I was paying for the car . . ."

I grabbed at Chigger round one side of Prometheus, but he ducked to the other.

"There I was, counting out my money . . . ," Prometheus went on.

I jumped round to the other side, reached for Chigger's ear, got a fistful of velvet instead. I hauled him out by the shoulder—him carrying on like a stuck pig—when Prometheus clapped his hand on my arm.

"Quiet, lad," he said real calm, and just like that Chigger shut up. He had never shut up so fast for me, and I was impressed. Before I could say a word of congratulations, though, Prometheus said, "Family squabble, not to worry," to the few people who had stopped to look at us. He tipped his hat and—one hand on Chigger, one on me—moved us up the street a piece.

"You could let go of me anytime," I said, and shook my arm free.

"Very well. But before you upset this poor boy again, you should know that when I was counting my money, I found a discrepancy."

I went all cold, but not because of anything Prometheus was saying. Past his shoulder, far up the street, a short orange-headed man was just tying his horse at the rail. I could tell his hair was orange, because the horse knocked it off with his nose and the man beat him about the head with it before he put it back on.

I shook my head, then looked again.

He was still there.

Uncle Beetle?

". . . one hundred dollars," Prometheus finished up, looking self-satisfied.

"Sure," I said. "Sure thing." Beetle stepped up on the walk, where another man stepped out of the shadows to join him. Uncle Glow, or maybe Uncle Wig—I couldn't tell.

"Clutie? What you lookin' at?" Chigger craned his head, but by that time they had gone back into the shadows again, maybe into a building.

Prometheus stuck his face between me and the scene up the street. "Did you hear what I said?"

"No. What time does the train leave?"

"An hour." He checked his watch. "Fifty-three minutes now. I think we need to settle the issue of young Chigger's clothing. He likes—"

"Fine," I said. "He can wear anything he pleases. He can go buck naked if he wants. Let's just get to the hotel and pack up, all right?"

Chigger was all smiles, but Prometheus said, "I must say, I find this about-face curious. And further, the missing money has me perplexed."

He gave me a look like he didn't find it perplexing at all, but I didn't have time to explain. I said, "We'll talk about it on the train," and hurried Chigger down the street to the hotel.

"This is better, isn't it?" Prometheus said with a sigh of satisfaction as the train pulled out of Abilene. He was sitting across from me in a red-and-gold brocade chair. Beside him on a little table sat a little double-globed reading lamp, glass prisms a-shiver with the train's movement, and a bottle of gin. He raised his glass and took a swallow.

"I suppose the car wasn't necessary, considering the short distance. But they had the rental just sitting there anyway, and I cannot resist temptation. And if I may say," he added, after wiping his mouth, "you look, uh, charming."

I had put on Agnes Ann's dress in the hotel, thinking that from a distance me and Chigger would not be recognizable. I had been right—my own mama wouldn't have known me. Agnes Ann had been a lot shorter than I expected, plus thicker through the waist and tinier in the bust. What I ended up with was a dress with a hem that fell a good six inches short, strained over my dinners, and needed a rope about the waist.

I hated to say it, but it had looked a lot better on Agnes Ann than me.

It had not really sunk into me what Prometheus meant by "private car" until that very minute, and now here we were, up to our ears and wallowing in gross and ungodly extravagance. There was a bedroom and a maid's room and a parlor, and a foldaway bathtub with spigots that shot water right out of the wall, hot and cold.

I do not want you to think that I was bedazzled by luxury, though—I had watched careful on the street, and out the windows once we got on the train. There was not an orange-headed person to be seen, much to the relief of my jittering hands. Now that we had cleared Abilene, I was beginning to wonder if I hadn't made it up, like Chigger had in Kansas City. Maybe I just had Bug Boys on the brain.

"You sure know how to travel, Prometheus," I said, as Chigger ran by us for the fifteenth or sixteen time. He had been doing that—running the full length of the car—ever since we left the station. I stuck out an arm to catch him.

"Enough running," I said. "You'll give yourself a spell." He leaped over my legs—a blur of black velvet—to sit by the window. I turned to Prometheus. "I sure want to thank you for having us along. Real neighborly of you."

He knocked back the last of his glass of gin, and poured himself another. "Think nothing of it, my dear," he said with a wave of his hand. He looked over toward Chigger John, who had his face pressed against the glass and was busy counting slow: "One, two, five, three . . ."

Prometheus smiled. "I have taken a strong liking to your young cousin." He leaned forward, motioning me toward him, and whispered, "You must tell me about the puke dogs someday. They seem to get him into a terrible state."

I guess I colored up some, but I whispered back that I would. Then I excused myself. I wanted to get out of the dress, for it was constricting my breathing so that I felt near to strangling. I motioned Prometheus back into his chair, found my bag, and retired to the bedroom. I was changed and just putting my things back in order—well, I was sitting there mooning over Joaquin's watch and chanting a gooey old love charm—when I heard a knock on the door.

I put the watch away quick and said, "Come in."

It was Prometheus. "I wondered if you would rather take luncheon in the dining car, or have it here," he said, and started to help me put my things in order. He was not yet staggered with drink, for which I was grateful.

"In here, I guess. How come there weren't any cattle in Abilene?"

"There were cattle. Just not nearly so many now that the cattle trade is shifted. Did I hear poetry?"

"Not exactly."

He looked at me.

"Sort of." When he just kept staring, I said, "Well, they're spells. Charms." I had no intention of spilling the beans about Joaquin, so I said fast, "Like if your arms are aching you, or you're lost in the piney deep, or if you want to make a wish."

He sat down on the bed. "Fascinating. How do you make a wish?"

I couldn't tell if he was making fun of me or not, but I decided to give him the benefit. "Well, for a little wish, you could just cross your fingers and spit twice. That'll work if you do it by the light of the full moon. Or if you see a snake track in the dust, you can spit in it. If nobody's around, that is. Somebody watching breaks the magic. For a bigger one, there's a rhyme, but you have to spit four times at the end and then slap the ground where you spat."

"Is expectoration usually involved?"

"You're making fun of me."

He smiled. "Sorry. Not at all. Go on."

"Well, OK. This is a rhyme you can say for a wish:

"Fry up the possum,
Boil up the fish,

> Meal up the table bread,
> Hark to my wish!"

Prometheus considered this for a moment. "Does it usually work?"

I didn't want to lie. I had not exactly had a hundred percent accuracy with my spells. More like less than fifty. I said, "There is one for rolling in the clouds and hiding a person, except that one only works in Missouri. But if a person is magic I expect most of them work pretty good."

"I see. And are you magic?"

I didn't know how to answer that question, so I said, "You want to hear another one? It's one to say when you find a dead bat. You hold it out in front of you and spin three times to your right, and you say, 'Lucky bat, lucky bat, Tell me where my beau is at!' Course if it's a fella rhyming if, he says 'gal' instead of 'beau.' "

"Clutie . . ."

"Or one for a safe journey. This one's old, Granny says her granny remembered it. I say it all the time to protect me and Chigger:

> "Spit on the fiddle
> Wind on the bone,
> Protect this gal
> Who's far from home.
> Spit on the zither,
> Wind on the sea,
> I'm out of the mountains,
> Protect ye me!"

Prometheus was smiling, just a little smile, although he was not looking at me, but at my quilt bag. He said, kind of distracted, "And do they work?"

"You asked me that already. If a witchwoman says them—"

"What's this?"

"What's what?" He had his arm in my bag, and I couldn't see.

"This," he said, and pulled out my deerskin quilt. Caught up in the folds, buckeyes rained upon the floor, but he didn't notice. He opened it out and held it up, and then he laid it on the bed and ran his fingers over it. The way he touched it was like the way Joaquin had run his hands over my skin. It was spooky, and I had to grab my arms to hold back the shivers.

"Where did you get this?" he said finally, like maybe I had stole it.

"I made it," I said, a little too defensive. "I made it in the woods, the winter I was twelve. I shot the bucks and tanned the hides myself. You dumped my buckeyes!"

"This is marvelous," he said, lifting it again, talking more to himself than me. He turned it over, handling it more carefully than I had ever thought to. "This pattern. Where did you—"

Chigger banged through the door in an abject panic. "Uncle Beetle's ghost! The Bug Boys is on the train!

eighteen

The bottom fell out of my stomach. I had been sure they hadn't got on the train. And where would they have found the money to ride? Uncle Beetle wouldn't have had time to sell his horse. Unless, of course, it was a stolen horse. Unless they had stole the train fare.

All those thoughts and about fifty others went flashing cross my mind, and by the time I had the presence of mind to speak, Prometheus was down on his knees and had Chigger by the shoulders, and he was asking just exactly where he had seen this ghost.

Chigger had pretty much stopped crying by then. "T-three cars up," he said.

"That could mean three or five or any other number!" I said, trying to keep from trembling and not having much luck at it. "He's got a loose idea of figures."

"There, there, lad. Your Uncle Beetle. Was anyone else with him?" Prometheus asked, just as soothing as could be.

Chigger sniffed, and Prometheus dug out a handkerchief and clamped it over Chigger's nose. "Blow." Then, "Were any of your other uncles with him?"

That was when it struck me. I said, "How come you know about Uncle Beetle? I never told you—"

"Do you suppose we might discuss this later?" Prometheus snapped before he turned back to Chigger. "Any others, boy?"

I said, "You don't need to go snarling at me. I only asked—"

"No," said Chigger to Prometheus, his face all squished from thinking. "Just Uncle Beetle."

Prometheus got up and led Chigger out the door, through the parlor with me close behind. "Show me where he is, Chigger."

"Just a goldang minute! What if Beetle sees you first? What if—"

"Then you'll keep the door bolted, won't you?" said Prometheus.

"What?"

"My dear, you are hysterical. Sit down. Calm yourself."

"How can I calm myself when there are Bug Boys on this very train?"

He looked at me for a second, then said in a low voice, "Personally, I feel the probability highly unlikely. On three separate occasions, Chigger sighted this Beetle in Abilene this past week alone. They turned out to be a ranch hand, a baker's assistant, and a bank teller, respectively."

"But I saw them," I said, and it came off me like a fifty-pound weight. "I saw them on the street this morning."

Prometheus stared at me. "In town?"

"Yes."

"In Abilene?"

"Yes!"

"Well." He pursed up his lips like he was giving it serious consideration. "This puts things in an entirely different light."

"I figured it might."

"Then you'd best bolt the door now," he said, and slipped out onto the platform with Chigger John.

I tell you, there is nothing so aggravating as a man who is dead set on taking charge of a situation he knows diddly-squat about. I was back in the bedroom in four jumps and grabbed Spider's pistol from its holster and stuck it in my belt—Prometheus might go out there unarmed and play the fool, but I would not—and then I started making my way behind them up through the cars.

I went slow and careful. Prometheus was so bullheaded that he was probably marching through there like Sherman through Georgia with no mind to the consequence. I was certain that each car door I opened would reveal Beetle with his knife to Chigger's throat, Prometheus already bleeding to death on the floor, and passengers all around frozen in apoplectic terror.

There was no sign of them in the first car, nor the second, nor the third. By that time I was as spooky as a green colt on a blustery day.

I was on the platform of the fourth car, back against the door, hand on the knob, ready to ease it open gentle, when it swung open fast and nigh on banged me off the train.

I saw a quick blur of grass rush by at thirty-five miles an hour before I caught myself on the railing, but I had my gun in hand and was ready to spring when a voice said, "I thought I told you to stay in the Pullman."

I stuck the Peacemaker back in my belt. "Dag-nab it, Prometheus!"

He offered his hand to help me up but I ignored it. I had just realized that I'd almost fallen off the train, and a thing like that can scare a person good. I got up by myself—by then Chigger had joined us on the platform—and followed Prometheus into the next car. I was real glad when the door closed behind us.

"It weren't Uncle Beetle, Clutie," Chigger announced with a big grin, and the front half of the car stopped their conversations to look at us.

"Hush," I said. "They can hear you in the next county."

"Well, it weren't," he said, pouting, but a little quieter. "It weren't him at all. It were a cigar salesman. He come from Ohio."

"Iowa," corrected Prometheus, guiding us down the aisle.

"Iowa," repeated Chigger. "He sold cigars."

I kept my trap shut until we were back in the Pullman. By then I had a lather worked up, and I let Prometheus—and Chigger—have it.

"What the Sam Hill are you doing charging up there when you know how Uncle Beetle is?" I was yelling but I didn't care. "Chigger, you look at me! Don't you know if he caught you he'd skin you alive or worse?" When that didn't work, I said, "He'd set the puke dogs on you, that's what! Sniffing and snuffing and baying and yapping!"

That got a rise out of him. "And their eyes all red!" he cried. "Comin' to eat me up from France!" He ran into the bedroom, crying, and banged the door closed behind him.

"Clutie!" Prometheus had drawn himself up to his full height, and I will say that it was impressive. "How dare you terrorize that child like that? I have a good mind to take you over my knee!"

"Just you try it, you crazy old drunk! If that really had been Beetle Jukes up in that car, my terrorizing that child would have been the least of your worries, for you'd either be dead or wishing you were. Beetle Jukes is not a smart man but he is meaner than a snake, and makes up in deadly what he lacks in clever. You are no match for him and don't go fooling yourself that you are. Further, I would like to know just how in tarnation you came to be in possession of so much knowledge about the Bug Boys. Just what's Chigger been telling you? How much do you know?"

Well, I guess that took the wind out of his sails, because he sat and motioned me down, too. He opened his bottle of gin, poured a splash into his tumbler, and drank it in one gulp.

"Perhaps you are right," he said at last. "Perhaps I did overstep my bounds. Perhaps I am a crazy old drunk, as you so poetically put it. But this Uncle Beetle, over whom you've lashed yourself into a frenzy, is dead. Dead, Clutie. It's likely that Chigger feels he's to blame, and perhaps that's why he keeps seeing Beetle's ghost. But I'm surprised at you."

I cringed a little at that. He was right. Maybe I'd made up the Bug Boys. Seeing them on the street in Abilene, I mean. Whoever it was had been pretty far away. Prometheus didn't give me time to apologize, though.

"Young Chigger and I became fast friends during your absence. I began to think—and I hope you will forgive me for saying it—that if you did not come back, I would take over his guardianship. It came as something of a shock—although not at all an unpleasant one, I assure you—when you were returned unharmed."

I couldn't think of a blessed thing to say. I just stared at him.

"Chigger told me something of his background. Yours, too. Well, I was able to piece it together from the scraps. But any man who could be banged over the head with a skillet by a twelve-year-old boy, particularly when that boy was Chigger, did not seem too dire an enemy."

I didn't say anything.

"I do have a question, though," he went on. "The Bug Boys. How on earth did they come by such an odious name?"

Well, I told him how all the Bug Boys had bug names on account of in the Jukes family, all the men of a generation got named after whatever misfortune had befallen the head Jukes of the generation before. Grandpappy Adder had been swarmed by wasps, so that was how Beetle's generation was named. When Beetle's older brother, Bumble, died from an ant bite that went septic, all the next generation of boys got named after bugs, too. I said it more drawn out than that, but that was the gist of it.

He mulled this over. "And the women? Just out of curiosity, you understand."

"Flowers. Birds. There was an Aunt Grizzly one time, back in the long agos, in Kentucky. But that was a mistake, on account of they thought she was an underhung boy until she turned thirteen and gave birth."

He just sat there.

All of a sudden I had a frozen feeling, like ice going up your spine. "What else . . . What else did Chigger tell you?"

He poured out another splash of gin and drank it down. "Besides the fact that you shot your husband, you mean?" Then, just like that, he turned toward the door and called, "Enter!"

I had not even heard a knock, I had been so flummoxed. It was a waiter with the midday menu, and Prometheus took and studied it like there was nothing wrong, like he hadn't just accused me—and rightly so—of murder.

He looked up from the menu and calmly said, "Shall I order for you, my dear?"

•   •   •

I took shelter in the bedroom, where I dried Chigger's tears. "No puke dogs," I soothed. "No puke dogs."

He looked up at me, those big blue eyes still welling with tears. "Ain't gonna come from France to eat me?"

"No, Chigger, no. There aren't any puke dogs. I was mean to say it to you."

"You was mean." He didn't say it like an accusation, just a fact.

"You forgive me?"

He paused long enough to blow his nose on the corner of his fancy collar. "OK."

"You'd better let me wash that."

His eyes narrowed. "Give it back?"

"Soon as it's dry."

Wearing a work shirt over black velvet britches, Chigger joined me and Prometheus for the midday meal, and all he could do was babble about the water. "It comes clean out the wall!" he said for the tenth time. "You just turns the doohickey, and out she comes! Whoosh!"

"Chigger," I said, "eat your string beans."

"Whoosh!"

"Chigger . . ."

"Whoosh!"

Prometheus salted his beef. "Mind Clutie."

"Yessir," said Chigger, and commenced to eat.

I stared at him. "How do you do that?" I said to Prometheus.

"Do what?" he replied. He was about done with the bottle of gin by then, having made heavy inroads while I was washing out Chigger's shirt. I figured three more splashes and the bottle would be empty. It was barely one o'clock.

"Never mind," I said. It had taken a while to catch up with me, but the more I thought about it, the madder I got. Gall, that's what it was, thinking that if something happened to me he'd get Chigger John!

I was in no mood to talk to him. I tried to bury myself in thoughts of Joaquin and Spanish weddings for I don't know how long. I had just about succeeded when Chigger tugged at my sleeve.

"Clutie? Clutie!"

"Sorry, Chigger. What?"

"Is it dry yet? Is my shirt dry to wear?"

Being jerked out of that daydream had got me crabby—well, I guess I was crabby already—and I said, "I don't know. Why don't you ask Prometheus?"

Prometheus shot me a look, to which I replied by staring out the window with my lips squished tight. I heard him say to Chigger, "Go and check, son."

Chigger scrambled out of his chair—he never could stand up without of lot of scraping and bumping—and after he left the room, Prometheus said in a low voice, "Stop it."

I turned toward him. "Stop what?"

"You know perfectly well what I mean, my dear."

I drew myself up. Well, as much as I could while I was sitting down. "I am sure I don't know what you—"

"Clutie?" Chigger was back with the soggy shirt, which he'd got all balled up. "Can I put it on now?"

I said "Yes" at the same time Prometheus said "No." Then I said "No" when Prometheus said "Yes."

After a silence in which Prometheus and I eyed each other back and forth, Prometheus finally gave an exasperated groan and went back to his bottle. I said, "Chigger, hang it back up and let it dry."

Prometheus kept his mouth shut except to pour liquor in it—he had opened a new bottle of gin—and he continued in the same vein until three-thirty that afternoon, when we reached Ellsworth.

If Abilene was no longer the Queen of the Cow Towns, then Ellsworth, which had been its successor, looked to be on its way out, too, although there was considerably more cow in the air than there had been in Abilene.

I took in a big lungful when we stepped down off the train. "Smells like home," I said.

"Cows!" said Chigger, back in his fancy shirt. The lace trim was not ironed, but he didn't care.

"Come along," said Prometheus. He picked up his valise, a brand-new one he had got in Abilene to replace the one he'd lost on the train, and started weaving up the street. There was a good-looking buckskin tied at the rail, and he remarked in passing, "Handsome mount."

"Johnnycake got sick," chirped Chigger. "Clutie shot him." He stopped dead in his tracks, as if he'd just remembered it for the first time that very minute, and burst out bawling. "Oh Johnnycake, oh Johnnycake's dead, won't give me no more rides . . ."

I grabbed him up just in time to keep a wagon from running over him, hauled him up on the walk, and dug in my pocket for a handkerchief. "Chigger, you never did ride on Johnnycake when he was alive."

It was a good thing I had the kerchief ready—I stuck it in between his face and his collar, and he had a good blow. "Now, don't think about it anymore. You go on up there and tell Prometheus to wait for me."

Chigger gave one last blast into the handkerchief, said "OK, Clutie," and ran ahead to where Prometheus was still ambling along, talking to himself. I picked up the bags I had dropped in order to snatch Chigger from in front of that freight wagon, and scurried to catch them.

"I wish you wouldn't go round bringing up things from the past," I whispered to Prometheus once I caught him up. "It makes him cry. If you want to talk about dead horses and such, talk to me."

He looked at me, kind of goggle-eyed, and said, "My dear young woman, I have not the slightest idea about what . . . about what . . . I don't know what you're talking about."

I plunked my backside on a bench and dropped my parcels. "Oh, never mind." Chigger was up the street a piece petting a dog, and I called to him to stop his fooling and get back. To Prometheus, I said, "Where you taking us now?" As long as it was west and in a hurry, I didn't much care.

He sat down next to me. Well, more like fell down. He got untangled from his valise, and then he said, "To the stage office. We seem to have taken the wrong train."

I stared at him until it sunk in. "The wrong what?"

"Train." It wasn't that hot out, but he produced a handkerchief and mopped at his brow. "I was a trifle . . . illuminated. When I paid the original passage."

It took a second for that to sink in, and then I got mad. "Illuminated? You have been lit up since I've known you, probably since God made water. I don't think that's a very good excuse! I don't think that is an excuse at all!"

The kerchief went round the back of his neck. "I assure you, it's very simple to correct. All we need do is take the stage—"

I got to my feet. "Prometheus, I have about had it! I have got half a mind to take Chigger and go on west without you. In fact, that's what I think I'll do."

He stared at the kerchief in his hand. Then he looked up at me, resigned. I all of a sudden had a bad feeling, a real bad feeling, and I wanted to take it back in the worst way.

He didn't give me a chance. With a sigh, he said, "Let me see. There's fraud. All those nice pilgrims, Clutie." He clicked his tongue and shook his head, slow. "That's probably not worth more than three years. Though three years, in the prime of a young girl's life . . ."

He paused, a pained look on his face, like he was contemplating my misspent youth. I was about to open my mouth when he said, "Horse theft. Oh, that's a bad one. It would depend on the jury, of course, and you might escape the death penalty, but . . . Well, best not consider it. Then there are the five double-eagles you stole from me."

My face went hot, just like that.

"That's a good long stretch in prison out here, you know," he continued, like he hadn't noticed. "And let us not forget your husband—Spider, wasn't it? So colorful. I'm afraid you would not be able to escape the hangman's noose in that case. I would be saddened, should I have to surrender you to the authorities."

There we were, faced off like two bucks during the rutting season. I would not have been surprised to see Prometheus lower his head and paw the ground.

I said, "You like Chigger John that much."

"I do," he said, just as Chigger came bounding up the walk. He stood up and gathered his valise and softly added,

"Let's not speak of it again," before he greeted Chigger with
a big "Halloo!" and set off up the street, me in his wake.

An hour later I had a new dress and a smile on my face, and
we were in a stage headed south, toward Dodge. The smile
was partly because of the new dress Prometheus had bought
me.

"We can't have you going round dressed like a farm-
hand," he'd said, just like that little discussion on the street
hadn't happened, and let me pick one out. It was yellow, like
buttered sunshine, with little white flowers and genuine rick-
rack trim. It fit me to a T and made me feel, well, like a girl.

Girlish was exactly my mood at the moment, not just because of the dress, but on account of what I had seen while
Prometheus was buying the tickets. There, on the wall of the
stage line office, on a board thick with papers for scofflaws
and desperados, had been a poster for the Spanish Kid.

I could scarce believe it, and had to bite my lips tight and
pinch my arm to keep from letting out a yelp. It said he was
a dangerous *pistolero,* and was wanted for murder and arson
and grand larceny and theft, and the reward was thirty-five
hundred dollars.

I was proud to know him. All the Bug Boys' crimes paled
in comparison. He was no donk-drunk, big-talking, penny-
swiping braggart, but the real thing, a man the Bug Boys
would get down on their raggedy knees to.

That's what I was thinking while the stage bumped and
bounced south and the sun eased its way toward the horizon,
the way the Bug Boys would do when they came after me
and found Joaquin. I would have on my yellow dress, all
sunshine colored and showing my figure, and the Bug Boys
would ride in talking tough.

Then Joaquin would come out with his tan skin and his
long horse tail, and his white sleeves billowing in the breeze,
like a pirate in novel. "Who is this," he would say, "to
cause harm to my Chrysanthemum?"

And the Bug Boys would recognize him at once as a man
to be reckoned with, and take off their hats and call him

mister and me ma'am, and back all the way out of the yard and never bother us again.

At least, that was the latest version, the ones where Joaquin whipped them with his pistol or shot them having been discarded. After all, he wasn't wanted in Colorado. I planned to keep it that way.

I was just settling in to play the daydream over again in my head when Chigger, who had been dozing next to me, said, "Clutie? Is we there?"

The stage was slowing, and Prometheus leaned out his window for a second. "It's not time to change teams. I . . ." Then his head came in and he stoppered his bottle with the heel of his hand. "Good Lord," he said, looking at me with something akin to horror. Or maybe it was befuddlement: he was so drunk it was hard to tell in the fading light. "Twice now, twice! What do you do to bring it upon you?"

Before I could ask what he meant, the stage came to a rackety halt and a man flung open the door. "Ever'body out," he said, his voice all gruff and muffled behind a kerchief. "This here's whatchacall a stickup."

nineteen

Chigger opened his mouth but I clamped a hand over it. "Just hush and do what they say."

Prometheus got out first, and you would not have known that he had been drinking at all but for that little stumble he made getting off the coach. Chigger and me picked him up, and while he was brushing the dirt off his knees, I'll be dad-gummed if one of the bandits didn't haul off and knock him back down with the butt of his rifle.

I cried, "You've got no call to do that!" and jumped on his shoulder and commenced to beat on him. It was a stupid thing to do, but I did not think twice about it: when you have been raised up in a family what robs for a living, I guess you are less-than-average scared of scofflaws.

"Hey there, wildcat!" cried a second bandit and pulled me off the first. He had me tight and I couldn't move. "By God, Yancy, I think she's trying to murder you!" He was laughing.

"Shut up!" The first man—he was older—felt his ear. His hand came away bloody. At least it looked like it. It was sunset, and we were on the shadow side of the coach. "Dammy!" he said. He began to climb up on the stage. "Just hold 'er there."

A third voice came from up by the horses: a third man. He was mounted and kind of skinny, and had a shotgun leveled at the driver. He was holding the other horses, too. He said, "Will you two shut up an' get on with it?" then wiggled his greener at the driver. The driver had his hands in the air. He looked plenty scared.

Chigger was bent over Prometheus, and he was wailing.

"Mr. Hyphen, don't be dead! Oh, Clutie, he ain't a-movin'!"

"You better not have killed him," I said to the one who had me, for even though he was not the one who had struck Prometheus down, I figured that he was guilty by association. Besides, he was closer. "You just better not. We have already been held up once on the train and once in Kansas City. Counting you boys, that makes three times in one state, and we are not all the way across it yet. That does not say much for Kansas."

He let go of me and pushed me out in front of him so that I was a rifle's length away. He was a middling-sized man, not nearly so old as the one who had laid Prometheus low. "You are makin' me tired. Turn out your pockets." He saw I had no pockets, being in a dress and all, and pointed to Prometheus. "Well then, turn out his." He had stopped laughing. I couldn't see his face on account of the kerchief, but there was a smirk in his eyes. It was getting on my nerves.

"Not as tired as you're making me," I said. I showed him Prometheus's pockets were empty. He did not even have his wallet on him, which I thought was strange, but I thought better than to remark on it.

"I said we have already been robbed twice before in Kansas. This wouldn't happen in Missouri. I'll have you know I am a personal friend of Mr. Frank James, and he would never strike down an unarmed man or rob a female."

"Oh. A personal friend of Frank James," he said. I could tell he didn't believe me. "That's different. Ain't that different, Yancy?"

His friend had climbed up on top of the stage, the sun at his back, and was busy tossing down our bags and the other freight. "Shut up. And quit saying my name out!"

Prometheus has started to come round, and Chigger was so preoccupied with him that he had about forgot that I was there. For some reason that made me even madder.

I turned back to the second man. "Frank James gave me two hundred and thirty-four dollars to travel out of Larkin County, Missouri, and I would have it still, if it hadn't been stole in Kansas City by my aunts who went to be whores in Chicago. Furthermore—''

''What the hell kind of rig has that young'un got on?''

He had not been paying the slightest bit of attention to me. He was staring at Chigger, who had Prometheus sitting up by then. Prometheus was moaning soft and holding his head in his arms.

''Got it!'' cried the first bandit, from up on top of the coach.

''About dang time,'' said the third man. I guess his arms were tired from holding the shotgun on the driver because it had drooped some since the last time I looked. He saw me looking and brought it level again. ''Hurry up!''

''Is that lace on that collar?'' said the one tormenting me. ''Well, ain't you a daisy! White stockin's and all!''

I stepped toward him, but he brought up that rifle quick. ''Easy, sister.'' He was still laughing.

''If the Spanish Kid was here you wouldn't laugh!''

Just then there was a loud crash. I jumped and so did the man with the rifle, and I think he would have shot me out of sheer startlement if the geezer on top of the coach hadn't hollered, ''Sure beats shootin' 'er open!''

He was talking about the box, which he had just thrown down from the rack on top of the stage. It had landed on a rock and busted, and was slowly giving up U.S. currency to the soft breeze.

The second man looked away from me long enough to say, ''Dang it, Yancy, you beat everything! How we gonna carry it now?''

The one called Yancy climbed down cussing. ''How many times I gotta tell you not to say my name out, Booker? Booker, Booker, Booker! How's it feel?''

''Shut up, both of you!'' cried the mounted man. ''By Christ, this is the last time I pull a job with either'a you! Yancy, find something to square that cash away in.''

Prometheus had regained part of his senses by then. Kind of weak, and to the one called Booker, he said, ''Do you intend . . . That is . . . please do not harm this girl or this child.'' He had his arm around Chigger.

I said, "He's not going to hurt anyone."

"Oh yeah? Why not?" He reached out and jabbed me with the rifle. "Frank James gonna save you?" He was smirking again, at least I think he was. "Frank?" he called out into the dusk. "Frank James! Yoo hoo! You out there, Frankie boy?"

There was no answer—nobody expected one, although I admit I was secretly hoping. From the shadows of the coach, Prometheus said soft, "Clutie, come here."

I paid him no mind. I said, "You are not going to hurt us, because the Spanish Kid will find out. He will track you down and see you die like a dog. He is a friend of mine, a special friend, so if you know what's best for you, you'll take your cash and leave us be."

Booker looked at me and I looked at him, and he was just about to speak when Yancy said, "Lookee here!"

I turned to see him on his knees, the contents of my quilt bag strewed on the ground, the bag itself stuffed with cash, and my deerskin quilt across his lap. He stood up and folded it across his arm, lucky buckeyes falling right and left. "Say, this is fine. I believe I'll have this, too."

I hollered, "You put that down!"

Booker poked me in the middle with his rifle. "Shut up."

I heard Prometheus say, "Clutie, please, I beg you!"

The bandit on the horse said, "Jesus *Christ*, will you hurry up?"

Yancy was on his horse with the money and my quilt. "C'mon, Booker."

Booker stood there for a second, then took a fast step forward and grabbed me by my elbow. He flung me down in the dirt. Chigger screamed. I landed against the wheel spokes just as I heard Prometheus, late as usual, roar, "Unhand her, you scoundrel!"

He charged.

Now, I have seen some darn fool things in my life, but that one had to take the cake. Booker thought so, too, because he turned the butt of his rifle around so that Prometheus ran smack into it and knocked himself out. As

Prometheus dropped, Booker looked down at me. "You're all crazy, you know that?"

Chigger was scurrying first to Prometheus, then to me, then back to Prometheus again, and he was wailing, "Don't you hurt my Mr. Hyphen! Don't you hurt my Clutie!"

Booker went over and got on his horse, then rode him the fifteen feet to where I was sprawled on the ground: rode him so close that his hooves ground my yellow skirts into the dirt. Then he bent down, right in my face, and said, "The Spanish Kid ain't gonna help you, missy."

I said, "Yes, he will!" and I was crying then, couldn't help it. "He'll hear what you did and make you sorry!"

He said, "Maybe you know him, maybe you don't. But you're just one in the crowd, darlin'. He's got a hundred girls, got a señorita in every town. So don't go thinkin' you're special."

The third man said, "Booker! We're leavin' without you."

Booker wheeled his horse, ripping my hem, and Chigger ran from Prometheus to me. Prometheus was coming round again, but he was confused on account of taking two thumps to the head on top of being so drunk, and he staggered to his feet, saying, "Ruffians! Blackguards!"

Booker said, "Jesus. If there's one thing I hate, it's a fancy man with no money," and shot him.

"Help me get him lifted."

The driver picked up his feet—I had his head—and together we managed to get Prometheus inside, which is no easy feat when you consider how narrow the door on a stagecoach is. Also when you consider that all the driver had done since the holdup men galloped off into the dusk was talk about his arms.

"I ain't a-teasin', I has about had it," he said. "I am goin' to tell those boys to stop puttin' payrolls on this stage. They has somebody in the office, that's all I can figure, somebody to tell 'em which coach it's on. Four holdups in as many months, and now on the night stage, and it's always 'Hands up!' My arms're old and creaky enough. I ain't a-gonna shoot 'em. Let 'em take their money, no skin off my nose. But can't it be 'Hands down!' just once?''

He had full enough use of them so far as I could see—the coach rocked with every bag and bundle he put back up there—but frankly I was too busy to care. Chigger, sniffling, held the lantern for me as I eased away Prometheus's coat and cut away his shirt. The wound was not terrible—although no wound is good—and after I hollered at the driver to stop rocking the stage for five minutes, I started to dig for the bullet with Chigger's pocketknife.

Prometheus was passed out. Whether this was from the pain or the drink I didn't know, but I was glad because that bullet was a devil. I was probing deeper and deeper with Chigger's pocketknife, biting at my lips and praying he wouldn't wake, when Chigger said, ''Clutie?''

''Hold the lantern still. I can't see when you wobble.''

''But Clutie . . .''

I looked up. ''What!''

He held Prometheus's coat in his free hand.

''What?''

He wiggled his fingers. Two of them. Sticking through the shoulder of Prometheus's coat like two white horns. ''Don't it look like a billy goat, Clutie?'' He started making billy goat bleats and swinging the coat around.

''Oh, Chigger!'' I heaved Prometheus over on his side, and sure enough, there was the wound the bullet had made on its exit. Chigger was still bleating like a goat, and after I got him hushed and made sure no bones were hit, I stopped the bleeding as best I could and started bandaging.

''How long ago did you find those holes in his coat?'' I said, Prometheus's sleeve in my teeth. I was ripping it up into bandages.

''Huh?'' said Chigger, staring out the window into the night. It was all the way dark by then.

''Never mind.'' I tied the bandage off. ''Help me fix him more comfortable.'' To the driver I yelled, ''You can go ahead and finish loading now.''

There was the sound of him getting up and grinding out a cigarette and grumbling, ''Hands up, load the coach, don't load the coach . . ." Then, "What you want I should do with all this stuff that feller dumped out on the ground?"

Prometheus got bandaged better at the next stage stop and was conscious for the doctor by the time we got to Dodge, which was in the middle of the night. Prometheus manifested enough money to pay for his services, plus extra for the inconvenience, and we left the doctor's house. I couldn't figure out where he had got his wallet from, but I knew better than to ask him.

We walked down deserted streets to the hotel. There was plenty of moon left, but dawn would be upon us soon. Prometheus woke up the proprietor and got us two rooms, but when Chigger made to come in with me, I stopped him.

"You stay with Prometheus tonight. In case he needs anything."

"OK."

Prometheus, looking white-faced and weary, didn't argue.

I struck a match and lit my lamp, locked the door behind me, and tossed my traveling poke, rattly with buckeyes from the long-gone quilt sack, on the bed. Then I sat right down on the mattress next to it and commenced to cry like my heart would break. I had held it in for so long, it was like a torrent. I don't know how long I had been at it when there came a knock on the door.

I said, "G-go away."

The knock came again. Through the door came, "Clutie, it is not wise to keep a man in my condition standing for too long."

I wiped at my face and blew my nose, and unlocked the door. "You should be in bed."

Prometheus smiled. "Not until you tell me what the trouble is." He sat down on the bed and patted the place next to him, and when I sat down he put his arm around me and said, "Now, what's all this, then?"

I don't know what came over me. Maybe it was that I was shy on comfort, maybe I was feeling overly sorry for myself. Whatever the reason, I broke down and wept even harder, and I told him about the Spanish Kid and how we had spent

our time on the prairie. I told him about the Indians and that
man and how we had ridden away, and how Joaquin had
given me his watch and taken a lock of my hair and my
buckeye and promised to find me. And then how that bandit
had said he had a señorita in every town.

I told him I had been jealous of Chigger and him when I
should have been grateful for somebody to take the load off
me, somebody to be Chigger's friend.

And I confessed about the five double-eagles I had swiped
off him while he was passed out, and how I had sewn it in
the hems of my pants. Well, he already knew about that, but
I felt better to say it out.

"I've still got it, I haven't touched a cent," I said, and
made a move to get it.

But he said, "Keep it. I won't miss the money, and it
might serve you well someday."

That set me off again. I tell you, back home in the Holler
I had always tried my best not to cry over things like hurt
feeling and beatings. But something about Prometheus sitting
there, with his arm round my shoulders and expecting me to
let go, well, it sort of made it all right. I think I cried as
much that night as I had in my whole life put together.

"And another thing," I sniffed, once I was capable of
speaking again. "Those men took my quilt."

I think Prometheus chuckled, although I cannot be sure, I
was weeping so hard. He still had his good arm around me,
and he gave me a squeeze. "There, there. Cry it all out, my
dear."

I did.

When I was run dry and had used up all of Prometheus's
handkerchief as well as my own and the best part of a pil-
lowcase, he wiped the last of my tears away. "All finished
now?"

I nodded.

"Clutie, I am sorry about your Joaquin. But you'll always
have those days to remember, won't you? That's more than
most people have, a good deal more."

I sniffed. "Yes." I felt a whole new wave of tears coming
on, but I dammed it up.

"Indeed it is. Most people wander through their lives with a vague feeling that something is missing, never knowing what it is. But you found it, didn't you? You'll always have that. I had my suspicions. You came back a little too well rested. And a little too chipper."

He squeezed me again and smiled. I tried to smile back at him, though I don't know how well I succeeded.

He said, "I'd like to offer you a proposition, Clutie."

I rolled my eyes, and he laughed, then had to grab his shoulder. "No, not that kind. Bloody hell, but my shoulder smarts! I don't suppose you'd have a drop of whiskey anywhere about, would you?"

"No, sorry." I *was* sorry, too—Prometheus was being real nice to me, and I knew that shoulder must hurt like a hot poker.

"Never mind that. I'll make it until the saloon opens. About this proposition. Not far from the end of the railroad is a little town called Goose Butte. It's where I live, when I am not . . . Well, it's where I live. I have taken a liking to you and Chigger, Clutie. More than a liking. I should rather say that I—"

He stopped and I thought his arm was paining him, but he was just staring into space. Then he shook himself out of it and said, "Anyway, would you do me the great honor . . . the great favor of . . . of . . ." He took a deep breath. "Of being my . . ." He looked like he had something on the tip of his tongue that was fighting him. Then "Will you be my housekeeper?" popped out, all in a rush.

I opened my mouth to say *Sure thing,* but I didn't get a chance, because he raced in real quick and said, "Of course, Chigger stays, too. Wouldn't do otherwise. I'll get him a pony. He'd like that, don't you think? And we could talk about books. I have many books, a library full of books, and I could teach you to play chess, and . . ."

He stopped, like he had said too much, and shifted his gaze to the floor. "Of course, if you are intent on going on to California, I'll understand."

Well, he was lucid for a change, anyway. I said, "Are there any Indians where you live? I mean, wild ones?" I was thinking about all that whooping, and the mortal fear on that man's face.

He looked up, kind of startled. "No. Certainly not. Well, not in town."

I figured to be on a roll. I said, "Where are you getting all this money? I mean I know you've got a mole on your neck and all—"

"A mole? What's that got to do with it?"

For somebody so smart, he sure could be ignorant. I said, " 'Moie on the neck, money by the peck.' Where'd you get yours?"

Serious as a judge, he said, "I have a trust."

I didn't know what that was, but it sounded important. I said, "How old are you?" It didn't matter, but since he was answering questions so handy, thought it a good time to ask.

"Thirty-six," he said.

I had figured he was older. I supposed it was the drink, making him seem haggard. As long as we were being so forthright, I said, "Prometheus, that night when I lifted your gold, I went through your wallet, too. There were some papers in it. Telegrams."

His gaze didn't waver. Maybe the pain was helping him think clearer. He said, "Yes, of course. Of course you would have seen them." He pulled himself up a little straighter and grimaced. "Fitzpugh's little missives. Actually . . . Oh, damnation. It's, well, it's a family curse."

Well, he had my attention. "A curse?"

"*The* family curse, I should say. One's enough." He looked a little uncomfortable. I thought I had asked too much and that he was going to leave, because he stood up and faced me, but instead he said, "We may as well get this over with. First things first."

He bowed deep, touching the bed for balance.

"I am Prometheus Gawain Burke-Jones, Earl of Dorsey. At your service. What with the Busby triplets, I skipped viscount entirely."

He bowed again, slightly this time, and it seemed to throw him off kilter worse that the big one, so he sat down again.

"All my titles have been bequeathed to me by my late

relatives," he continued. "It's quite confusing even to me, and frankly, I have no wish to understand it. I wasn't a baron. No, that title went to someone else, thank God. I was perfectly content with barnonet. I was a baronet for some years, through nine Burke-Joneses."

I just stared at him. His head wounds had affected him worse that I thought. Maybe it was the liquor twisting his brain.

It must have showed on my face, because he said, "No, I assure you, I'm quite sane. Father—he was British—died when I was young, and Mother brought me to her home in America. I have never been back. Strange things happen to the men in our family."

"Strange things?" I figured to humor him.

"You asked about the telegrams? The story has it," he said, "that the curse was laid on by a French gypsy during the Napoleonic Wars. Caught pilfering and sentenced to the firing squad. They say she cursed the captain of the squad and all his male descendants. That was Great-grandfather Demetrius. Lord Demetrius. He was a tad dotty, and had run off to war on a lark. Unfortunately, he was forty-four years old and already had a great many children, some of whom already had children of their own. Demetrius survived the war long enough to inherit the dukedom, but he was run over by a cabbage wagon soon thereafter."

I was pretty interested by now, for true or not, it was a real fascinating story. I said, "You should write this down. This beats *Ivanhoe* all to pieces!"

"No, it doesn't." All of a sudden, he looked real tired. "The point is, we started dropping like flies thereafter, and there are only three males of Burke-Jones lineage left alive. The Marquess of Wembly—"

"Marquess? That sounds like a woman."

"I assure you, my cousin Zeus is very much a man. Where was I? Oh yes. The Duke of Pemwell. And me. It was the death of the Busby triplets—they even changed their name, to no avail—that set me . . . Well, I drank. More than usual. I'm sure you understand the shock of it—three at once! And

I ended up in Kansas City with those aunts of yours, God help me.''

He took a breath and said, ''I am going to die, Clutie, sooner if not later.''

Well, I had not been expecting that. I started to tell him that he was crazy, then thought better of it.

''Everybody dies'' was the best I could come up with, and then I tried to save it. ''You're young yet. Well, sort of young. I mean, thirty-six isn't too old.'' Then I grabbed my poke, stuck in my arm, and pulled out a buckeye. ''Take this,'' I said.

He took it and rolled it in his fingers, studying it. ''And what, may I ask, is this?''

''It's a lucky buckeye. From back home. You carry that in your pocket, and no harm can come to you.''

He smiled a little, and tucked the buckeye into his vest pocket. ''Thank you, Clutie. I shall carry it always. But you haven't answered my question.''

I studied his face. It wouldn't be so bad, working for him. I liked him, even if he was crazier than a stump-tailed cow in fly season. Earl of Whatsis, my foot.

But California could wait.

I said, ''I'll keep your house, Prometheus. But don't you go buying Chigger a pony.''

''A dog, then?''

''Maybe a dog.''

The next day Prometheus was in bad shape. The doctor came to the hotel and administered laudanum. This gave him some ease, although he was fit to be tied when he found out he couldn't chase it down with whiskey.

The sheriff came up and asked us questions about the robbery. I told him what I knew, and said I entrusted him to retrieve my quilt for me. I further gave him instructions to send it to the town of Goose Butte in Colorado Territory when it was found, care of Mr. Prometheus Burke-Jones.

It was nice, having a destination and a place to call home, even if I'd never seen it. When he asked my name and I told him, he said, ''Jukes? Seems to me I've heard that before.''

I crossed my fingers behind my back and told him there were tons of Jukeses back home. Might be a few of them had wandered west. He studied my face for a spell, then said he supposed so. He eyed Chigger—who was sitting in the corner shooting marbles, and who had refused to take off that stupid velvet outfit, even to have it washed—and said, "Takes all kinds" and left.

By the next day Prometheus was well enough to travel, but we did not leave. He hired a private car for us which had to be brought in from some other town down the line, and so we whiled away the time in Dodge.

It was a pretty nice town, although rough and small and just getting under way. It wasn't so tiny that Chigger didn't spot a man he swore was Uncle Beetle.

He turned out to be the mortician.

The Pullman arrived the next afternoon, and we all trained west in the lap of luxury, even if we could not get an express and had to put up with stops in every backwater town in Kansas. The landscape rolling past the windows got less green and more bleak. And it was none too green or cheery to begin with. It looked so poor and infertile that two red-headed women couldn't have raised a ruckus on it.

As for me, I was still feeling bad about Joaquin, still crying for him in the night.

Early the next morning we gained the end of the railroad, which was in Las Animas. I had not realized it was so near. If we had taken an express train we probably would have made it in four or five hours.

"Welcome to Colorado!" Prometheus exclaimed as we climbed off the train. He had given up laudanum in exchange for scotch, and was feeling expansive. I was just happy to be rid of Kansas.

Chigger took off down the track, shouting, "Where's our house! Where's my dog, Clutie?"

While I corralled him and explained—for the fifteenth time—that we weren't there yet, Prometheus had already got us tickets for the stage and they were loading our bags.

"Don't you ever take time to breathe?" I said as he hurried me along.

"Not today," he said happily, and gave me a hand up into the coach. "Tallyho, Chigger!"

Across from me, Chigger echoed, "Tallyho! Tallyho!" as the stage pulled out of Las Animas, headed for Goose Butte.

twenty

There were no buttes at all near Goose Butte. Prometheus said that one of the first fellas there had had the dysentery. He always joked that he was loose as a goose, and the other boys started calling him Old Goose Butt. It turned out he had the sugar diabetes something terrible and died, and they named the town Goose Butt in his honor, since nobody remembered his true moniker. When the first ladies came out, they pitched a fit about living in a town with a profane name, so after due consideration—and a few nights of sleeping in the front room—the town fathers tacked on the E.

Goose Butte had been a dusty ranching and farming town, then a serious gold mining town, and now it was back to ranching again, the gold having run out. Where they had found it—the gold, I mean—was in a series of vugs.

Now, as Prometheus explained it, a vug is like a geode: you know, one of those rocks where if you break it open with a hammer, it's hollow and lined with crystals, like a secret fairy world. Well, a vug is like that, only big. Sometimes more than thirty feet long and forty feet high, big enough to stand up and jump up and run around in—big enough to ride a horse in—and all lined solid with gold crystals and gold flakes, and the floors chockablock with pure gold boulders, no fooling.

When gold is found like that it mines out rich—sometimes upwards of two million dollars, U.S.—but it mines out fast.

The town got transformed. I do not mean to say it had any sort of patch on Kansas City, but it had gone from ten or twelve structures to over two hundred, practically overnight.

There had not been much time for planning, so the buildings were pretty much a hodgepodge, from Spanish to clapboard to Queen Anne to adobe hut, surrounded by terrain so unable to sustain anything more than scrubby bushes that they had to freight in the lumber.

Anyway, just as the last nail was pounded in and the last abode brick set into place, the gold ran out. At least, that was what Prometheus said. The last vug was scraped clean, leaving not a single flake or nugget, and people packed up their silver tea sets and lace curtains and cherrywood breakfronts and were just about to move on to the next boomtown, when word filtered down that the railroad was coming.

Some people left, of course, the railroad being nothing compared to the glory of bright metal, but others stayed on. I saw several empty storefronts on the way from where the stage dumped us out, and there was a ''For Sale'' sign on about every third house. The streets seemed empty, although there was a spanking new depot, half-finished, and men working on it.

Prometheus's house was about the fanciest one on a street of fancy houses, about half of which were for sale and empty, their shutters banging. Although we had people living in the houses next to us, an adobe and a frame house across the street were vacant.

Most of the places had big lots, and Prometheus's was no exception. There were three acres, most of it behind, and it sat up from a rocky, shallow stream called Dollar Creek, which marked the edge of town. The yard was in grass and prickly pear and, out back, several big old mesquite trees, all dark-trunked and gnarly and twisted.

Anyway, Prometheus's house was not an adobe but was made of wood, three stories of it, with a wraparound porch and geegaws and two turrets and, just like he promised, a library crammed full of books. I was kind of shocked that Prometheus thought one person could take care of it all, and somewhat daunted by the prospect. Also, it was in a sorry state of disrepair, a fact upon which I remarked as we pulled Chigger up through the staircase after a riser caved in.

"I've been meaning to fix that," said Prometheus, scratching his chin.

"Again, Clutie, again!" cried Chigger, even as I was picking the rotted wood chips out of his hair.

About the first thing I did was to take two buckeyes from my bag and snug one up in a corner of the front porch, and another on the back stoop.

Now, don't go thinking that I was superstitious. I'd step right on a crack and never think twice, and cut my fingernails of a Sunday, and nothing bad has ever happened to me for it. When I spilled the salt, I didn't pitch it over my shoulder or douse it with water. I didn't go round stringing up lucky buttons, and I wasn't afraid to sing in the outhouse or step in somebody else's footprint in the mud, or to throw a hat right on the bed.

No, that kind of foolishness never cut any truck with me. Although I did spell-charm the place right off:

> "Douse the mouse,
> Souse the louse,
> Christ in Heaven,
> Bless this house."

I said it at all four corners of each floor, with a spit and a slap thrown in.

It's just better to be safe than sorry, where buckeyes and charms sayings are concerned.

Coming from a one-room cabin, I thought Prometheus's place was like out of a book. I had my very own private room for sleeping, about as big as our whole house back home, with two big windows and a four-poster bed with these blue curtains hanging down at the corners, all fancy. I had never had a bed before, outside of rented ones in hotels, and it was like sleeping on clouds.

Chigger had his own room, too, which Prometheus soon filled with hobbyhorses and play soldiers, and a wooden train that went round and round on a track if you gave it a good enough shove. Sleeping by his lonesome made Chigger nervous at first, and he would come into my room of a night and camp on the floor. That stopped after about a week, though.

In the attic was a trapdoor that took you out on the roof, and from there you could about see the whole of the world. To the south were far-off mesas, hazy yellow and soft blue with green. Back the way we came was flat to the end, all dusty brown plains with hardly a bump. Low on the western horizon were the mountains, all blue-purple and misty. Sometimes I'd go up there and sit and stare at those mountains, and try to imagine the other side. California.

For the next few weeks I lost myself in that house, and in work. I was a slave to its majesty. I dusted myself to sneezing fits, washed my hands red, and waxed and polished and painted. I oversaw a carpenter and a chimney sweep, and had a man come in to teach me how to put up wallpaper.

It was not exactly that Prometheus was untidy. He was a real stickler about his personal appearance. He wore tailored suits that came all the way from Boston and New York, he was always shaved real precise, and his blond hair was always clean and tidy and pulled back at the nape. It was just that, well, the house sort of escaped his attention.

Sometimes I would look out the window and see Prometheus down by the creek leading Chigger on the fat pinto pony he had bought for him. It didn't take more than two days for him to break his word, but I guess I didn't mind so much when I saw how happy it made Chigger.

And he loved that pony. He brushed it until it was so glossy that its coat was like a mirror and we had to stop him, lest he brush it bloody. He named it Chub, and was content to let Prometheus see to the feed. We had padlocked it away after I put Prometheus wise to the story of Johnnycake and his untimely demise.

After Chigger heard the story of the vugs—well, after he made Prometheus tell it eight or ten times—he decided to be a miner, and when he was not brushing his pony, he tunneled.

At first he dug in the yard, but a yard full of holes and a

drunkard are a risky combination at best. After the third occasion of Prometheus nearly killing himself, I directed Chigger to dig in the cellar. Sometimes there was no stopping him once he had a thing in his head, and this was one of those times. It kept him out from underfoot, and it was pleasant to hear him singing as he worked away.

Prometheus had bought Chigger a slew of new clothes, too, and without telling them, I burned up that fancy velvet suit with the trash. Chigger didn't even miss it.

I don't mean to let on like Chigger was the only one to profit by knowing Prometheus—I had never imagined living in such elegant surroundings. Besides the furniture and books and a room of my own, there was pump water right in the kitchen and the backhouse was ten steps from the door. Even Agnes Ann Roebuck never had it so fine.

Chigger, when I could catch him, was teaching me how to cook. It shamed me that he could do it natural and that I couldn't, but Chigger had the patience of a saint, and before ten days I had made a roast that you could actually eat, once you cut the black parts off.

I had new clothes, too, a passel of them. Ready-made dresses in green and pink and blue and lavender, and more cloth for when I had time to sew. I tell you, I felt just about like a princess, like I had fallen into the lap of luxury.

The day I finished the house I had a big fire out back, and the last things I pitched in were my old work clothes, once I had taken the gold coins out of the hems. Boots and britches were Jukes Holler togs, and I had put Jukes Holler and everything that went with it far behind me. I got kind of choked up while they curled and turned black, but it was a good kind of choked up.

Now, this house had rooms with names, and they were named for what you did in them, mostly. There was a library for the books, and a dining room for eating your meals, and a parlor for when you had company. There was a morning room—for to sit in of a morning, I guess—and a cloakroom for cloaks, although that one was real little. Most all of them had been closed up, but I aired them out and dusted them up, and soon the house was full of light again.

I also found the gun room. There were cases on the wall filled with rifles, mostly presentation models, and they were pure-dee beauties. When I remarked to Prometheus that I had never seen the like, he told me to pick out one for my very own.

I chose a Winchester '73, and it was a handsome firearm indeed, all engraved special, and with a rear sight for extra accuracy. One afternoon, to have a vacation from cleaning, I took it out in the scrub to test it out. Prometheus came, too, Chigger tagging at his heels, and he was fair amazed at my marksmanship right up until he passed out.

All that time, the time I was getting the house back in order, I tried not to think about Joaquin, which meant that I thought about him most of the time. Sometimes I would miss him something terrible and I would cry, my tears dripping into the soap suds. Other times I would be mad at him—a señorita in every town!—and beat the rugs with extra fervor.

But mostly I missed him. I missed him something fierce.

"How come nobody ever comes to call?" It had just struck me. I set down my book—I was all tucked up in my new blue dress in one of those big leather chairs in the library— and peered at Prometheus over the lamp.

He rustled his newspaper, then set it down. It was one of the few evenings that he was sober enough after dark to sit and read with me.

"What are you reading?" he said, like I hadn't asked him a question.

I held up the cover. I had got sick of Dickens and Sir Walter Scott, and was taking a break with *Two Fisted Shooter: Buck O'Malley Rides Again*. It was pretty good.

I said, "How come nobody comes to visit? In books folks are always payin' a visit or swappin' each other's cards."

He said, "Where's Chigger?"

"Gone to bed after a good scrub. He was hog-dirty from digging up the cellar. I believe he has hit bedrock—at least, I hear a lot of banging. And you are getting me off the subject. You didn't answer my question."

He picked up his newspaper again and raised it up so I couldn't see his face.

"Prometheus!"

Real quiet, he said, "Because, my dear, I am the town drunk."

That didn't come as any news to me. I said, "And?"

He lowered the paper again.

"I'm the town drunk, don't you understand? That's one thing when a town is wild and wooly and growing and rich, and the gold is flowing. Everybody's drunk then, by God! But it's another thing entirely when things have settled down and the Women's Temperance League or the Christian Anti-Liquor Union or whatever it is has taken root, and a grown man has to sneak into the Handy Jack Saloon through the back door to have a shot of whiskey at three in the afternoon."

Well, that was about the most he had said to me in one chunk since we got there, what with him being either soused or with Chigger or both, and me busy settling the house or weeping over the Spanish Kid.

I said, "That's no skin off your nose. I don't see anybody stopping you from going in the front door of the Handy Jack. And what has the Women's Temperance Whatyamacallit got to do with you?"

He said, "That's just the point," and raised up his paper again.

I let that cryptic remark stand, for I could see that he was in a mood, and there would be no arguing with him.

Now, strange as it may seem, I had not left the house at all, up until that time. First, I had been sort of busy, and second, Prometheus had everything delivered. But the next day, for the first time, I went into town, and I saw what he meant.

I went with a shopping list—I had heard that's what ladies did, and I wanted to do it right. I had buttons and thread and penny candy for Chigger all written down on a proper list, and I had Miss Alvinetta Hanker's copy of *Ivanhoe*, too, trussed in brown paper and ready for mailing. I had finished it a long time ago—and I was mad on account of the hero ended up with the wrong gal—but I felt bad about keeping it for so long.

I was not halfway down the main street when, being pre-occupied with watching the toes of my new shoes peek out from under my skirts as I walked, I bumped into a woman and knocked her flat. She was shorter than me, although she was tallish, and corseted up tight—it was like running smack into a wall—with her dress all buttoned right up her throat and little spectacles on her nose.

"I sure am sorry, ma'am," I said as I picked her up and tried to dust her off. I say "tried" because she shoved my hands away like they were poison.

"Oh, bother!" she said, looking annoyed out of all pro-portion. "Botheration!" She had her hankie out and was making these little stabs at her dress with it, without much effect, and she had not straightened her spectacles.

I said, "I believe you'd have more luck if you'd—"

"You're that . . . that *creature,* aren't you?" A snake couldn't have spat it better than she did, and I was kind of startled.

"Creature?" I managed finally.

"Prometheus Burke-Jones's . . . strumpet." She fixed her spectacles on a long, thin nose and eyed me up and down. Then she said, "Trash!" and stuck her chin in the air and walked off, skirts still dusty and hat askew. About a half block up the street a tumbleweed blew into her, and she swatted at it with her purse for about a minute and a half before it let go and she got on her cranky old way again.

Well, I went from startled to shocked. Not about the tum-bleweed, but about how anybody could have known about the Jukeses clear out in Colorado, let alone that I was one. It got me depressed, and I guess I was still down in the dumps when I reached the post office—that being at the Butterfield office—because the man there looked at me funny, and said, "Anything wrong, miss?"

I handed him my package and I said, "No," and then I said, "Yes," and then I was afraid to say anything more lest he, too, know that I was a Jukes, and think low of me.

He took my parcel and weighed it and told me the fee, and while I counted out the coins, he said, "I see you met Miz Gensch."

"Beg pardon?"

He took my coins and put them in a drawer behind the counter. "I was out gettin' a breath of air. You ran into her down the way a piece?"

"Oh. I didn't know her name."

"Yup, Miz Little Dove Gensch 'bout runs this town. Don't look like you got off to a very good start. Course you could always remedy that by joinin' the C.W.T.S. That's the Christian Women's Temperance Society to you."

For a clerk, he was awful chatty, and he didn't look like he was going to run down anytime soon.

"I don't suppose you're the type, though," he went on. "You're that gal livin' up at His Highness's place, are you? Having some times up there, I'll bet." He wiggled his eyebrows real lewd, and I would have slugged him had not the counter been between us.

"What do you mean, His Highness?"

"Whatever he's callin' himself now." You could tell he thought he was real funny. "His Lordship. The Prince. Whatever."

"I'm the housekeeper, nothing more," I said, "And it's an earl. That's what he is, an earl." I didn't believe it for a second, but it seemed to me Prometheus's honor was in need of defense.

"Then I reckon we don't got to curtsy to you, being just the hired help."

"What?"

"Whatever you say, miss."

"That's Missus." I guess I was kind of huffy by that time. He had me all mixed up. "I am a widow."

"All the merrier, then," he said, still smirking, and then he looked past me and said, "Sendin' another parcel to your ma, Zeke?" I had not even realized there was a line. Well, one man.

My face burning, I went out and past the windows and leaned back against the building in a heap, only to see two ladies across the way point at me, then whisper behind their hands as if that made them invisible.

It wasn't fair. I had thought I looked real high tone, wearing a twelve-dollar dress and real shoes instead of boots, and my hair fixed nice in a knot on top of my head, but I guessed I was just plain doomed to Jukesness. It made me mad. It kind of made me want to cry, too.

From inside the door came the sound of men laughing loud, and I knew they were laughing at me. That made me even madder, but I had other errands to run, and a Jukes is tough, if nothing else. I stood up, rubbed my nose on my sleeve, squared my shoulders, and proceeded to Hoskins General Store.

The lady there was nicer than the man at the Butterfield, if you count nice as more polite. She was no friendlier that a baked carp, though: she sold me my buttons and thread and penny candy and then disappeared into the back of the store, which was all right with me because it gave me time to read the circular unfettered.

It was tacked up next to the door, and said in bold black letters:

CHRISTIAN WOMEN'S TEMPERANCE SOCIETY
Battle Evil Drink Shoulder to Shoulder
With Your Sisters!
Denounce the Demon Rum!
Meeting Thursday Night
At the Residence of Mrs. Gensch
(Covered Dish)

I heard a voice from behind me say, "I don't think *you'd* be interested in that." It was the clerk. She was standing in the curtained doorway, half in and half out.

Well, she was right, I wouldn't. But I said, "Why not?"

Her head gave a little jerk and she puffed out air as if to say *Oh, Law!* real disgusted. And then she jerked the curtains closed between us.

It seemed like the whole town was on Mrs. Gensch's side,

and I went home feeling pretty low, all right, with my head down, scurrying along the boardwalks.

When I got home, Chigger was busy tunneling in the cellar, as usual, and Prometheus was out to the carriage house, mucking out Chub's stall with a pint bottle in his hip pocket.

"Prometheus?"

He jumped a little. I guess he had been lost in thought. "Ah, Clutie!" he said, leaning on his pitchfork. Even for cleaning out stalls, he was dressed real natty. He had taken off his suitcoat, but there was a red brocade vest underneath, and he had not got one speck of grime on it.

He eyed my bag, and said, "You've been to town, I see. What do you think of our fair metropolis?"

I sat down on a hay bale. "Not much. There was a woman named Mrs. Little Dove Gensch who has a twist up her backside for anybody named Jukes. I didn't know word had got this far. And she doesn't care much for drinkers, either. She's having a big meeting at her house out to some place called Covered Dish on Thursday night for those of a like mind."

Prometheus stared at me for a minute, and then he said, "Oh!" and then he explained about the covered dish. I did not have too much time to feel stupid, though, for Prometheus launched into a stream of vitriol about the Christian Women's Temperance Society in general—and Mrs. Gensch in particular—that lasted some time and was a thing of beauty. Prometheus could orate up a storm when he was of a mind. In the end he had to sit down and mop his brow and loosen his collar and take another swig, that's how much steam he had worked up.

I said, "Well, that doesn't explain how she heard of the Jukeses. She looked me square in the eye and called me trash!"

Prometheus put his handkerchief away. "Oh, I dare say the Jukes name means nothing to her. She called you that because you're staying with me."

For a second there I felt like Chigger. "Huh?"

Prometheus stood up, grabbed the fork again, and turned away from me. "She thinks—Well, she thinks you're a . . ."

"What?"

Prometheus sighed. "Best leave it alone, my dear."

But after I thought about it for a while, I knew what he meant. She thought I was a whore.

I lay in bed awake for a long time that night, and not just because I had burnt the beef again. According to Prometheus, Little Dove Gensch was a force to be reckoned with. Single-handed, she had about got the whole town turned round to temperance thinking. Prometheus was well stocked against the possibility of Goose Butte going dry, having laid in case upon case of liquor. I was not so fortunate. I would have to stay sober and get called a whore.

That got me to thinking about back home, about Granny Wren and the Bug Boys, and I got a little homesick—not for them, curse their hides, but for the green of Jukes Holler, the everlasting deep and mossy green of it. Where we were, it was green, too, I supposed, but in a real pale way, kind of like God had just drawn a veil of color over the stunted trees and grass to fool a person into staying.

I thought about Joaquin, too, although I had vowed I wouldn't. I thought about his eyes and his mouth and the way his skin felt, and the way his voice sounded, all deep and exotic. I thought about the smell of him—musky and full of mystery and gun battles and wild chases. As much as I had tried to hate him, I couldn't. I could be mad, but I couldn't hate. I had made a sketch of him, just a little one of his face, and I slept with it under my pillow.

And I worried that my curse hadn't come. Six weeks between a woman's flowers can be normal when she's young, but I didn't think puking every morning was. Nobody knew of my dilemma, Chigger always being off to see his pony or tunnel to China or something, and Prometheus laying abed till all hours.

If I was with child, it was Joaquin's—though I figured if worse came to worst, I could probably palm it off as Spider's. I had not lain with him for months and months, but nobody knew that except me and Spider, and he was dead.

Then again, maybe I was just letting my imagination run

away with me. Maybe I just had a touch of the ague.

Or maybe Mrs. Little Dove Gensch was right about me.

Thursday night I wrestled Chigger into a bath.

"What are you doing to get so dirty, Chigger?" I asked as I washed behind his ears. He was solid dirt, and I was just beginning to find the pink of skin.

"I's gonna find me a vug, Clutie," he said real matter-of-fact. "I's gonna make you 'an Mr. Metheus rich. Vug, vug, vug," he added, and stuck his head under the water to repeat it, all full of bubbles.

Sometime during the last couple of days, Chigger had stopped calling Prometheus Mr. Hyphen. I was glad of it. Even though he was still a syllable short, it was a big improvement.

I hauled him up and I said, "Chigger John, Prometheus is already rich. And there aren't any more of those vug things. They found them all. Besides, I half suspect Prometheus made them up."

"Vug, vug, vug," he said, and started to stand up.

I sat him back down with a slosh. Giving Chigger John a bath was as good as taking one yourself. "Hold still!"

"Don't wanna hold still. Wanna go riding!"

"It's dark. Your old Chub pony is asleep." I stood up and wiped my hands on my apron, though what with the apron being soaked, it didn't improve them much. "I think I have about got all of you scrubbed that's fit to see. You finish up now, and call me when you're done."

I went out into the main part of the house, leaving Chigger to finish up in private in the kitchen. Prometheus was snoring away in the big leather chair in the library, probably from all the work it must have taken to get Chigger to call him Mr. Metheus, and I let him be. I stared out the window until Chigger called "Clutie! I's done and dry!" and all the time that I was combing his wet hair and putting him to bed, I was thinking about that meeting at Mrs. Gensch's house.

I determined to go. It was crazy, but sometimes you just have to do a thing. I waited for Chigger to go to sleep—that took all of two minutes—and changed into something dry and crept out the back door.

That afternoon, while he was spewing and spouting, Prometheus had described the Gensch house, and I recognized it, having passed it on my way into town. It wasn't as far as a rock throw by Jukes Holler standards, just a ways down the street and then over one block, and I got there in no time. I settled down in the bushes until the ladies had all gone inside. Then I crept up underneath a window. Actually, it kind of tickled me to do it. I kept thinking about Agnes Ann Roebuck, and wondering if Mrs. Gensch would give me a dress to keep quiet.

I peeked over the sill. I couldn't exactly hear what they were saying, on account of the window was closed—leave it to the Christian Women's Temperance Society to close down the windows when there are thirty ladies in the room and you know it has to be stuffy as all get out! I could see them real good, though.

And that's all I wanted to do, really, see them. I wanted to see what kind of ladies would call me a tramp and a slut, just for taking care of a poor old drunk. Well, I guess he wasn't so old, or so poor, but you know what I mean.

Anyway, there was Mrs. Little Dove Gensch holding court in her black dress, this one buttoned up just as tight as the one she'd been wearing when I knocked her flat on the sidewalk. She was skinny, and tinier than I remembered—I guess she looked more intimidating in the street. She was talking up a storm, gesturing wide with one arm while all the ladies nodded their heads. I caught a word or two now and again—"Sin!" and "the devil's tonic" and "vile corruption" and the like—when she'd get real excited. She could have been a fine preacher had she been fitted to it by sex.

And then somebody came over and opened the window, just a crack, and I decided she would not be such a good preacher after all. She was off liquor in general now, and talking about me in particular, about how I'd had the nerve to show my face in town on a public sidewalk when everybody knew what kind of woman I was.

"This common harlot!" she said, by way of underscoring,

and then asked everybody what they planned to do about me.

Now, I was pretty much flabbergasted. Not counting Mr. Foot, I had only been with one man without benefit of clergy—well, marrying cord—in my life, and he had been my own true love—even if I wasn't his—and I did not think that justified calling me names, or "doing" something about me.

I was just starting in on a spell to give her the dysentery— it starts out, *Beets through a baby, Grease through a sieve*— when hands grabbed me, covering my mouth.

I flailed out in all directions, sure it was Mr. Little Dove Gensch come to take me in and plop me in the middle of the room so his wife could point out the wages of sin in person. But then, over my struggles, I heard someone whisper, "*Querida!*"

I just went limp. I couldn't help it. He turned me round and kissed me, and I found my strength again and I kissed him back like I never kissed anybody before—and then I hauled off and slapped him across the face, just as hard as I could.

twenty-one

He put his hand to his cheek and whispered, "Ouch!
Chrysanthemum, what are you—" He stopped right
then to drag me into the bushes, for a crowd was
gathering at the windows.

I guess we did not dive soon enough, for Mrs. Gensch
looked me right square in my eyes and then gasped, her hand
to her mouth. And then, just like that, her eyebrows knotted
together in the middle and she pulled the shade.

Joaquin twisted me round to face him, my back having
been against his chest in the bushes, and said, "What is the
matter with you!" He was still rubbing at his face, at the red
marks from my fingers.

I started walking. I was afraid Mrs. Gensch would set the
dogs on us, if she had any. "You have got a lot of nerve,"
I said. "Riding in here like—How did you find me clear
down here?"

"First I have to find the town. I have to go to many, and
this is not easy. Then I have to find the house," he said,
catching me up and clamping a firm hand on my arm. "Then
some drunken old man—it takes the whole of ten minutes
for him to answer the door—he looks all over and doesn't
find you—and he is not in a very pleasant mood, *querida*—
then he sends me down here . . ."

"Don't you call Prometheus a drunk!" It was true, but it
was one thing for me to call him that and another for Joaquin
and the rest of the town.

He stopped, and stopped me with him. "If a thing is a
tortoise, you do not call it a jackrabbit. Where did you get
this dress?"

I turned my head and stuck my nose in the air—if I had looked at him I would have kissed him, and I was too mad for that.

When I didn't answer, he shook me a little, and when that didn't work, he took my face in his hand and turned my head. "Why are you so angry?"

"Because you've got a señorita in every town, that's why." I started to cry. I couldn't help it. "Because you've got a señorita in every town, and you're never going to come back for me!"

He cocked his head. "But, Chrysanthemum, I am here."

He had a point, but I was not going to be put off so easily. I said, "What about all those girls? He said if you had one you had a hundred. He said—"

"Who is he?" Joaquin broke in angrily. "Who is this man who spreads slander?"

"I don't know his name. He held us up on the coach between Ellsworth and Dodge." Then I thought better of it and said, "Booker. That was his name. And his friend, Yancy, stole my quilt, the one I told you about. It was deerskin, the only one like it. I thought . . . I thought you were never coming back." I was crying full tilt by that time. He dug a handkerchief out of somewhere and gave it to me as we walked past the houses, past wrought iron and white picket fences set into dust and gravel.

"Booker. Chrysanthemum, Jake Booker will not bother you again. Does this please you?"

I gave my nose one last good honk, then handed the handkerchief back. "What do you mean?"

"I mean, he is taken care of." He had that knowing look. "He will not bother you again."

I shook myself free and faced him. "You mean you shot him? Goldang it, Joaquin, this is Colorado! You can't just go round shooting people because they dance on Sunday!"

"*Qué?* You are talking crazy."

I started to say something, but he hushed me and tipped his head toward the Matheson's front porch, which we were passing at the time, and where the Mathesons were sitting out, taking in the air. I said, "Real pleasant evening, isn't it?"

Mr. Matheson had been the one to come over and teach me how to wallpaper, Prometheus having hired him, and he smiled and started to say a pleasantry. But through clenched teeth, his wife said, "Cornelius!" and he didn't, although he shrugged his shoulders apologetic.

We walked on a bit, until we were out of Mrs. Matheson's earshot, it being clear that she was in Mrs. Gensch's camp, and the whole time Joaquin kept a firm grip on my arm. If the truth be told, I was torturing so over his return that I was nigh on peach-orchard crazy. That hand on my arm was about to drive me out of my skin: it was all I could to not to pull him to the ground and do the deed right then and there. I had been arguing with him, but sometimes argument can be a funnel for passion.

I said, "Race you to the house!"

It wasn't very far by then and I beat him to the gate—being unencumbered by boots and spurs—whereupon he kissed me again.

"Chrysanthemum," he whispered into my hair, "you are a strange woman. I think you smoke the loco weed." He kissed my ear. "How do you come to be so beautiful?"

I eased open the gate. "I could listen to you talk all night."

He followed me in. "Tonight I do not plan to talk."

Slow, arm in arm, we went up the walk, then up the steps to the front door. I put my hand on the knob to open it, but Joaquin gathered me up into his arms again. "Ah, *querida*," he said.

I tell you what, I nigh on melted then and there. And I would have, too, if the door hadn't swung in. It was Prometheus, and he did not look one bit pleased.

"Young love," he said. "How quaint." And ushered us inside.

The Spanish Kid took off his hat and nodded a curt bow. "As you can see, señor, I have found her. I thank you for your assistance."

For somebody who had been passed out not one hour ear-

lier, Prometheus appeared wide awake. "My pleasure, sir."
He did not look like it was his pleasure at all. In fact, he
looked about two hairs away from slugging Joaquin in the
jaw or calling him out for a duel or something.

I said, "Prometheus, this is my friend Joaquin, who saved
me in the wasteland."

"I am aware of that," said Prometheus, frosty as could
be. "We must thank him properly."

Joaquin gripped my arm harder, stood up taller. "I assure
you, señor, there is no need."

Prometheus stared down his nose. "I think there is."

"No, no," said Joaquin through clenched teeth. "It was
my pleasure, entirely."

I swan, what with all the bravado in the room those two
had both gained a couple of inches, and I would have
laughed had not the situation been so perilous.

I shook Joaquin off my arm and stepped in between them.
"Honest-to-Jim! A person would think they were at the Den-
ver Mint cockfights for all the gold-plated strutting in here.
Prometheus, stand down."

He had the good sense to look embarrassed just a little bit,
which was enough for me, but Joaquin appeared like he
wanted to get his two cents in.

"We're retirin'. Aren't we?" I took Joaquin by the arm
and turned him toward the stairs. Well, I didn't exactly turn
him, but after a second he came along.

I looked back down the stairs when we reached the first
landing, and Prometheus was still standing there, glaring up
at me.

The next morning I was up and dressed before everybody
except Chigger, who I saw through the window when I came
down into the kitchen, and he was knee deep in Dollar Creek.
If he didn't look a picture down there—the sun sparkling
gold highlights in that setter-red hair and playing silver off
the water and the scrubby trees—I don't know what did.
Right then, Colorado looked pretty good to me. Satisfied that
I was done throwing up for the day, I hollered him in.

"Don't you know you aren't going to find a frog in

there?'' I asked after he skidded in the back door and plopped into a chair.

There were barely any fish in that creek, and I'd had to look long and hard for a minnow to put in Prometheus's whiskey. Now, this is a sure cure for drunkenness. You put it in the bottle and let it die—that is a sad part, but it's for the better good—and take it out, and when a person drinks any whiskey from that bottle, they are cured forever. I was just waiting for Prometheus to work his way round to that bottle.

"Weren't lookin' for no frogs," Chigger said, studying on a salt cellar. "I were dumpin' my diggin's." He twisted his head at the frying pan in my hand and grimaced. "You gonna cook, Clutie?"

I said, "I aim to try. Joaquin's back. The Spanish Kid? Do you remember him?"

He screwed up his face and set to pondering it.

"He was with Frank James. On the road back in Missouri. He rode me on his horse."

Chigger's face lit up. "I remembers! Your feet was hurtin' you terrible. You reckon he's got a candy for me?"

I ruffled his hair and he made a face. I said, "I don't know, Chigger. I'll ask him when he wakes up."

He pushed back his chair. "Well, I's going minin'." He threw back his shoulders with self-importance and marched out of the house, and a second later I heard the cellar doors bang open.

Well, it kept him out of trouble, but I was kind of disappointed. I had hoped for some help with the cooking. I persevered, though, and a half hour later I opened the bedroom door with my hip, tray balanced before me, and sat down on the edge of the bed.

"Joaquin?"

"Um?"

If he didn't look glorious! Half-tangled in white linens and his hair all fanned out on the pillows, the sun streaming in through the windows to paint him bronze on the tanned parts, and golden on the parts the sun never reached. I was real tempted to forget about breakfast entirely—for I found myself thinking how nice it had been to lie with him on a genuine bed instead of blanket-covered dirt—but just then he opened his eyes, scootched himself up, and yawned.

"What is this, Chrysanthemum?" He was looking at the tray. I had used Prometheus's best silver and china.

"Breakfast." I set the tray on his lap.

"Ah, good! I have an appetite this morning." He said it with a wink that set my insides all aflutter, and then he lifted the sterling top off the first dish. And then the second. And then the third.

He said, "*Querida,* this is very . . . nice. What is it supposed to be?"

"Eggs," I said. I guessed it was pretty burnt. It hadn't looked so awful bad in the kitchen. "With bacon and sausage and grits."

He just kept staring at the tray. "Which is the bacon?"

I snatched the tray up, and two of the lids fell back on the bed. "I never claimed I could cook." Tears were pushing at the backs of my eyes, but I willed them away. It seemed like everything of late made me want to cry, even that stupid breakfast. "Back home, I shot the game and somebody else cooked it. I never learnt. No, I take that back. I couldn't learn. I just don't have the Jukes knack."

I picked up the lids that had fallen and covered my eggs back up. Or maybe it was the grits. "I'll get Chigger to fix you something, I guess," I said and started to leave, but he took hold of my skirts.

"Chrysanthemum, I have a surprise for you." His sheet had fallen away, but it was like he didn't care. I have never in my life seen a man so unconcerned about being stark naked in the broad daylight, a quality which I do not share.

I couldn't help admiring it in him, though.

I said, "What surprise?"

"You will see." He kissed me, just a little peck on my cheek, and said, "Now, go and clean up the mess you have undoubtedly made, and I will be with you."

I went on down and did like he said, cursing myself the whole time for my lack of womanly skills and trying not to cry and knowing for pretty sure why I felt like that, but trying

not to think about it. I was convinced that I was about to
find pups, as Granny Wren used to say, but I was also fair
certain that nobody would want to hear about it, at least not
yet.

Joaquin came down about ten minutes later—he had
clothes on, for which I was relieved—and let me tell you,
he rolled up his sleeves and got busy as a tick in a tarpot,
no fooling. Chop, chop, chop went the cleaver, faster than
the eye could see, on tomatoes and peppers and onions. Eggs
were cracked one-handed and scrambled while bacon fried
and sausage sizzled. I just sat down and watched with my
mouth open, he put on such a show.

Not that there was any need for talk, for Joaquin sang the
whole time he cooked, and I'll be danged if he didn't have
a patch on Chigger for the sweetness of his voice, only his
was baritone. He had hummed while we danced under the
Kansas moon, but I had never suspected the full glory of it.
It kind of made my insides seize up, hearing him sing like
that. He sang in Spanish and in French and I didn't understand a word, but considering that for all I knew his songs
could have been full of murders and scalpings, it was just as
well.

He was about done and just dishing up the eggs—all full
of onion and peppers and tomatoes and mysterious things
he'd found in the pantry, and smelling past wonderful—
when Prometheus walked in, pulling up his suspenders.

Just like that, Joaquin stopped singing.

Prometheus stared at me, then he stared at Joaquin, then
he stared at the food. He looked at Joaquin again. "Was that
you? Were you singing?"

Joaquin said, "*Sí,*" and that was all, but there was an
unspoken "and what are you going to do about it?" in there.

Prometheus pointed at the eggs. "And am I to understand
that you are responsible for this?"

Joaquin's eyes narrowed, but as he had a plate in each
hand I didn't think there'd be any gunplay.

He said, "I am."

Prometheus put his hand on the back of a chair and stared
at Joaquin, real flat. I held my breath. Who knows what goes

through a man's mind? Then all of a sudden he pulled out the chair and sat down.

He said, "You can stay if you cook. Lord knows we need one. But stop wearing those Spanish spurs in the house or you'll ruin my floors. Pass the bacon."

The next day, we got a call from Mrs. Gensch. Well, sort of a call. And only sort of from Mrs. Gensch. Actually, what it was, was a rock thrown through the window with a note tied to it that read, "Limey drunkard go home and take your whore and the Mex with you."

I was kind of offended that they left off Chigger, but it was not a big rock.

Prometheus shrugged it off. I guess it had happened before. But Joaquin was madder than a scorched bear. "Who is this person?" he ranted. "Why does he not sign his name?" Then he'd spout a knock-you-down stream of Spanish cusswords that even had Prometheus blushing.

"How dare they call my Chrysanthemum a whore!" he said, once he got around to English again. "How dare they call me a Mexican! I was not born there, I did not live there until I was eight! Do not I look American to you? Do not I speak the English perfectly?"

I noticed he didn't have any argument with the "limey drunkard" part.

Prometheus ordered new glass for the window, and I hid Joaquin's pants to keep him from going into town and starting trouble. I guess normally a little thing like that wouldn't have stopped him. But for my sake, he stayed home, muttering in Spanish and pacing up and down in the library in his drawers.

Well, Prometheus's drawers, which I'd borrowed for him. He didn't own any.

That afternoon I decided to see to the rose garden. Prometheus had roses planted all along the front fence, but nothing had been done with them for a coon's age. I found some heavy gloves and went to work pruning and weeding, and I had worked the whole morning away and was about to go in and see if Joaquin had started lunch yet, when a shadow fell over me.

I looked up to find Mrs. Little Dove Gensch glowering at me from the outside the fence. There were three other ladies with her, all with the same disgusted expression on their faces. Mrs. Gensch was closest—close enough that I could have reached out and touched her had I'd wanted to, which I did not. But we had to live in the same town with her, so I swallowed my pride and determined to be nice.

I stood up and dusted my gloves off. "Morning, Mrs. Gensch. Ladies," I said, making myself smile. "We got your rock."

"This is a civilized town," she said, ignoring my stab at light conversation entirely while her three friends nodded. "All the other 'ladies' of your ilk have left."

That annoyed me, but I kept my tone level. I said, "I don't know what you mean. I am my own woman. I took a job as housekeeper here, and I intend to stay on and do my work, and keep my own business."

She studied my face for a minute, during which her expression didn't change one jot. "You keep your business with Mexicans and drunkards."

One of the women behind her muttered, "Yes."

"You keep your business under decent people's windows."

Another lady nodded and said, "Scandalous."

"We will not stand for that in Goose Butte," Mrs. Gensch finished up, and she looked at me like I was dirt on a stump.

Now, she was beginning to get me mad, but I clamped a lid on it. She would be sorry indeed if I let my Jukes side out.

Real calm, I said, "First off, that man is not a Mexican. He is Joaquin Gabriel Mondragon Delacroix." I pronounced each syllable with the utmost care. "He was born in the U-S-of-A. His daddy was French and a Jew, and his mama was Spanish. I think if you are going to call people names, you should at least call them the right ones."

I let her chew on that for a minute, and while she was thinking I added, "And you should be nicer to Prometheus.

I mean, Mr. Burke-Jones. He is a real fine man, civic minded and rich to boot. I think you could profit by currying his favor instead of harping on one tiny little flaw. For a drunkard, he is a good man.''

I thought on that a second, and added, ''I shouldn't have said that part about the drunkard. Even for a regular man, he's awful nice. And you should be ashamed, throwing rocks through people's windows.''

Well, the ladies were upset clear out of proportion, to my way of thinking. One had her gloved hands to her ears; another had turned bright red. The third one had turned red, too, with her mouth hanging open, and Mrs. Gensch looked about to explode.

She stammered and she huffed, as if she was too mad to get the words out straight, and then she said, ''Of all the nerve! Of all the unmitigated gall! How dare you—''

She stopped mid-sentence and stared past me, up at the porch, and her jaw dropped open. Her friends followed suit in rapid succession, each with mouth open or eyes popped.

I turned and followed their gaze, and I had to cover my mouth lest I laugh out loud. Joaquin had just stepped out the door.

''*Querida,* you have trouble?'' he said, staring at Mrs. Gensch, for the two of them had locked eyes. Joaquin didn't look away, I suppose because he was looking for an excuse to shoot her or something, and Mrs. Gensch and the ladies couldn't shift their gaze because Joaquin didn't have any pants on. They focused on his face out of sheer panic.

I said, ''No, it's all right. Mrs. Gensch just called me trash and got mad when I didn't agree with her. You can go on inside now.''

But he didn't. He said, ''Chrysanthemum, I think you had better come in the house.''

''In a minute.'' I was enjoying the look on the ladies' faces too much to leave now. They might as well have been turned into four pillars of salt, and over such a teensy thing as a man in his underdrawers. I felt sorry for their husbands.

''No, now,'' said Joaquin, real serious. ''Something has happened.''

I nodded my head to Mrs. Gensch, although she did not see me—being transfixed by horror or admiration, I couldn't tell—said, "You'll be excusing me," and went up the steps to join him.

I whispered, "Remind me to give you back your pants," as I looked over my shoulder to the street. Mrs. Gensch and company were already halfway up the block. I had never seen four ladies move so fast without breaking down and running.

"Pants?" said Joaquin, as if he had just remembered, and was shocked at me for being so petty at a time like this, whatever "this" was. "Come quickly."

He fair dragged me to the back of the house, to the kitchen, where Chigger sat at the table, legs swinging.

"Clutie!" he said around a mouthful of jawbreaker, "Mr. Kid give me a candy!"

I said, "That's fine, Chigger John." And then, to Joaquin, who was hopping boot to boot, and Prometheus, who had his hands clasped before him and was wringing them, I said, "What's so important?"

To Chigger, Prometheus said, "Oh dear. Oh dear, oh dear. Show her, son. You lovely boy!"

Chigger rolled that jawbreaker around in his mouth a minute, and then pushed it halfway out with his tongue to let me see.

"Chigger!" It was Joaquin this time. "Show Chrysanthemum what you have found!"

The jawbreaker rolled back in. "Chrysan . . . Chrysan . . . ?"

"*Clutie!*" both men cried in unison.

"Oh. OK." He shifted to dig in his pocket. His hand came out clenched around something.

I whispered, "This better not be a dead frog," and Prometheus shushed me.

Chigger held forward his fist, then sprang it open. It was a perfect nugget of gold, as big as his palm.

He smiled wide. "Vug, vug, vug!"

twenty-two

Two days later the news of the strike was in the papers, but by then half the neighborhood was dug up. It seemed that Mrs. Crandall, next door to the east, had been spying on us with her husband's old Army binoculars on behalf of Mrs. Gensch. When she saw all four of us trundle out of the house and into the cellar, sober as judges, then emerge whooping and hollering and shouting jubilation to the Lord and covered in gold dust, she dropped those binoculars and grabbed her husband's pickaxe and commenced to tunnel.

All over the neighborhood the dirt piles grew slapdash, till they were thicker than warts on a pickle. They tunneled in the fronts, they tunneled in the backs, they tunneled underneath the houses. Four lots down, the Dietrichs dug under their foundation and caved in the south wing. Over on Ash Street, the Winklemans pickaxed their way straight into the shaft under their outhouse, and they said that Mrs. Winkleman was doing nothing but laundry for the next two days.

We all thought it curious that Chigger had made no such mound—after all, his tunnel was twenty feet long if it was an inch. It turned out that he had deposited every last bit of his diggings in Dollar Creek, where the fast-moving waters had whisked it downstream forever.

"Don't want no dirt piles," he said, all serious. "Mr. Metheus, he falls over 'em in the yard."

We brought a few chunks of gold up from the vug, just to look at, but Prometheus said to let it lay until the railroad came to town, for it was due any day.

This made me kind of mad at first—all that gold, just

sitting there!—but his explanation was that if we mined it, it would be easier to steal. Let the railroad come to town first, so we could get a crew in and get it out of town fast. Since Goose Butte's smelter had been long since closed and razed, I saw his point. It didn't stop me from going down there just to savor the beauty of it, though.

We had widened the tunnel—Chigger having dug it boy-sized, which did not leave room for manly shoulders—but that was all, and sometimes I would just go down there all by myself with a lantern and sit for hours.

It was a middling-sized vug, being perhaps twenty-two or-three feet long, fifteen feet wide, and seventeen or eighteen feet to the ceiling in the highest part, although most of it was eight or ten feet tall. There was a kind of tilting floor, so that the back was higher that the front.

The floor and walls and ceiling were frosted thick in gold crystals and flakes, some as big as a man's thumbnail. This was mixed in with milky quartz, but not much, and combined with the practically solid gold rocks scattered on the floor—everywhere from pea-gravel size to a couple of boulders you could sit on—it had a powerful effect by lantern light. It was just like Prometheus had said: like being in a fairy cave.

We took turns at night guarding it, lest somebody slip down and hammer off a few thousand dollars' worth, and when it was Joaquin's turn to watch or mine, the other of us would slip down and spend the night. We would make love, and then he would tell me exciting tales of his exploits, and then we would have at each other again.

Now, I have got to tell you that I was more used to Joaquin by then, and some of his adventures were beginning to sound a little far-fetched to me. Like the time he claimed he outran a posse by daredevil dodging all over Arizona Territory and disappearing into the Apache Nations. Or the time he stood off thirty or forty bloodthirsty Comanches and came out without a scratch. I didn't say anything, though. He could have read a seed catalog to me for all I cared, I loved the sound of his voice that much.

Prometheus, much to my satisfaction, had finally hit the minnow bottle and had given up the drink. It was about two days before I noticed it, being so preoccupied with Joaquin and the vug and all, but then I began to wonder that the level in the library decanters hadn't gone down, and that the bottles he had hidden in the pantry had only decreased by one. Sure enough, it was the minnow bottle, and I congratulated myself.

Also, he suddenly got a whole lot testier. He complained about the sheets being scratchy. He railed that the library books were dusty, that the figurines on the mantel weren't straight, that his chair wasn't comfortable, and what had I done to it?

"I didn't do a dad-blasted thing to it, you old fool," I said. We were in the library at the time, and he was shifting this way and that in his chair and grumping something fierce.

"You're driving me crazy," I said. "No, I didn't put starch in your underwear or hide your shoes or your razor. The only thing I ever hid was Joaquin's pants, for all the little good that did, and that was only for a day."

He had broken out in a sweat—he sweated near all the time now—and I said, "Give over your hankie."

"I would if someone hadn't hidden it," he grumbled.

I went to him and mopped his brow with my sleeve instead. "I'm glad you stopped, but you are driving me crazy. Lately I'd as soon shin up a thorn tree with an armful of eels than ask how you're feeling."

He smiled a little—well, I think it was a smile—and patted my hand. "I'm sorry, my dear. I fear this is more difficult than I thought it would be." He looked around. "Is there water?"

I fetched him a glass, and he took it with trembling hands and bade me sit opposite him. "I suppose you are wondering why . . ." He trailed off, and I waited. "It seemed like the proper time," he said finally. "It seemed, dear Clutie, with everything . . ." There he was, trying to take the credit when I knew it was the poor little minnow that had sacrificed its life for him. I kept my mouth shut, though.

He sipped at his water, and I remembered the time he'd asked me to be his housekeeper, how nervous and stuttery he was then. Not big and flamboyant at all, like usual.

"It seemed like the time, with Chigger finding the vug and all?" I said, trying to be helpful.

"That, too." He took a sip of water from the glass. It shook in his hand, sending little quivery waves down his chin. He wiped them absently with his cuff and said absently, "Everything tastes of fish." Then, "Clutie my dear, is there . . . is there anything you want to tell me?"

That took me aback. The only secret I had was still a secret, and I hadn't even told Joaquin yet. It seemed there was never a good time. And I sure as shooting wasn't going to tell Prometheus first.

I said, "No, there's nothing. Nothing at all."

"I am not so old as you think," he said, frowning. "I am a young man. Well, relatively young. I'm rich! I have a title and lands. I could . . . I could . . ."

He trailed off again, which was just as well because I couldn't for the life of me figure out where he was going. Probably neither could he.

I got up and kissed him on the forehead, and said, "That's right, Prometheus. You're a young, rich man and you've got a title. And I'm a young, poor girl who has got a bucket of spuds to peel if you want any dinner. You call me if you've got something besides complaints to spout."

"Why do you put up with this?" Joaquin said. He was playing with my hair at the time, down in the vug. We had the watch. "With Prometheus and his temper?"

I snugged the blanket up under my chin, and curled myself tighter under his arm. It was cool in the vug. "Because . . . I don't know. I can't explain it. He's not got such a bad temper, it's just that he's stopped drinkin'. That can make a man touchy. Besides, he's good to Chigger."

"Not reason enough, *querida*. A man can be nice and not deserve such devotion."

I craned my head to look at him. "Why, I do believe you're jealous!" It made me feel proud to inspire such a dastardly emotion in the heart of a man, especially Joaquin's heart. "You're jealous of Prometheus!"

I'll be dad-blasted if he didn't color up some. "Certainly

not!'' he said with vigor. He got to his feet and began to pace up and down, naked as a jaybird. Normally that might have bothered me a tetch, but there was something about being in the vug. Surrounded by lantern light, gold, and shadows, he looked like the king of the world. He looked like Apollo or Adonis or one of those old-time heroes come to life again.

He did not notice my admiring gaze, though. He was too busy pacing and working himself into a tizzy. He said, ''I would not be jealous of one such as this. He is old. He is like a banker, never working in the sun, all pasty and white.''

''He's not even ten years older than you.'' I was pleased with the entire proceeding. I sat up, taking my blanket with me. ''And he's white because he doesn't have to go outside unless he wants to. He's rich.''

Joaquin stopped pacing. ''Ha! I see the truth now. It is the money. He is rich.'' ''Rich'' came out like a dirty word, and I was shocked.

I sat up straight, hugging the blanket to me. ''I don't believe I like your tone, Joaquin. If it wasn't for Prometheus, me and Chigger would still be walking across Kansas, if we hadn't got scalped or starved to death on the road. He waited for me in Abilene when I was in the wasteland and he took good care of Chigger, even if he did buy him that stupid outfit.''

Joaquin's eyebrows crunched together. ''What stupid outfit?''

''And if he offered me a job taking care of his house, I can't see that it's any skin off your nose. What was I supposed to do until you came for me? Why, it could have been months, even years!''

Well, that shut him up, sort of. He was looking the other way and I could hear him muttering under his breath in Spanish, but after a minute he turned his face toward me and said, deadly serious, ''You have no love for him?''

''Well, sure I do! But not like—It's different. Not like you.''

He thought a minute. ''Like an uncle, maybe?''

Right off I was covered in shivers. "No, for sure not like an uncle. That was a bad choice, Joaquin."

He said, "Like a father, then?"

Now, never having owned a father, at least a live one, I was not sure. But things were getting out of hand, and I said, "Yes. Like a father."

Joaquin looked down, and I could see his nostrils flaring. Suddenly he looked up. "Forgive me, *querida*. I did not think."

He looked so dejected that I had a hard fight to keep myself from laughing. Real serious, I said, "That's all right, Joaquin."

He sat down next to me on the blankets and put his arm around my shoulders and hugged me tight. "I am a fool. You are too good for me."

I said, "That's likely the truth."

Joaquin laughed and let loose of me, reaching for his cigarette papers and pouch.

I said, "There's something else. Maybe I shouldn't say anything . . ."

He lifted an eyebrow. "Say it."

"Well, it's just . . . Well, so long as we're on the subject of Prometheus . . . Well, there's this curse."

A grin took possession of his face, and he wiggled his eyebrows. "Oh, a *curse*!" He tapped in the tobacco. "I am much interested in curses."

I smacked him in the arm and nearly spilled his smoke, but he just kept smiling.

"Don't be thataway, Joaquin. It's for real. Well, it probably isn't. But Prometheus thinks it is, and I reckon that's what counts."

I told him all about that old French gypsy woman and how she put the hex on the Burke-Joneses, and how I found all those telegrams about his kin dying strange and unusual deaths, including that last one about the Busby triplets, who had got killed even though they changed their name.

"What's a topiary?" I asked.

His cigarette was finished, and he stubbed it out on a solid gold floor. "I do not know. I think maybe it has something to do with the bushes."

"Well anyway, now he thinks he's royalty or something. An earl or a baron, I forget, and the whole town's laughing at him, calling him Highness and Prince and whatnot. I tell you what, Joaquin, that man needs me."

He lay back down, pushed away my blanket, and pulled me onto his chest, skin on skin. "I know another man that needs you, Chrysanthemum." He gathered my hair in his hands.

"Joaquin? That Booker fella. The one that shot Prometheus?"

"Mmm." He was nuzzling my throat.

"Did you . . . did you really kill him?"

"Chrysanthemum, you talk too much."

"But did you?"

He sighed and drew my head back so he could look me in the eyes. "I saw him arrested. He is in the jail for ten years. No, I did not kill him. He is not one of the seven."

"The seven?"

He sighed and shook his head. "Chrysanthemum, what am I to do with you?"

I didn't know what he was talking about, but it didn't seem like the time to start a lengthy conversation about it.

He kissed my forehead. "Are you finished with the talking now?"

I said, "Yes. But, Joaquin?"

He stopped the next kiss a inch away from my lips. "Yes?"

"You couldn't've got my quilt back?"

"You are so greedy, beloved," he said, smiling, his face an inch from mine and coming nearer. "We will see. Now, hush."

Two days later, Prometheus was over the worst of the shakes, and we had news that the railroad crew had been sighted twelve miles east of Goose Butte. Between the railroad and the gold strike, people poured into town, and I guess Mrs. Little Dove Gensch and her ladies were so busy checking everybody's credentials that they didn't have time to bother with the likes of me.

I should have been happy. The gold would soon be mined and off our hands, and Prometheus would be even richer than before. Since Chigger had found it, Prometheus had provided him with a generous income, and him and me would never have to worry about money again.

But still, I was troubled in my mind. Soon I'd start to swell up, and while I could pass it off for a while as a result of Joaquin's good cooking, that wouldn't do for long. Joaquin had not brought up the subject of marriage, and I felt funny to tell him about the baby. Like I was trying to trap him. Maybe I was afraid that if I told, he would just get on his horse, say adios, and ride off.

And I would surely die if he did that.

It rained that day, which was good because we needed it, but it was a certified toad strangler. The clouds rolled in from the west at about five o'clock. The air grew still and the sky clabbered up, and all of a sudden it fair burst open, and I do mean burst. It poured for maybe twenty or twenty-five minutes, and it was a good thing it didn't last longer, or I would have been hammering up an ark.

After, the sun came out just long enough to check on the world—to see if it had got drowned or not—before it went to bed. Dollar Creek was a muddy, roiling monster, having overflown its natural bed and come twenty feet up the yard. I don't know how the others fared, but I could hear the Crandalls, next door, shouting to each other as they bailed out their diggings.

Joaquin and I were on the back stoop, surveying the damage and listening to Archie Crandall call, "Another bucket, Mother!" when Prometheus came out. He tucked a shawl over my shoulders. I was glad, for although it had been hot that afternoon, it had all of a sudden got real chilly.

He cocked his head toward the creek and said, "Behold the beast."

I said, "How long before it goes down?"

Both him and Joaquin, at the same time, said, "By morning." Then they looked at each other, kind of snarly at first, till Joaquin grinned.

Prometheus raised an eyebrow and said, "Hmm."

The next day the creek was down, though there was still a lot of mud, and I was feeling restless. Come afternoon it had dried up some, and I took down my Winchester. I borrowed Joaquin's horse—unbeknownst to Joaquin, who, having talked Prometheus into a chess game, was occupied in the library—and set off, across Dollar Creek and into the scrub, looking for something to shoot.

The day was warm and clear and Peligroso was frisky, Joaquin having only worked him a few times since his arrival, but he soon cleared out the kinks and settled down. I don't know what Joaquin had done to him, but he was the best-trained horse I had ever ridden. He had a mouth like butter, and you barely had to lay a whisper of rein on his neck to spin him like a top.

I rode out about three miles—cursing my skirts the whole time and wishing I hadn't burned up my britches and especially my boots—and ended at a rise, sparsely wooded with low scrubby trees, if you could call them trees at all. I tethered Peligroso to a bush, and then I sat down on a rock and proceeded to cry my eyes out.

I thought about home, not all yellow and brown and dry like this—the rain had helped a little, but not much—but solid dark green and moist; the way the woods were full of birds and critters; the dark, shrouded holiness of it, with the sunlight falling through the treetops in beams and spikes; and the soft way it lit the ferns and woody undergrowth, like a magic carpet.

Home seemed safer, somehow. What with the trees and the hills and all, sometimes you could not see ten feet. Here, you could see forever. It made you feel naked.

I thought about my old camp up at Tickled Bear Hill, and the cave sparkling with reflected light from the Little Shy, and the big old oak and how I'd shinnied up it to spy on Agnes Ann's rainbow dresses on the wash lines.

I thought of Miss Alvinetta Hanker, too, so patient and

kind, and so nice to loan me books—I still wore the little gold heart she'd given me for graduation, never took it off. I could remember a time not so very long ago when there was nothing I wanted more in the world than to be like Miss Alvinetta Hanker.

Well, things were different now.

I cried for my stolen quilt. I cried for those lost drawings hidden in the chicken coop—I had only looked at my drawing paper three times since I bought it in Kansas City, and only lifted a pencil but once. I even cried over Frank James saying I should be a forger, I was so good at it. I had not lived up to my potential at all.

But mostly I cried because Joaquin hadn't mentioned wedding bells, not once, and I just knew he was going to up and leave me. It did not bother me half so much that I would bring a baby into the wilderness to raise by my lonesome as it did that I would never see Joaquin again or have his arms around me or hear him telling me all those whoppers.

Well, a person only has so much water in them and can only cry for so long, and after a bit I was run dry, if not feeling any less sorry for myself. I wiped my face on my skirt and picked up a couple of pebbles. The lucky bones of crawdads are the best for fortune-telling, but I hadn't seen one crawdad in the whole state of Colorado.

I drew a circle in the earth, closed my eyes, rattled the pebbles in my hand like dice, and said, "Will he stay or will he go? Tell me yes or tell me—"

Hands grabbed me from behind.

My first thought was *Indians!* and I lashed out every which way, figuring to inflict the most possible damage before losing my hair, and cursing myself for having left that fancy Winchester in my gun boot. I flailed back with an arm and caught somebody alongside the head, and was genuinely shocked to hear him say, "Jesus-kick-the-bucket, Clutie!"

It was Uncle Glow, all five-foot-nothing of him. That skinny orange braid trailing down his back, he held the side of his head and moaned, "What'd you wanna go and do that for?"

He wasn't alone. Someone said, "You gonna be a good girl, or should I just knock you silly?" It was Beetle. He was just limping over the rise, into sight.

I expect my mouth was hanging open.

Glow was still hanging on to his skull, but that didn't keep him from batting me with the other hand. "Speak when you's spoke to!"

I made a sign against evil and witchery. "U-uncle Beetle? Is it a ghost?"

He came toward me, lashing out with that peg, chopping grass and weeds with every stride. It was no ghost. Beetle was flesh and blood, and I knew right then I was in the deep fat and it was coming to a boil.

Beetle said, "I's hard to kill, you little shithead. Ain't no little whomp over the skull goin' to do me in."

I said, "What do you want? Why have you followed me all the way out here?"

Another voice sounded from the scrub and I clutched my throat. "What makes you think we'd follow a big ol' ox like you?" It was Spider, sure enough, risen from the grave.

Quick, I made the sign against witches again. I said, "I know *you* were dead! Has Granny witched you?"

He laughed, and it was pure evil. "You hardly hit me, wife. It were just a graze. Skittered straight across my ribs. And Granny ain't witchin' nobody no more."

Glow picked his old Reb cap up off the ground and laid it across his heart. "She was took two days after you run off."

"Bear," said Beetle, real matter-of-fact. "She were in the woods pickin' curin' herbs when it come upon her. She give as good as she got."

"That bear were tore up somethin' horrendous," added Glow with a toothless look of keen admiration. "Guts ever'where!"

Spider leaned a dirty elbow on his saddle horn. His right eye still looked in at his nose. Some worse than before, I believed. He said, "Jeez, Glow, get on with it!"

Glow put his cap back on his head. "See, it's like this, Clutie. We read in the papers—"

Beetle backhanded him and knocked him flat. "I does the talkin' around here!"

"You found her!" It was Uncle Wig, riding up the rise from the other side and just coming into view. If Gnat and Violet and Mama had been there, it would have been a family reunion entire. I admit I was encouraged by the sight of him. He, at least, would speak in my behalf if their plan was to murder me and leave me to rot.

"Uncle Wig!" I cried. "What are y'all doing here?"

He rode up and got down off his horse and came over and put his arm around me. He said, "You're bleeding! Beetle, you been roughin' this little gal up?" He took out a rag and daubed at my lip.

Spider said, "Little? She's as big as a skinned horse, and she's got fat, too! I say we don't need her. I say we just ride in whoopin' and hollerin' and just take it."

Beetle hollered, "Shut up, the lot'a you!"

Spider slouched down on his horse. Glow plopped his butt on the ground and commenced chewing on his braid.

Uncle Wig dug in his pocket for a minute, then brought out a scrap of paper, all folded up. He straightened it out, then handed it to me. He said, "This is why we come."

It was a newspaper clipping—Wig would have been the only one who could read it, and then haltingly—about the finding of the vug. It was soiled and smudged, but I saw that the find had been attributed. "The rich strike was made by young Chigger John Jukes, aged 12," it said, "a houseguest of Mr. Burke-Jones."

"What paper is this from?" I asked. The *Goose Butte Gazette* would hardly have been so nice.

"Abilene," said Wig, taking back the clipping and folding it real careful. "Though I hear it's made the papers all the way to New York City. I reckon you's famous, Clutie. Chigger John, anyway."

"We want it," said Beetle, always impatient. "Get it for us."

"How can I?" I said. "It's not even dug yet!"

"Dig it," said Beetle.

"Myself? I do not think you know how big this strike is."

Just like that, he flipped up the butt of his rifle and knocked me in my underjaw. I flew back and landed on my backside to the sound of Spider laughing.

Everything looked hazy for a minute, but I heard Beetle clear. "You dig it, or Chigger is gonna be cold as a pump handle. I'll slice him to ribbons and mail you the pieces. Don't think I won't."

Now, they had me scared. Beetle was uncommon mean, and now there was no Granny Wren to hold him back. He would come right up to the house and kill Chigger—and Prometheus and Joaquin and me, too—to get his way. I knew Joaquin was as hotheaded as he was brave, but I didn't know that he could hold his own against four Jukes men who were mad, despite his tales of boldness and backbone on the plains.

"All right," I said from the ground. "But I can only get out a little at a time."

Beetle appeared pleased, if wary. "How much is a little?"

"More money than you've ever seen."

He studied on this for a minute, during which time Wig helped me up to my feet.

"You send somebody—send Uncle Glow—down across Dollar Creek come dawn. I'll meet you and bring you some gold."

"I'll say who's comin'," said Beetle with a scowl. "I'll choose. And don't think you're gettin' away with nothin'. We's gonna come every morning. You'd better be there. We's gonna come every morning till our saddlebags is full up."

Spider said, "You tell 'er, Beetle," and reined his horse away.

Glow stopped chewing on his braid. "We's gonna be rich! Yahoo! We's gonna be richer than Weevil, who went to Arizony!"

"Shut up, Glow," said Beetle. He turned on his heel and stomped off into the brush, peg leg slicing. The rest of their horses must have been down the hill, for I did not see them.

Uncle Wig was still beside me. "Your jaw achin' you?" he said, not unkindly.

It was, but I said, "No." I reckoned I'd have one golly-whopper of a bruise.

"We been watchin' the house," Wig went on, as we watched Glow pick himself up and scurry after Beetle. "You don't go out much."

I didn't say anything.

"Who's that feller? The one with the long horse tail."

I figured he must mean Joaquin. Both him and Prometheus wore their hair tied back, but Prometheus's was shorter and wouldn't show from a distance.

"Nobody," I said. "Just a friend." I figured it best to change the subject, so I said, "I thought I saw Beetle in Abilene a few weeks back. He been chasing me?"

"Why would he be chasin' you, Shortcake? Cause'a that little ruckus?" He shook his head. "They was over that by the time Spider could get outta bed, or so I hear. I guess Beetle was pretty mad over the horse, though. Till they found it shot dead."

I cringed. I said, "Chigger gave it the colic. He didn't know."

"Beetle said it served you right, and the horse, too. I hear they barely got Granny covered with dirt 'fore they rode on west, and left the farm for your mama and Gnat and Violet to tend. No, you didn't have much to do with it. It was the legend of Weevil what inspired 'em."

A hawk circled overhead, and I turned my face up to it. So Mama was the new head Jukes. It seemed fitting. I said, "Then how come it took them so long to get this far?"

Wig shrugged. I half-wished he'd pluck a coin from behind my ear, or maybe roll one over his fingers, just for old time's sake. And he'd had a bath sometime, too. He wasn't near as ripe as the others.

"The usual," he said. "They got arrested for petty thievery in Abilene. Stole a box of cartridges and a jar full of horehound candy. Well, half-full. They'd'a been in jail yet if I hadn't rode through accidental and paid their fine. Showed 'em the clipping, too."

I looked away from the hawk, looked at him. "Then this is all your fault."

From over the hill, Beetle bellowed, "Wig! C'mon!"

He scratched his head, and with a wink he straightened his hat. "Reckon so, Shortcake. See you come dawn."

twenty-three

I was so mad that after they rode out of sight I shot four jackrabbits, and I named each one. Spider, Glow, Wig, and Beetle, Beetle being the biggest and the ugliest.

It was coming dark when I splashed back across the creek and up to the barn, and Joaquin was fit to be tied.

"Where have you been?" he said, and fair pulled me from the saddle. "Why do you take Peligroso without asking? This country is no place for you to be alone!" Then he pulled me into his arms and held me tight. "Ah, *querida,* do not ever do that again," he said against my ear. "What would I do if you were lost?"

I clung to him, torn between telling him about the Bug Boys and losing him, telling him about the baby and losing him . . . This whole dad-blasted thing was just getting too complicated, and I hugged him as hard as I could.

"*Querida,*" he whispered, half a joke and half surprised, "you will crush me!"

It had been a spell since I packed a deer out of the woods on my back, but I guessed I still had my strength.

He led Peligroso into the stable, and despite everything, I laughed out loud. There stood little Chub, saddled and bridled and at the ready. I said, "I would like to see you on that pony. I'll bet you could walk and ride at the same time."

He smiled, all sheepish. "It is a foolish picture, no? You see what you bring me to?"

He had a couple of lanterns lit, so it was brighter in the barn. I was careful to keep my head turned to the side, or at least cover my bruised jaw with my hand. Uncle Beetle had whomped me good and I knew it would be beginning to show.

Joaquin was real pleased with the rabbits, and while he gutted and skinned them, Chigger came down from the house and plunked himself on a hay bale.

"I thought you was lost, Clutie. Is you found now?"

I petted his hair. It was all full of fire in the dying sunlight. "I'm found. Joaquin, who won the chess game?"

He looked up from the rabbit he was gutting. "We are not yet completed. That Prometheus, he plays well. I think maybe I like him."

Something about his tone told me that more than chess had transpired, but I was smart enough not to ask. Instead, I turned to Chigger. "What have you been up to? You been guarding the vug?" I wished I hadn't said it. Just like that my innards were in a turmoil again.

"Mr. Metheus got a paper," he said. "A man come to the door and give it to him."

Joaquin threw another handful of rabbit guts to the side. "Paper? The newspaper."

"It was little," said Chigger, sticking his nose closer to see what Joaquin was doing. "He's done locked himself in the room with the books, an' he won't say nothin'."

Gently, Joaquin pushed Chigger away from the rabbit and the knife. "A little paper? Telegram, maybe. Chigger." Chigger's nose was back in the rabbit, and Joaquin put a hand on the top of his head and pushed him away. "Hold onto your horses, *muchacho*. I tell you what. You will sing a little song with me, no? And stay out of the trouble?"

I stood up quick. Prometheus getting a telegram could only mean bad news. As they launched into a spirited rendition of "Green Grows the Grass on My Rebel Love's Grave"— Chigger having been teaching Joaquin songs of back home— I excused myself and started for the house.

Honest-to-Jim, I didn't see how things could get any worse. As I walked up past the mesquite trees and into the house, I turned it over and over in my mind. Should I tell Prometheus about the Bug Boys? If I did, would he make a stand and maybe get somebody killed? I didn't mind so much about the Bug Boys, even if they were kin, but I minded a whole lot about Prometheus and Chigger and Joaquin. And, I was surprised to find, me. Especially the unborn life I carried.

I hadn't made up my mind by the time I gained the library, which did not surprise me in the least. I set it aside for the moment, squared my shoulders, and knocked on the door.

There was no answer.

I knocked again. I figured that Prometheus had a bottle in there, the telegram having knocked him off the wagon, and he was passed out. I wondered how long it would take for Joaquin to take it off its hinges.

I knocked one last time and called to him, and I was about to fetch help when I heard footsteps, slow and heavy. The door creaked open an inch. He said, "Come in, Clutie."

He wasn't plowed, much to my surprise. He hadn't been drinking at all. He slumped down in his chair and announced, "The end . . . is nigh."

I turned up the lamp. Leave it to Prometheus to make a drama. "What do you mean, the end is nigh?"

"I mean," he said, combing fingers through his hair, "that is it near."

I said, "I *know* that, you crazy fool. I mean, what's got your tail in a twist?"

He pointed to a wadded-up piece of paper on the floor. "Read it. And, as the wags say, weep."

I picked it up and straightened it out. It said: "REGRET TO INFORM YOU ZEUS BURKE-JONES MARQUESS OF WEMBLY EXPIRED TUESDAY LAST STOP TUMOR SPRANG UP OVERNIGHT STOP HOW ARE YOU FEELING STOP ANDREW FITZPUGH ESQ."

"You see?" he said after I looked up. "There is no hope. I might as well order my casket and be done with it. White satin lining. Make sure they use white satin. They can bury me in the vug after they mine it out. Toss me down there and throw the dirt on top of me. You shall have my fortune, of course."

I put my hands on my hips. "If you don't beat everything! Believing in some silly curse—"

"I remind you that it has wiped out nearly the entire male populace of my family. Only two remain, counting myself. That is hardly a frivolous matter."

"The curse didn't wipe them out. They got drowned or fell off horses or hit on the head with one of those topiary things."

He arched a brow.

"This last one is a tumor," I went on. "Likely on his liver. Which he likely got from drinking himself to death, which you have stopped doing, I very kindly remind you. So you stop talking about being buried in white satin in the vug. I don't want to hear it."

He put his head in his hands. "Two left, just two left," he moaned. "Take me now."

I would have laid into him again, but there was somebody knocking at the front door. Pounding, more like. I yelled to Joaquin before I remembered he was down to the barn skinning jackrabbits and singing, and so I said, "I am not done with you yet," and went down the hall, carrying the lamp with me.

"All right, all right!" I said, for they were banging so hard as to rattle the glass. I set the lamp on a table and yanked the door open.

There stood my aunts Carnation and Myrtle, all rigged out in cheap Chicago dresses, spangled and gaudy, and Carnation was greatly swole with child.

I believe I just stood there, bug-eyed.

And then Carnation burst past me and ran down the hall and threw her arms about the neck of Prometheus, who had wandered to the library door.

"Oh, my lovin' husband," she cried. "We's together at last!"

"Unhand me at once!" Prometheus cried, and pried her hands off his neck. I didn't know whether he looked more scared or repulsed.

"Oh, Mr. Jones, doncha remember me, honey? Doncha remember your ever-lovin' wife?"

Prometheus was backed to the wall. "Help!"

Carnation was all feathers and ruffles and green silk and grasping little Jukes fingers. "Oh, Peaches, woncha take your lovin' Carrie back? Our baby needs his papa!"

"Madam!" Prometheus threw up his hands, aghast.

Now, in the excitement I had forgot all about Myrtle Marie, but suddenly she shoved her way past me, into the house and to Carnation's side, and said, "Carrie!" She jerked her head in my direction.

"What!" snapped Carnation. Then she squinted and got a better look. "What's she doin' here?"

They forgot all about Prometheus.

"Claim jumper!" said Myrtle.

"Thief!" said Carrie.

"Dirty rotten claim-jumpin' whorin' little thief!" said Myrtle.

Prometheus ran down the hall the other way, shouting, "Joaquin! Joaquin!"

Myrtle jumped me. I cannot say she took me by surprise, for she was a Jukes and I half-expected the slugging to break out anytime. I didn't figure her to land on my head, though, and that is exactly what she did.

She knocked me to the floor before I even thought to fight back, and commenced to batter me about the skull. I got a fistful of brittle orange Jukes hair and yanked hard. She let out a bellow and went to slug me again, but I had got her off balance and rolled on top.

Now it was me slapping her, and it felt good. I smacked her for Beetle, I slapped her for Glow and Wig. I smacked her for Spider, too, and I was just about to haul off and slug her a good one for Granny, when Carnation kicked me in the ribs.

She started in to do it again, real quick, but I grabbed her foot and yanked and she went *bang* on the floor on her backside, holding her belly. Myrtle Marie let out a yell and clawed at my face, and I believe she might have done me serious damage if Joaquin had not at that moment lifted me off her. Pried, more like.

She came up off the floor and started after me again, but

Prometheus grabbed her by the shoulders and pinned her back against his chest. I believe he got kicked in the shins a couple times for it, but he did not let go.

"Stop it!" Joaquin thundered. "*Madre de Dios,* stop it now!"

We both stopped flailing—Joaquin had a real commanding way about him that made my heart flutter, even then—and hung there, panting. Carnation pulled herself up off the floor, still holding a protective arm around her belly.

Prometheus said, "Somebody close the door."

It was standing wide open, and a little crowd had gathered on the sidewalk. Kids with dogs, men on their way home from work, ladies out for evening air—all of them leaned over the fence to see better. And right in the middle of them, arms propped akimbo and with a satisfied smirk on her face, was Mrs. Little Dove Gensch.

Joaquin let go of my arms. I went to the threshold and stared back at the crowd. We must have been putting on a real show for them, what with the hall lit so bright with lamplight and all. So I bowed from the waist, real ceremonious, and said, "Thank you very much." Then I slammed the door.

"If you have come here to cause trouble, you have sure succeeded," I began.

"You're the troublemaker!" cried Myrtle, still restrained by Prometheus. Her eye was ticcing to beat the band. "Here I brung poor Carrie to you—swole up, she is—and first thing you try to punch her out!"

"Swole up?" I cried. "She's no more comin' fresh than—" I was about to say, "than I am," but thought better of it. "Than . . . than Chigger is," I said. "She's all full of pillows, probably stolen, too! She's—"

"Who *are* these women?" Prometheus thundered.

There was a silence. Joaquin said, "I would like to know this myself."

Then everybody started to talk at once. I was trying to say how they were my whore aunts who had robbed me in Kansas City.

Carnation professed her undying love for Prometheus and

kept saying, "Doncha recollect me, sweetie pie?"

Prometheus kept stuttering and backing closer to the wall.

Chigger, coming in late, figured it was a family reunion and kept asking everybody if they had a candy.

Myrtle Marie said some story about how Carnation and Prometheus were married, and how Carnation therefore had half of everything, and all the time she talked she made eyes at Joaquin, in between the tics.

Joaquin was the only one not to join in the tumult, and finally, when the volume had about reached its peak, he lifted up his arms and thundered, "*Silencio!*"

Just like that, it was quiet. He could sure hold a crowd. He pointed at Carnation and said, "This one says she is with child and the father is Prometheus."

Carnation smiled and crossed her arms.

He pointed at me. "Chrysanthemum calls her aunts soiled doves, and says they stole her money."

I looked at Carnation and made a face.

He pointed to Prometheus. "He says he has never seen you before."

Prometheus straightened and tried to look imperious.

"And this one?" He looked at Myrtle Marie, who was winking at him real broad and making lewd gestures. "I think this one is *loco.*"

Myrtle Marie huffed and stamped her foot.

Chigger tugged at his sleeve, and he added, "I know, *muchacho.* You want a sugar candy." Then he looked up. "The best thing is . . ." We all waited. "The best thing is, I think you should go."

Carnation looked at me like I was the one who was leaving.

"No, *you.* And you," he added to Myrtle. "I think this is something that cannot be satisfied in a hallway at night. Come tomorrow, in the light."

Well, I didn't want them coming again tomorrow or any other day. I said, "Joaquin! They're nothin' but a bunch of whores after the vug!"

Carnation batted her eyes real innocent. "Vug? What vug?"

"And that baby! It's a good foot lower than when she first came in here!"

She wrapped an arm underneath it and heaved it up with the flat of her hand. She smiled. "Oh, he's kickin', all right."

Myrtle said, "Sure to be a boy when they moves around that much," and sidled up to Joaquin.

I said to Carnation, "It's been no more than six weeks since I met you in Kansas City, and you weren't lookin' piggy then. You said Prometheus was so drunk he didn't even diddle you!"

Prometheus cleared his throat. "I take umbrage at that."

"Ha!" cried Myrtle Marie.

By that time, she had managed to sidle over and press her body tight against Joaquin, who was making a face like she might have nits or something and he didn't want to catch them. I reached over and flung her away from him. "Don't be hanging all over him. Get your own fella!"

Well, she came at me again, but as luck would have it, Prometheus caught her from behind and Joaquin stopped me, and we never did make contact.

"I have heard enough," said Joaquin, once I quit struggling. "You ladies, you leave this house." Then he looked over at Prometheus. "If that is your wish, señor?"

"What? Oh yes, indeed!" said Prometheus.

"*Bueno*. There will be no coming back *mañana*, either. Or the day after. This is finished."

"Well, if that don't beat all!" cried Carnation, with a lot of hand waving. "Here we go and travel through the perilous whatyacall, desert, at risk of our lives and very limb to bring tidin's of joy, and here you go, givin' us the rush. I don't suppose it makes you no nevermind that my sweet little one will get borned without a father."

Just then she looked down. While she had been hot and heavy in oration, her baby had slipped to the floor.

"It's born, it's born!" she cried, and made a dive for it, but I was quicker.

"Towels!" I said as I scooped them up and showed the men. "Honest-to-straw-walkin'-Jim on a crutch, but you beat everything! Towels and a hotel pillow, just like I thought! Out, get out!''

I threw her pillow at her and shoved them out the door and slammed it behind them and caught the hem of Myrtle's dress and heard it rip, but I didn't care. I leaned back against the door and slithered to the floor. All the starch had gone out of my legs.

"Hold still," Joaquin said, and dabbed at my jaw again.

"Ouch!" I pushed away his hand. My jaw had caught up with me—the place where Beetle had crashed into it with his rifle butt, I mean—and it was fast turning purple. "That's not helping. It's not cut."

Joaquin put his rag down and got up to check the rabbit, which we were frying on the stove. "I do not remember your aunt landing such a blow in the face," he said. "It is very strange."

"I did it on the desert," I replied. And when he looked at me strange, I said, "Rifle kicked."

We were all sitting round the kitchen table. It seemed it had become a natural gathering place. It wasn't so formal as the dining room with its flocked wallpaper and linen table-cloth and display of china. The kitchen was nice and homey, especially now that you could eat the food.

I had just finished explaining who the aunts were—or trying to. I had left out the part about Carnation being Chigger's true mama, though, since he was in the room.

Prometheus sat across from me, newspaper at his elbow, rubbing his temples. "You say I was in a hotel with these girls?"

I turned toward him, wincing with the effort. "The Wigwam Hotel in Kansas City. You remembered it fine when you were still drinking. At least, you kind of remembered it. It's where I met you."

"Really," said Prometheus, his face all screwed up. "I thought that was on a train."

"Close enough," I said. I supposed anything that took his mind off that telegram from Mr. Fitzpugh was a good thing.

"I reckon we'll have to be ready when they come back. The aunts, I mean."

"They will not be back," Joaquin said. Chigger tried to snitch some rabbit from the pan and Joaquin gave his hand a little swat with his turning fork. "Later, *muchacho*."

"And what, may I ask, is to stop them?" Prometheus asked.

Joaquin shrugged. "I have said they are not to."

"I see. And people just naturally do as you say." Prometheus said it flat and kind of sarcastic, but Joaquin didn't notice.

"*Sí*," he said, just as serious as a judge. "Always. This reminds me of a time when I was in the mountains of California," Joaquin started, and I knew we were in for another tale.

I was in no mood for it. I had to think about what to do about the Bug Boys, who were going to ride in come dawn expecting a sack of gold. It was my turn to stand watch, which meant Joaquin would be down there with me. The gathering part would be easy, since there was so much of it just rattling loose on the floor, but how to do it without him waking? He was ever on the alert, and each little rustle and sound got his attention, and I did not know a spell for making people sleep heavy.

"... up north, you know?" Joaquin was saying as he poked at the rabbit pieces sizzling in the pan. "Where there are many great pine trees, and in winter the deep snows. This was in a famous blizzard, the worst blizzard anyone could remember. The snow, it was so deep a man could step into it and sink up to his armpits, and this is where it was shallow. I and Red Bob Dugan were hiding out in a—"

"Stop it," I said before I knew the words were leaving my mouth. "Just stop it. It's always the worst blizzard with you! The driest drought, the hottest heat, the most Indians, the most steadfast, hell-bent-for-leather, ride-'em-down posse the world has ever known. Doesn't anything *normal* ever happen to you?"

Boy, that kitchen got quiet. Prometheus froze, and even Chigger held his breath.

Joaquin didn't say anything, either. He stood with his back to me, silent, and I knew I had done it this time. I comforted myself that at least he would not hit me, but I sort of wished he would.

Slowly, he turned to face me. I was surprised, because his face was real thoughtful. At last he said, "And what is normal? The things that happen to a man, happen. They are."

Then he shrugged his shoulders and laughed. "*Querida,* my love, you ask the hard questions. Chigger, how about we sing for your Clutie and Prometheus? You want to try '*Los Lobos Loco*'?"

Chigger joined him with enthusiasm. It beat me how Chigger could remember all those Spanish words perfect when he couldn't recall a thing you said to him unless you said it eight times. It also beat me how Joaquin could take a question that any other man would have shot you for asking and turn it into a philosophical problem, but there you are.

The rabbit was cooked and dished up along with potatoes and good rabbit gravy and warm tortillas and fresh peas, to the sound of soprano and baritone. My jaw was hurting more by the minute, so I was chewing slow. It was just as well. My stomach was so tied up in knots, if I'd eaten faster I probably would have foundered. Prometheus finished first—his appetite not yet having picked up since he quit the bottle—and he started reading the newspaper aloud.

" 'President Grant Dedicates Monument.' Ho hum. 'Bandits Escape Tres Rosas Incarceration'." He rolled the ash off his cigar onto his plate, then gave the newspaper a shake to straighten it. "Price of sugar going up. Price of paper going down. Price of gold rising." He smiled and gave his paper a jaunty jiggle. "Good news for us. By the by, I'm getting some men from the railroad in two days. Temporarily, to start the digging."

I was relieved at first, then, just as fast, nervous. What if the Bug Boys hadn't gone away by then?

Joaquin had stopped eating, with his fork in the air, halfway to his mouth. Slow, he said, "Read to me of the Tres Rosas."

"What? Ah yes. *Someone* is interested in what's going on

in the world." He gave me a look. "Here it is. 'A daring escape was engineered Tuesday in the town of Tres Rosas, New Mexico. Deputy Vance Hartung was injured and over two hundred dollars in damages were incurred when associates of Morgan "The Albino" Pomeroy stormed the jail. Pomeroy, who was awaiting execution—' "

"Give it to me!" said Joaquin, snatching the newspaper away so fast that both me and Prometheus jumped.

"W-what is it?" I said.

Joaquin did not answer. He glared at the paper, reading to himself. Slow, his fists curled tighter and tighter, until that paper held no recognizable shape. His mouth opened once, and I poised my hands to cover Chigger's ears lest he start cursing, but there was no need: he sprang up from the table and went outside, newspaper crushed in his fist.

We all just sat there. I had never seen Joaquin so mad, not even when that man had the Indians after him and the bullets were flying all around us.

"Go out to him, Clutie," said Prometheus quietly.

"Not yet," I said, and I was trembling. "Not yet."

twenty-four

I t was a half hour before I could make myself go look for
him. By rights I should have been down in the vug—to
guard or rob it, one or the other. Maybe both. But Prometheus had padlocked the cellar that morning, and the lock
was still on.

I found Joaquin in the stable. By lantern light, he was
saddling Peligroso. I stood in the doorway for a moment,
listening to the wind shift lazy through the mesquite, watching him.

I couldn't read his face. He tightened the girth a last time,
then dropped down the stirrup. He gathered the horse's reins
and started to back him out of the stall.

I said, "You weren't even going to say good-bye?" And
then, before he could answer, I guess I sort of lost my mind,
because the next thing I knew I was pounding on him, beating on his chest. I was not up to snuff, the Bug Boys and
the aunts having taken the edge off my natural strength, and
he caught my arms after no more than six or eight blows.

"Chrysanthemum!" he said in shock, and then hugged me
close. "*Querida, querida,*" he said soothingly, "I would not
go without saying good-bye. I was coming to the house."

"But why? Why?"

"You know."

"No, I don't!" I was crying then, but not the kind where
you bawl out loud. It was the hopeless kind with no sound,
where the tears just fall from your eyes and there's nothing
you can do to stop them. "All I know is one minute you're
standing in the kitchen reading the newspaper and the next
you're saddling your horse and lighting out!"

"But I told you! I—" He stopped short and started beating his pockets. Out came what was left of the newspaper, all crumpled, and he smoothed it out. "This man." He jabbed a finger at the sheet, at the story about the jailbreak. "This man is the last. He must die. I have vowed it."

I slumped against a post. "What the Sam Hill are you talking about?"

"But I told you of this! I told you of this in the vug, and on the prairie. I avenge my father. Each man in the gang that my grandfather hired, each man who spilled my father's blood upon the land, they have all met their ends. These are the seven. They are bad men, who bring death to everything they touch. I thought this Albino would be taken, too, if by the hangman. This is why I was free to come to you. And now he lives."

You could have knocked me down with a goosefeather. It all knit together now. All those stories, they must have been true. At least, part of them.

I said, "Joaquin, don't go. Don't leave us. We—I . . . need you."

"I must go." He led Peligroso out of the stable, and I ran after him.

"Please, Joaquin!"

He cupped my head in his hand and smoothed away the tears with his thumb. Not that it did much good. "I will not be gone long. I have the full moon for a head start. And Tres Rosas is not forty miles from the border."

"But you don't know where they ran off to!"

"I will find him. And this time I will not rely on some *gringo* marshal. I am leaving my things, *querida*. I take only what I need for the trip." He patted his saddlebags. "Do you think I would do this if I did not plan to return?"

"But you don't need to—You can't—Joaquin, can't you let this one live? Mayhap he'll run off to Mexico."

"And kill Mexicans instead of Americans?" He shook his head. "No. It must be done." He started to mount, but I grabbed his shoulder.

"Aren't you just like them, then? Just like your seven?"

He stopped, considering this. At last he said, "Perhaps

yes, perhaps no. I think it is no. And after the Albino? The killing, it stops. And I will have my beautiful Chrysanthemum. And Chigger, who will sing us to sleep at night.''

''That's not all you'll have,'' I said, not meaning to. ''You'll have . . . I'll have . . .''

''What?''

It was too late to back up now. ''Joaquin, I'm going to find pups.''

He just looked at me.

''I've come fresh. I've swallowed a watermelon seed. I've ketched!''

His eyebrows scrunched.

''Crimeny! We're goin' to have a baby, Joaquin.''

His mouth opened, but no sound came out. I couldn't tell if he was glad or angry. Then, all of a sudden, he swooped me up into the air and laughed big and twirled me around and around. ''This is true? You? And me?''

I nodded. I felt ten pounds lighter for having told him.

''You think it will be a boy? Try for a boy, Chrysanthemum. He will be a king! He will be President of the United States! He will be so handsome that all the señoritas will swoon!''

He kissed me, full and hard on the mouth, then gentle and sweet, and when at last he pulled away I knew that I had changed his mind, that he was going to stay.

''I never loved anybody the way I love you, Joaquin,'' I whispered. ''Not anybody. I'll do my best. I'll try for a boy.''

He said, ''Chrysanthemum, lie on your back. The Spanish women, to get a boy they lie on their back at night and drink limeade for breakfast. Or maybe that was a girl. No, I think for a boy.''

I didn't know where I was going to get limeade, but I said, ''I will.''

He kissed me again and whispered, ''This is all the more reason I must hurry back to you.''

I couldn't believe it. I said, ''No!'' and tore at his clothes. ''You can't go, Joaquin! You can't leave me!''

He grabbed my wrists. ''Stop! Stop it!'' He was shouting then and his face had grown dark, as dark as it was carefree before. "Chrysanthemum, you are foolish." He gave me a shake, just a little one. "Don't you know that I would never leave you? I may go away, yes, but going away is not leaving. I would never leave, never. Know this."

I couldn't speak, his expression was that terrible and serious. I just nodded, tears streaming down my face.

He pulled me to him and held me close against his chest. Into my hair he whispered, "Ah, my funny little Chrysanthemum, my love," and then, just as sudden, he released me and swung up on his horse.

"*Adios, querida!* I will not be long!"

He goosed Peligroso in the ribs and had cantered down the yard and was wading the creek before I knew what had happened. I ran after him, calling, "Joaquin! Wait! Come back!" but by the time I reached the creek he was over the rise. Out of sight. Gone.

Slow, I walked back up to the house, each footstep feeling like I was wearing anvils for shoes. When at last I reached the back porch, Prometheus was waiting with the key to the cellar padlock and a lantern.

I took them from him, not saying a word, head down, afraid he'd see my tears.

So quiet I barely heard him, he said, "I'm sorry, my dear. So very sorry."

I kept my head down. "You heard?"

"Yes. Is it true? You weren't just saying it to make him stay?"

"It's true."

He paused, his head down, like he was thinking something over.

I said, "I guess we have both had bad news today." I meant his telegram.

"Yes. You shouldn't be down in the vug in your condition. Here, let me—"

He started to take back the lantern, but I pulled it to me. "No! I mean, I'd like to stay down there tonight. Alone. I mean, I'd be thankful for the solitude."

"Yes," he said. "Yes, I see. Well, if there's anything, anything at all I can do . . ."

"Sure, Prometheus. I'll let you know."

• • •

That night after everybody was asleep, I snuck up to the barn and found a sturdy sack. Down in the vug, I filled it up until I could barely lift it—and that happened faster than I'd thought it would, gold being awful heavy.

I took only pebbles from the floor, a little here and a little there, and it was so little by comparison that a body would never know that any was missing. I took the pebbles with the most of that white milky quartz, too, so at least I had the satisfaction of knowing that the Bug Boys would not get the highest grade.

I felt pretty raw about it, though. Prometheus had been awful good to us, better than anybody ever, and here I was, swiping his treasure. But it was for Chigger. Surely he'd understand.

I tossed and turned all night, going in and out of sleep, sometimes waking up with my eyes wet and bleary. I woke up mad a few times, too—mad at Joaquin, mad at the Bug Boys, mad at the aunts—but the night passed.

Just before dawn came, I dreamt of a white horse. Now, a white horse is the worst kind of omen. It portends death or grievous illness, either for the dreamer or close kin. In the dream was a row of young corn, and the white horse was trampling it, pawing it into the ground, breaking all the fresh young stalks like it had gone mad.

I woke up with a start, a prayer against demons on my lips. That horse felt important to me, about as important as Granny Wren's dream where the big snake wrapped round the cabin and foretold the war. It was a while before the shaking subsided, before I could start up the tunnel with my sack of gold.

I dragged and stopped, dragged and stopped. It was heavier than I'd thought. I made a whole lot more noise than I was comfortable with, especially when I got to the cellar and had to hoist it up the stairs and out to the yard, but I didn't have time to be too quiet. Dawn was racing up fast, and the Bug Boys would be impatient.

At last I got it down the long yard and to the edge of the

creek, and I was about to sit down in a heap when I heard a voice from the bushes.

" 'Bout time." It was Uncle Glow. He rode over and held down his hand.

I said, "You're gonna have to split it out. It's too heavy."

He said, "I'll be the judge'a that!" and got down off his horse, skinny braid swinging. The sight of that orange string set me to thinking about Joaquin's horse tail, and how much nicer it was, and then about the white horse and the dream. I had to fight to keep from crying again. I tell you, if I had had a scissors, I would have reached over and cut Glow's off, just for spite.

He gave me one of those "Useless female!" looks and went to lift the sack, but it didn't budge. Neither did it move the second time he tried to lift it, or the third. Finally, he opened it and started scooping gold into his saddlebags.

He was so stupid he did not even remark on it. Now, you'd think a person who'd never had squat would have at least said "Golly!" at the sight of all that gold, but all he said was, "There, Miss Smarty," after he'd heaved the bags onto his poor horse and shouldered what remained in the sack.

"That's about all there is," I lied, while Glow fumbled his way back up on his horse. "Take it and leave us be. You can't come back for more,'cause there isn't any."

"Oh, you done told a big fib, Clutie!"

I sucked in air and my heart went up in my throat. Dang that Chigger and his Indian sneaking! I turned all around, my eyes searching quick in the bushes.

"There's a whole lotta gold, and Mr. Metheus, he says—" His words turned into a shrill scream. I started toward his voice.

I stopped before I had gone three steps.

Beetle rode up out of the creekbed, out of the brush, and he had Chigger John under his arm, thrashing and kicking. "Be still!" he said, and when Chigger kept on wiggling and screeching, he cracked him over the head with the butt of his pistol.

Chigger went limp.

"Tomorrow morning." He hoisted Chigger's little body across the horse's withers. "And the next. And the next. Till it's all we can carry. You got that, Dung-for-Brains?"

He didn't wait for a reply. He yelled at Glow to get a move on, and then he loped his horse across Dollar Creek and up the hill, Chigger's little red head flopping.

I tore up the yard, into the house, into the gun room, and I was cursing Chigger for sneaking down to the creek, cursing Joaquin for leaving, cursing Beetle for being born. Cursed myself most of all, for not telling somebody, for thinking I could handle it on my own.

I raced to the rack and pulled down the Winchester. Hands shaking, I loaded it, crammed extra cartridges into my skirt pockets.

Out to the landing, down the stairs, out the back door— in a flash I was to the creek and wading across it. The water sucked at my skirts, weighing them down. I clambered up the far bank, my skirts dragging like wet mortar and hair hanging in my face, but I gained my feet and I kept going.

I ran until my chest was heaving, ran until my breath was coming in ragged gasps, ran until I was took with a stitch in my side that brought me to my knees. I lay there panting till the pain subsided a bit, and then I dogtrotted on, following the tracks.

I hated those dad-blasted skirts. Once the panic had worn off and I had started some serious tracking, I tied them up betwixt my legs. When that failed, I started ripping them off. Well, part of them got ripped off by brambles or cactus and the like, but I helped. Soon I was practically down to my underwear, at least below the waist. This suited me fine, except that I had to carry all my extra cartridges down the front of my dress top and they were a botherment.

I ran through scratchy scrub where the tracks were hard to follow, up and down low rolling hills covered in tall, weedy grass and prickly pear. Back into the scrub again; slower all the time, that rifle like an anchor, weighing me down, holding me back.

I don't know what was wrong with me. Maybe it was the baby, maybe I was too long out of the woods. But by mid-morning I was sunburnt and down to a draggy walk, and still no sign of Beetle or Chigger John except their tracks. I could not for the life of me figure out why they had gone so far out, considering they were planning on coming back each morning.

And then I had a real sinking feeling. They. *They* were planning on coming back. *They.* I checked the tracks again, and then I sat right down in the hot dirt with my head in my hands.

I had been following the track of a single horse, not two, and it was headed south, straight for the New Mexico line. Peligroso's tracks. Joaquin. The Bug Boys must have veered off miles back, somewhere in the scrub.

How could I have been so stupid? I had been so scared and crazy and mad that I had missed what any kid would have seen plain. I would have cried if I had owned the strength. After a while of just sitting there, all sore and hope-less, not to mention tattered and hungry and thirsty and hot, I stood up and turned around and started limping back.

I walked and walked and walked some more. I had come out farther than I realized, and my legs were feeling like they were filled solid with fishing weights. By noon I was so dry that wisps of hair had stuck to my open mouth, and when I pulled them free, bits of skin came with them.

I guess it was not long after that when I heard the horse. I had labored almost to the top of a rise, and the sound being on the other side, I hunkered down behind a low bush, rifle at the ready.

Closer and closer it came. It stopped just short of the top of the rise—short of me seeing it—and I could hear leather squeaking, like somebody was looking all around and turning in the saddle.

I held my breath. It could be an Indian. A Noble Savage on the prowl. Prometheus had said there weren't any in town, but I was a long ways out. I was pretty sure that Colorado Indians were wilder than Kansas ones, it being farther west and all, which meant they wouldn't exactly be friendly to white women on foot. But then, just as fast, it came to me that it was leather I'd heard. I was fair certain an Indian wouldn't use a white man's saddle.

That left Beetle. If it was him, I would have him in two shakes. I was sort of dizzy from the sun and thirsting something fierce, but all of a sudden my head got real clear.

This wasn't the old days. I wasn't scared of him—especially compared to Indians. He had my Chigger, and I aimed to get him back, and blast the consequences. I wasn't afraid of any dream white horse. That big old Winchester suddenly felt light in my hand, like a bird, and I knew I could do it.

And then somebody called, "*Cluuuutie!*"

Well, shoot. All that hot blood wasted. I got to my feet. I could see him now. He was standing in the stirrups on a strange horse, looking the other way.

"Prometheus?" My voice came out in a dry croak.

He took his cupped hands away from his mouth and fair leapt from the saddle. "Are you all right? Are you hurt? What happened to your dress? What were you *thinking*?" The questions rolled out of him so fast and furious that I couldn't answer, though I tried some there at the first.

Finally I just put my hands over his mouth and whispered, "Water."

That gave him something to do. He ripped the canteen from his saddle and opened it, sloshing some out in his haste and muttering, "Yes, water. How idiotic. Water!"

I gave him my rifle and took the canteen, and by the time I finished drinking—and let me tell you, warm water out of a canteen never tasted so good—he had regained some presence of mind. He looked cross, like the time he had accused me of starching the linens, only worse. He said, "All right now?"

I handed back the canteen. "I reckon." My voice still sounded broken but it was better. I looked out over the plains. I didn't want to meet his eyes.

"Clutie? Where's Chigger?"

I couldn't say it.

He put his hand on my arm. "Clutie?" When I didn't answer, his fingers tightened. "Clutie!"

In a whisper, I said at last, "Gone."

He gave me a jerk, turned me toward him. "What do you mean, 'gone'!"

I finally lowered my gaze to meet his. "Stole," I said, and then I couldn't stop the words from pouring out of me. "Uncle Beetle stole him to make sure I'd swipe more gold from the vug. I didn't take much, Prometheus; I mean, I only took the worst grade. Well, maybe I took a lot, but I thought it'd be enough. I thought they'd go away. And then Chigger followed me down to the creek and there were two of 'em instead of one, and I dreamt the white horse, and—"

"Stop!"

"—and I thought I was following the right track, but it was Joaquin not Chigger, and—"

"*Stop!*"

He grabbed hold of my other arm and shook me then, shook me hard. I shut my mouth. He was glaring at me something fierce, and I looked down lest I be swallowed up by the raging in those terrible blue eyes. He stopped shaking me, and it seemed like we stood there a long time, his hands on my arms, me staring at my feet, nobody saying a word.

At last he let go. He said, "Let us go home. On the way, you will tell me—slowly and from the start—how Chigger came to be kidnapped. He is kidnapped, I take it?"

I nodded and looked up. Now they were just regular eyes. Maybe it had been my imagination.

He said, "We will go home, and then we will decide what to do."

He mounted the borrowed horse with some difficulty, it being a willful mare, and then stretched a hand down for me. It took three tries, what with the horse skittering around and such and Prometheus shouting, "Quandary! Steady there, beast!" but at last I climbed up behind him.

"This is a terrible horse," I said. It had bucked out twice, and we were not yet fifty feet from where we started.

Prometheus jerked her head up just in time to keep her from getting it down and really bucking up a storm. "Steady, Quandary! Steady, girl!" he said, then, "I agree. She is, indeed, a terrible horse. I borrowed her from Cornelius Matheson after I determined you were gone.''

"You tracked me out here?" As soon as the words left my mouth I knew it was stupid—how else had he found me, if not by tracking?

But he didn't say it. Instead, he confided, "I was in the army.''

I was about to say I knew that, that I had seen his discharge papers, when the horse took it in her head to reach back and bite Prometheus in the foot. He was too fast for her and kicked her in the head.

"Besides,'' he continued as she got back to business, "your skirts are tattered over the landscape for miles. You look a sight.''

I supposed I did. I had shed the petticoats, too, for the most part. I was glad I had worn underwear, because it was what I was down to, aside from a few shreds and scraps of calico or white cotton. I said, "Well, I still have the bodice part. I could sew a new skirt to stick on it. I guess.''

I wished he'd kick the mare into a lope. I had wasted too much time already, what with following the wrong tracks like a prime fool.

It was like he read my mind. As we skirted a thicket of some new kind of sticker bush—and I swan, I had blundered through plenty that day—he said, "I'm sorry we cannot proceed more quickly. Quandary bucks if you ask her to move at a faster pace. I think you have been jolted quite enough.''

He meant the baby. I guess he thought that it'd get shook out of me somehow, like Carnation's pillow. I said, "Quandary's a funny name for a horse.'' Personally, I thought Sour Bitch would have been a better choice.

"Matheson says it's because you have to be drunk to get on her, but sober to ride her. Thus, the quandary.''

Again, she swung her head to bite, ears pinned, but he was too quick for her. He stuck out his foot and the force carried her into it, landing her a sharp blow along the cheek piece of her bridle. She shook her head and kept on walking.

"Now, start from the beginning,'' he said, like nothing

had happened. "The very beginning. Speak slowly, and don't leave anything out."

Quandary brought us home about mid-afternoon, during which time she had nearly bucked us off four times and got in one good bite on Prometheus's boot, and in which time I also told Prometheus everything, with every *t* crossed and every *i* dotted.

As we splashed across Dollar Creek, it occurred to me that I scarce recognized the neighborhood. Dirt piles were everywhere, so high and so numerous that you could not see some of the houses, and I could hear the hollers of people hoisting up dirt and rocks. They had dug up so much land that it was a wonder they had left any houses standing at all.

The padlock was still safe on the cellar door, I noticed as we neared the house, and there were a couple of strange men there, armed to the teeth.

"Prometheus?" I said.

"I forgot. Mr. Hargrove and Mr. Stitch. I hired them to guard the cellar. I'll not have you sleeping down there anymore. I should have done it days ago."

We rode up the yard to the house, whereupon Prometheus bade me get down. "Mind the horse," he said just as she nipped my sleeve.

I jumped back. I said to the mare, "You didn't once happen to have a cousin in Missouri, name of Johnnycake, did you?"

In reply, she tried to bite me in the face. I ducked just in time.

Prometheus handed down rifle. "I shall return Cornelius's mount. I suggest you get in the house and change your clothes before some busybody spies you. And don't worry, Clutie. Chigger will be safe."

Quandary, sensing the nearness of her stable, bucked twice before Prometheus got her under control. At last she set off at an annoyed walk across the field, ears pinned flat, head swinging side to side, Prometheus as straight-backed in the saddle as if he had a rod up his spine. I had not realized how accomplished a rider he was. You would think somebody who rode that good would have a horse of his own.

Mr. Hargrove and Mr. Stitch both looked like they would skin their grandmother for a nickel, and seemed not a bit shocked to see a lady get off a killer horse in her underwear. I nodded to them, figuring the ammenities could wait, and went in the house. After so long in the sun, it felt cool and homey, about as nice as anything.

Despite Prometheus's promise that Chigger would be all right, I was still worried. But, besides feeling like a bobcat that's been dragged tail-first through a briar patch, I was perishing with hunger. I stopped in the kitchen. There was a plate of the fried rabbit Joaquin had made the night before. Just looking at it made me cringe with remorse.

If there was a prize for stupidity, I surely was the leading contender. Why hadn't I told him about the Bug Boys? Why, what with them being so easily impressed by famous men, just the sight of him might have caused them to drop Chigger and run.

Then again, maybe not.

Well, what was done was done, as Prometheus had pointed out till he was blue in the face. I poured myself a tall glass of water and drank it down—it seemed I could not slake my thirst—picked up a piece of rabbit, and stripped it of meat in three bites. I grabbed another piece while I was still chewing on the first, and started up the front hall, to the stairs. That Joaquin was a good cook. I hoped he'd get back before we ate all the rabbit.

I hoped he'd get back before Beetle hurt Chigger.

I had just turned to go up the staircase when somebody knocked on the door. Shadows falling through the curtained panels told me they were too tall to be Carnation and Myrtle, so I just kept on up the stairs. I was in no mood for company, and I figured company would be in no mood for me.

But the banging kept up. I stopped halfway to the landing and hollered, "Go away!"

"We will not be put off!" cried a female voice, and I knew it right away for that of Mrs. Gensch. "Open the door this instant!"

There was a man's voice. He said, "Now, Little Dove . . ."

I heard her say, "How many times do I have to tell you, Hiram? No familiarities. Open up in there!" She commenced to bang on the glass with her knuckles.

"Go away!" I called from the stairs, around a mouthful of half-chewed rabbit. "I'm not decent!"

But the banging and the shouting got worse. I was afraid she'd break the glass. So I went down and flung the door open. "What! What is it this time?"

Mrs. Gensch started right in. "It has come to our attention that there is a wanted man in this house!" She waved a sheet of paper. "A killer by the name of the *El Dragón*, and we— that is, the ladies of the Christian Women's Temperance Society, will not . . . will not . . ." Her eye had finally fallen on my skirts, at least where my skirts were supposed to be.

"Will not what?" I said, taking another bite of rabbit.

"Ma'am? I'm Sheriff Jenkins," said the man with her. He was dark-haired, mustachioed, dressed nice in a gray hat and pin-striped suit with a badge pinned on the front of it. He was smiling, although I couldn't tell if it was at her or me. "Miz Gensch, here, has got herself into a swivet over some feller she thinks—"

"I *know* it's him. Mrs. Wannamaker definitely recognized him. And she herself told me his name!" She had recovered from whatever shocked condition she had worked herself into, although I noticed she did not let her eyes fall below my face.

I said, "You mean Joaquin. The Spanish Kid." It made tears of pride and longing come to my eyes, just to say it.

"You see?" Mrs. Gensch cried triumphantly. "She's fully complicitous in the situation! A dangerous *pistolero* is loose in our town!"

The sheriff snatched the paper from her and handed it to me. It was a wanted poster for Joaquin, out of New Mexico. Seeing his picture on it made my heart grow warm, but reading what was underneath chilled it again. They had set his reward at $5,000, and said it was for murder, among other crimes.

I decided to play it bold. "This doesn't mean anything," I said to Sheriff Jenkins. "He is not wanted in Colorado. Besides, all those men he killed got killed for a reason. They were in a gang, a long time ago, what murdered his daddy. They were vicious killers."

"Clutie? Why are you at the door in your underwear?" Prometheus had just come up from behind me. "Hello, Hiram." The two men shook hands.

"I want him out of here!" cried Mrs. Gensch.

Well, Prometheus shooed me upstairs to change, but I crouched on the landing to listen. Mrs. Gensch carried on awhile longer about Joaquin and harped on as how everybody at this house was drunken and went around with no pants or skirt and it wasn't *decent* and we were all going to perdition in a handcart, and didn't anybody have *values* anymore.

By the time Prometheus could get a word in edgewise, he explained—real patient, too, considering how he felt about Mrs. Gensch—that Joaquin had been a model citizen during the time of their acquaintance, and although he had unfortunately been called away on a matter of urgent business, Prometheus was certain that upon his return, Joaquin would put all Mrs. Gensch's fears to rest.

Up on the landing I smiled, thinking that he meant Joaquin would put her fears to rest with pistol or blade, but such was not the case, as he offered her a sherry.

She turned it down kind of huffy—I suppose she had to, being the head of the Christian Women's Temperance Society and all—and after she banged off toward home in a snit, he asked the sheriff in.

"Would you care to see the vug, Hiram? It's opportune you should call today. We've had a bit of excitement."

"Don't mind it I do, Prometheus. But first, would you please tell me why that little gal answered the door all dirty and sunburnt and scratched up, and eatin' fried rabbit in her hootchie-coos?"

There was a scrape of boots in the hallway. "All in good time."

''And don't you have a kid runnin' round here someplace, 'bout eleven or twelve?''

''That's what I want to talk to you about. Drink?''

''After we see the vug. If you don't mind my sayin' so, you don't hardly seem lit up at all. I hope sobriety ain't catchin'.''

twenty-five

As Prometheus told me later, the town was not going to be much help in getting Chigger back. We could count on Sheriff Hiram Jenkins—he was the law and had to help whether he wanted to or not, although I thought he seemed the sort that would've helped Prometheus even if he didn't have to. We had Mr. Hargrove and Mr. Stitch, although somebody had to stay behind and guard the vug.

It was a ragtag crew, near as ragtag as the ones we were setting out after.

The plan was that come dawn, Mr. Hargrove and Mr. Stitch were to hide, and I was to go down to the creek like usual and give the Bug Boys more gold. Sheriff Jenkins said we were to wait a bit, then follow along after them, slow, and let them lead us to their hiding place. We would then surround them and that would be that.

I said we might as well follow the tracks now, but the sheriff said the Bug Boys would most likely move their hide-out. I said he did not know the Bug Boys very well, for they were not smart enough to move their camp, but I was ignored. When I said that they were plenty mean enough—Beetle, anyway—to shoot Chigger in the head if we surrounded them, the sheriff asked me to pour him a cup of coffee.

I put in a restless night. Although Chigger carried a lucky buckeye, the Bug Boys had them, too, and they had been blessed by Granny Wren. Well, Chigger's had been, too. But there were more Bug Boys.

I dreamt of Chigger John in the hands of the Bug Boys and woke with a start when Beetle's knife slit his throat. I dreamt uneasy dreams of home and Granny Wren poisoning one soldier and intestating the other, and that woke me up, too.

And I dreamt the white horse again. He was tearing at the corn once more, but this time I couldn't wake up. I watched, helpless, as he ripped at it in his madness and ground it beneath his hooves, and then a pack of black, wild dogs came down out of the woods and began to savage him, clawing at his flanks and haunches with their terrible teeth, snapping at his throat.

I finally woke in a cold sweat. When Prometheus came in, I was already up and dressed. I was afraid to dream anymore.

Down into the vug I went, Prometheus with me this time, and we gathered up the nuggets. Not a quarter so much as before, but a goodly amount. Then he bade Mr. Hargrove and Mr. Stitch join him in the cellar.

"I can't imagine what's keeping Hiram," Prometheus said for the fourth time, checking his timepiece and mopping his brow, though the predawn was chilly. "He should be here. He's bringing the horses!"

Me, I went down to the creek to wait.

The sun was just peeking over the hills when I looked up to see Wig wading the creek on his horse. I had been waiting so long—and slept so badly the night before—that I guess I dozed off. At least I didn't dream.

He smiled down at me as I clambered to my feet. "Some less than yesterday," he remarked as I handed him up the bag.

"If I take more, they will notice. How's Chigger?"

"He abides," he replied. "He's got a womanly influence now."

"What do you mean?"

"Myrtle and Carnation's camped with us. I swan, I don't know how they knew, but they was on us like ducks on a June bug. Hard to believe a woman like Carnation could have a motherly instinct, but there you are. You tell 'em where we was?"

I shook my head. "How could I tell when I don't know?"

"Well, you keep it that way." He hauled his horse about.

I said, "Uncle Wig, I dreamt a white horse tearing up the corn. I dreamt it twice."

He reined in the horse and sat there for a minute, his back to me.

Finally, without turning round, he said, "You shouldn't tell such whoppers, Clutie. I ain't gonna pass that along," and rode across the creek, up the hill, and out of sight.

I trudged up the yard to the house. By the time I got there, Prometheus was up from the cellar. I said, "Myrtle and Carnation have caught wind of this somehow, and they're out there at that camp. I think we're going to need more men."

Sheriff Jenkins, who must have arrived while I was asleep, was just coming up from the stable with three mounts. "Saw the whole thing. By God, that's a ratty lookin' nag he's riding."

I looked at the horses, then at the sheriff. "I thought Mr. Hargrove was going with us. Or Mr. Stitch. You've only got three horses."

Prometheus put his hand on my shoulder. "Mr. Stitch will accompany us."

"But there's—"

"Go in the house, Clutie. You're not to ride . . ." He lowered his mouth to my ear. "I'll not have you roughriding in your condition."

"But these are the Bug Boys, and they've got the aunts there with them!"

The sheriff looked up from the girth he was messing with. "What's this? Who's with 'em?"

While Prometheus explained about Myrtle and Carnation, I tried to think what to do. If this bunch of fools thought they would just ride out there peaceable-like and kindly ask the Bug Boys to pretty please hand over Chigger—and the gold, too, so long as they were at it—they had another thing coming.

I thought about asking Prometheus again, but I knew what he'd say—ever since he'd stopped drinking, you could hardly get round him at all. I didn't even consider Mr. Stitch, since he looked about as smart as a pump handle and mean-er'n a sack of snakes to boot.

"Sheriff," I said, "you don't understand about the Bug Boys. You have got to let me go along. What we have got to do is—"

"Now, Miss Clutie," he said, cutting me off. He put a hand on my shoulder. "I reckon I know how to take care of a bunch of mud turtles up out of the swamp."

I said, "That just shows how much you know about it. There's no swamp in Jukes Holler."

"Go in the house, Clutie," said Prometheus, real stern. "I mean it. Mr. Stitch is a good tracker, and the sheriff knows what he's doing. We'll have Chigger and be back before dinner."

I could tell they were set on it. I had no choice. I said, "All right," and went in the back, banging the door behind me. I walked straight up the front hall and up the stairs to my room, and leaned out of the window.

"Well, go if you're going!" I called, and slammed the window.

I found Spider's Peacemaker and gunbelt and put them on over my skirts.

I dumped out all the rest of my buckeyes—I was down to five now—and put them in my pockets. All told, that made six.

I walked down the stairs to the library, opened the gun rack, and took out my Winchester and ammunition.

Then I went out the front door and ran up the street in the rising light to the Mathesons' barn, and commenced to steal their horse.

I'll bet Quandary was the worst horse west of the Missis-sippi. Not only did she blow herself up so terrible when I saddled her that I had to tighten the girth five times—and that is no fun in a dark barn, especially when you are getting bit and stepped on a'purpose every five seconds—but she would not take the bit until I buried it in a palmful of grain, and even then she chomped on me.

I had the devil's own time even getting on her—I could

scarce call it "mounting up," since that implies some command over the situation. She about bucked me off twice before I even got out of the Mathesons' yard, and she made such a ruckus I was sure they'd wake up and find me swiping her.

But they didn't, and I finally got her out of the yard, across Dollar Creek where it cut across the back part of their lot, and up the hill.

Prometheus and the others had already left. I could see their tracks where they made a mess of Wig's, and as the sun gained on the horizon, I could make them out, too—three little hazy dots in the distance. I stayed well back, which was easy, Quandary owning no gait but a cranky walk.

We traveled like that for about an hour and a half, losing sight of them for long periods, then getting a glimpse. I was getting antsy.

Not because of Quandary—we had established a routine whereby I whopped her over the head with a switch every five minutes and reminded her not to buck—but because I couldn't imagine the Bug Boys being hid so far out. My stomach was hurting, although I had not thrown up, and I could no longer see Prometheus and the others.

Then I heard a shot. Then another. And then all hell broke loose. It was faint, coming from up ahead. Without thinking, I kicked Quandary in the flanks and hunched to take off at a run. Instead, she bolted straight up in the air and started to sunfish and crowhop like there was no tomorrow. There just about wasn't, either, for I was hanging half out of the saddle and sweating through my dress by the time I got her stopped.

She was lathered up pretty good, too, and was past minding when I leaned across her neck and lost my breakfast. I had lost Spider's pistol in the ruckus, too, along with three buckeyes. I decided to leave them lay. I still had the rifle and plenty of charms, and I would not chance dismounting.

By then the shooting had long since stopped. I didn't know what to think. I wiped my mouth on the back of my hand, wishing I had brought a canteen: I was still queasy in my stomach, and thought water would settle it a little. But I hadn't any, so I started forward, at a walk this time. Quandary didn't argue. She was still blowing hard from putting on her show.

I said, "I hope you feel as rotten as I do, you rank old bitch," and swatted her one between the ears by way of emphasis.

I cut a wide path to the south, watching all the time for signs of an encampment and praying that they had not put a bullet in Prometheus or Chigger, that all that shooting meant Prometheus had saved the day and that the Bug Boys were on their way to prison.

I didn't have much hope, though.

Before too long, I saw smoke coming over a rise, a little thin trail of it from a fire just started. I rode up closer, then got off Quandary—who was still tired enough that she only pretended to nip my arm—and crept forward.

Then my bones froze. On the breeze came snatches of music. A mouth harp. And I didn't believe Prometheus played one.

I tied Quandary to a sticker bush without much hope she'd stay for long, took down my rifle and the box of ammunition, and then I got down on my hands and knees and snuck up the rise, to the crest.

They were all down there. There was a buckboard wagon. Sheriff Jenkins was tied to the front wheel, his arms splayed out in a T. His head lolled on his chest, like he was passed out. Carnation and Myrtle were up in the wagon bed, dressed in canary yellow and bright purple. They each had a parasol, and were fanning themselves leisurely, their backs to the body of Mr. Stitch, who was sprawled on the ground about fifty feet behind them, stone dead.

They had scalped him, and he was half-naked. There was a bloody place at his crotch were they had taken his privates. My stomach turned over and I gagged.

I didn't think I had anything else left to puke up, but I found it.

Chigger was tied to the picket line by his hands. There were two horses dead. Prometheus's mount and the other two were there as well.

Spider sat on the ground over to the far side, holding his arm. I believe he had been hit, for there was blood on it. There was a blanketed body beside him. It had to be Glow on account of the size, so small, and the orange braid trailing out the top. I thought of Glow gone, and how nobody'd ever yell "Yankees in the corn patch!" again, and how he'd never again run to defend the honor of the South, and I got a lump in my throat.

That was, until I saw Wig and Beetle over by the fire. It was Wig playing the mouth harp. He put it away and poked at the little blaze. Beetle was poking at Prometheus with a big old knife, and Prometheus's suitcoat was gone, his sleeves tattered and dirty.

I couldn't hear what Beetle was saying, but I could guess. I had hunkered outside the barn back home and overheard too many tales of tortured and mutilated Yankees to give Beetle the benefit of the doubt, especially now that Granny Wren no longer held him in check.

And there was Wig—my Wig, who called me Shortcake and danced coins across his knuckles, who was the only one of them ever to be nice to me—about to aid and abet him.

I could barely hear what they were saying, what with the wind whisking it away. Prometheus appeared staunch, though. Trussed and hogtied though he was, he sat straight and proud, like he did not give a fig for the blood seeping from the corner of his eye, or for the knife Beetle now held to the fire.

I was proud of him. I guessed he would have made a fine officer.

Wig got to his feet. The look on his face was fierce, like I'd never seen it before. He took two steps away, then wheeled and kicked Prometheus in the side. The aunts giggled and Myrtle applauded. "Another!" cried Carnation, and Wig complied.

I checked the rifle.

Wig crossed the camp and untied Chigger, and hauled him, kicking and pitching a fit, back to the fire. He threw him down in a heap. I heard him say, "Watch," but the wind snatched away the rest of it.

Chigger was looking around, dull-like, and then he looked square in my direction. I don't know how he spied me, on my belly in the brush, but he did. His face lit up and I thought for sure he'd holler "Clutie!" and Beetle would kill him dead, but instead he cupped his hands to his mouth. His secret Indian whistle carried over the wind, bringing up gooseflesh on my arms.

Until Uncle Wig smacked him, that was. He landed several feet away, on the ground between me and Beetle.

I stared down the barrel of the rifle, breathing hard, sights on Wig. But as mad and scared as I was, I could not make myself pull the trigger. A squirrel or a rabbit is one thing, your own kinfolk another. As murderous as they were, I just couldn't shoot.

Beetle and the others didn't pay Chigger any mind, because just then Wig leapt upon Prometheus and grabbed his head and forced a wood block in the side of his mouth.

I knew they meant to cut out his tongue, and that would be just for starters.

I swung the rifle to Beetle, who held the knife, blade glowing red in his hand. He leaned over Prometheus and pressed the flat of the red-hot blade to his upper arm, where the sleeve was torn.

Prometheus screamed.

I whispered, "God forgive me." My finger tightened on the trigger.

"No! Mr. Metheus!" Chigger popped up between us.

I backed off just in time, or the shot would have taken off the top of his head.

I whispered, "Get down!"

Instead, he ran to Prometheus and threw himself upon him. Beetle slugged him in the head so hard he rolled off, and then Wig hauled him up by the arm. Chigger just hung there like all the stuffing was gone out of him, and Wig tossed him to the side.

The aunts cheered.

With all the attention on Chigger, Prometheus had struggled to his feet, and he kicked Beetle in the arm. The knife went sailing. Beetle howled and yelled something at Wig, of which I heard "pig-suckin'."

The aunts waved their parasols.

Wig knocked Prometheus to the ground again, farther away from me, then got behind him and took him in a choke hold, and dragged him to the wagon. They lashed him to the back wheel. His burnt arm was an angry red.

Beetle picked up his knife.

I sighted Beetle again. I knew I could not shoot just one of them. I would have to kill them all. And I couldn't do it, not even with Prometheus hogtied for torture. They wouldn't have given me a chance, that was for sure, but I had to give them one. Just one.

Beetle motioned to Wig to hold Prometheus still. He pulled a rusty pair of pliers from his back pocket and brought them near Prometheus's gaping mouth, I expect to hold his tongue still for the chopping.

My knees were shaking, but I made myself stand up, on legs that felt like jelly, and tried not to look at Mr. Stitch.

I called, "Stay your hand, Beetle Jukes!" I don't know how it came out so bold.

Both Beetle and Wig whipped round. Wig saw me first. He hollered, "Clutie? Is that—"

Then Spider started shooting. I had forgot him entirely. He was shooting wild, not in my direction at all, but crazy, here and there. I didn't even think. I hit the ground, drew a bead, and fired.

He dropped and lay still, blood seeping from his head.

I wiped at my eyes to get the tears out of the way. Spider had always been the worst kind of polecat to me and he had murdered my Daisy cat in the coldest of blood, but he was kin. And I expect that no matter how bad your kin are, blood is thicker than water.

Still, I whispered, "And *stay* dead this time, you grimy little peckerwood."

A bullet whizzed over my head.

Well, so much for last chances.

Myrtle and Carnation were still in the wagon—I could see a purple bustle and a snatch of yellow where they were hun-

kered down—but Wig was under it, pretty much, Beetle was
on his way in, and they were firing, or at least Wig was.
Most of the shots went wild, but a few came too close for
comfort.

I sighted on Beetle first, Wig being pretty much hidden in
the shadows behind Sheriff Jenkins, behind the front wheel.
Beetle had fallen and was skittering on his side—his bladed
peg leg was bad for traction, but good for me. I fired just as
he got to his hands and knees and pulled the greater part of
his body behind Prometheus.

For a second I thought I'd missed—a spoke of the wheel
near Prometheus's face splintered—but then I heard Beetle
whoop and saw his hand flop into the light.

There was just Wig left.

For what seemed like a real long time, but was probably
less than a minute, nobody fired. Nobody did anything except sweat. Well, at least I did.

Then Wig called, "Shortcake?"

His voice sounded good to me, homey-like, but I reminded
myself that he had done his worst on poor Mr. Stitch, lying
cut up on the plain. I didn't look at the body, though. I
couldn't look.

I said, "Throw out your gun, Uncle Wig. I am not fooling."

He said, "I can see that you ain't. What kind'a gun you
usin', Clutie? That my old Navy? Don't seem like that old
pistol'd do in a circumstance like this. Did you get you a
new one?"

"Winchester," I said. "Throw out your gun." I could see
him moving around behind the sheriff and the wheel. Not
clear, just snatches of motion.

"Well now, I don't believe I had better do that," he called
back. "Seems to me that Winchester a'yourn has a hair trigger on it. You been at work on it with a file?"

"Wig?" wailed a female voice from the wagon. "Wig!
What's goin' on!"

I heard him snarl "Shut up!" real vicious before he said
to me, greasy-like, "Shortcake? Clutie, honey? Why don't

you just step out into the open real slow, so's your old uncle can see you mean him no harm?''

I reckon that was what did it for me. That oily edge to his voice, like I was some mark that he was setting up for the take. Except he wasn't out for my pocket watch. He was out for me.

I hollered back, ''I believe I'll have to think about that, Uncle Wig,'' and brought up that Winchester.

I had him in my sights once, for just half a second, but then he ducked back into the shadows. I could only sight on a piece of him at best, between the wheel being in the way and the sheriff tied to it and all. And that was in the shadows. I couldn't even be sure it was him.

I thought about the dream, how I'd thought me and Chigger were the corn and the Bug Boys were the white horse, trampling it into the grounds. I was beginning to think I'd been wrong. Maybe I was the dogs, ripping at the horse's flanks. The puke dogs.

I dug in my pocket and took out the last of my buckeyes and lined them up in a row before me. I said a quick spell for luck, spat twice, slapped the dirt, and picked up the gun again. I seated it against my shoulder and waited.

After about three minutes, he called, ''Clutie Mae? You think it over yet?''

I don't know what possessed me, but I said, ''What?''

He called again, ''I say, did you think it over?''

I stared down the sights of that Winchester. I said, ''I can't hear you! Speak up!''

His face appeared between the wheel spokes—just a little sliver of pink and one blue eye. ''Are you gonna step out like a good—''

I fired.

It was a good shot, like a turkey shoot. The bullet took him above the eye, and he flew back. I didn't reckon there was any way he wasn't dead.

Still, I waited a bit before I collected my buckeyes and stood up. The aunts were still bustle-end up in the wagon bed, but for all I knew, they were carrying, too.

I called, ''Carnation and Myrtle Jukes! I'd appreciate it if y'all would stand up and put your hands in the air."

Nothing.

I shouted, "I'm going to give you till I count five, and then I'm going to started peppering that wagon bed."

Myrtle stood up on the three count. Carnation on four. They were empty-handed.

I got up then, and slowly walked down into the camp. I did not mean to be so deliberate, but I could hardly make my legs move.

I had nearly forgot about Prometheus, being so occupied with the uncles and all, but I went to Chigger first. He was still breathing, but he was out cold.

I was just about to stand up and go untie Prometheus when there sounded such a screech as I had never heard, and I was knocked flat, the rifle flying.

Beetle! I twisted to the side fast and hard, even as that rebel yell was leaving his throat.

It was a good thing, for his knife missed me by inches.

I grabbed his knife hand by the wrist. I guess I was still fair strong, for though it didn't retreat, it didn't come forward, either. For a second he stared at me—surprised at my strength, I guess—and then he made to slap me with his free hand.

I pitched to the side, and we rolled over and over in the dirt, tangled in my skirts, fast getting shredded by his peg leg.

I felt the slash when he got me with it, like flash fire in my calf, but the knife was coming too near my face to worry about it.

I jerked to the side again, and he cursed, yelling, "Damn woodscolt!" and somehow he got his knee up high enough to jab me in the belly.

It near took the wind out of me, but not quite, and he was in such an odd position that all of a sudden, I had leverage.

I took the chance and brought my other hand into play. I jerked up on his wrist with both hands, up and away, rolling under him, then on top. He flailed out with his free arm to stop us, and when he did, I jerked the knife down with all my strength.

Even with him fighting me, the knife sank halfway into his chest. He looked up at me, pure unadulterated evil in his eyes. He curled his lip and said, "You goddamn bastard dunghead! You've stuck me!" like it was the last thing he had expected.

I guess I was hysterical. I cried, "Die! Why won't you die!" I leaned forward and shoved that knife in the rest of the way, all my force behind it.

I buried it to the grip.

His eyes were still full of rage, still glaring at me like the Devil himself. "You . . . you go to . . ." And then the strangest thing happened. His face got real soft, just like all the mean was draining out. He said, "Ma? Mama?" real soft.

I sat up, straddling him. I saw then the wound my bullet had made. It was in his shoulder, just a nick.

I don't know why, but I said, "Yes, son?"

His eyes weren't looking at me, then, but straight up. Just like a little kid, he whispered, "Mama? Wig took my . . . He took my . . ."

I waited a second, but he hadn't the strength to finish. I said, as kindly as I could, considering I was crying, "Then we'll get you a new one, son."

Then he stopped breathing and I closed his eyes.

Finally.

I crawled off him, sweat matting my hair and tears streaming down my cheeks, and looked up straight into the face of Prometheus. I guess we had rolled there during the struggle. If he didn't look a sight! Mouth gaping wide and white all round his eyes, he stared at me like I was an avenging angel sent straight down from heaven. Or up from hell.

I said, "Hold on," and got my rifle from under the wagon, and then I heaved myself up to my feet. The aunts were still standing in the wagon bed. I guess they were in shock that I had bested Beetle, for Carnation had both her hands over her mouth and Myrtle's eye was ticcing a mile a minute. I hadn't noticed before, but Mr. Stitch's scalp was nailed to the side of the wagon seat, making bloody flutters in the breeze. I looked away quick. I didn't want to know what they done with the other parts.

I said, "Get down." Every word was an effort.

They just stood there.

I brought up the rifle and fired a shot over their heads. They got down, all right.

I sent them out about twenty feet, where they wouldn't be near any weapons, and then I crouched down beside Prometheus and commenced to untie him, careful not to touch his arm.

I had him almost free—the Bug Boys tied some gruesome knots—when there came a disturbance from out over the rise.

It was Quandary, who got herself free of the sticker bush to jog down into the camp and join in the mayhem. She proceeded down toward us, and Carnation, sensing a golden opportunity, made a dash for it. Flinging herself into the saddle, she give a mighty kick.

It took the mare by surprise, I guess, because she actually broke into a canter. Myrtle yelled, "Pick me up, Carrie, pick me up!"

But Carnation didn't get that far, because after the whole of one stride, Quandary all of a sudden came to her senses. She stopped short and bucked out high in the rear.

Carnation didn't stick. She flew through the air like a big yellow bird and smashed against the side of the wagon, not three feet from Prometheus, headfirst. Quandary gave herself a shake and wandered off to graze.

Myrtle said, "Dang blast you, Carrie!" but Carnation was dead, and past caring.

Me, I finished untying Prometheus before I passed out.

We rode back in the wagon. The bodies were piled in back with the horses tied on behind. Myrtle rode on a horse, tied back in the line, so we would not have to listen to her carry on.

All those dead Jukes and poor Mr. Stitch heaped up behind me, I sat on the tailgate with Chigger's head in my lap. I tried everything to wake him up, but to no avail. I was not feeling so good myself. My leg hurt like the devil, and I was feeling all strange in my belly. I threw up again, sitting there with him, and I would have given anything to hear him cry, "Puke dogs! Puke dogs!"

As it was, I was just sick and lonely.

Prometheus drove us right straight into town, Sheriff Jenkins having a broken arm and a bunch of cracked ribs, and therefore being in need of immediate medical attention. Well, I guess the rest of us were, too.

Town had sure changed since the last time I was there, and all because of the vug. The railroad, too. The street was fair thick with people going every which way, but they made a path for us once they saw our cargo. Some wag called out, "Howdy-do, your Princeliness," and another, "That what they's wearin' to court these days, Duke?" and a couple of kids made a big show of bowing, then laughed and ran. But Prometheus looked straight ahead and kept driving.

They sent for a doctor as soon as we got to the jail. Myrtle was put in a cell in the back room over the protests of the deputy, who said they weren't equipped to deal "with no female wrongdoers," and wouldn't the hotel be a better place? Prometheus told him to shut up and do it, and to close the door, for Myrtle was still carrying on something terrible. I don't believe she took a breath the whole way in.

They laid Chigger out on the sheriff's desk, after sweeping it clean of paraphernalia. His breathing was even, but he was still out cold. I sat in a straight chair beside him, holding his dear little hand while the doctor bandaged my leg. I watched Prometheus get his arm doctored while he told everybody what to do. He was barking orders and running the whole show.

I had to smile. I could scarce believe that this was the selfsame man who had got on the wrong train and then fallen off it because he thought he smelled gin. I was glad he had, though. His getting that whiff of juniper had changed our lives, me and Chigger.

Of course, maybe I hadn't a right to feel happy—after all, Chigger was passed out, cold as a turnip, beside me. I had just murdered nearly the lot of my male kin. And I was in a family way and feeling more poorly by the minute. But without Prometheus, I wouldn't have met up with Joaquin again, wouldn't have had dresses, wouldn't have lived in a nice house—practically a mansion—and wouldn't have had the vug. Not that it was mine, but I swan: just looking at it gave a person renewed faith in the majesty of the Lord.

And most of all, I never would've known Prometheus for what he was when the demon run, as Mrs. Gensch called it, wasn't upon him. I blessed the day I'd put the minnow in his whiskey. Dirty, tattered, cut up, and skin-sizzled though he was, he ran those fellas in the sheriff's office dizzy, and they listened to him. He never had to say a thing twice. I could almost believe those tales of English titles, seeing him like that.

I was going to have some kind of story to tell Joaquin when he got back.

The doctor was bandaging up the sheriff, and Prometheus came over to me. "My dear," he said softly, "you look a fright. Come."

He started to help me up. I felt dizzy and put an arm out to steady myself. "What about Chigger?"

"He'll be fine. Don't you worry. Now, come along."

I leaned on him, too tired to argue and feeling all strange in my innards. I just wanted to sleep. I stood up and started toward the door with heavy feet, but then Prometheus said, "Oh God!" and scooped me up in his arms so quick I scarce knew what was happening.

"Doctor, quickly!" he cried. "She's bleeding!"

twenty-six

W hen I came to, I was in my bed, in my room. I knew it was morning, for sunlight was streaming between the pulled-back curtains. Somebody had dressed me in a linen wrapper. I went to pull myself up on the pillows, but Prometheus came out of nowhere and said, "Lie still." I guess he had been sitting over in the corner.

I said, "But I have slept all of yesterday afternoon away, plus the whole of the night. It's wash day."

Prometheus sat down on the edge of the bed, and studied his hand as he smoothed the coverlet with long fingers. He was dressed real nice again, in dark gray pants and a vest with a gray silk front. Tall and lean, he cut a fine figure, and I was impressed by his handsomeness all over again. Giving up the drink had done wonders for him.

And then he said, "You've been in . . . You've slept six days."

I could not think of a reply. I just lay there.

"The doctor says you must rest, Clutie." He looked up then, and his brow was furrowed with concern. "You nearly lost the baby."

I swallowed hard. "Chigger John?"

His forehead smoothed. "Oh, he's up and pestering the miners. Yes," he added when I lifted a brow, "they've been here for the last four days, stripping the vug."

"How's your arm?"

"Oh, that. Nearly healed. Not to worry."

I looked toward the window. "I wish I could have seen it one last time. The vug, I mean."

He didn't answer. He got up and fussed with the curtains

a bit. "The pressure's off us. Ed Sherwood, over on First Street, hit paydirt. It's only a little vug, but now they're all digging over there. Just in time, too." He chuckled. "We had visitors."

"Visitors?"

"Archie Crandall, from next door. He tunneled through from the other side." He smiled and winked. "Archie cried, 'Thunderation, Mother, we've struck the Big One!' And then he saw our workers and demanded to know how they came to arrive in the void ahead of him."

I was grinning. My stomach was growling, too, and Prometheus put his fingers to his brow. "How stupid of me. You must be starving. I'll bring you up a tray, shall I?" I started to make a face, but he added, "Mrs. Matheson has come in to cook for us."

"Mrs. Matheson?" I could scarce believe it. I said, "I think you had better have a food taster, then. She's liable to poison us!"

He smiled. "I think you'll find that Mrs. Gensch has lost a lot of ground with the local ladies."

Not ten minutes later they were both in my room with a tray. Mrs. Matheson shooed Prometheus out and helped me tend to myself, and then she tucked me in all proper with her busy little hands and brought me the tray.

She was chubby and all smiles, and I have got to say she was prettier than I had thought. A whole lot nicer, too. But then, when the only knowledge you have of a person is them leaning forward on a porch and telling their husband not to talk to you, I suppose you can get the wrong idea.

She lifted the lid off my eggs and toast. "Dr. Killfish says you're supposed to eat light, hon."

She uncovered the fried ham and hash browns. "Just broth." Away came the top off the flapjacks.

She poured me out a cup of coffee, then, as an afterthought, took the lid off a little bowl of beef soup.

"I suppose you'd best eat this first, then."

In silence, Mrs. Matheson watched while I demolished my soup and dived into my eggs. I noticed she was shifting from foot to foot, kind of nervous, and I said, "Thank you, Mrs. Matheson, ma'am. This is past fine."

She cleared her throat. "I just wanted to say how sorry . . . Well, I just wanted to say. That's all." And then I'll be jiggered if she didn't choke back a sob and leave the room.

I wondered what she was sorry for. For being rude, maybe? Perhaps it was because all of my uncles had got killed, albeit by my hand, although I didn't much think she'd be sorry for that, just grateful. Maybe it was just because I was sick.

After three days in that room, I was ready to scream. I had terrible dreams about poor Mr. Stitch, even though Prometheus told me over and over that he had been dead before they started cutting on him. I suppose that men who have gone to war have seen things as bad—worse, maybe—but I had not. Prometheus said that Mr. Hargrove cried like a baby when he heard what had happened to his friend.

Chigger, who seemed to have forgotten the whole thing, came up to visit me six or eight times a day. I just thanked the Lord, and didn't remind him. Prometheus was always around, of course, and Mrs. Matheson brought me my meals regular. The doctor came a couple of times, but wouldn't let me out of bed no matter how many times I told him I felt fine.

There was nothing to do but sleep and wake up sweaty and scared, or read books and listen to the sound of the men working on the vug.

They had not even brought me up any papers, and finally, after I threatened to go downstairs and get them myself and generally raised a ruckus, Prometheus caved in.

We had made ourselves famous, all right. "MURDEROUS JUKES GANG THWARTED!" read the headline. "Grisly Murder of Septimus Stitch" it said underneath, and then "Sheriff Jenkins Routs Ruffians." I shook my head. The sheriff had been passed out for the whole thing.

I read the article anyway—you couldn't help it, as it took up most of the first page. Prometheus was in it, and they called him a "prominent local businessman," which was sure a step up from "limey drunkard."

The details, though, were all confused. They said that the sheriff had done the killing, aided by a wounded Prometheus, and that "the gruesome scene was discovered by Mr. Burke-Jones's housekeeper, Chrysanthemum Chestnut."

I thought that was real odd. Now, maybe Prometheus had told them my name was Chestnut to keep me from being connected with the Bug Boys, and as I saw it, that was fair. But I had done the killing, right or wrong, and I figured I should get the blame or the glory.

I was disgusted with the story, and turned the page. The articles were mostly boring, being "Mrs. Thacker Grows Prize Tomato" or "Henry Boy Best in Church Attendance" and the like. One story was missing, though. It was just a little one, maybe three inches long and just a column wide, and it had been scissored out neat and proper.

It was on page three, where they usually put stories about what was going on in the territories, and I thought it unusual that Mrs. Matheson had cut a recipe from there. They were usually in the back. I knew, for I had made a mess of Easy Chokecherry Pie and set the oven on fire with Lazy Day Six-Layer Casserole.

I had a few days' wait for the next paper. I swan, news is stale when the local news comes out only once a week. Our story only took up half the front page, and I didn't read it. The other story was about the second vug being found, with a picture. I didn't read that either.

On the third page, there was another hole, this one a good bit larger than the first. I thought it was funny, but I was too tired to think about it much. I yawned and closed the paper.

Outside, I heard Chigger whooping, "Faster, Mr. Metheus, faster!" and I smiled, knowing Chigger was riding the range on the end of Prometheus's lead rope.

I leaned back and closed my eyes. There was nothing else to do.

Evening came. I'd had my supper and was so crazy from being in my room that I could have spit. I figured it couldn't hurt me to go sit out on the back stoop for a spell. The fresh air would likely do me a kindness.

I poked around in my dresser for something to put on over my night shift so I would not shock the neighbors more than necessary, found a wrapper, threw it over my shoulders, and poked my head out the door. Nobody. I smiled. With luck Prometheus would be in his study, and he'd never be the wiser that I'd been downstairs at all.

I tiptoed down the staircase—my leg having had a chance to heal up good—and was just stepping off down the hall when I heard voices, coming from the library.

Now, normally, I am not one to snoop. Well, I spied on the Bug Boys a lot, but that was different, on account of they were criminals and kin and all, and I was younger then. But generally speaking, when I hear voices, I just go my way and mind my own beeswax.

This time I stopped because I heard my name being spoke.

The door was open, and it was Prometheus doing the speaking. "I don't know how I'm going to tell Clutie. I've thought about it—agonized, actually—and it's been days now, but I still can't. There's no gentle way."

"You got time, Mr. Burke-Jones." It was Mrs. Matheson. "She's not strong enough yet to hear it. I cut those stories out of the paper, and if there's any more, I'll cut—"

"Not strong enough to hear what?" I said, stepping into the doorway, clutching my wrapper.

Prometheus appeared stricken. Mrs. Matheson hurried over to me with a "Child, child!" and tried to hurry me back upstairs, but I would not be budged.

"Not strong enough to hear what, Prometheus?" I repeated. My eyes did not leave his face.

After a long minute he said, soft, "Mrs. Matheson, leave us."

"All right," she said warily, "but I'll be in the kitchen." She walked down the hall real slow and then the kitchen door clicked closed behind her. I only heard this happen. I was still watching Prometheus's face. I could not read it, and it scared me.

He said, "Sit down."

I perched in one of the big leather reading chairs, then curled my feet up under me like if there was less of me sticking out, there was less that could be hurt.

"What is it? What's wrong?" All sorts of things went through my mind in a flash, like maybe I had lost the baby and they hadn't told me, or maybe Prometheus was sick and going to die, or maybe *I* was going to die.

And then he said the thing I hadn't thought of, a thing that froze my heart.

"Joaquin . . . ," he started, his voice shaking, "Joaquin is dead. I don't know how else to say it. It was in the paper. It . . . it happened in Mexico. There was a gun battle, and . . . they said . . . they said . . . Oh my dear, I am so very, very sorry."

They told me later that I screamed and tried to hurt myself. I do not know that this was true, for I don't remember anything past the telling of it, not much for a good week.

I do know that once I was allowed to leave my bed again, I looked for the herbs to flush a baby. But Colorado being an arid place, they could not be found, though I searched among the yucca and prickly pear for days, and all my spells didn't work.

At last I gave up looking, and in time came to covet the life within me once again. It might have his laugh, so big and broad, or the way his eyes got all crinkly at the corners when he smiled, or his swagger, or his gentleness. Joaquin would live again through me, at least a part of him.

Sometime in there, during the time I was looking for herbs, Prometheus started asking me to marry him. At first I just turned away without a word. I was not talking much then.

Then I said no. His proposals got more elaborate, and he kept coming up with reasons why we should be wed. He said I would have no wifely chores—on account of the Burke-Jones curse—and that Joaquin's son would be titled and wealthy and bear his name—though not the curse—and that Chigger would be taken care of forever and always.

I still said no. I held out hope that Joaquin was coming back, that the story in the newspaper had been lies or a mistake. Every day I'd ford the creek and climb to the top of the hill and stand in the high yellow grass, chanting spells and looking toward Mexico. And every day I'd come down alone to find Prometheus standing out in the yard, his arm around Chigger's shoulders, waiting for me.

It seemed like in no time I was four months along and showing some. Then five months, and getting obvious. Fall, such as it was, set in, and turned to winter. We lit the fires at night, and still I wore black.

The next time Prometheus asked, I said yes.

He wept, and the sight of it got me all teary, too. A big man like that, crying. He said, "Clutie, do you think you could love me a little? In time, I mean?"

I said, "I already love you, Prometheus. It's just . . ."

He put his arm around me. "I know." We were in the library, sitting on the leather couch. The fire crackled soft, pushing the shadows back.

"Prometheus? I can't figure, that is . . . Well, why me? Seems to me you could get any lady you wanted. A real lady, not Jukes trash. Course, I know how you like Chigger, but—"

He took me by both shoulders and looked me square in the eye. "Don't ever say that again, Clutie."

"Which part?"

"You know what I mean. Clutie, there is a deep and abiding goodness in you, a goodness that all the Jukes blood in the world couldn't muddy. Without you protecting and nurturing him, would Chigger be the sweet, ingenuous child he is? Would he even be alive? And I shudder to think what would have become of me if you hadn't happened along. My life, Joaquin's, Chigger's—all our lives would have been different without you. And so much poorer."

He stopped and took my face in his hands, like he was studying me. Firelight washed up over his face.

"You cannot cook to save your life, and I very much doubt you know a fish fork from a frog gig. But, darling, you are my heart. And Clutie?"

I whispered, "Yes?" I was fascinated.

"Well, to use your vernacular . . . Clutie, you clean up mighty fine."

I laughed, and he got all bothered.

"Clutie, you little goose, you're beautiful!"

I said, "I am?" I guess I had never thought about it. All those years in the Holler had got me too convinced that I was big and lumpy and plain as a mud fence. Of course, Joaquin had said I was pretty, but I chalked that up to hot blood. "I'm not a rawboned lump?"

Prometheus tilted his head and one brow went up. "The only thing even remotely lumpy about you is your stomach, my dear. A wholly temporary matter." He let a hand drop from my face, then paused. "May I?"

I said, "Sure."

Gently, almost like he was afraid of it, he settled his palm on my stomach. He sat real still, like he was listening though his hand, not looking at me, but at my belly.

Real quiet, he said, "I'm tired of names like Prometheus and Daedalus and Apollo. They smack of the curse. What would you think of Robert? If it's a boy, of course."

He was so serious, staring at my belly like he was certain it contained the Second Coming and any minute it was going to speak to him.

I said, "Well, I don't know, Prometheus. I have always admired the name Aphid, myself."

He looked up, aghast.

"Praying Mantis?" I said. "We could call him Mantis for short. Or Bluebottle. That's a fine strong name. Or—"

"Clutie, you're teasing!" He broke out in a grin that faded as fast as it had come. "Aren't you?"

I gave him a little shove. "Prometheus, you old—" I felt it then, like always, that little foot hammering my ribs from the inside. Prometheus felt it, too.

He breathed, "Is that . . . ?"

"Your son." And at that moment, I consigned him to Prometheus, lock, stock, and barrel. It surprised even me.

"My son," he repeated, so breathy and faint it was more felt than heard. Then louder, "My son, Robert. If it's a boy."

I put my hand on top of his. "It will be."

I had promised Joaquin.

• • •

We got married in the front parlor the next Sunday afternoon, with Mr. and Mrs. Matheson as witnesses and Sheriff Jenkins to give me away. Chigger John caught the bouquet, and after, we repaired to the library for cake and ice cream—which was Chigger's favorite part—and champagne, which was everybody else's.

Except for Prometheus. He stuck to lemonade.

Prometheus looked proud enough to bust his buttons. He was so happy to have me sewed up, legal, that he got misted up a couple of times, and made about a thousand toasts, and gave everybody a party favor of a solid gold nugget as big as a robin's egg.

I know you will find this hard to believe, but I did not until that day realize how terrible lonely he must have been till we came along. It made me awful happy to see him so resurrected. It made me cry, too. Of course, about everything made me cry in those days, on account of the baby and all.

Anyway, we had eaten about all the cake and were polishing off the ice cream when there came a knock on the front door. Mrs. Matheson, being closest, went to answer it. When she came back, she had with her a real curious person.

He was short, although not so short as the Bug Boys, and skinny and pale. He had on a dark suit, real proper except for where it was dusty. His hair was parted down the middle and slicked back, he carried a bowler hat and a silver-headed cane and a big leather envelope, and he had these little glasses just perched there on his nose. They were tied to his pocket with a long string.

I believe I stared.

It wasn't more than a half minute before everybody else was staring, too. Prometheus stepped forward. "May I help you, my man? Have some ice cream!"

But the newcomer waved it away, and said, "Burke-Jones? Prometheus Burke-Jones?"

Prometheus hiked an eyebrow. "Yes. And who might you be? I believe, sir, that you appear to be a process server!"

He had said it for a joke, and everybody laughed except the little man, who said, "Oh dear me, no!" He had an accent, kind of like Prometheus's only a whole lot more of it, if you take my meaning.

He said, "I've come to . . . That is . . ." He pulled himself up straight and announced, "I regret to inform you that Mars Henry Burke-Jones, ninth Duke of Pemwell, has expired. I have traveled across an ocean and the greater share of this beastly country to convey this message to you, and to convey you back to England with me. It was my feeling that you would not come otherwise, my lord."

And then I'll be danged if he didn't bow from the waist.

We were all kind of shocked, I guess. Everybody except Prometheus, who said, "Oh dear. Poor Mars. I'm the last then."

"Indeed," said the little man. "And really, sir, wouldn't you rather like to spend what time you have left as a duke? There is the estate to be settled and so on, and you will have to determine an heir unless . . . unless . . ." His eye had just fallen upon me, still rigged in my wedding dress with my belly pooched out. He turned pink. "I'm terribly sorry, my lord! Have I interrupted someone's wedding?"

I said, "Could I ask your name, mister?"

"Fitzpugh. Andrew Fitzpugh, at your service, madam."

Prometheus put his arm around my shoulders. "Ah. Fitzpugh. We meet at last." He held out his spare hand and Fitzpugh took it. "This is Clutie, my bride. The Lady Chrysanthemum. And from what you say, the new Duchess of Pemwell."

Well, poor Mr. Fitzpugh was so shocked he passed right out and had to be given smelling salts. I almost keeled over, too. I always figured that all this royalty business was Prometheus's little make-believe hobbyhorse, that a snake would have a better chance at growing feathers than Prometheus did of being a real earl or a duke.

But it was true, all right, and inside a week we had packed our bags. By that time, Prometheus had explained the circumstance to Mr. Fitzpugh, who understood completely, or said he did—he was real proper—and swore to keep our secret. That the baby wasn't Prometheus's, I mean.

He said at first he'd do it for England, and a couple of

days later he confided that he'd do it just because he liked me so much. He said I reminded him of his grandmother. I guess maybe she came from the Jukes part of England.

Prometheus had put the house up for sale and sold off the furnishings except for his books and a few personal things, and he was raring to go.

I was surprised at his attitude. You'd think he would have approached the trip—not to mention life in general—with dread, seeing as how he was the only target left for the family curse. But he said he figured he was going to die anyway, and if that was the case, then he was going to do it in style, not hidden away in some backwater town in a drunken stupor, waiting for Mr. Death to find him.

Me, I had mixed feelings. The house reminded me of Joaquin. It seemed I could still smell his good cooking and hear the echo of his laugh. From the corner of my eye, I caught glimpses of him in vacant rooms, and I would have given my soul to hear him call me *querida* one more time. And it reminded me, too, of the Bug Boys, and how I had shot them down, all cold and heartless and Jukes-like.

It wasn't a healthy thing, living in that house.

Still, I felt awful sad to go. Goose Butte did not seem like some backwater town to me. It was the first real city I had lived in, and the finest house I ever could have dreamt, and if the folks were mean and snotty, they came round. Well, some of them did: we had not seen hide nor hair of Mrs. Gensch.

But all in all, leaving was for the best.

As we set out for the new depot, Chigger roosting high on the luggage like the Prince of Persia and Chub tied on behind, I couldn't help looking back at the empty house, past it to Dollar Creek, and past that to the rolling, yellow, cactused land Joaquin had disappeared into forever, the land that had swallowed him up like a frog does a fly.

Prometheus's arm came around me. "Feeling low?"

"I wish I could have seen his grave, Prometheus. Put flowers on it or something."

He didn't say anything, just looked straight ahead and rubbed my back.

I looked ahead then, too, and put the house and thoughts of it behind me. It was all east now. East across a whole continent, the most part of which I'd never seen, never dreamt I would. Then a ship that would take us across the sea to England, where all those Jukeses came from long ago, back when they were regular Jukeses, before they started marrying each other and took to the hills. Then to Pemwell Park, which Prometheus said was so grand that I would not believe him even if he told me, so he'd let me wait and see for myself.

Mr. Fitzpugh met us at the depot. Bags and trunks were loaded and Chub was seen to and Chigger was, at some length, convinced not to ride with him in the livestock car. After saying a weepy good-bye to the Mathesons and the few others that had come to see us off, we climbed up into a private car, this one brand as brand new and spit-polished as Prometheus was sober. The whistle sounded, and we pulled out of Goose Butte forever.

"Would you care to stop in Missouri?" Prometheus came over and sat beside me on the divan. "See your mother?"

"No." I had already thought about it long and hard. I just couldn't face Mama, what with having murdered the rest of the family and all. "I want to send her some money, though. And a letter. I want to tell her I love her, and that me and Chigger are going back to where the Jukes came from, all the way over to England. I'm going to send it care of Miss Hanker. She can read it out for Mama."

Chigger, who had been running poor Mr. Fitzpugh ragged since we stepped up on the depot, banged through the door all out of breath.

"Clutie? Clutie, can I have me a candy? Mr. Fitz says I has got to ask you."

Chigger had taken a liking to Mr. Fitzpugh, and I was real grateful he had settled on calling him Mr. Fitz. I didn't think I could handle hearing Mr. Pugh forty times a day for the rest of my life.

"Yes, Chigger. You can have a candy."

"Can I play with Chub?"

"At the next stop."

"OK. And Clutie?"

"What?"

He came close to my ear and whispered, "I's glad you wed up with Mr. Metheus. I like's havin' me a daddy."

Prometheus heard. He turned away, but I could see that he had got all misty again.

Me, too.

twenty-seven

Well, Robbie, that's how you got made. I am sorry that Prometheus wasn't your true daddy and that we lied to you, but you can see why we did it. And you can be sure that no father ever loved a son more than he loved you.

I guess, when you come right down to it, I was Chigger's puke dogs. I don't mean that I was slavering or red-eyed, or that I traveled on all fours—well, I did, sort of, there at the end with Beetle. But I don't mean anything like that. I mean that the Bug Boys were as vomitous a bunch of pig-sticking vermin as ever came down the pike. They were that white horse, grinding the young corn under foot. And I was the dog that did them in.

You know, in all the years since, I have never had another dream that I could remember, and Chigger's never mentioned those puke dogs again. Not once.

The year that you were four, I got a parcel, all the way from the U-S-of-A. It had been in transit for some time and was stuck so full of stamps that you could scarce see the paper.

It was my quilt, Robbie, my deerskin quilt that I made when I was twelve, and that was stole from me off the Ells-worth-to-Dodge stage.

And there was a letter with it, from Joaquin. I tell you, my heart just about stopped. I sat there for a long time just holding it, afraid to read, afraid of what it might say. When I finally did read it, I cried.

He was sorry, he said. He had been in a Mexican prison. He said thinking of me was the only thing that kept him alive during those horrible years. When he got out, he went up to Goose Butte, found strangers in the house, and talked to the Mathesons. She told him I had gone. She told him everything.

He asked about you, Robbie. He said, "How is my son?" He knew you were a boy without being told. He trusted me to make one.

I hid that quilt away and I never told Prometheus, but he knew, just like he knew that I was writing back and forth with Joaquin. It was like the time he knew I was carrying you practically before I did. He had that way about him.

You were only five when Prometheus was took with fever. At the onset we sent you up north, to your Aunt Penelope at Elm Tree, for Prometheus knew the curse had come to claim its final victim.

That last night, as I sat vigil beside his bed, Prometheus roused and took my hand so tight I thought he'd squeeze it to pulp.

"Clutie," he whispered, pulling me close, "tell Robbie."

"Tell him what?" I asked. "Lay back and rest. Let me say another charm."

"Tell him," he said to me. I wanted to reach the bell rope to call for help, but he had me too tight. "No more chants and talismans. I'm dying, Clutie. The curse took Mars, and now it's taking me."

I said, "Stuff and nonsense. Mars was eighty-two."

He wasn't listening. "Robbie has to know everything. About you and me, and your family. Especially about Joaquin."

His words were awful faint by then. I had my ear right down to his lips. I said, "I will, honey, I will. Do you have your buckeye? It'll keep you safe. It won't let you die."

"Promise you'll tell him," he breathed.

"I promise," I said, and "I love you," and I was crying then.

"My dear," he whispered, so faint. "My very dear. Go back. Joaquin needs . . ." He gripped me tighter with one hand, and opened the other fist. His buckeye rolled out along the bedclothes, onto the floor. And then the breath went out of him for good and all.

You once asked me why the ring finger of my right hand was crooked, and I think I made up some story. But the truth is that your daddy broke it that night, he was holding me so tight. It never did mend right, but I didn't mind.

I had every intention of keeping that vow when I made it, Robbie, but you were so little that I couldn't tell you right off. You wouldn't have understood. And then, when you got older, I never could seem to find the right moment.

Joaquin was writing me, "Come! Come!" all the time, but I stuck it out for seven more years, and when you were twelve and more concerned with boarding school and your friends than me, I took Chigger and left. I asked you and you said all right.

You were the duke, after all.

I guess I was sort of mad. Now I know it was only your age, but when a boy doesn't want to bring his friends home for holidays 'cause his mama is a colonial and talks funny, it hurts.

I know you thought I was stupid. You laughed at my paintings because they didn't look like England, like the country you knew. And you asked me why I didn't get rid of that heart I wore round my neck, the one give to me by Miss Hanker. You called it cheap.

I heard you call me provincial and rustic, and you imitated Chigger John more than once. Although now I can say that you were a real good mimic, it sorrowed me something terrible at the time.

Those were bad years for us. You were as obnoxious as you were handsome, and it hurt me to look at you, for you favored Joaquin so much. And you were laughing at me all the time. Worse, you were mean to Chigger, who never loved anybody better in the world than you.

I had no one, no friends, for society had turned its back on me the minute Prometheus died. The only one what was civil to me was old Queen Vic, but it's not like she can just drop everything and come for a chat and cookies.

Anyway, I never was a part of it before, but after, it was

worse. Chigger was a comfort, but you were my only son, Robbie. And you were ashamed of me.

I took the easy way out. Your Aunt Penelope was glad to have you. She never thought much of me, anyway.

So me and Chigger sailed back across the sea. We stopped off in Missouri to see the folks. The old house at Jukes Holler was falling down and overgrown, the land having been sold off long since and all the Jukeses dead or gone, nobody knew which. Nobody cared, I guess, save for me. And Chigger. I just hoped Mama had moved on and had a nicer life. I had sent her a lot of money over the years, but she had never answered.

A good speck of the woods had been cleared to make farmland, but my cave at Tickled Bear Hill was still there, and the tree I hung my quilt in, though the big oak up top had been struck by lightning long since. It was split clean down the middle.

The town had not changed one bit. I asked after Miss Alvinetta Hanker—I had written her a few letters, but never had a reply. It took me a few folks before I found one that remembered her, and then he said he believed she had gone up to Des Moines, or maybe it was Des Plaines. He didn't remember exactly when or where.

We ran into Agnes Ann by accident, and didn't she bow and scrape when she heard I was a duchess! She had married a fella, name of Hunsucker, who took over the hog farm when her daddy died, and she had her oldest boy with her. He had orange hair and light blue eyes and looked about as smart as a box of rocks. Strange, but it made me kind of happy to see him. I guess Spider finally sowed a crop that Granny couldn't dig up.

We went to see Frank James. He was not hard to find. He looked older than his years and he had lost his brother to those back-shooting Ford brothers, but he remembered me all right.

He had Chigger sing a song for him. He hadn't forgot Chigger's voice, although Chigger was a grown-up man by then, about the same age as you are now, and his range had long since changed from soprano to tenor. But it was still pure beauty. Chigger picked "The Amputee's Lament," which is also called "Bury My Leg at Calico Creek, Don't Throw It in the Fire," and had both me and Frank honking our noses and thinking about the old days, and the war.

After Frank had a good wipe at his eyes and a last blow on his handkerchief, he offered us a lemonade and asked whatever had become of the rest of my family.

I said, "I shot most of them."

"Fair enough, little sis," he said, right out. "A bigger batch of back-stabbers never lived."

I slipped a buckeye under his porch.

Finally we came out here to Colorado, and Joaquin was waiting for us at the depot, hat in hand. I tell you, he was a sight to make the angels sing. After we had hugged and kissed for God knows how long right there on the platform, he took me straight to a Justice of the Peace and we got hitched, with Chigger for the witness. Nothing ever felt so right in all the world.

Now, I guess that comes as a shock to you, too, doesn't it? Especially since I waited three whole years—until you were fifteen—to tell you I got married again, and even then I said I had just done it. You didn't write again until you were twenty. I bless your Caroline every day of my life for getting you to answer my letters. One a year is better than nothing.

Anyway, I had a lot of pictures of you, of course, and he was eager to know all about you, and if you were a good shot and such. I said you didn't shoot but you played cricket, and after I explained that, I told him you were in the school choir. You always had a wonderful voice, Robbie, clear as a bell. Now you know where it came from.

I wish you had sent more pictures in the years since. I ache for the sight of you. I guess a letter every year isn't near enough, after all. We will take what we can get, though.

I reckon I should say here that the reason Joaquin went to jail in the first place was because of Mr. Foot's brother Lester, so I guess it was my fault, too. He was chasing that Albino fella—you remember him? He was the last of the seven, the ones who killed Joaquin's daddy.

Anyway, he had chased him lickety-split, clear down into Mexico, and caught him with the expected results. He was hurrying north again when he ran across a Mr. Foot, down on the border country.

He didn't know if it was the right Mr. Foot until a little ten-year-old girl came to serve them supper. She was on a crutch with one leg all drawn up funny, and acting scared.

Joaquin stood right up. "Are you Lester Foot, señor? The brother of Ezra Foot?"

Lester got up, too, and said yes he was, by Christmas, and what was it to Joaquin? The rest of it was just like Joaquin had said he would do, all that time ago in Kansas, except he did not shoot Lester through the head. It was the heart, and Lester fought back.

He took that poor little girl to a mission, and was on his way to the border when he was apprehended, after a lengthy battle, by the Mexican authorities. He got shot up pretty bad. He nearly died.

News has a long trip from Mexico, and I expect it got scrambled along the way. That was why the papers thought he was dead.

You know, if I hadn't told Joaquin about Mr. Foot, my whole life would have been different. Yours and his, too. But then I think, what if Prometheus hadn't got on the wrong train and then fallen off it, and what if Joaquin's crew hadn't decided to rob it, and what if Chigger hadn't taken it into his head to tunnel? That and about twenty other "what if's."

You just never know.

Anyway, nobody around here knows I'm a duchess, although the postmaster thinks something funny's going on. I write back and forth with Queen Vic now and then—and let me tell you, she understands about love. It's Albert this and Albert that, and him dead since 18-and-61.

What with your having come of age and married up with Caroline, I guess that makes me the dowager duchess or something, anyway. I know she's a whole lot better at it than I was. Not that I didn't know which fork to use and all that, because Prometheus taught me, and he taught me good. But there's a whole lot more to the art of being civilized. I guess you have to be born with it, or at least brung up on it. According to the way I was raised, it's a wonderment I knew that spoons weren't for digging the wax out of your ears.

I wish you would come and see us, Robbie, or maybe the other way round. We raise cattle and horses—Joaquin's the big horse trainer in our part of the world. We have got a middling-sized ranch, about twelve thousand acres, and it is beautiful. We are near the mountains—well, within a hundred miles—and they are real majestic on the horizon, all purple and blue and permanent, and we have lots of extra space.

We built it that way a'purpose with extra bedrooms, thinking we'd have more kids, but we were never blessed. You were our one and only.

I hope that after you read this story, you won't hate me, or think less of Prometheus. Maybe it will help you understand your father a little better. He wanted the Burke-Jones line to go on—but without the curse—and you filled the bill perfect. You aren't under the curse, Robbie, nor your little James, so you can just forget all that hogwash your Aunt Penelope's surely fed you. You'll probably both live to be a hundred and ten.

And I want you to understand something else.

I loved Prometheus. It was a different kind of love than Joaquin—with him, it's all fire and sparks and whoop-de-doo. But with Prometheus, well, it sort of snuck up on me. It was quieter, but just as strong, and just as deep.

He loved you with all his heart, Robbie.

So do I.

postscript

Cat's Cradle, Colorado
May 1900

Dear Robbie,

It's been only a week since we received your letter dated the 11th
of February, and here it is, almost the end of May. It seems the mails
are slower all the time.

First, I want to say how sorry I was to hear about old Queen Vic.
It was in all the papers here. I wish she had held on a little longer,
so she could know we've got things patched up. But I expect she is
with Albert now, and that'll make her happier than any news I'd
have.

I can scarce believe you are coming to see us! All is forgiven, you
write, and you are sorry that you were a "sniveling, snotty little
fool." Son, you weren't. It was me, not fitting in. But that is all
behind us now. How I yearn to see you and Lady Caroline and little
James!

I will forever be grateful to your Caroline for making you read
my story. You said she read it first, after you cast it aside. "Robert,
if you love me, you will read this." That's what she said to you. I've
turned it over in my mind a hundred times, till I can almost picture
it like I was there.

God bless her, and God bless you.

You write that you are anxious to meet Joaquin, and he is more
than anxious to see you. With him, it's always, "I must show Roberto this!" or "Roberto will be pleased, no?"

I hope you ride. He has got a real pretty bay picked out for you, and he's been working it, special. But don't go thinking that he is a "magnificent bandit," as you put it. He was true to his word. He settled down and never shot another fella again. Well, except for those three in that little range war we had, but that was self-defense.

They proved it in court.

Joaquin is still straight and tall, and he still wears his hair in a horse tail down his back, more often a braid these days. There's some gray in it, but it's real appealing. Me, I have got a little fat because we have a good Mexican cook, but Joaquin says there is more of me to love.

From where I sit I can see the road, and there's a buggy coming down it. I swan, the dust is kicking up good today! That's the eastern way, down the road. If you stand up on top of the house, you can see practically to where the earth drops off. Joaquin says you can see all the way to Kansas City, but then he's prone to exaggerate.

Did I tell you about Chigger? I can't remember. A couple years after Joaquin and me got married, I'll be jiggered if he didn't find himself a gal. Her name is Amanda, and she used to be a schoolteacher. I guess you could have called her an old maid if you had a cruel streak, seeing as she was 31 to his 26 when they got hitched. But she has a heart as big as the Rocky Mountains, and she saw the goodness in Chigger right off.

We built them a house here on the ranch, and they have two little boys, ten and four, that are as cute as a bug's ear, although they have regular names. Charley and Sam. Sam's the baby, though he gets mad if you call him that. And both of them are above-average smart.

That buggy's pulled up in the yard now. Joaquin's strolling out to meet it. I always let him do that first. He admires company—more folks to tell his stories to, I expect. I'm getting more retiring in my dotage. I'll be 43 this year and still have all my own choppers, but I'm starting to slow down a little. I guess I'll make it a good long spell yet, though. I reckon to go down fighting like Granny Wren, with my teeth all full of bear.

Land sakes, there's a woman in that buggy! Joaquin's kissing her hand—he always was a gentleman—and helping her down, and my goodness, but she's pretty! She sure doesn't look like any kind of ranch wife. Maybe they're new, come to buy horses. Joaquin's got some fine ones, and folks travel in from all around. Reining, roping, cutting: you name it and his horses can do it. That lady's got a little child with her, and honest-to-Jim if he isn't a ring-tailed tooter! Feet barely on the ground and he's already chasing the chickens!

There's a man, too. A big, strapping, broad-shouldered fella, just stepping down from the buggy. Got on a suit. Can't see his face, but he's turning, and—

Can it be?

Oh, Robbie. Oh, my son!